I0740429

David Hogg

Life of Allan Cunningham

With Selections from his Works and Correspondence

David Hogg

Life of Allan Cunningham
With Selections from his Works and Correspondence

ISBN/EAN: 9783337278045

Printed in Europe, USA, Canada, Australia, Japan

Cover: Foto ©Raphael Reischuk / pixelio.de

More available books at **www.hansebooks.com**

LIFE

OF

ALLAN CUNNINGHAM,

WITH

SELECTIONS FROM HIS WORKS AND CORRESPONDENCE.

BY THE
REV. DAVID HOGG,

AUTHOR OF "LIFE AND TIMES OF THE REV. JOHN WIGHTMAN, D.D."

DUMFRIES: JOHN ANDERSON & SON.
EDINBURGH: JOHN GRANT, 34 GEORGE IV. BRIDGE.
LONDON: HODDER AND STOUGHTON, 27 PATERNOSTER ROW.
1875.

PREFACE.

THE object aimed at in this volume has been to let Allan Cunningham, as much as possible, tell his own Life, by giving selections from his works and correspondence, with a link where necessary for connecting the narrative. This is generally considered the best kind of biography, and a distinguished critic, Dr. Johnson, says,—"Those relations are commonly of most value in which the writer tells his own story." Whether the selections have been well chosen it is not for me to say, but they have been made with the intention of showing not only the literary, poetic, and social character of the man, but also of preserving the remembrance of some Scottish customs and ceremonies which have now passed away. The work has been written *con amore*, from admiration of "Honest Allan," and his intimate connection with

the district of Nithsdale. I have been greatly
assisted in its production by the kindness of many
friends, in allowing me the use of letters, and in
communicating important information with respect
to the subject of the Memoir, which I did not
possess. To them I tender my sincerest thanks for
their generous interest in the work. I would
specially mention Mr. Anthony C. M'Bryde, artist,
Edinburgh, grand-nephew of Allan Cunningham, who
voluntarily supplied the portrait and the two sketches,
engraved by himself, and who also contributed the
poem inserted at the end of the first chapter. To
Mr. Allan Cunningham, nephew of the Poet, my
warmest acknowledgments are also due, for the use
of the bust from which the photograph was taken,
and for other favours. I now entrust my book to
the public, hoping that, for the sake of the subject,
it will receive their regard.

D. H.

KIRKMAHOE MANSE.

CONTENTS.

CHAPTER I.

CHAPTER II.

CHAPTER III.

CHAPTER IV.

CHAPTER V.

CHAPTER VI.

CHAPTER XX.

CHAPTER XXI.

LIFE

OF

ALLAN CUNNINGHAM.

CHAPTER I.

POETIC FERTILITY OF NITHSDALE—POWER OF SONG OVER LEGISLA-
TION—NO BIOGRAPHY OF ALLAN CUNNINGHAM—LITERARY
APPRECIATION OF HIM—PARENTAGE—FAMILY TALENT—THOMAS
MOUNSEY CUNNINGHAM—EDUCATION AT A DAME'S SCHOOL—
"THE HILLS O' GALLOWA'"—HIS SENSITIVENESS AS TO
CRITICISM—CONTRIBUTIONS TO THE "EDINBURGH MAGAZINE"—
TIFF BETWEEN HIM AND THE ETTRICK SHEPHERD—PETER
MILLER CUNNINGHAM—HIS LITERARY PRODUCTIONS.

THERE is no district of equal compass within our ken
which has been so prolific in poetry and song as that of
Nithsdale, and it continues as fertile as ever. Apart
from Burns and Cunningham, the *Dii majores* of song
in the vale, the number of minor minstrels whom it has
produced is almost incredible. Some of these are, of
course, very inferior, though, all things considered,
deserving of commendation for their efforts. Some,
again, are highly respectable in their effusions, but
circumstances, not always under their own control, have

A

prevented them from soaring into fame. Some are forgotten. Some were never known to be forgotten, except by a limited circle, and some were known only anonymously, if the bull may be excused, through the medium of the local newspapers, and the magazines of the day. One generation has gone, and another come, hastening to go again, transmitting, as if by hereditary descent, the poetic faculty, and the old woodlands are still vocal with song.

We have sometimes puzzled ourselves with the endeavour to discover the *why* and the *wherefore* of this, without, however, coming to any satisfactory conclusion on the matter; and we have asked ourselves if there can be anything in the atmosphere, or in the local scenery, to account for it? or if it is altogether a mere matter of chance, a caprice of nature under heaven-born inspiration? We know parishes which, for half a century, have been prolific in producing preachers, while those adjacent never sent a single youth to college. Nor can it be said of either that the profession has run in the blood, as very few instances of this are found. From whatever cause, or whether there be a cause at all, the fact is certain, that the spirit of poesy is still hovering, as of yore, over the length and breadth of Nithsdale.

When Fletcher of Saltoun wished to have the making of his country's songs, and he would let any one else have the making of its laws, he meant veritable songs, expressing in appropriate terms his countrymen's sentiments and feelings, amorous, patriotic, pathetic, courageous. He knew that only such would take hold of the public mind, and produce the effect he desired. These must have free and unbiassed sway to maintain a permanent footing throughout the land, and not, as it is said in the present day, by paying a high royalty to some distinguished professional to sing a doggerel into temporary popularity. That will never transmit any song from one generation to another. Our songs, to become part of the country's existence, must be sung, not on the opera stage, with instrumental accompaniments, but lilted in the gloaming, and at the milking hour, warbled with the song of the lark behind the plough, or on the hill-side with the sheep, and they shall live, though it may be a matter of no concern to many whether their authors' existence is secured or not. Now, whose songs are they that we hear chanted at our rural merry-makings, at our wedding-feasts, on the harvest-field, or at the farmer's ingle in the long evenings of winter? With some exceptions, they are those of Ramsay, Burns, Scott, Hogg, and Cunningham, though probably the fair songstress knows nothing of their author. They are all one to her, the sentiments they breathe are those of her own heart, and she pours them forth with a melody and a cordiality which stir the very souls of all around her. She sings them to her children in the cradle, and, in process of time, they to theirs, so that they are handed down to posterity with a reality of feeling which forms part of our national character.

It has long been a subject of wonderment and remark that no biography of Allan Cunningham has yet been given to the world, notwithstanding the abundance of materials for that purpose within the reach of almost any one qualified to collect and arrange them. His varied abilities, natural and acquired—his endowments, physical and mental—his rise from obscurity to an eminence which gained for him the intercourse and friendship of the noble—his connection with the metropolitan press—his association with a distinguished sculptor—his diversified literary productions—as well as the reminiscences of his early life, floating through Nithsdale and elsewhere, might have tempted some ready pen to produce an interesting record of the stone-mason, poet, novelist, biographer, and sculptor, all in one. But no! A slight sketch written by himself, and of limited extent, is all that exists for the information of posterity, and which has been eagerly drawn upon by those permitted access to the treasure.

Yet Allan Cunningham was not without high appreciation in his day, as well as now, by some whose favour was worth the winning, and his society was courted in the circles of the literary and the great. Miss Landon said that "a few words from Allan Cunningham strengthened her like a dose of Peruvian bark." Mrs. S. C. Hall "remembered how her cheek flushed, and how pleased and proud she was at the few words of praise he gave to one of the first efforts of her pen." Sir Walter Scott characterized him as "Honest Allan, a credit to Caledonia." The Ettrick Shepherd described him as "the very model of Burns, and exactly such a man." Tom Hood said, he "used to *look up* to Allan Cunningham, who was formed by nature tall enough to snatch a grace beyond the reach of art." Talfourd said of him, that he was "stalwart of form, and stout of heart and verse—a ruder Burns." And Southey apostrophized him thus—

> "Allan, true child of Scotland; thou who art
> So oft in spirit on thy native hills
> And yonder Solway shores, a poet thou!"

Still, notwithstanding all this appreciation, no biography has been written. We fully feel our inadequacy for such a task, and agree with the poet that "fools rush in where angels fear to tread;" but from our admiration of the man we are willing to make the attempt rather than that the work should remain undone. What we shall throw together may at a future time be useful to some one capable of doing our countryman justice.

Allan Cunningham was descended from an ancient family, who held possessions in Ayrshire bearing their name. After the battle of Philiphaugh his more immediate ancestors thought it advisable to dispose of their inheritance rather than run the risk of losing it by forfeiture, as one of them had served as an officer under the great Montrose. Having done so, they became tenants of the farm of Gogar Mains, in the neighbourhood of Edinburgh, where they remained for several generations. It was here that Allan's father, John Cunningham, was born on the 26th of March, 1743. When he had reached his twenty-third year his father died, and being unwilling at so young an age to undertake the responsibilities of the farm management, he surrendered the lease, sold off the effects, and went into the county of Durham to improve himself in the knowledge of farming, as England at that time was considered ahead of Scotland in agricultural progress, and that he might qualify himself for the office of land-steward or overseer wherever Providence should cast his lot. After some time he returned to Scotland, and became overseer to Mr. Mounsey of Rammerscales, near Lochmaben, in Dumfriesshire.

He then married Miss Elizabeth Harley, the daughter of a Dumfries merchant, who had formerly been a farmer in Berwickshire. She was a lady of great personal attractions and accomplishments, shrewd in judgment, poetic in fancy, and altogether possessing a very superior intellect, which she transmitted to her family, both sons and daughters. John Cunningham, having now acquired considerable experience in agricultural pursuits, resolved to improve his condition along with his young wife, and with this view took a lease of the farm of Culfaud, in the parish of Kirkpatrick-Durham, in the Stewartry of Kirkcudbright. This enterprise, however, not proving so successful as he had anticipated, he was forced to relinquish farming on his own account, and became factor to Mr. Syme of Barncailzie in the same parish, upon whose death he removed to Blackwood, to fill the same situation there under Mr. Copeland, the proprietor, and finally he went to Dalswinton in the same capacity, where he greatly assisted Mr. Miller in his agricultural improvements on the estate, and with whom he remained till his death in 1800, in the fifty-seventh year of his age. He had nine children—five sons and four daughters—who all gave evidence of superior talent and high intellectual ability. He himself "was a man fond of collecting all that was characteristic of his country," and, doubtless, the continual witnessing of this by his sons, tended, in no small degree, to inspire them with a similarity of taste.

All the sons were more or less distinguished for their love of literature, and their contributions to the periodical press, a circumstance rarely to be met with in the family of a cottager, where few opportunities for writing were afforded, and little leisure was at command. They are deserving of something more than a passing notice.

James, the eldest son, was brought up to the mason trade, and afterwards, by his integrity, skill, and perseverance, he became a master-builder with very gratifying success. He was a great student of antiquarian lore, and as leisure allowed he wrote articles for the newspapers and magazines within his reach. He also maintained a considerable correspondence on literary matters with the Ettrick Shepherd, and others with whom he was acquainted, but none of his writings are forthcoming, as duplicates were not kept, and his magazine articles were without signature. He was a great favourite with his brother Allan, as we shall afterwards see, and with whom he kept up a most affectionate correspondence. He died at Dalswinton village on the 27th of July, 1832, in the fifty-seventh year of his age, being exactly that of his father at the time of his death.

Thomas Mounsey, the second son, was only a year younger than his brother James, and was born at Culfaud, on the 25th of June, 1766. He received the first elements of his education at a Dame's school, kept by one Nancy Kingan, whose whole stock of instruction consisted in the alphabet, the Shorter Catechism, the Psalms of David, and the Proverbs of Solomon. Spelling was considered useless, and a mere waste of time. Writing and arithmetic she did not pretend to, and as for grammar, she had never heard of it. Her great boast to any occasional visitor to her seminary was, "the bairns when they lea' my schule hae unco little to learn o' the Bible." Having finished with Dame Kingan, Thomas was next placed under the tutorship of Dominie Gordon, at Kellieston, who had the strongest belief that knowledge could be imparted to a pupil through any part of the body by means of physical appliance, as well as by oral instruction.

One way and another the education was completed, or, as the common phrase went, "the maister could gang nae farther," and young Thomas, at his own request, was apprenticed to a millwright in the neighbourhood. He now began cultivating the acquaintance of the Muses, and submitted his poetical productions, from time to time, to the inspection of his father, who was proud of his son, and gave what counsel and encouragement he thought judicious. By-and-by he found opportunity of getting some of his effusions brought before the public notice, through the medium of the local journals, which greatly stimulated his efforts to further success. After his apprenticeship was finished he resolved to push his own way in the world, and directed his steps to England, with the sage counsel of Mr. Miller of Dalswinton to abandon all poetical aspirations. Here for a considerable time he followed desultory employment in his trade, as we find him at Rotherham, King's Lynn, Wiltshire,

Cambridge, and Dover, but at last he had the good fortune to become managing clerk in the establishment of Sir John Rennie, the celebrated engineer in London. After nine years' poetic dormancy, he woke up in the pages of the *Scots Magazine*, to which he made frequent contributions, and which, at the request of the Ettrick Shepherd, he allowed to be inserted in "The Forest Minstrel." He composed several songs which attained great popularity, but by far the most popular was "The Hills o' Gallowa'." In short, it was the great song of the day, and as it is still chanted in the South we shall insert it here:—

"THE HILLS O' GALLOWA'.

"Amang the birks sae blythe and gay,
    I met my Julia hameward gaun;
The linties chauntit on the spray,
    The lammies loupit on the lawn;
On ilka howm the sward was mawn,
    The braes wi' gowans buskit bra',
An' gloamin's plaid o' gray was thrawn
    Out owre the hills o' Gallowa'.

"Wi' music wild the woodlands rang,
    An' fragrance wing'd alang the lea,
As down we sat the flowers amang,
    Upon the banks o' stately Dee.
My Julia's arms encircled me,
    An' saftly slade the hours awa',
Till dawin coost a glimmerin' ee
    Upon the hills o' Gallowa'.

"It isna owsen, sheep, an' kye,
    It isna goud, it isna gear,
This lifted ee wad hae, quoth I,
    The world's drumlie gloom to cheer.

> But gie to me my Julia dear,
>   Ye powers wha rowe this yerthen ba',
> An' O! sae blythe thro' life I'll steer,
>   Amang the hills o' Gallowa'.
>
> "When gloamin' dauners up the hill,
>   An' our gudeman ca's hame the yowes,
> Wi' her I'll trace the mossy rill
>   That owre the muir meand'ring rowes;
> Or tint amang the scroggy knowes,
>   My birken pipe I'll sweetly blaw,
> An' sing the streams, the straths, and howes,
>   The hills an' dales o' Gallowa'.
>
> "An' when auld Scotland's heathy hills,
>   Her rural nymphs an' jovial swains,
> Her flow'ry wilds an' wimpling rills,
>   Awake nae mair my canty strains;
> Whare friendship dwells an' freedom reigns,
>   Whare heather blooms an' muircocks craw,
> O! dig my grave, and hide my banes
>   Amang the hills o' Gallowa'."

This song was so thoroughly popular and appreciated that several authors got the credit of its composition. It was especially attributed to Burns, and appeared in an edition of his poetical works which was published by Orphoot at Edinburgh in 1820. The same honour was also accorded to the Ettrick Shepherd in the "Harp of Caledonia," edited by Mr. Struthers; but the real author was unknown. The Julia of the song was a Galloway maiden with whom Cunningham was in love, and upon her death he wrote another, entitled "Julia's Grave," very beautiful and pathetic, which appeared in the *Scots Magazine* for 1807. That his affection for this young lady was deep-rooted and sincere is evident from the fact that he made her the subject of several of his songs besides those noted above. Though he afterwards became the happy husband of a loving wife, yet the name of poor Julia Curtis was ever deeply impressed on his heart.

He was extremely *touchy* on the merits of his compositions, so that editors and he were frequently at variance. A writer in the *Scottish American Journal* of 7th September, 1871, says of him, " Mr. Cunningham was somewhat whimsical in his tastes, and rash in his judgments. He could not bear to hear any of his productions criticised, even by his most intimate friends, and considered professional criticism the most contemptible and worthless of occupations. He made the acquaintance and corresponded with the Ettrick Shepherd, but somehow a dryness arose between the two, and when Hogg visited London about forty years ago, there was a mutual desire to meet, but nothing could bring them together. Hogg sat in solitary dignity in London, and Cunningham, equally obstinate, in Southwark, and who was to cross the Thames was the all-important question. The man of Nith invited him of Yarrow, and the man of Yarrow invited him of Nith, but neither of them would stir; and when a mutual friend interposed, he was repulsed in a style that made him almost wish that both worthies were tumbled into the Thames. They never met."

His literary taste extended to prose as well as poetry, and when the *Edinburgh Magazine* was started in 1817, he contributed several interesting articles on ancient and modern times, under the title of the

" Literary Legacy," but falling out with the editor, he withdrew. It was, however, in lyrical poetry he was fitted to excel, had his extremely sensitive temperament allowed him to persevere. But it is often found that superior genius is clogged with some insuperable failing which impedes the flight to fame. This idiosyncrasy of his character was greatly lamented by his brother Allan. In a letter to the Ettrick Shepherd on this point he says, " My brother's want of success has surprised me too. He had a fair share of talent; and, had he cultivated his powers with care, and given himself fair-play, his fate would have been different. But he sees nature rather through a curious medium than with the tasteful eye of poetry, and must please himself with the praise of those who love singular and curious things." In private life he was highly esteemed by a wide circle of friends, and his business habits were regular, punctual, and faithful. He died of cholera on the 28th October, 1834.

John, the third son, was also trained a mechanic, and evinced considerable talent for poetry, and literature in general, but he was prematurely cut off, while still in his teens.

Allan was the fourth son, but we shall merely mention his name at present, as he is to engage our special and whole attention afterwards.

Peter Miller, the fifth and youngest son, was born at Dalswinton, in November, 1789, and was first educated at a school similar to those at which his elder brothers had been taught. After passing through the curriculum of medical study at the University of Edinburgh, he was appointed Assistant-Surgeon in the Royal Navy. "In this capacity," says an obituary notice of him in the *Gentleman's Magazine*, June, 1864, "he saw service on the shores of Spain, where the great war was raging, and on the lakes of America, where he became the close friend of the celebrated Clapperton. He also served for some years in the Eastern Archipelago, and had ample opportunities of observing the effect of tropical climates on the European constitution. Of this he profited when, peace having arrived, he was thrown out of the regular line of duty, and would have been left to vegetate on half-pay if he had not sought other employment from the Admiralty; in the course of which, to use the words of the *Quarterly Review*, he ·'made no less than four voyages to New South Wales, as Surgeon-Superintendent of convict ships, in which was transported upwards of six hundred convicts of both sexes, whom he saw landed at Sydney without the loss of a single individual—a fact of itself quite sufficient to attest his judgment and ability in the treatment and management of a set of beings not easily kept in order.'—*Quarterly Review*, January, 1828.

" The result of his observations during this period was embodied in his 'Two Years in New South Wales,' which was published in 1827, in 2 vols., post 8vo, and rapidly ran through three large editions. This work is both amusing and instructive, and although necessarily superseded by more recent works on the same ever-extending subject, is still frequently quoted, and some centuries hence will afford a mine of information and speculation to the correspondents of the *Sylvanus Urban* of the Antipodes. Mr. Cunningham added the profits arising from this work to his early savings in the navy, and expended them in an attempt to open up a large tract of land, in what he then fondly regarded as his adopted country. But the locality was perhaps badly chosen ; the seasons were certainly unpropitious, and he soon abandoned the struggle, as far as his own personal superintendence was concerned. His well-earned reputation at the Admiralty, however, speedily procured him employment, and he served successively in the ' Tyne,' 18, on the South American Station, and in the ' Asia,' 84, in the Mediterranean. In the course of these years he published a volume of essays on ' Electricity and Magnetism,' and another on ' Irrigation as practised on the Eastern Shores of the Mediterranean.' He also contributed an account· of a ' Visit to the Falkland Islands' to the *Athenæum*, and was a frequent writer in other periodicals. He was a man of remarkable powers of observation, and of the most amiable and conciliatory disposition, and, it is believed, passed through life without making a single enemy. His attachment to his brother Allan was particularly strong, and although death had separated them for more than twenty years, the name of that brother was among the last articulate sounds which passed his lips." He died at Greenwich on the 6th of March, 1864, in the seventy-fourth year of his age.

Of the four daughters, one now survives (April, 1874), the sole representative of the family, with her dark eyes as lustrous, intelligent, and penetrating, as if she were only twenty instead of fourscore.

On the death of John Cunningham, his widow removed with her family to Dalswinton village, where, through the generous liberality of Mr. Miller, she was allowed a free house and a small field for a cow's grazure during her lifetime. This she did not long enjoy, however, for her daughter Mary, Mrs. Pagan at Curriestanes, kindly prevailed on her to remove from Dalswinton and reside with herself, which she was probably the more easily induced to do from the circumstance that she had not been well provided for at her husband's death. It will be seen afterwards how affectionate and mindful of his mother, in this respect, was her son Allan, till the day of his death. She was a little woman, with sharp black eyes, and retained her faculties till the age of ninety, when she died. During her lifetime she was greatly respected, both on account of her own sterling qualities, and as being the mother of Allan Cunningham.

The following verses on the ancestral family are contributed by a grand-nephew of Allan Cunningham, Mr. Anthony C. M'Bryde, artist, Edinburgh, who seems to inherit a portion of the genius of his great kinsman :—

"THE CUNNINGHAMS OF CUNNINGHAM.

" The Cunninghams of Cunningham, in good old days of yore,
Were doughty barons stout and bold as ever drew claymore ;
Who for their King and Country's right in battle foremost stood,
And gave to dye full many a field the Sassenach's best blood.

" Within their halls at festive board, in many days langsyne,
When freely passed the jest and song, the usquebae and wine,
Amid their leal retainers, so merry, free, and gay,
They were the blythest of the blythe, none merrier were than they.

" That night on Carrick's rock-bound shore the warning beacon burned,
To drive the invader from his throne the royal Bruce returned—
And Cunningham of Cunningham, like lion bold let loose,
Dashed gallantly across the hills to fight or die with Bruce!

" In Killiecrankie's mountain pass they fought right gallantlie,
In favour of King James's cause, by the side of brave Dundee—
And many a well-contested field their valour did engage,
No nobler name than Cunningham exists on history's page!

" And well, I wot, the lion heart survives those 'good old days'—
The patriotic spirit breathes in kinsman Allan's lays;
His 'Hame and it's hame,' and his 'Wee, wee German laird,'
Shall live with Scotland's lyric fame while the Scottish tongue is
    spared.

" O ! let us cherish proudly now their virtues manifold,
And strive to emulate the deeds they did in days of old;
For never shall we know again men of superior worth,
Than the Cunninghams of Cunningham—none nobler lived on earth."

CHAPTER II.

ALLAN CUNNINGHAM'S BIRTH—EDUCATION—APPRENTICED TO THE MASON TRADE—GEORGE DOUGLAS M'GHIE—HUMOROUS MEMORIAL TO MR. LENY OF DALSWINTON—BURNING OF CUNNINGHAM'S LETTERS—FEAR OF FRENCH INVASION—MYSTERIOUS MARKING OF THE HOUSES—DISCOVERED TO BE A HOAX, AND REWARD OFFERED—FIRST EFFORTS IN SONG—MEETING WITH THE ETTRICK SHEPHERD ON QUEENSBERRY HILL—INCIDENT AT ALTRIVE— TRAVELS ON FOOT TO EDINBURGH TO SEE SIR WALTER SCOTT —ATTENDS THE FUNERAL OF BURNS.

ALLAN CUNNINGHAM was born in a cottage near Black-wood House, on the banks of the Nith, in the parish of Keir, Dumfriesshire, on the 7th of December, 1784. The cottage has long since disappeared, and its site is now covered with a gigantic yew, but he who there first became a citizen of the world cannot be forgotten. He was but a child, scarcely two years old, when the family removed from Blackwood to Dalswinton; and, conse-quently, he always looked upon Kirkmahoe very much as his native parish—where his oldest memories took their rise, his boyish days were spent, his youthful associations formed—where his education was acquired, and his apprenticeship served—where his poetic fancy first burst into song, and the flame of love first kindled in his breast. These, and such as these, constitute home, and make the place where they were experienced the scene of our nativity, though it may not be strictly and literally the true place of our birth. So felt Allan

Cunningham when, in after years, and far away, he sang—

> " Dalswinton hill, Dalswinton holm,
> And Nith, thou gentle river,
> Rise in my heart, flow in my soul,
> And dwell with me for ever!"

Allan, like the elder members of the family, was also trained at a Dame's school, which was of the usual order, and conducted in the village of Quarrelwood by a Mrs. Gray. These schools were not only useful but absolutely necessary in their day, as parochial schools were "few and far between," but they were not by any means of a high educational character. This, indeed, was not required. Ability to spell one's way through the Bible was considered all that was necessary, and when this was attained, the pupil was sent out to country service, to herd the cows, or nurse the children, till age and strength fitted for higher and weightier duties. Writing was not considered essential, as few parents could "read write," and letter postage was entirely beyond reach. The Bible was the grand climax, and when a scholar was "once through the Bible," his education was finished, and he was removed.

At the age of eleven, or rather before he had attained that period, Allan was taken from school, and put under the care of his brother James, resident in Dalswinton village, to learn the trade of a stone-mason, while his physical frame, as may well be imagined, was yet scarcely strong enough for handling the mallet and the chisel with anything like effect. However, in his case the maxim was true, "Learn young, learn fair," as his

handiwork afterwards proved; and though his education was sadly curtailed as regarded both quantity and quality, yet his insatiable thirst for knowledge induced him in great measure to become his own instructor. At this time he knew nothing of English grammar, which was afterwards to be so necessary in his connection with literature and the press; but he supplied the defect by private study, while experience in reading and writing brought him into the art of what was required for correct composition.

In the evenings, after the labours of the day were over, as well as at the mid-day hour, he read with avidity every book within his reach, listened eagerly to every snatch of old ballad he heard sung, treasured up every story told—his own imagination amply supplying any omission in the narrative, or any failure in the memory of the narrator. As he got into the middle of his teens he began to manifest somewhat of a roving disposition when the stars came out and the moon arose. At kirns, trystes, rockings, foys, bridaleens, weddings, and such like merry-makings, he was always an invited guest, and was sure to be present, for the fun and frolic they afforded, as well as for the opportunity of hearing lilted some old Scottish ditty, or narrated some tradition of the feudal times. But besides this, he was suspected, along with some of his companions, of occasionally play-ing pranks at the farm-houses in the neighbourhood, to the annoyance of the inmates, though it was never known to their injury either in property or person. Yet, however bold or venturesome in his frolic, he always managed to escape detection.

His chief companion in these days was George Douglas M'Ghie, a youth about his own age, the son of a weaver in Quarrelwood, and engaged in the same occupation as his father. It is necessary to notice him here, from the future reference we shall have occasion to make to him in his correspondence with Allan Cunningham during the greater portion of his life. M'Ghie had very considerable talent, but his education was limited and imperfect, though it was afterwards improved, and it was thought by many in the place, that had circumstances permitted, he would have been more than an equal to his friend Allan, but he early involved himself in the cares of matrimony, and so there was an end to all literary aspirations. He was full of humour, and was always in request when public, social, or charitable petitions were to be drawn up. Besides being considered qualified for the composition of the document, he wrote a beautiful hand, which was an additional inducement to apply for his service.   As a specimen of his ability in this way we append the following, premising that the inhabitants of Quarrelwood had long playfully constituted it a burgh, and appointed Magistrates and a Town Council:—

" To James M'Alpine Leny, Esquire of Dalswinton.

"The Petition of the Magistrates, Town Council,
and Freeholders of the Burgh of Quarrelwood,

" Humbly Showeth,
·" That your Memorialists cannot contemplate without feelings of just indignation, the reckless manner in which Mr.

Rodan, like the Destroying Angel, has torn down and erased the ancient fabrics of Gothic and Grecian architecture which for time immemorial have been the boast and pride of the Burgh; even the College, which has sent forth men whose names will flourish to immortality on the page of their country's history, has been swept away by this ruthless invader of a Burgh's rights; hence your Memorialists may, with great propriety, be compared to the ancient Jews lamenting over the ruins of Jerusalem. Much, however, as these doings are to be regretted, we beg leave to call your Honour's attention to that which more immediately concerns the preservation of human life.

"Your Memorialists have long viewed with pride a magnificent Ash tree everhanging one of the principal streets and thoroughfares of this ancient and venerable Burgh, which, for stately grandeur and symmetry, might rival the boasted Cedars of Lebanon. Your Memorialists have lately observed, with unfeigned regret, the ravages which time and the many angry storms it has encountered have made on its large and elevated trunk, being literary split into halves, and every blast threatens its total annihilation. Had the funds of the Burgh permitted, your Memorialists would have employed Daniel Hunter, or some modern Archimedes, to have secured it by hoop or screw; but since the Free Church mania has seized a great proportion of the ratepayers the revenues of the Burgh have rapidly declined.

"Your Memorialists, having carefully examined their Charter, find that it gives them no right or control over the growing timber, although standing within the boundaries of the Burgh. Your Memorialists, therefore, humbly solicit that your Honour will either cause the tree in question to be taken down, or otherwise secured, as to your Honour shall seem fit, so that the lives and property of Her Majesty's liege subjects may in future not be thereby endangered, and your Memorialists, as in duty bound,

" Shall ever pray.

" GEO. DOUG. M'GHIE,
          "Burgh Chamberlain.

" Council Chambers, April, 1844."

The application of the terms *Gothic and Grecian architecture* to the hovels of Quarrelwood is humorous in the extreme. So also his appellation of *College* to the Dame's School. But M'Ghie was something more than humorous. For withering satire he had scarcely an equal; and in his capacity of Inspector for the Poor, an office which he had long held until incapacitated by the infirmities of old age, his official correspondence must have excited the risibility of the Board of Supervision, as well as troubled the serenity of his brother Inspectors. On his retirement from the Inspectorship he was entertained at a public dinner in the parish, as a mark of esteem, and in recognition of the valuable services he had performed in his official capacity, as well as a land-measurer in the district. In returning thanks for the toast of his health, he very modestly said, in his own humorous and graphic way,—

" Mr. Chairman and Gentlemen,—I presume that the most of you are aware that nature never designed me for a rhetorician, but still this deprivation has peculiar advantages, for where little is given, little can be expected. I feel myself much in the predicament of Sir John Falstaff, when, on the morning preceding the battle of Shrewsbury, he wished it was bedtime and all well. I am under the same tribulation of mind, but from a very different cause. Sir John, whom Shakespeare represents as no hero, was apprehensive of personal danger, while mine is from a moral conviction of my unfitness to express the deep sense of gratitude I feel for the unlooked-for, and, I may add, unmerited testimony of your kindness. From the very flattering and eulogistic manner in which our Rev. Chairman has been pleased to introduce my health, I am beginning to feel grave doubts of my own identity, as he has given me credit for much to which I never considered myself to have the remotest claim. In the discharge of my duties as Inspector I am conscious of many shortcomings, but I have had the good fortune to be favoured with an intelligent Board, and what is of primary importance, an intelligent Committee, always ready to aid me with their counsel and direction in cases of difficulty. It is certainly very flattering to the feelings of an old man, verging on the confines of another stage of existence, to be considered deserving of such a mark of your esteem, the remembrance of which may well cheer the remaining period of life."

He died at Quarrelwood in 1868, at the age of eighty-four, and a few weeks before his demise he burned upwards of a hundred of Allan Cunningham's letters, extending over a period of many years, because a promise that he would do so had been exacted by the writer. No persuasion of ours could prevent the holocaust. "I promised Allan that I would do so!" he said, and he did it.

During the first few years of the present century the

South of Scotland was in a continual state of ferment and alarm, from the reports every now and again arriving of a threatened invasion by Napoleon Bonaparte. The inhabitants of Kirkmahoe, like others within easy reach of the Solway, were always in dread, night and day, of being in the hands of the French without a moment's notice. When the alarm was at its height, it was found one morning that every dwelling was marked with a mysterious number, indicating too certainly that the foe had secretly landed, and had sent forth their emissaries to make preparations for a sudden attack. Neighbour ran to neighbour in the greatest consternation, but only to find that the one was as bad as the other. Every door was marked, and that must mean something, and therefore a watch must be set to prevent being taken by surprise. So all set to watching, every man his own house, with the arrangement, that, in the event of anything happening to one, the alarm should at once be given, that all might run to the rescue. The sun slowly ascended the sky, slowly crossed the meridian, slowly descended to the west, and darkness gathered around, while the sentinels faithfully stood at their posts. They were relieved by another guard during the night, and when the morning came, all being safety and peace, it was at once surmised that a cruel hoax had been played upon the parish. This was speedily confirmed, and great was the indignation shown, but who had perpetrated the deed no one could tell, no one was suspected at the time, but afterwards.

One farmer—Thomas Haining of Townhead—a very worthy and God-fearing man, felt his spirit greatly roused within him at what he considered a most cruel, heartless, and unholy deed; and loudly declared that if he could discover the perpetrators, as it must have required more than one, he would assuredly bring them to justice. In the course of the week a placard was secretly posted up in various parts of the parish to the following effect:—

"Whereas some person or persons unknown, with no fear of God before their eyes, have been guilty of wantonly, maliciously, and profanely imitating David's numbering of the people, and the marking of the dwellings of the Israelites on the eve of their departure from Egypt, to the great annoyance and trepidation of the inhabitants of this parish, a reward of £50 is hereby offered for such information as may lead to the conviction of the offender or offenders, as aforesaid.—Apply to Thomas Haining, Townhead, marked No. 14."

The offenders were never discovered, but soon universal suspicion pointed only in one direction. What added to the mystery at first was, that during the same night all the houses in the Kirklands of Tinwald were marked in a similar way. Without any expectation of receiving the reward, we now give the information solicited, though it may be rather late. The "perpetrators," both of the house numbering and the placard, were Allan Cunningham and George Douglas M'Ghie. The secret was told us by M'Ghie a short time before his death, when he said he had never told it before. We deeply sympathize with these fear-stricken inhabitants of Kirkmahoe, who fancied themselves doomed to destruction on that woful morning, but we are not quite prepared to say what sentence should have been passed, in the event of discovery, upon the delinquents— Cunningham and M'Ghie.

The term of Allan's apprenticeship has expired, and he is now a journeyman mason, and to a certain extent, therefore, his own master, that is, he is free to choose his own master; but the literary aspiration is growing with his growth, and strengthening with his strength, while the poetic *afflatus* has already kindled into song. His effusions found the best of all circulating mediums, in being chanted by the peasantry at their wedding-parties and other merry-makings, and strangers present wished to hear them repeated, so that they might carry them into their own district. Many amusing attempts were made by the buxom damsels to transfer them to writing for the benefit of their friends, but the general method adopted was to have two or three encores by which they could be impressed upon the memory. It is not to be wondered at that in these ballad singings under difficulties varieties should occur, according to the ability of the fair songstress to tax her memory aright. These liltings, however, had become pretty widely diffused, though they had not yet received the dignity or the assistance of print.

Allan had an ardent desire to meet with the Ettrick Shepherd, of whose poetic abilities he had heard so much; and as they both belonged to nearly the same class of peasantry, and had also been imperfectly educated, he was the more anxious to have a meeting. The Shepherd had now come within ordinary reach of him, being engaged with Mr. Harkness of Mitchelslacks, in the parish of Closeburn, and he resolved to embrace the opportunity lest he should never have another so convenient. The distance, however, from Dalswinton to Mitchelslacks was by no means inconsiderable. The Shepherd himself describes the first meeting with enjoyable gusto. It took place one summer day on the side of Queensberry Hill, where he was tending his master's sheep, and cultivating his muse in the leisure time. Here he had erected a hut of the smallest dimensions to shelter him from the weather, and take his meals in on stormy days. To get inside he had to crawl on hands and knees, and this effected, the roof was so low that it would only allow him to sit upright, not at all to stand. Within was a bench of rushes which served the double purpose of seat and bed, and just the length of himself, on which he could recline at ease when the sheep were all right. So one day, to his great surprise, he saw two men ascending the hill towards him, who, from their gait, he at once knew were not shepherds, and he was at a loss to conceive who could stumble into such an out-of-the-way place. His dog Hector saluted them in his usual hostile manner, and he himself would much rather have avoided them, as he was not in dress to receive strangers, being bare-legged and bare-footed, and his coat in tatters.

"I saw by their way of walking," he says, "they were not shepherds, and could not conceive what the men were seeking there, where there was no path nor aim towards any human habitation. However, I stood staring about me till they came up, always ordering my old dog Hector to silence in an authoritative style, he being the only servant I had to attend to my orders. The men approached me rather in a breathless state, from climbing the hill. The one was a tall thin man of fairish complexion and pleasant intelligent features, seemingly approaching to forty; and the other a dark ungainly youth of about eighteen, with a buirdly frame for his age, and strongly marked features—the very model of Burns, and exactly such a man. Had they been of the same age, it would not have been easy to distinguish the one from the other.

"The eldest came up and addressed me frankly, asking me if I was Mr. Harkness' shepherd, and if my name was James Hogg? To both of which queries I answered cautiously in the affirmative. . . . The younger stood at a respectful distance, as if I had been the Duke of Queensberry, instead of a ragged servant lad herding sheep. The other seized my hand and said, 'Well, then, Sir, I am glad to see you. There is not a man in Scotland whose hand I am prouder to hold.'

"I could not say a single word in answer to this address; but when he called me SIR, I looked down at my bare feet and ragged coat, to remind the man whom he was addressing. But he continued: 'My name is James Cunningham, a name unknown to you, though yours is not entirely so to me; and this is my younger brother Allan, the greatest admirer that you have on earth, and himself a young aspiring poet of some promise. You will be so kind as to excuse this intrusion of ours on your solitude, for, in truth, I could get no peace either night or day with Allan till I consented to come and see you.'

"I then stepped down the hill to where Allan Cunningham then stood, with his weather-beaten cheek toward me, and, seizing his hard, brawny hand, I gave it a hearty shake, saying something as kind as I was able, and, at the same time, I am sure as stupid as it possibly could be. From that moment we were friends, for Allan had none of the proverbial Scottish caution about him; he is all heart together, without reserve either of expression or manner: you at once see the unaffected benevolence, warmth of feeling, and firm independence of a man conscious of his own rectitude and mental energies. Young as he was, I had heard of his name, although slightly, and, I think, seen one or two of his juvenile pieces."

The afternoon was spent cheerfully within the hut, the two visitors freely partaking of the Shepherd's bread and sweet milk, while they in turn treated him to something they had brought with them, which was *not* milk. Allan repeated many of his songs and ballads, and heard many in return. "Thus began," says Hogg, "at that bothy in the wilderness, a friendship and a mutual attachment between two aspiring Scottish peasants, over which the shadow of a cloud has never yet passed. From that day forward I failed not to improve my acquaintance with the Cunninghams. I visited them several times at Dalswinton, and never missed an opportunity of meeting with Allan when it was in my power to do so. I was astonished at the luxuriousness of his fancy. It was boundless; but it was the luxury of a rich garden overrun with rampant weeds." The remembrance of this meeting was referred to by Cunningham twenty years afterwards, in London, on a renewal of correspondence with the Shepherd, as we shall afterwards see, since it was a day never to be forgotten on either side.

' An intense and lasting friendship henceforth subsisted between James Hogg and James Cunningham, which was greatly strengthened by the various visits of the former to Dalswinton, to which reference has been made. So much so, indeed, that the Shepherd and his wife, Maggie Philip, were desirous of adopting as their own child, one of Cunningham's daughters, Jane (Mrs. M'Bryde), a sprightly girl some nine years of age. She lived with them for three years at Altrive, and had many opportunities of observing the character of the Bard of Kilmeny. There she had the proud satisfaction of being introduced to Sir Walter Scott, as the "niece of Allan Kinnikem." He would take her hand tenderly into his, pat her on the head, and look with his soft loving gray eyes into hers, asking some kind question. She said "he was just a douce, plain, hamely-spoken country gentleman." An incident in connection with one of Sir Walter's visits to Altrive, while she was there, is not known, but is worth relating. The Shepherd had a greyhound which he sarcastically named "Claverse," after the hero of Scott and Aytoun's love. Hogg's servant lassie, a little maid of all work, and, perhaps, for a girl, not over well-fed, had been making black puddings in the kitchen. While Sir Walter and Hogg were seated at the parlour window, their attention was suddenly arrested by the appearance of Mary the servant, running like the chief witch in "Tam o' Shanter," to recover a pudding which she alleged the dog had stolen. Sir Walter laughed heartily, and slyly insinuated that he feared poor " Claverse," like his great namesake, got the credit for crimes which he perhaps did not deserve.

Young Allan's admiration of poetic genius was enthusiastic, and could scarcely be restrained within reasonable bounds. He had the strongest desire to see face to face those who in this respect had acquired fame. As an instance of this, in addition to the above, may be mentioned the following incident:—When Sir Walter Scott's "Lay of the Last Minstrel" was published, Allan purchased a copy at 24s., out of his scanty earnings, which he committed to memory, and when " Marmion " appeared, in the height of his ecstasy, he started off on foot from Dalswinton to Edinburgh, that he might catch a stealthy glimpse of the author. He kept pacing up and down opposite Scott's house in North Castle Street, when an adjoining lady tenant from Dumfries recognized him and invited him in. There he stood for a time, when at last his curiosity was gratified by a sight of the great author on returning home from the Parliament House. Allan immediately thereafter departed again on foot for Dalswinton.

Another instance of his poetic enthusiasm for genius was in reference to the burial of Burns. He was then an apprentice under his brother James, and both were working in Dumfries at the time Burns returned from the Brow-Well worse than when he left for it. All saw he was dying, and the poet knew that himself. On the third day after his return his spirit passed away to the "land of the leal." Allan took a position in the funeral procession, and walked with head uncovered all the way to the church-yard. He remarked afterwards to one of his sisters, that while he saw some shedding tears as the mournful cortege moved along, there were not so many as should have been. This was his estimation of the great departed. It could not arise from personal friendship or much intercourse, for although the two residences were almost opposite each other, Sandbed and Ellisland, yet the river Nith flowed between, and there was no convenient way of access between the two. Besides, Burns was only three years in Ellisland, and when he left, Allan Cunningham was only seven years old. At the time of the funeral he was consequently only twelve. So that, as we have said, Allan's enthusiasm arose not from personal friendship, but from admiration of the poet's genius.

At the same time, there was personal knowledge of the poet, if not personal intimacy, at such an early age, for Burns and John Cunningham, Allan's father, were on the most friendly terms as neighbours. It was at John Cunningham's table, in the farm-house of Sandbed, that Burns first recited his glorious epic, "Tam o' Shanter," while one of his best future biographers stood in the ingle-neuk, listening with eager and sympathetic interest to the eloquence with which it rolled forth from the lips of its great author.

CHAPTER III.

LETTER TO THE REV. JOHN WIGHTMAN—MR. WIGHTMAN'S ANSWER—
SECOND LETTER TO THE REV. MR. WIGHTMAN, CONTAINING A
POETIC EFFUSION—CONTRIBUTES TO A LONDON LITERARY MAGA-
ZINE—COMMENDATION OF HIS PIECES—"THE LOVELY LASS OF
PRESTON MILL"—LETTER, WITH NEW POEM, TO HIS BROTHER
JAMES.

IN a letter to his parish minister, the Rev. Mr. Wightman, Allan gives an account of the way in which
he spends his leisure time, and requests advice as to the
best manner of improving his intellect, and raising his
position in the world. He is now in his twenty-second
year, a journeyman mason, but with a strong desire for
literary distinction in the annals of his country, although
the path before him seems rugged, and the atmosphere
around him hazy in the extreme:—

"Dalswinton Village, 11th April, 1806.

"Reverend Sir,—According to promise, I have sent you
Sharp's edition of 'Collins, Gray, and Cunningham's Poems,'
and I am well assured they will give you in reading them
the same degree of satisfaction and pleasure which they gave
to me. I would have been happy to have seen you at the
manse on purpose to converse about some important and
laudable matters—particularly to get your advice concerning
my future course of life—to direct my reading, &c., for I am
in a manner entirely left to my own inclinations in pursuit
of what we term happiness, and I may go wrong. I shall

be directed entirely by you in everything that tends to my welfare and improvement; for I am not above nor below advice. I shall give you some idea of what I make of time when among my hands that you may form in your mind what kind of being I am. My daily labour, I may say, consumes it all, except what is allotted for sleep, and the short intervals for meals, and considerable portions of these are dedicated to reading any entertaining book, provided it says nothing against our religion. Such I carefully avoid. Poetry especially gives me most delight—Young, Milton, Thomson, and Pope, please me best.

"Social converse with my fellow-creatures I never avoid on any rational subject that improves the mind, and sweetens the bitters of life, of which, though young, I have had my share. Sometimes I write a. few lines on any pleasing subject that strikes my fancy. I have even attempted poetry, but mostly failed. After public worship is over on the Sabbath, you may find me reading in some sequestered spot, far from the usual haunts of bustling mankind, where I retire by myself to be more at liberty in my reflections and contemplations upon the works and goodness of Him who made me. I am for the most part cheerful, except when musing upon, or reading some affecting book. After returning thanks to God for my preservation, I retire to the embraces of sleep, and rise with a cheerful mind, judging it part of my tribute to my Maker. An honest and cheerful heart is almost all my stock. I fervently adhere to truth, and, to close all, I .have an independent mind.

"These, sir, are the outlines of my way of life as near as I can draw them. Now, to be candid with you, I wish to have your advice concerning books which are most proper to peruse; how to use my time, and in short, whatever you deem useful to me in life. If you would be so good as to direct my small share of abilities to flow in their proper channel, I would esteem it the greatest favour your goodness could bestow. I am certainly much in want of education. I was taken from school and put to learn my trade at eleven years of age, and I really begin to feel the want of it much. English grammar I never learned—indeed it was not in use in the school I was at. I have spoken of the Library to several of my acquaintances here, and they will become members of it as soon as it is instituted. I spoke with all the eloquence I was master of in its favour.—I ever am, reverend and worthy sir, your devoted servant, while

"ALLAN CUNNINGHAM.

"Rev. John Wightman,
    "Manse of Kirkmahoe."

Now, passing over the immature style of this letter, which, all things considered, is rather to be admired than faulted, it is valuable as giving a glimpse of the writer's inner life at this time, as well as an outline of the manner in which his leisure hours were spent. It was just such a production as gratified the heart of the minister, and he was not long in replying to his young parishioner. He might have said, "Go on as you are doing, and you will prosper, your conduct is commendable;" but a request had been made, and therefore he wrote as follows:—

"Kirkmahoe Manse, 20th April, 1806.

"My dear Allan,—I return you your two volumes, with many thanks. These poems have long been great favourites of mine. The picture you have drawn of yourself in your letter to me is exceedingly interesting. I wish you to have a happy journey through life—a smooth road and a serene sky. We must, however, lay our account with a chequered scene. The wisest and best of Beings has seen this to be most conducive to our true interests. I approve of your reading poetry. Goldsmith, in his 'Deserted Village,' says something very fine on the subject of poetry—

> 'And thou, sweet poetry, thou loveliest maid,
> The first to fly when sensual joys invade.'

The reading of poetry should be mingled with other pursuits. It is a liberal recreation, but should not be a business. It is said to be apt to foster, in elegant and ingenuous minds, a romantic delicacy, and a morbid sensibility inconsistent with the sober and industrious pursuit of the useful arts and professions. This can be the effect only of an excessive fondness for the creations of fancy; but I think there is not much reason to fear this excess in one who is so much confined, and so properly, to the duties of his employment as you are. You would do well to read books of practical science, and history, and travel, which will guard you effectually against any danger of loving poetry too much.

"Such books as the following may be worth your perusal, as they may fall in your way, or as you may find it convenient to purchase them: Dr. Robertson's 'History of Scotland;' Hume's 'History of England,' with one of the continuations; Dr. Henry's 'History of Great Britain;' some of the best tours in Great Britain, or different parts of it; the travels or tours of Moore, Cox, Swinbourne, Brydone in Sicily and Malta, Niebhur in Asia, Vaillant and Sparrman in Africa; Captain Cook's and Anson's voyages, &c., &c.; and I shall mention a book or two in divinity: 'Evidences of Christianity,' by Dr. Porteous, Bishop of London, by Dr.

Beattie of Aberdeen, and by Mr. Addison; Dr. S. Clarke's 'Commentary and Paraphrase on the Four Gospels,' with Dr. Pyle's continuation through the New Testament; or, the 'Family Expositor' of the pious and amiable Dr. Doddridge; Dr. Gisborne's 'Survey of Christianity,' and his other works; the sermons of Blair, Walker, Seed, and Sherlock. These, my dear sir, are a few of the books which you may read at your leisure, and still be steady and unremitting in attention to your profession. It is a well-balanced rather than a well-stored mind which bids fairest to be happy. Never lose sight of your religion. This is the grand recipe for happiness:—

> 'Let fouk bode weel, and strive to do their best;
> Nae mair's required: let Heaven make out the rest.'

"While you preserve your independent mind, consider always that stubbornness has no right to the title of independence. I am *convinced your* mind is not of that character. That rude and savage independence which does not attend to the mutual subserviency of the branches of human society, is apt to meet, in an evil hour, with a rude blast to break it, and ruin follows. Mingle with your virtuous contemporaries and friends, and convince them that one may be cheerful, and yet 'unspotted from the world.' I will be glad to give you my best advice at any time, and am, dear Allan, yours truly,

"JOHN WIGHTMAN.

"Mr. Allan Cunningham,
     "Dalswinton Village."

The following week Allan sent the minister another letter, enclosing a poem which he had just composed :—

"Dalswinton Village, 27th April, 1806.

"Reverend Sir,—You will no doubt think me impertinent in writing to you again, but you must forgive me. Your fine ideas on the pleasures of solitude, on the Sabbath of 20th April, so charmed me, that whenever an opportunity offered itself, I determined to write thanking you for so many useful hints on life and the sweets of retirement, &c. But your letter arriving, for which I sincerely thank you, overthrew my resolutions entirely. I instantly resolved to show my love of solitude, of nature, and of virtue, in a kind of rhyming, prosaical poetry. It but poorly expresses my ideas, but it is sincere enough:—

"THE NITH.

" Nith, sacred Nith, beside your hermit stream,
   Your rocks and foliage bright with summer's beam,
   How do I love to walk and raving muse
   Upon the balmy fragrance Heaven bestows!
   How dear unto my mind your foaming pride,
   Where spreading hazels drink your blushing tide!
   How sweet the morning mist that wraps your woods—
   How pure the orient sun that gilds your floods!
   Wild in his beams your sportive tenants stray,
   And show their gold-tinged sides in wanton play.
   Sweet to the smell your honey-suckled trees,
   That fling their dew-dipt odours on the breeze;
   Mild blooms your primrose on the shelving rocks,
   And sweet the hawthorn shakes her dewy locks.
   Like beauty is the dew on yonder thorn,
   That as a meteor vanishes in morn.
   Your beeches high their lofty heads uprear
   Unto the heaven, and threat the middle sphere;
   The scented birks bend too their tressy locks,
   And form cool arbours o'er the moss-girt rocks.
   The woodbine anxious clasps the cavern's brows,
   Where rustic heaven-taught genius loves to muse.

O how the mind is fired in nature's fields!
What virtuous peace this to the bosom yields!
O ever welcome to my soul ye groves,
Ye rushy fountains, and ye green alcoves!
Ye hermit glens, ye haunts of peaceful rest,
That soothe the soul, and calm the tortured breast;
Ye teach the melting passions how to move,
And charm the heart of man to heavenly love.

  " Blest solitude, by kindred nature given,
Amidst thy peaceful walks I've talked with heaven !
But oh! too few, alas! its sweetness feel—
Man's giddy brains in maddening tumult reel;
His soul rough-cased in ignorance and whim,
Floats wildly on, and reason swells the stream;
His life he prizes as if life were given,
To swell his pride, and shake him off from heaven.
His heaven-erected face is given in vain—
He drags his reason 'neath the bestial train;
In life's deep mire, in search of gold he plies,
He grasps the shadowy phantom fast and dies:
This is the foolish man's unthinking end,
With too much vanity to think and mend;
With too much wisdom to do aught amiss—
Too happy for to taste of happiness;
Too well informed for to inform his mind,
And too quick-sighted for to see he's blind.

  " O, what's the source of prideful thoughts and vain?
'Tis self-struck reveries of a vacant brain.
What can we boast of, for vain thoughts to swell?
We grasp at heaven and plunge ourselves in hell !
Go, ask yon graves where our great forbears lie—
' Come to your kindred dust,' they all reply.
Look to yon blasted oak, low in the vale,
Its moss-grown trunk, gray, whistling to the gale;
Its many arms reached wide, its top touched heaven;
Its forked roots into earth's centre driven;
Its foliage green embalmed the dawning mild,

Wild flowers and shrubs beneath its fragrance smiled;
But lightning came, and scattered it around,
And strewed its blushing honours on the ground.

"And so is man, tall as an oak he shows—
Pure vernal odours from his foliage flows;
Vain in his strength, he mocks the lowly thorn,
And opens wide his giant arms in scorn.
He shakes the neighbouring woodlands at his nod,
And grasps the echoing winds, aërial load;
But death in form of thunder cleaves his pride,
And widening ruin hurls on every side:
The brambles, wild-insulting, o'er him grow,
And nameless streams deep-eddying o'er him flow.

"This is ambition's end, this folly's fall,
Thus certain vengeance overwhelms them all;
Thus they stand trembling on the brink of death,
And shudder at eternity beneath.
O dreadful chance! but no dread chance to those,
Whose mind with virtue and religion glows.
Let tyrants threaten, boreas tempests howl,
And nature tremble, 'twill not shake their soul:
Death, gloomy death, to them no terror seems,
Their nature sinks in paradisian dreams.

"Thus, O my soul, pursue fair virtue's road,
Keep peace with honour, and revere your God;
And though in life's rough ocean luckless starr'd,
We read that 'virtue is its own reward.'"

"You are in the right with respect to poetry. Reading
it too much and nothing else certainly softens the mind; but
I have a very good collection of other books which I read at
times. At another time I will give you a list of them.
I shall avail myself of your courteous offer of advice
without reserve, and you may often expect to hear from

me on that head.—I ever am your obedient and obliged servant, while

" ALLAN CUNNINGHAM.

" Rev. John Wightman,
　" Kirkmahoe Manse."

The discourse alluded to above, containing the "fine ideas on the pleasures of solitude," was an exposition of the Twenty-third Psalm, in which the minister, himself a poet, gave a graphic description of the scenery that the King of Israel saw around him, while tending his father's flocks on the hills and in the solitudes of Judah.

Encouraged, as we have seen, by the genial countenance and sage advice of his parish minister, who was himself endowed with the spirit of poetry, and published many admirable pieces anonymously, Cunningham now began to give rapid flight to his muse, and to look for a channel through which he might try his poetic strength, and "tempt his new-fledged offspring to the skies." Lilting lassies, at kirns, and weddings, and other merry-meetings, might be good enough in their way, but as an advertising medium they were not in his mind sufficiently extensive for what he thought himself capable of producing. So he looked elsewhere and succeeded.

There was at this time (1807) a London periodical entitled *Literary Recreations*, conducted by an Irish gentleman, Eugenius Roche, which seemed to him a likely vehicle for the gratification of his desire; and, accordingly, he despatched a few pieces to the editor for insertion, under the signature "Hidallan," the name of one of Ossian's heroes, describing their origin, and intimating that it was the writer's first attempt to have his verses put into print, so as to obtain the high title of an author. These were readily accepted, and received insertion in due time. Not only so, but in one of the monthly notices to correspondents, special reference was made to him in the following terms:—" We really feel proud in having the pleasure of ushering to public notice, through the medium of our publication, the effusions of such a self-taught genius as Hidallan." Mr. S. C. Hall, in reference to this matter, says:—" I knew Eugenius Roche somewhat intimately in 1825. He was an Irish gentleman, of a very kindly and genial nature. At that time he was editor of the *Morning Post*, and had all his life been a labourer for the press. He was proud of the small share he had in advancing the fortunes of Cunningham; and long before I became acquainted with Allan, described to me the surprise he had felt on the discovery that so young and so apparently rough a specimen of the 'north countrie' was the writer of the poems he had read with so much delight."

This notice of Mr. Roche was highly encouraging, and stimulated the youthful poet to further efforts of a similar kind. But it had not the effect of inducing him to relinquish the hope of eminence in his special profession. As a tradesman he was distinguished among his fellows, and in Dumfries he always received higher wages than they, as he was put to the execution of work which required peculiar skill and delicacy in the manipulating, such as carving, moulding, and like ornamentation, for which he had a decided taste, and an artistic hand.

A new era is now about to dawn upon him, as well of love as of literature, and rural quietude is soon to be exchanged for a city's fermenting din. Still he knows it not. He is chiselling away during the daytime, and in the evening pluming his muse's wing. He has left the superintendence of his brother James, with whom he had served his apprenticeship, perhaps because of the scarcity of work which often occurs in the experience of a country mason, or probably because he had a great ambition to rise in the pursuit of his trade. As we have seen, he had a decided taste for the execution of ornamental work in buildings, to which he was always assigned; and as country employment was generally precarious, and as plain as possible, there was no encouragement for him to follow it. So he went here and there and everywhere, as his taste directed. He is now twenty-five, and has sobered down from the moonlight escapades carried on by his friend M‘Ghie and himself, when both were in their teens.

His master in Dumfries is anxious to assume him as a partner in business, but this offer he declines. He has other projects simmering in his mind which he keeps to himself. A new mansion was to be erected at Arbigland, in the parish of Kirkbean, and as carved ornamentation was essentially necessary for such a building, we find Cunningham there. While engaged in this work he lodged in the neighbouring farm-house of Preston Mill, where he met for the first time with his future wife, Jean Walker, in the capacity of a domestic there.   The intimacy by degrees ripened into affection, and then into love, but they did not unite their fates together for a considerable time afterwards.   She is the subject of one of his finest songs:—

"THE LOVELY LASS OF PRESTON MILL.

" The lark had left the evening cloud,
    The dew fell saft, the wind was lowne,
Its gentle breath amang the flowers
    Scarce stirred the thistle's tap o' down;
The dappled swallow left the pool,
    The stars were blinking owre the hill,
As I met, amang the hawthorns green,
    The lovely lass of Preston Mill.

" Her naked feet amang the grass,
    Shone like twa dew-gemmed lilies fair;
Her brow shone comely 'mang her locks,
    Dark curling owre her shoulders bare;
Her cheeks were rich wi' bloomy youth;
    Her lips had words and wit at will,
And heaven seemed looking through her een—
    The lovely lass of Preston Mill.

" Quo' I, 'Sweet lass, will ye gang wi' me,
    Where blackcocks craw, and plovers cry?
Six hills are woolly wi' my sheep,
    Six vales are lowing wi' my kye:
I hae looked lang for a weel-faured lass,
    By Nithsdale's holmes an' monie a hill;'
She hung her head like a dew-bent rose,
    The lovely lass of Preston Mill.

" Quo' I, 'Sweet maiden, look nae down,
    But gie's a kiss, and gang wi' me:'
A lovelier face, O! never looked up,
    And the tears were drapping frae her ee :

'I hae a lad, wha's far awa',
    That weel could win a woman's will;
My heart's already fu' o' love,'
    Quo' the lovely lass of Preston Mill.

" 'Now wha is he wha could leave sic a lass,
    To seek for love in a far countrie?'
Her tears drapped down like simmer dew :
    I fain wad kissed them frae her ee.
I took but ane o' her comely cheek ;
    ' For pity's sake, kind sir, be still !
My heart is fu' o' other love,'
    Quo' the lovely lass of Preston Mill.

" She stretched to heaven her twa white hands,
    And lifted up her watery ee ;—
' Sae lang's my heart kens aught o' God,
    Or light is gladsome to my ee ;—
While woods grow green, and burns rin clear,
    Till my last drap o' blood be still,
My heart shall haud nae other love,'
    Quo' the lovely lass of Preston Mill.

" There's comely maids on Dee's wild banks,
    And Nith's romantic vale is fu';
By lanely Cluden's hermit stream
    Dwells monie a gentle dame, I trow !
O, they are lights of a gladsome kind,
    As ever shone on vale or hill;
But there's a light puts them a' out,
    The lovely lass of Preston Mill."

We are informed, in a note by the author, that "Preston Mill is a little rustic village in the parish of Kirkbean on the Galloway side of the Solway; it consists of some dozen or so of thatched cottages, grouped together without regularity, yet beautiful from their situation on the banks of a wild burn which runs or rather tumbles through it, scarcely staying to turn a mill from which the place takes its name."

While his thoughts seem to be intent on love, the Muse is not forgotten, as, in addition to the above, the following letter to his brother James shows:—

"Arbigland, 1st July, 1809.

"My dear James,—I would have seen you upon the 'Siller Gun' day, but I was so fatigued that I really could not attempt the journey. As I will not possibly be up from here before a month or six weeks, I will send you a few of the rhymes I have been composing in my leisure moments. The following opens with the arrival of intelligence to Lord Maxwell of our *own* Nithsdale of his Queen's escape from Lochleven, and the summons is sent by him at midnight to warn his military tenantry and vassals:—

> "'Twas midnight when, at portgate barred,
> The clanging tread of hoofs was heard
>   In Maxwell's hilly tower—
> And soon, 'To arms,' the chieftain cries,
> And soon, the nimble courier hies,
> Dashing through Nith's dark stream he flies,
>   To raise the Nithsdale power.
> Fast by Dalswinton's woody hall
>   The bugle blast was blown—
> Its gallant baron heard the call,
> And bounded forth his vassals all,
> A spearmen forest gleaming tall
>   Into the star-beams shone.
> While o'er the Nith's lone stream they bound,
> By Tinwald towers was heard the sound,
>   The warrior's rousing cry.
> The woodman on his rushy bed,
> Lone-bosomed in his woodland shed
>   Uplifts his toil-slept eye,

And rushing from his jangling brakes,
His six-ell Scottish lance he shakes.
Sad sight it was to see dismayed,
In midnight hurry, loose arrayed,
Each young and lovely Nithsdale maid,
       Waked with the hour's alarms.
All by their cottage doors they shook,
Whilst in their arms their lovers took,
And on them fixed each tearful look,
       And sank within their arms.
Adown their ready spears they threw—
But short the promised love—the vow—
And short the farewell interview,
       For louder waxed the note.
And soon to morning's breaking beam,
The battle banners dimly gleam,
As o'er the Nith's fair-valleyed stream
       The gairy pennons float.
Soon by their various barons led,
Lord Maxwell's pavement sound their tread,—
Above the rest the veteran stands.
With aged smile he eyed his bands,
       And shook his hoary hair.
Tall, like an ancient oak he stood,
Whose stubborn trunk the storms have bowed,
       With branches shorn and bare;
Rejoicing 'neath Spring's milder skies,
Views round his vassal woodlands rise,
       Outstretching green and fair.
Oh, ne'er again on tower or height,
Shall stream that reverend banner white,
Or rustic bard, with heartfelt strain,
Welcome his gallant lord again!
Long, long, each lovely Nithsdale maid
May stretch her white arms from her plaid,
       And bare her breast of snow.
The aged matrons long may mourn,
Yearly upon that fatal morn,
       Which saw their banners low.

> They'll march at midnight's solemn hour,
> Their corpse-light quivering round the tower,
> And weep for all the gallant flower
>   Of lonely Nithsdale low.
> And long in rustic tale or song,
> At coming 'mongst the peasant throng,
> Will all their loss their tears prolong,
>   Thy spring, O Nithsdale low!

   *   *   *   *   *

"I would have sent you the *Edinburgh Review*, but I suppose you will get the loan of George M'Ghie's. I had a letter from one of the editors of the *Recreations*, wishing me to send him all my poetry, and he would get it published for me in London. This offer I have declined.—With my respects and good wishes for you and your family's welfare, I am, dear Brother,

"ALLAN CUNNINGHAM.

"Remember me to my mother, and my sister-in-law, and any of the 'lave.'—A. C.

"Mr. James Cunningham,
 "Dalswinton."

CHAPTER IV.

FIRST MEETING WITH CROMEK—LETTER FROM MOLLANCE TO HIS BROTHER JAMES—FIRST INSTALMENT OF THE "REMAINS OF NITHSDALE AND GALLOWAY SONG"—"SHE'S GANE TO DWALL IN HEAVEN"—"BONNIE LADY ANNE"—CROMEK'S LETTERS— LEAVES FOR LONDON.

IN the summer of 1809, Mr. Cromek, a London engraver, and a great enthusiast in antiquarian lore, paid a visit to Dumfriesshire in the company of Mr Stothard, the celebrated landscape artist. "The object of their joint-visit," says Mr. Peter Cunningham in his introduction to an edition of his father's Poems and Songs, "was the collection of materials and drawings for an enlarged and illustrated edition of the Works of Burns." Mr. Cromek had published, a few years before, a supplemental volume to Currie's edition of the Works, and, pleased with the success of the "Reliques" (so the volume was entitled), was preparing for publication, at the same time, a select Collection of Scottish Songs, with the notes and memoranda of Burns, and such additional materials as his own industry could bring together.

"Mr. Cromek brought a letter of introduction to my father from Mrs. Fletcher, of Edinburgh, herself a poetess, and the friend of Sir Walter Scott and Campbell. A similarity of pursuits strengthened their acquaintance; their talk was all about Burns, the old Border Ballads, and the Jacobite Songs of '15 and '45. Cromek found his young friend, then a stonemason earning eighteen shillings a-week, well versed in the poetry of his country, with a taste naturally good, and an extent of reading, for one in his condition, really surprising. Stothard, who had a fine feeling for poetry, was equally astonished.

"In one of their conversations on modern Scottish Song, Cromek made the discovery that the Dumfries mason on eighteen shillings a-week was himself a poet. Mrs. Fletcher may have told him as much, but I never heard that she did; this, however, is immaterial. Cromek, in consequence of this discovery, asked to see some of his 'effusions'; they were shown to him; and at their next meeting he observed, as I have heard my father tell with great good humour, imitating Cromek's manner all the while, 'Why, sir, your verses are well, very well; but no one should try to write songs after Robert Burns, unless he could either write like him or some of the old minstrels.' The disappointed poet nodded assent, changed the subject of conversation, and talked about the old songs and fragments of songs still to be picked up among the peasantry of Nithsdale. 'Gad, sir!' said Cromek, 'if we could but make a volume—gad, sir!— see what Percy has done, and Ritson, and Mr. Scott, more recently, with his Border Ministrelsy.' The idea of a volume of imitations passed upon Cromek as genuine remains flashed across the poet's mind in a moment, and he undertook at once to put down what he knew, and set about collecting all that could be picked up in Nithsdale and Galloway. Cromek foresaw a volume of genuine verse, and entered keenly into the idea of the Nithsdale and Galloway publication. A few fragments were soon submitted. 'Gad, sir! these are the things;' and, like Polyphemus, he cried for more. 'More, give me more; this is divine!' He never suspected a cheat, or, if at all, not at this time."

O! Allan, shall we call you *honest* Allan any more? thus to play upon the credulity of one who was so enthusiastic in his admiration of your own national poet, and who desired to save from oblivion the remains of the minstrelsy of your own native dale. Still, Burns confesses that he did something of the same kind with some of the same songs which he contributed to Johnson's Museum. He gave them to the world as old verses, to their respective tunes, while, in fact, little more than the chorus was ancient, though, he said, there was no reason to give any one that piece of intelligence. Motherwell also did the same thing, when he published in the "Harp of Renfrewshire" his "Cavalier's Song," commencing with the lines—

> "A steed, a steed of matchlesse speede!
> A sword of metal keene!"

and prefaced it by saying—"The following lines are written, in an old hand, in a copy of Lovelace's Lucaste, London, 1679," while all the time it was an original composition of his own, after the antique manner in phraseology and spelling. Now, though two blacks, or rather three, don't make a white, we mention this merely to show that Cunningham was not alone in this kind of literary imposition, or mystification, or by whatever euphemism it may be characterized. We have no doubt that this meeting with Cromek gave a stimulus to his muse, to carry out the project he had so suddenly and secretly devised, and we can easily account for the "eleven split new songs" referred to in the following letter to his brother James, from Mollance, near Castle-Douglas:—

"Mollance, 3rd August, 1809.

"My dear James,—I have been 'holding high converse' in the path of song since I saw you. I have composed eleven 'split new ones,' one of which I have enclosed. Want of time prevents me from sending more, which I deem of superior worth. I have no place to compose my mind in, but in the Babelonian slang of tongues which compose a workman's kitchen. I am, however, much at my ease, and comparatively serious! I hope my sister-in-law is quite well, and my young namesake. I do not know when I will see you, probably not these six weeks.

"I am begun to my old trade of building whinstone. We have had an untoward time of it, working away late and hard. I care not much for hard work, but I meet it with unconcern. I see my lot is predestinated, and I cannot deviate from the path laid out for me. So, welcome labour, welcome toil, divine heaven sends them! I had better have a contented and easy mind although my carcase be wrapped in 'Muirland raploch, heplock plaiden,' than have an unquiet heart pranked out in superfine linetorum. Is not my idea good? Were a better plan to cast up I should accept of it; if not, let me be humbly wise.—With my kind respects to my sister-in-law, to my mother, to Peter, and all the rest, I remain, dear James, your affectionate brother, while

"ALLAN CUNNINGHAM.

"Mr. James Cunningham, Dalswinton."

Mr. Cromek had not long returned home when he wrote to Cunningham on the subject which was so entirely engrossing his head and heart. His first communication was, "How are you getting on with your collection? Don't be in a hurry. I think between us we shall make a most interesting book." In reply to this Cunningham sent the first instalment of the so-called Remains, entirely an imitation only, but a very fine one, of the old ballad style:—

"SHE'S GANE TO DWALL IN HEAVEN.

"She's gane to dwall in heaven, my lassie,
    She's gane to dwall in heaven;
Ye're owre pure, quo' the voice o' God,
    For dwalling out o' heaven !

"O what'll she do in heaven, my lassie?
    O what'll she do in heaven?
She'll mix her ain thoughts wi' angels' sangs,
    An' make them mair meet for heaven.

"She was beloved by a', my lassie,
    She was beloved by a';
But an angel fell in love wi' her,
    An' took her frae us a'.

"Lowly there thou lies, my lassie,
    Lowly there thou lies;
A bonnier form ne'er went to the yird,
    Nor frae it will arise !

"Fu' soon I'll follow thee, my lassie,
    Fu' soon I'll follow thee;
Thou left me nought to covet ahin',
    But tuke gudeness sel' wi' thee.

> " I looked on thy death-cold face, my lassie,
> 　I looked on thy death-cold face;
> Thou seemed a lily new cut in the bud,
> 　An' fading in its place.
>
> " I looked on thy death-shut eye, my lassie,
> 　I looked on thy death-shut eye;
> An' a lovelier light in the brow of heaven,
> 　Fell Time shall ne'er destroy.
>
> " Thy lips were ruddy and calm, my lassie, ,
> 　Thy lips were ruddy and calm;
> But gane was the holy breath o' heaven
> 　That sang the Evening Psalm.
>
> " There's nought but dust now mine, lassie,
> 　There's nought but dust now mine;
> My soul's wi' thee i' the cauld grave,
> 　An' why should I stay behin'!"

This very beautiful imitation of the ancient ballad was despatched to London, we have no doubt, with a feeling of pride, but, at the same time, we are certain, with a consciousness of trembling and fear on the part of the author as to the future success of the work, and the risk he ran of having his imposition discovered. Had it been for a song or two, or even half a dozen, but a whole volume of contraband lyrics was not a " consummation devoutly to be wished," and we cannot therefore do otherwise than believe that it was with some misgiving that the first song was transmitted to London. Whether this was so or not, it was speedily succeeded by the following ballad:—

" BONNIE LADY ANNE.

" There's kames o' hinney 'tween my love's lips,
    An' gowd amang her hair,
Her breasts are lapt in a holie veil:
    Nae mortal een keek there.
What lips dare kiss, or what hand dare touch,
    Or what arm o' love can span,
The hinney lips, the creamy loof,
    Or the waist o' Lady Anne?

" She kisses the lips o' her bonnie red rose,
    Wat wi' the blobs o' dew;
But gentle lip, nor semple lip,
    Maun touch her lady mou';
But a broider'd belt wi' a buckle o' gowd,
    Her jimpy waist maun span—
Oh, she's an armfu' fit for heaven,
    My bonnie Lady Anne!

" Her bower casement is latticed wi' flowers,
    Tied up with silver thread,
An' comely sits she in the midst,
    Men's longing een to feed.
She waves the ringlets frae her cheek,
    Wi' her milky, milky han',
An' her cheeks seem touch'd wi' the finger o' God,
    My bonnie Lady Anne!

" The morning cloud is tassl'd wi' gowd,
    Like my love's broider'd cap;
An' on the mantle which my love wears,
    Is mony a gowden drap.
Her bonnie eebree's a holie arch,
    Cast by nae earthly han',
An' the breath o' heaven's atween the lips
    O' my bonnie Lady Anne!

> " I am her father's gard'ner lad,
>   An' poor, poor is my fa';
> My auld mither gets my sair-won fee,
>   Wi' fatherless bairnies twa;
> But my Lady comes, my Lady goes,
>   Wi' a fou' an' a kindly han';
> Oh, the blessing o' God maun mix wi' my love,
>   An' fa' on Lady Anne!"

In a note to this ballad it is said that there is a variation in the last verse well worth preserving. Indeed, a deal of unseemly chaff had intermixed with the heavy grain, which has cost a little winnowing and sieving.

> " I am her daddie's gardener lad,
>   An' poor, poor is my fa';
> My auld mither gets my sair-won fee,
>   Wi' fatherless bairns twa.
> My een are bauld, they dwall on a place
>   Where I darena' mint my han',
> But I water, and tend, and kiss the flowers
>   O' my bonnie Lady Anne."

The enterprize on which Cunningham had ventured was not only in a moral point of view daring, but it was also one attended with considerable difficulty and hazard. He had undertaken to furnish a number of ancient ballads, sufficient to make a volume, collected in the districts of Nithsdale and Galloway, but he knew they were to be the productions of his own brain, from such traditional snatches as were floating about, and some of them not even that; and as his only time for composition was limited, even were the Muse willing, which it was possible might not always be the case, his engagement might, therefore, fail. Besides, he might infer, from the enthusiasm which his friend·Cromek had shown in the matter, that it would not be long ere a demand would be made upon his poetic resources. This consideration might have upset the nerves of many a more highly gifted and experienced poet than he was at the time, still he never flinched, but set himself with all ardour to the work, building by day, and writing far into the night, or rather the morning, till he got so far ahead that final success appeared to him certain.

If he sent off the foregoing pseudo-antique specimens to his London friend, with a feeling of doubt and hesitancy, not only as to their reception, but also as to the propriety of the act, we may be certain that he awaited with great anxiety the nature of the verdict which would be pronounced upon them. He had not, however, long to wait in suspense. On their receipt, Mr. Cromek wrote back in the most grateful and glowing terms, acknowledging the arrival of the valuable treasures he had secured, at the same time making some critical comments on certain words and phrases which they contained, showing that he was by no means an incompetent judge, and that he was well versed in ancient ballad lore. In the course of correspondence he occasionally put to his Nithsdale friend certain interrogatories which could not be very agreeable in the position assumed as a hunter of poetic relics, such as the one inquiring what the fragment of " A Tocher " was extracted from, and again earnestly requesting the names of the poets which Nithsdale and Galloway had produced. These were trying questions, and as a

"Don't remember" might have aroused suspicion, it is probable that the answering of them was considered "more honoured in the breach than in the observance." Here is Mr. Cromek's acknowledgment of the first instalment:—

"64 Newman Street, 27th October, 1809.

"Thank you, very, very kindly, my good Allan, for your interesting letter, and the very fine poem it contained. Your *short* but *sweet* criticism on this wonderful performance supersedes the necessity of my saying a word more in its praise. I must, however, just remark that I do not know anything more touching, more simply pathetic, in the whole range of Scottish song. Pray, what d'ye think of its age? I am of opinion, from the *dialect*, that it is the production of a Border minstrel, though not of one who has 'full *ninety* winters seen.'

"In *old* ballads *abstract ideas* are rarely meddled with—an old minstrel would not have personified 'Gudeness,' nor do I think he would have used compound epithets, 'death-cold,' 'death-shut ee,' &c.; much less would he have introduced the epithet 'calm' as it is applied in this song. A bard of the olden time would have said *a calm sea, a calm night*, and such like.

"The epithet 'Fell' ('Fell Time' in the last line of the 7th verse) is a word almost exclusively used by *mere* cold-blooded *classic* poets, not by the poets of nature, and it certainly has crept into the present song through the ignorance of reciters. We *must* remove it, and its removal must *not* be mentioned. We'll bury it 'in the family vault of all the Capulets.'

"'Ye're ower pure'—I do not recollect the word pure in

old, or, indeed, in modern Scotch ballads; but it may pass muster. I have read these verses to my old mother, my wife, sister, and family, till *all our hearts ache.*

"The last verse of 'Bonnie Lady Anne' contains a fine sentiment.

"The Jacobite Songs will be a great acquisition. I am pretty sure that among us we shall produce a book of consequence and interest. I have now arranged the plan of publication. I shall place Burns and his remarks, with the songs remarked on, at the front of the battle. These Songs will afford hints for many notes, &c. You and I will then come forward with our budget in an appendix, introduced with some remarks on Scottish Song, which *I much wish* you would try your hand at. I think you will succeed in this much better than myself. I would then conclude the book with a selection of principally old songs and ballads, from Johnson's 'Musical Museum.' This selection will consist of about five-and-twenty or thirty of the best songs, which lay buried alive amid the rubbish of that heterogeneous mass.

"Speaking of the 'Museum,' I hope you will receive safe a copy of this work, six volumes, which I have got bound for you. The 'Museum' has become scarce since I published the 'Reliques.' Do me the favour to accept of these books, which I send under the full persuasion that to *you* they will be a mine of wealth.

"Your brother (Thomas) dined with us on the Sunday before last. He is a very good fellow. He desired me to remind you of an old woman, living (I hope) at Kirkbean, 'ycleped *Margaret Corson.*' She has, or had, a budget filled with songs. If you see her, ask her for what she may happen to recollect of an old fragment beginning—

> 'D'ye mind, d'ye mind, Lady Margery,
> When we handed round the wine,' &c.

"From this woman you may also learn many particulars respecting 'Mary's Dream,' and its author. If she lives at any distance, hire a horse and ride at my expense as boldly as 'Muirland Willie,' when he went a-courting. Pray get what you can from her respecting the history of this song and its author.

"My family beg their kindest wishes. Whether my wife will be able to welcome you to London *in broad Scots* I cannot tell; this I will venture to say for her, that she, as well as all of us, will welcome you in the simple old style language of the heart.

"On the subject of your *crossing the Sark* I will write fully in my next. At all events the spring must introduce *you* with other *wild* flowers to the notice of my London friends.

"I was glad to find you were pleased with the present of the song ('The Blue-Eyed Lass'), in Burns' handwriting. You may safely consider yourself a favourite to receive such a thing from *me*, I can assure you. Remember me very kindly at home. God bless you.

"R. H. Cromek.

*   *   *   *   *   *

"I begin to feel anxious to see what you have done. I beg of you to take a week from your employer, and sit down leisurely to the papers; for which *week* I will send you, by Johnson's next parcel, a £2 note, with this old proverb as an apology for so doing, 'He may well swim that has his head hadden up.'

"Adieu again,

"R. H. C.

"Mr. Allan Cunningham."

Mr. Cromek is now more urgent than ever for Cunningham's departure to London, and even fixes the very time when he must appear in the great metropolis. His letter on that point is very jubilant, and must have greatly influenced the young stonemason in taking such an important step. Still we cannot help thinking that in the mind of Cunningham, from his careful moral training at home, and his regular observance of public religious ordinances after leaving his father's roof, there must have been a little misgiving as to what might be the result of this daring speculation. What if his so-called ancient ballads should be discovered by London critics to be spurious, mere imitations, and an imposition be charged upon him! Where could he hide his head, and would not his endeavours after literary fame be quenched, in so far as moral principle was concerned! Something of this sort must doubtless have passed through his mind ere the great undertaking was finally resolved on. But Mr. Cromek is urgent for him to go, and, besides, he has promised to use all his influence to obtain for him some permanent situation of emolument; a promise, however, which was not fulfilled, from some cause or another:—

"Friday, 27th January, 1810.

"My dear Allan,—While I recollect, I will tell you that I shall not put the Nithsdale Ballads to press till I am able to announce to Great Britain the arrival of your worship in the Metropolis, which I hope will be soon. You must be here by the 1st, 2nd, or 3rd of April or so. We will then sit down and make a good book.   I have arranged the materials already come to hand, and have written several *spruce* notes. I am absolutely dying to see ' Billy Blin',' and his many companions. ' The Lass of Inverness' is quite lovely. When you are here I will point out to you the beauty of these things as I feel them.

" The fragment of ' A Tocher' is curious and interesting. What is it extracted from ? The History of the Pipers will tell well. As you say, ' Notices Concerning By-past Manners' are valuable. ' The Border Minstrelsy' hath scarcely any other merit. ' Muirland Willie' is *braw*. The picture of the Country Ale-House is so faithful that it might be painted from. Thank you for it very kindly. ' Maggie Lauder' will do *fine*. ' Blythsome Bridal'—sensible observant remarks. I envy you the sight of Lady Nithsdale's letter—pray steal it. At all events mark its date, and compare it with the printed copy, but don't talk about it, and inform me who possesses it. Let me have the History of the Fairies of Nithsdale and Galloway, and the Brownie. Adieu, my good friend, in great haste, your sincere

" R. H. C.

" Mr. Allan Cunningham."

[No date.]

" Pray what are the names of the poets Nithsdale and Galloway have produced ?

" I shall introduce ' Bothwell Bank' as the production of a friend, and you may claim it ; but say nothing about it till it appears and you will hear it remarked on. It is too good to be thrown away ; you must have it.

" Since I wrote the above, I have read your ' Bothwell Bank' to Mr. Stothard. He is delighted with it. His taste is perfect. He wishes me to allow it to be shown to Mr. Rogers, the author of the 'Pleasures of Memory,' which I shall do. Adieu.

"R. H. CROMEK.

"Mr. Allan Cunningham."

" 64 Newman Street, 8th Feb., 1810.

"I congratulate you very sincerely, my dear Allan, on the *good things* your two last contained. Your 'Brownie' is very fine. Something near the outline of your story Scott had picked up, but yours is so *rich* and *full* that I do not think it worth while, when I print it, to give the reader notice of any resemblance. I have now a clear ken of a *curious* book, on which we can pride ourselves, notwithstanding much *criticism*, which I plainly see it will get. I have got a famous motto for the book—Remains of *Nithsdale* and *Galloway* Song; with Historical and Traditional Notices relative to the Manners and Customs of the Peasantry, now first published by *R. H. Cromek.*

> ' We marked each memorable scene,
> And held poetic talk between;
> Nor hill, nor brook, we paced along,
> But had its LEGEND or its SONG:
> All silent now.'

" The variations of ' Tibbie Fowler' are very good, and the Notices also. From the specimen you have given in your ' Brownie,' I have every hope, from your other characteristic Tales, they will do wonders for our Ballads. I think you show the richness and pleasantry of your genius in these stories as much as in any sort of composition.

" Do let us see you as *early in April* as you can.   I think it would be best to go to Leith, and thence by sea to London; but more of this in due time.   You may return by Liverpool when you do return.

" I have engaged a scribe to make a fair copy of the materials for our volume, with the various notes, &c., in their proper places.   Let me remind you not to forget the games of ' *England* and *Scotland*,' &c., &c.—there is no haste for them.   As to the *Cutty Stool*, I don't know if it would be *politically* good to write about it; if I should, I shall do it with a ' noble daring.'   I fear I am not sufficiently *familiar* with it to do it justice.   Try *your* hand, *i.e.*, if you think it worth shot.   What a grand thing in the hands of Burns!

" I beg you will not be afraid your communications will swell my volume too much: even a *small* volume has a *great* swallow.   Did I ever ask you to write six lines (when I say *six* I only mean that number) of introduction to the old ballad, 'The Wife of Auchtermuchty!' It is a fine thing, and I wish to use it.

" I beg of you not to approach me without some *Relique* of *Burns*.   The plough that he turned up the mouse's nest with *will do*, or if you can trace any of the descendants of his ' Mountain Daisy,' bring one in the button-hole of your coat, or *his* ox, or his ass, OR ANY THING THAT WAS HIS.'— Adieu, very sincerely, your affectionate friend,

" R. H. CROMEK.

" As to Burns' Apostrophe to old and forgotten Bards, it is exquisitely beautiful and tender.   I do not think it would do as a motto, because, if you *reason* on the effect produced on your feelings, you will find that much of its beauty arises from the circumstance of so great a poet as Burns himself sympathising with those sons of genius. Coming from a mere editor, the effect would be considerably diminished.

" Mr. Allan Cunningham."

" 64 Newman Street, 22nd Feb., 1810.

" My dear Allan,—I have got safe your last, containing the account of the Cutty Stool. Though 'rude and rough,' yet it is 'ready-witted,' and exceedingly to my wishes and purpose. I have been rewriting, and I hope you will think well of what I have done. I *think* I have given *still more* vigour to the strong parts. I have heightened the *pathos*, and I have aimed at a burst of eloquent indignation. But you shall see it and judge for yourself. I say you shall see it, because I have the work fairly transcribed, and I mean to indulge your longing een with a sight of this precious volume by Johnson's next parcel. But, except your own, take care no *mortal eyes keek in.* However, in this act as you think fit, only BE CAUTIOUS not to divulge the *secrets* of the PRISON HOUSE. I shall send you the book, because you will then see my plan, and you may suggest hints of improvement, such as we further want in illustration.

" You will see that I have enriched the text wherever I could by notes, and I have connected my remarks with the text, and this incorporation will preserve whatever consequence and value they may have. I regret that the notice of ' Brownie ' must appear in a note, but it cannot be helped, it is too curious and novel to be overlooked, even by the most indolent reader. You will see we want the *sports* and *pastimes* alluded to in some of the poetry, and the Life of Lowe (author of ' Mary's Dream'), but if you have the materials, bring them with you, and write the descriptions here.

"The Cutty Stool you have done with *great ability*. I want a short notice of your lassie, which I will introduce by way of note to the bottom of the ballad of ' Derwentwater.' As to Lady Nithsdale's letter, I hope you have not been at the trouble of copying it, as I have got from Edinburgh the number of the *Scots Magazine* in which it originally appeared. I only wish you to compare a printed copy with the manuscript, and mark the difference, if any. I want the date of it and the direction.

" You have not yet informed me of the authority on which you found the interesting anecdote of Murray's treachery. It is absolutely necessary. When you have read this book I shall be miserable if it is not to your taste. It *must* excite much curiosity. I have a notion it will prove a precious crust for the critics.

" God bless you, my dear friend.

" R. H. Cromek.

" Mr. Allan Cunningham."

" 22nd March, 1810.

" My dear Allan,—As the booksellers are *determined* to put our Nithsdale book *immediately* to the press, I write to beg that, if it suit you, you will set off as soon as possible. You *must* ' buckle an' come away.' Pray send me the book by the *very first* mail, and ' *taking the beuk* ' with it.

" Mr. Grahame, the author of ' The Sabbath,' is in town. His opinion is high indeed of the volume; it will do us all good, I hope. Write to me by return of post if you can, if but a line, and say when you think you will leave Scotland; at all events forward the book. The verses on Cowehill will be a great acquisition, from what you say of them.

" I am not angry with the booksellers for their resolute conduct; on the contrary, I think the sooner the volume is out the better.　Indeed, if it is not ready in two months, the season, as it is called, will be lost.—God bless you with all my heart.

"R. H. C.

"Mr. Allan Cunningham."

" 28th March, 1810.

" My dear Allan,—I have received by this day's mail the welcome news of your intended departure from Dumfries. My family rejoice most heartily with me.　The firing of the Park and Tower guns, announcing a grand victory, would not have interested any of us *half as much.*　I am very glad you showed the volume to Mrs. Copeland and her niece, and, from what you say, I am also happy that the printing has only just begun, and shall stop the press till I see you.　I hope to receive the volume by to-morrow's mail, and, be assured, I shall hold your pencil-marks most sacred.

" One of the luckiest things that could have happened was the late visit from Mr. Grahame.　The work will derive infinite advantage from his remarks.　He augurs it a most warm reception from the public.　But when you come, and when we lay our heads together, I am certain several things will be added, and others materially improved.

" Now for your *amphibious* journey.　I advise you not to stop at Edinburgh at all, and, as I know you will take this counsel, I have not enclosed a letter—except, on second thoughts, you *must* call for a moment on Mrs. Fletcher; and in case she should not be in town, and to guard against the carelessness of servants, write your name on a slip of paper, and leave it, with the message — that you were passing through Edinburgh to London.　If you see her, say you are coming to me on a visit, and make my kindest respects to her. Then proceed to Leith, and stay all night in an inn—don't attempt to come in any part of the ship but the principal cabin on *any account.* I mention this, because, from some mistaken idea of saving a guinea, you may suffer much personal inconvenience. Keep as much on the deck as possible.

" R. H. C.

" Mr. Allan Cunningham."

There is something warmly affectionate in the instructions and advice here given with reference to the voyage, and one's heart gratefully reciprocates the sentiments of kindness expressed towards the aspiring poetic Scotchman. Having always had a hankering after literature, and for some time back having cherished a desire to substitute mental for manual labour, he was the more easily persuaded to accept the invitation by the pleasing prospect which Mr. Cromek held out, and to try the great metropolis as a field for fortune and fame. He accordingly began to make preparations for leaving, amid the remonstrances of friends, and their admonitions on the folly of surrendering a present good for an uncertain future. They urged the dangerous tendency of a great city's temptations to lead the inexperienced astray; the difficulty of a stranger finding employment where thousands of native citizens could scarcely sustain life; and, lastly, the cutting off, as it were, by distance, all connection with kindred and home. But their efforts to restrain him were of no avail. Go he would.

When his arrangements were completed he took a temporary farewell of the lass o' Preston Mill, turned his back upon Nithsdale, upon kith and kin, and bade his native land adieu! He was to sail from the port of Leith, the usual and most convenient mode of transit in those days, especially when anything in the shape of luggage had to be taken along. Having arrived there, and, being on the point of starting, an affectionate "Good-bye" was accorded him by comrades and friends. He himself thus describes the scene:—

"The hour of fame and distinction seemed, in my sight, at hand. I turned my eyes on London, and closed them on all places else. In vain my friends urged me to study architecture, and apply the talent, &c., &c. . . . . On my way to the pier of Leith I met one of my old Edinburgh comrades, Charlie Stevenson by name, who was rejoiced to see me, and tried, over 'a pint of the best o't,' to persuade me to become his partner in the erection of two houses in the New Town, by which he showed me we should clear, by the end of the season, a hundred pounds each. I declined his kind offer. 'If,' I said, 'undertakings of that nature could have influenced me, I need not have left Dumfries, where, with certainty of success, I might either have begun business for myself, or been admitted into partnership with my masters, who would have been glad both of my skill and my connection. So I parted with worthy Charlie Stevenson, and committed myself to the waves in one of the Leith smacks, bound for London. Several of my comrades from the Vale of Nith, then at the University, waved me from the pier, and away I went, with groves of laurels rustling green before me, and fame and independence, I nothing doubted, ready to welcome me to that great city which annually swallows up so many high hopes and enthusiastic spirits."

Good-bye, for the present, Allan Cunningham, we shall soon meet again in the new field of your operations. Remember and act up to what you said some four years ago, in a letter to your parish minister, the good Mr. Wightman of Kirkmahoe, when you were giving an account of how you spent your time, and asking his advice for the future—"After returning thanks to God for my preservation, I retire to the embraces of sleep, and rise with a cheerful mind, judging it part of my tribute to my Maker. An honest and cheerful heart is almost all my stock. I fervently adhere to truth, and, to close all, I have an independent mind." Adieu! we shall soon meet again in the great metropolis.

CHAPTER V.

ARRIVAL IN LONDON—PREPARATION OF THE VOLUME—CROMEK'S LETTER TO A. CONSTABLE ON THE SUBJECT—TESTIMONY TO CUNNINGHAM—CROMEK'S DEATH—CUNNINGHAM'S OPINION OF LONDON LIFE—ENGAGES WITH BUBB A SCULPTOR—BECOMES A REPORTER IN PARLIAMENT—LETTER TO HIS BROTHER JAMES, ENCLOSING NEW SONG—LETTER TO M'GHIE—LETTER TO HIS BROTHER JAMES.

CUNNINGHAM arrived in London on the 9th of April, 1810, a day never to be forgotten in the annals of England, as being that on which Sir Francis Burdett was sent to the Tower. His first experience in the great metropolis was not at all what he had anticipated. The laurel groves of which he had so fondly dreamt were nowhere to be seen. Every one seemed intent upon his own affairs, and had neither time nor inclination to regard the interests of a stranger—even Mr. Cromek was scarcely an exception, save for his own ends. His promised influence came to nothing—he had either none to exercise, or he had no opportunity to use it. However, he entertained Cunningham at his house, while he prepared for the press the forthcoming volume of the "Remains of Nithsdale and Galloway Song." When it was all but ready for publication, Mr. Cromek wrote regarding it to his friend Mr. Archibald Constable, publisher, Edinburgh, in the following terms:—

"You will rejoice with me that my volume of Nithsdale Ballads is on the verge of publication. I wish you had had it, because it should have issued from a Scotch house, and because it is a most curious and original book, and will most certainly have a very wide circulation. I have so high an opinion of it myself, that I think Mr. Jeffrey will and must say it is the most valuable collection that ever yet appeared. I have now given—what I think was never given—the real history of the Scottish Peasantry; and as far as relates to the twin districts of Nithsdale and Galloway, I have ventured to describe at some length their manners, attachments, games, superstitions, their traditional history of fairies, witchcraft, &c., &c., taken down from the lips of old cottars. One of the most interesting and valuable of these was a Margaret Corson, an old woman, aged ninety-seven. The title I send you. The whole 1000 will be printed on India paper. Pray give one, with my kind respects, to Mr. Hunter, to add to his collection, as it is a wonderful group, drawn by Stothard from the peasantry."

Now, in the above letter there appears an amount of selfishness which detracts considerably from the character of the writer. He arrogates the doing of the whole work himself, without even hinting at a coadjutor, while the truth is he had almost no hand in the matter, with the slight exception of a passage or two. Cunningham composed the Ballads, wrote the Introduction, as well as the descriptive Notes, and corrected the proofs, toiling at the work from morning to night, and was rewarded for all his labour with—how much does the reader imagine?—a single bound copy of the volume, with the assurance that the work had been very costly in the production, but he would get something more when another edition appeared!

We fear we have been too rash in asserting that Mr. Cromek made no reference to a coadjutor, and that only a passage or two in the volume was his own, though we have Cunningham's authority for the last statement. But surely Cunningham could not have written the following two sentences in the Introduction:—"To Mr. Allan Cunningham, who, in the humble and laborious profession of a mason, has devoted his leisure hours to the cultivation of a genius naturally of the first order, I cannot sufficiently express my obligations. He entered into my design with the enthusiasm of a poet; and was my guide through the rural haunts of Nithsdale and Galloway, where his various interesting and animated conversation beguiled the tediousness of the toil; while his local knowledge, his refined tastes, and his indefatigable industry, drew from obscurity many pieces which adorn this collection, and which, without his aid, would have eluded my research." It is possible that this was inserted at Mr. Cromek's dictation, nay, almost certain, from the character of the parties engaged in the work.

This, however, may be said in Mr. Cromek's behalf, with regard to the small remuneration which Cunningham received, that he had been all his life in pecuniary embarrassments, and scarcely a week before his death, which occurred within fifteen months after the publication of the "Remains," he wrote to Mr. Constable a very grateful letter acknowledging receipt of his benevolent assistance:—"Your letter and enclosure of Saturday relieved me from a pressure of anxiety almost insupportable. . . . My family are tremblingly alive to your goodness. God reward you!" He died six days afterwards, on the 14th of March, 1812. No one can surely read this letter of Mr. Cromek's, so full of gladness, gratitude, and affection, and say that all came from a selfish heart. Straitened circumstances alone, we believe, prevented him from remunerating Cunningham as he deserved. It is understood that he died without being aware of the mystification wrought upon him with regard to the volume of which he was so proud. The pecuniary condition of Mr. Cromek on his death-bed, and his gratitude to a friend for relief, strongly remind us of the case of our own national poet, Burns, in similar circumstances.

While the volume is still in the hands of the printer, and will not be issued till December, we may turn our attention for a moment to his opinion of London life. No doubt he was greatly disappointed in his prospects, and a little exaggeration of the character of what passed before him may be palliated, if not entirely excused. When his literary engagement with Mr. Cromek terminated he did not, however, sit down in despondency, or, in moody melancholy, make the dark future darker than it was in reality. He visited the public places of amusement, examined the great sights of the city, watched attentively the various grades of society, and formed an estimate, which he thus briefly expressed in a letter to his brother James five months after his arrival:—"Amid all the bustle of existence, and the noise, the gaieties, and frivolities of cities—the hue and cry which Patriotism has after her, and the hideous rumour which Hypochondriacism awakens when she mounts the "louping-on-stane" to the other world—from all these soul-afflicting things I cast back my thoughts on my native Nithsdale, and sigh for her fair fountains and poetic vales. I enter into delightful converse with my dear friends whose kindred blood I inherit, and in whose hearts I hold a place. I feel something like that unsettled agitation of mind which might be nursed into despondency, and now and then a severe touch of that romantic and characteristic feeling which is mixed by the hand of God in every Scotchman's heart. The English have not that vehement warmth, that vigorous originality, which the Scottish peasants have. Scotland is an age or two behind in corruption, and she has hitherto preserved her ancient character from villanous foreign intermixture." So wrote Allan Cunningham, when evidently suffering from home-sickness disease.

> "It's hame, an' it's hame, hame fain wad I be,
> An' it's hame, hame, hame, to my ain countrie!"

In a similar strain he also wrote to his friend George, a short time afterwards, with regard to his dissatisfaction with the great city:—" I have been at all the great theatres, and I have heard the 'Messiah' of Handel, but I would prefer to hear your father singing 'Bonnie Barbara Allan.' It is only the beauteous alliance of words with music which delights or affects me. I cannot feel my heart's-blood coming warm, and my soul leaping to my lips, in any other music than that of my native country; which induces me to think, nay, believe, that our hearts were formed entirely for the delights of our parent kingdom—for the music thereof, for the ideas thereof, and, last and dearest, for the maidens thereof. Indeed, I cannot find that dear communion of kindred sentiment, in either man or woman, which I found in Scotland. Their manners are not those of nature, but of artifice. The men are all punsters, and have no mercy on words which they can in any way hang a pun upon. They are hurried and impetuous in conversation, and unmercifully addicted to listen to themselves." We believe the reprehension here made is not necessary now, if even then, and that Cunningham afterwards saw he had been too severe.

We are informed on the best authority that it is not true, as has been hinted by one writer, that in his destitution and desperation for employment, he became a common pavier in Newgate Street. Allan Cunningham a common pavier on the streets of London! Impossible! After hanging about in comparative idleness for some weeks, with no prospect of the horizon clearing, and Mr. Cromek now listless or uninfluential, he engaged with an inferior sculptor of the name of Bubb, in Caermarthen Street, at twenty-five shillings a week, afterwards increased to thirty-two, on account of his superior skill as a workman. Nevertheless, he was greatly chagrined at having been led away on such a wild-goose chase, especially so much in opposition to the entreaties of his friends at home, and he was, therefore, desirous of concealing his position from their knowledge till better fortune arrived, if it ever should.

In the midst of his dissatisfaction he began casting in his mind what other employment, more congenial to his taste, he should look out for instead. While thus ruminating, he says—"I now thought of Eugenius Roche and the *Literary Recreations,* a work which I never could persuade myself died from want of the breath of genius. I found him in Carey Street, a husband and a father, and as warm-hearted and kind as his correspondence had led me to imagine. He was well acquainted with foreign, as well as with English literature; wrote prose with fluency, and verse with ease and elegance; and was in looks and manners, and in all things, a gentleman—tall, too, spoke with a slight lisp, and was of a fair complexion. He had in other days expressed a desire to serve me, and pointed out the newspapers as a source of emolument to an able and ready writer. As he was now the conductor of a paper called the *Day,* he told me he would give me a permanent situation upon it as a reporter as soon as the Parliamentary sessions began, and in the meantime he would allow me a guinea per week for any little poetic contributions which I liked to make. What the duties required of me were, I could form no opinion, but as I concluded that Roche must know I was fit to fulfil them, I was easy on that point. I was now well off as to money matters, and in a position to indulge in a wish dear to my heart, namely, to bring my lass of Preston Mill to London, and let her try her skill as a wife and a housekeeper."

That Cunningham, who knew nothing of shorthand, and had never learned grammar in his life, should undertake the heavy and responsible duties of a reporter in the Houses of Parliament, is almost beyond our belief; but yet he did so, until he was obliged to surrender the occupation on finding it prejudicial to his health.

We have just seen that, despite his desultory and uncertain employment, he had serious thoughts of taking a wife, as he deemed it impossible to live economically otherwise, and, notwithstanding his mind had been long made up on the subject with the lass of Preston Mill, he now, cunningly, writes to his brother James, desiring him to look out for a proper helpmate among his acquaintance:—

"London, September 8th, 1810.

"My beloved James,—. . . . I am glad to find you all so well, and I am 'unco weel mysel,' God be blessed for it, and praised too. I have got four shillings a week added to my wages. We had designed a general *strike*, and many are yet out of employment. One of our men was turned off, and I am now considered the soul and nerve of the shop, and the master has taken a great regard for me, so I live very well and happily. I have left my old lodgings, and a young man called Thomas Lowrie, a Cabinetmaker from Dumfries, has joined me in taking a neat room, where I will be cheaper and more heartsome. Indeed, London is in no way suitable to any but a married person. I breakfast in one house, dine in another, sup in a third, and go to bed in a fourth. In every one of these places extortion must have in her accursed hand. The thing is, everybody must live, and we buy one another like other vermin. So, it would be no wonder were I found married in some letter or another soon. The truth out is, I want you to 'look owre' the register book, and choose me a wife from among the mid-leg kilted daughters of Caledonia. I cannot admire the City English, nor do I care for spoiling the proverb of a certain prophet, 'and, behold, thou shalt take unto thee a daughter of whoredoms.' O fie! It is the Scripture says so, and not I.

"Well we have at last printed that volume of 'Remains of Nithsdale and Galloway Song.' It is beautifully printed and hot-pressed in octavo, and contains 400 pages. I am convinced it will edify you greatly, but it may not be made public until December. I will try to send you a copy, so don't buy one. The thing which pleases me in it, every article but two little scraps was contributed by me, both poetry and prose. You will see what the *Edinburgh Review* says about it, for it must be noticed and highly too. You must send me, with Peter, a little twopenny book of old songs in the handwriting of my beloved Mrs. Copeland. I forgot it, I dare say, among my papers in my chest.

"Peter will find Thomas just at the entrance into the new London docks, half a mile below the Tower, and only a quarter a mile from Miller's wharf, where the Edinburgh smacks anchor at. I am sorry to find that Mrs. Copeland is poorly. I had a letter from her a week ago, and she complains of indisposition. Burns certainly thought of her when he wrote—

'Nature made her what she is,
And never made anither.'

"You inquire about Cromek. Why, my dear James, he speaks as generous words as you would wish to hear from the pulpit. O! the bravery of the lips, and the generosity of words, are the current coin with which naked bards are ever paid; and as a specimen of his critical discernment, I wrote a queer song, ycleped, ' A Song of Fashionable Sin,' beginning—

> ' My ladie has a golden watch—
> On my ladie's breast's a diamond broach—
> Her hair prempt in a rubie knot,
> And siller-tasselled petticoat.
> But my lord can quat thae siller bobs,
> Thae costly jukes wi' trinkets laden,
> For petticoats of hodden gray
> An' laced jimps of hamely plaiden,' &c., &c.

" Now, I inserted this in a newspaper, and it was printed among a great number of offices. I was at Mr. Cromek's, and a lady was praising it highly. He did not know it was mine, and condemned it as a base thing, and of bad Scottish ! I never heeded him, but marked it down as a precept, that a man may talk about the thing he does not understand, and be reckoned a wise fellow too.

" I expect to publish a volume of old ballads if I once had them collected. For this purpose I have composed a ballad called 'The Battle of Cheviot Wood,' on the popular story of Chevy Chase. It is 129 verses long, and the finest poetry I ever composed. I could cheat a whole General Assembly of Antiquarians with my original manner of writing and forging ballads. Indeed, the poetry of our ancestors is become all the cry. Romance and chivalry will again begin their adventures—distressed damsels relieved— unaccomplishable exploits of knighthood—and a whole Lapland winter of heathen darkness will overspread the land ! from which may the Lord deliver us ! and let Scotland ' hae

ac blink' of true poetic sunshine. Here's the song you
wanted—

"THE THISTLE'S GROWN ABOON THE ROSE.

"Full white the Bourbon lily blows,
    Still fairer haughty England's rose;
    Nor shall unsung the symbol smile,
    Green Ireland, of thy lovely isle.
    In Scotland grows a warlike flower,
    Too rough to bloom in lady's bower;
    But when his crest the warrior rears,
    And spurs his courser on the spears,
    O there it blossoms—there it blows—
    The Thistle's grown aboon the Rose.

"Bright like a steadfast star it smiles
    Aboon the battle's burning files;
    The mirkest cloud, the darkest night,
    Shall ne'er make dim that beauteous sight;
    And the best blood that warms my vein,
    Shall flow ere it shall catch a stain.
    Far has it shone on fields of fame,
    From matchless Bruce to dauntless Græme,
    From swarthy Spain to Siber's snows;—
    The Thistle's grown aboon the Rose.

"What conquered aye, and nobler spared,
    And firm endured, and greatly dared?
    What reddened Egypt's burning sand?
    What vanquished on Corunna's strand?
    What pipe on green Maida blew shrill?
    What dyed in blood Barossa hill?
    Bade France's dearest life-blood rue
    Dark Soignies and dread Waterloo?
    That spirit which no tremor knows;—
    The Thistle's grown aboon the Rose.

F

> " I vow—and let men mete the grass
> For his red grave who dares say less—
> Men blither at the festive board,
> Men braver with the spear and sword.
> Men higher famed for truth—more strong
> In virtue, sovereign sense, and song,
> Or maids more fair, or wives more true,
> Than Scotland's ne'er trode down the dew;
> Unflinching friends—unconquered foes,
> The Thistle's grown aboon the Rose.

" I now and then get a guinea for writing a song, which helps me to live and array myself. I have laid out a great deal of money on tools, &c., &c. I enclose you Peter's notes, which he will, I dare say, need much. You once mentioned to me that Captain Miller was wishing to write to Porry concerning my songs, &c. Now, I do not know a better hand I could make of my songs than get a guinea a piece for them. I will likely apply to Porry. I know he is a lover of Scottish song, and I hope he is a judge.

" Present my love to my dear mother, to my sister-in-law, and to Jenny, &c.; also to Dr. Patie. I had a letter to-day from Miss Harley. She says that she has written to James Dalzell, and she hopes he will soon get a situation. Direct to Cromek's, for I am not yet stable enough for direction.—I remain, dear James, yours through good and evil times, while

" ALLAN CUNNINGHAM.

" I have delayed writing, or rather, as you will see, of sending my letter, hoping that by this Peter will have some permanent hope of a place, as it is a risk to come to London in uncertainty.

A. C.

" Monday Morning.
" Mr. James Cunningham, Dalswinton."

The song contained in the above letter, "The Thistle's grown aboon the Rose," appeared in the *Scots Magazine* of February, 1811, with the signature "Hidallan," which he had used in his poetical contributions to the *Literary Recreations*.

It seems the "Remains of Nithsdale and Galloway Song" has been published, but marriage is in the ascendant, though both subjects are in his head and his heart, and in the exuberance of his joy he writes to his quondam companion, George, respecting both. It would appear that he had to *purchase* presentation copies of the volume:—

"London, 10th December, 1810.

"Dear George,—I write in a most unfriendly-like hurry, because I am writing post-haste, against both wind and tide, and coach-time to boot. O man, you pleased me in your last letter. I want folk to write me as much as you do—sly, humorous, and enthusiastic. Why, it gives a lift to my mind, and makes me more merry and conceited. I am going to be married soon. My weel-faured lass will hang like a tassel of gold on a shepherd's plaid, only for the dogs to bark at.

"You will find some songs on her weel-faured face in that volume of Nithsdale and Galloway Songs, where the poets of the last century have, by the divine gift of inspiration, anticipated and commemorated the beauties of this. It will make me proud, thinking that my songs in her praise will drop from the lips of a dear friend, and from one too who can appreciate their worth, and modulate his voice to suit the rapture and enthusiastic admiration of beauty which pervaded the poet when he wrote them.

"I could have wished to have sent you a volume, but I had so many to give that even gratitude itself gave way at last to the necessities of want, and my means ran short, but not my inclination. I will sometime soon, perhaps, find means to get you one; and if you correspond with our James, you will find him proud in lending you what he most dearly values.

"Read, then, my volume through, with a most acute and critical eye, and combine your own ideas of it along with those of James M'Ghie, my dear old friend, and the friend of my father. He will tell his mind, and tell yours. Let me know what things please you, and tell your reasons for being pleased, because I want to learn.

"I will write you more at leisure, sometime after you have answered this. I am very well. I have left my old trade, and engaged for two guineas and a-half per week to write along with my friend Mr. Roche. Do not say ought about this to anybody but to my brother (James), for I do not want it to be known.

"Give my respects to your sister, Rachel. Tell her to sit down seriously and learn some of these songs. I know she will lilt them like a starling. Your brother James, too, claims my regard in being in love with my Jean; but tell him to bide in Kirkmahoe and admire her, as I would be jealous were he to go to Kirkbean. . . . Give my respects to your father and mother. I think often on the pleasures I enjoyed at their fireside. Let them remember in their prayers one who is happy in saying how much he esteems them, and values their children. In break-neck haste. Write me soon.

"ALLAN CUNNINGHAM.

"Mr. George Douglas M'Ghie."

Time wore on. He contributed poetry at a guinea a week, and did other things besides, which were absolutely necessary for a man with marriage in view, and the exchequer at a low ebb. He was determined to be married, and, as we shall by-and-by see, he carried his purpose into execution. But, in the meantime, what we are most concerned about is, his ability and success as a Parliamentary reporter, without the qualifications now considered indispensable for informing the public of what nightly takes place in the great House of the nation. In these times, however, reporting had not attained its present high state of efficiency. The substance only was given, and not the *ipsissima verba*, except by a very few. Others besides Cunningham had to depend entirely upon a good memory, and as many long-hand notes as they were able to take. From these two sources they had to frame speeches as they best could, so as to give the gist of what had been said. We understand that some of the best summaries of what takes place in both Houses of Parliament at the present day, are written by parties who trust to a retentive memory and a few notes, without calling in the aid of stenography. In the following letter, addressed to his brother James, Cunningham tells us his experience and appreciation of the Reporters' Gallery :—

" London, December 29th, 1810.

" My beloved James,—I have placed myself down to write at what Shakspere calls 'the witching time of night.' The seasons unto me are now changed. I owe my allegiance to the moon and to the stars. The blessed sun of heaven himself I count now no more on than on an oilman's greasy lamp. I gain nothing by his light. My new business has completely overturned that ancient system of prudential economy recommended by the precepts and examples of our ancestors, to observe the great order of nature, by sleeping in the evening, when nature slept, and wakening when the sun, coming gloriously forth, quickened the world into life, and resumed all the functions of awakening nature. However, as I do not believe in predestination, I do not deem it probable that our Creator thought of reporting speeches of certain men for newspapers, else He would have made some little provision in the economy of nature for their benefit, to show they were not utterly neglected. Thus, had He contrived a blink of sunshine to have dropped down in this wicked metropolis, peradventure about three in the morning, I should have adored Him, and prayed ere I went to bed. Now this is, in plain words, that I go to bed mostly at three in the morning, but I took this pompous way of telling you about it to show you how I can perplex a plain tale into bombast and extravagance, and go to the utmost limits of comprehension. To this I am humbly indebted to my new system of education, wherein I have to varnish with mighty words the fierce and uncourtly language of political iniquity. Now, you will perhaps lift up your voice against this wicked way of life. I pray you have mercy, and consider me as a person who has already half-forded a deep and dangerous river, where there is equal danger in turning back as in proceeding, so let me wade through.

"I have written a number of speeches for both Lords and Commons. I find it quite easy, for I collect notes for one hour from what is said, just, I mean, as the speaker delivers it. This outline I have to return to the newspaper office with, and write out into three columns of debate. These columns will take me four or five hours, and then I return to my home. Now, this is pretty severe work, but I have so many days of leisure to sweeten all this that I enjoy my situation with much satisfaction.

"I am proud to find you are in such brisk employ, and that you have the prospect of more in future. There is one thing which pleased me, though, perhaps, it may not be so edifying to yourself, which is, that you have got into the Captain's business, who, I doubt not, will employ you for his farming transactions for the future. Now, this will rub off that indolence, that diffidence, that rust of the mind, which belonged to you, nay, to us all, so much. Impudence, I mean genteel impudence, is so very necessary for pushing us through life that I wonder it is not laid down as a precept of education in our public schools.

"I was so extremely bashful when I came to London that I really could not utter a known falsehood above three or four times a day. Now, I could assert in the face of a congregation that the sun derives his light from the moon, and make the dullness and paleness of her evening Majesty a leading proof of it. Nay, I could, if required, almost make oath on't.

"I am pleased with your remarks on the 'Nithsdale and Galloway Songs.' They were very short, but I mean not to let you escape this way, for you must write me a long letter on purpose, showing wherein I have erred or done according to my duty. Choose out all your favourites, and write fully about the songs of the two rebellions. Now, you must mind one thing, and I beseech you mind it, that these songs and ballads being written for imposing on the country as the reliques of other years, I was obliged to have recourse to occasional coarseness, and severity, and negligence, which would make them appear as fair specimens of the ancient song and ballad. This being considered, I beg you will not visit me as I would deserve had they been my avowed productions.

"I am glad Peter has got himself thrust into a place. I am much afraid he will never make a great figure in the polite business of surgery. He can do nothing for himself unless he has the "drawn dagger" of necessity at his back, pushing him to adventure. I do not argue this from his conversation, but from his writing. A man may have so much diffidence or natural modesty in his composition as will prevent him from being eloquent in conversation; but if there be anything like genius in his composition, it will break out in a letter, where he has the free and unhampered exercise of all his powers, and time for studying propriety of expression, and the proper use of his own feelings. Now, Peter, however stupid and vulgar in conversation, is ten times duller and more perplexed in his letters. His thoughts seem like a printer and types before they are adjusted—a heap of confusion and misplaced beauties; for this, that if counsel could have amended or corrected it, he would have been a master of conversational eloquence, and a proverb unto all the sons of Nithsdale. Counsel can correct but cannot bestow genius, it is a gift of God; and many a person has reason to be thankful for the little he has got, for that little might have been less.

"With regard to the books I want—Blair's Lectures on Elocution — Dryden's Virgil's Æneid — Burns' Poems — Sir William Wallace — Ossian's Poems — and the two volumes of 'Elegant Extracts.' Now, pack them up, and direct them to lie at the office until called for, else the expense of bringing them by a porter is equal to the charge of a waggon. Now, you will write to me when you send them off, and I will know when to call for them.

"I must not forget to tell you that I have planned and begun a work of Poetry and Criticism. I mean to restore all our Scottish songs to their uncorrupted purity, to alter and amend others, where correction is necessary, and to produce upwards of a hundred original ones of my own to be sown among them. Along with all this, notices will be given to elucidate manners, customs, and opinions which belonged unto our ancestors, or which at present may exist. The name of every author will be printed at the title of the song, and, where accounts of them can be got, such things will be given. Now, what think you of this?

"Three volumes in the style of that I sent you, and closer printed, will hardly contain them. Mention this to none! else it will ruin the work. Give my love to my dear mother, and to my dear sister-in-law. I am glad the bairns are 'gush, and ramp, and ranting.' When you see Jenny present my respects to her. Do the same to William Miles, and to Adam Ferguson; and, my dear brother, accept of the united wishes of my heart, head, and soul, for your welfare. God bless you. Direct to Cromek's; I am going to shift.

"ALLAN CUNNINGHAM.

"Mr. James Cunningham."

CHAPTER VI.

SOME ACCOUNT OF THE VOLUME—EXTRACTS—"THOU HAST SWORN BY THY GOD, MY JEANIE"—VARIATION ON "TIBBIE FOWLER"—THE "SALT LAIRDS" OF DUNSCORE, AND THE "GUSTIN BANE" OF KIRKMAHOE—PRIVATE CRITICISMS—PROFESSOR WILSON—THE ETTRICK SHEPHERD—SIR WALTER SCOTT—THE "SCOTS MAGAZINE"—"A WEARY BODIE'S BLYTHE WHAN THE SUN GANGS DOWN."

THE volume of "Nithsdale and Galloway Song" made its appearance in December, and was not only favourably, but enthusiastically, received by the general public and the press. Before, however, we state the opinions of the great critics as to its merits, we shall give a brief account of the character of its contents, with a few extracts as specimens of the work. It was not only important with regard to what it professedly treated of, ancient ballad lore, but it was also important as being the starting-point in Cunningham's literary career, a career which he himself, with all his sanguine aspirations, could not anticipate or foresee. It consisted of an Introduction, thirty-two pages in extent, four classes of Ballads, arranged under the headings of Sentimental, Humorous, Jacobite, Old and Fragments, with an Appendix. The songs were professedly gathered among the peasantry, taken down from their recital of them, or were related by others who had obtained them from the same source. We believe that with regard to a considerable number of them this was the case, in so far as the old proverb has it, that the poet "having got a hair made a tether of it," a single scrap swelling into a goodly song.

The Introduction is a very accurate and graphic description of what the peasantry in the south of Scotland then were as to their customs, habits, superstitions, and beliefs. Matters of this kind are now much changed, but it may, therefore, be the more interesting to readers of the present day to have a glimpse of these :—

"The condition of the inland peasantry was easy, and comparatively affluent. Almost every one had a cow, and a few acres of land. Oatmeal, pease, delicate mutton, fish in every stream, and milk and butter, furnished the necessaries and some of the dainties of existence. Their clothes were all of home manufacture. The men's dress was mostly a fine mixed gray, from wool of a natural dye, a large chequered plaid and bonnet; their shoes were formed of leather tanned by the shoemaker. The women's gowns were of lint and woollen, fancifully mixed, and frequently of exquisite fineness, which is still a popular and becoming dress. . . From their fathers and from their ministers they learned to contemplate the sacred mysteries of the Bible with submissive veneration. Unskilled in the figurative language of poetic instruction, or lost in the raptured soarings of historic inspiration, they took poetic license for truth, and the wild, unbridled flights of Eastern personification were the revelation of Heaven, written with the finger of the Deity. The Bible was put into every youthful hand, with ' *This is the handwriting of God.*' Every sentence was taken as it is written, in the close fidelity of translation. Hence arose that superstitious belief in wizards, witches, and familiar spirits, the popular creed of heathenism.

"The Cottars devoutly opened the Book of God every evening, and on every Sabbath morning, to offer thanksgivings and praises, and to instruct and admonish their children. The holy Songs of David were committed to memory, to be allied to the church melodies. The mind received from these a cast and an impressure of thoughtful melancholy which often exalts it to the noblest conceptions. A rigid moral austerity, and severity of religious conversation, were the consequences of their long struggles with English supremacy, and formed no part of their natural constitution; on the contrary, they were ever ready to mingle in the pleasant mirth of society. Their ancient music still lingered among them, a proscribed fugitive of religious zeal; wedded to those old songs and ballads, the favourites of every age, it was beyond the power of banishment. This love of music and poetry was privately fostered by the old men and women. It had been their own delight and amusement, and they loved to cherish the fond remembrance of other years. They appointed meetings at each other's houses for dancing and singing, to which, at the close of day-toil, the lads and lasses would hasten for several miles round. Here they sang, accompanied by the violin or lowland pipe. The old men recounted the exploits and religious struggles of their ancestors, and mingled in the song, or joined in the dance.

" Enraptured with their music, and emulous of praise, the youths cultivated those seeds of poesy which are more or less to be found in every lover's heart. In the presence of those whom they loved they strove to excel in the strains of tender complaint or pathetic appeal, which were sung and so much admired by their mistresses. Inspired with such sensations, they caught up the prominent features of their adventures, and sang of their jealousies and wooing felicities in numbers worthy of remembrance. To the heart of a Scottish peasant it is a sensation of divine rapture to listen and behold his beloved lass warble, and sweetly modulate those strains to which her tender heart and beautiful face had imparted sympathetic loveliness. The interview at some favourite secluded thorn, in the dew of gloaming; the stolen looks of love; the midnight meeting of chaste affection; the secret kiss and unheard whisper in the dancings and trystes, are the favourite themes of poetic record. These songs were sung before the aged; and their praise, with the kind looks of approval from their mistresses, was a reward sufficient to stimulate to nobler exertion. Old songs were altered to suit some more recent occurrence; their language was frequently minted anew, and the song would take a novel appearance from a small incident of love, or a gallant exploit.

"To these public dancing trystes the daughters of the chieftains would sometimes go in peasant's disguise; possibly to partake in the rural felicities of unrestrained gaiety and frolic; or, perhaps, smitten with the charms of some young peasant, they wished to listen to the natural eloquence of love, and the fervent pathos of rustic wooing. There are yet some remnants of songs which evidently allude to rencounters of this kind, and many more might, perhaps, have been collected on a more diligent search.

"The language of the peasantry has none of that vulgar broadness so disgusting in those sea-coast towns which commerce has corrupted. Imagery drawn from the select sources of nature will clothe itself in chaste and becoming language —the summer wind, the gloaming dew-fall among the loose locks of a lovely maiden, the flower-tops bent with dew, the balmy smell of the woods, the honeycombs of the wild bee, afford fine poetic figures, which nought but profligacy can pollute or misapply. The crimson brook-rose, the yellow-freckled lily, the red-lipped gowan, the pale primrose, the mealy cowslip, the imbedding thyme, are flourishing in rustic pastoral; and the rich-scented hawthorn, the honey-leafed oak, the tasseling honeysuckle, and the bloomy promise of the orchards and bean-fields, embalm themselves in song as pure as the dew which the hand of evening drops on them. But the tender eloquence of the new-paired birds, and the infant song of the new-flown nestlings, were happily caught by peasant discernment:—

> ' The new-paired laverocks among the bloomy howes
> Sing kindly to my, Mary while she ca's hame the ewes.'

" The lark is a chief favourite, and being the herald of morning, sings overhead to the swain returning from the errands of love, who naturally puts his own felicities into her mouth. The wild and mellow mavis, the loud-lilting black-bird, the familiar rose-linnet, the lively gold-spink, are all classical songsters, whose warblings are pleasing to a lover's ear. From the sacred pages of the Bible the peasantry drew many of their finest ideas and imagery. It imparted a tone of solemn sincerity to the promises of love, and gave them a more popular currency among the aged and decorous. Another source of instruction was the select code of proverbs which wisdom had stored up in the progress of society; these, being short and happily figurative, were the current coin of primitive converse. Owing to the great distance between the chieftain and the cottar, these productions never passed into the notice of the great. Composed and sung in unaspiring obscurity, their authors never attempted to hold them up to public notice. The applause at a country wedding, at a kirn dancing, at a kirk-supper, after a bridal, satisfied the bard's vanity; and perhaps the secret assurance that his sweetheart would live in his verses among her great grandchildren was the utmost bound of his ambition."

This extract is quite sufficient of itself to show that Mr. Cromek could not possibly be the author or compiler of the volume. The deep, penetrating insight into Scottish sentiment which it contains, and the thorough acquaintance with Scottish manners and customs which pervades it, are entirely beyond the reach of anyone but a native of the soil; and no Englishman, however great his enthusiasm, or his love for ancient lore, could have so identified himself with the subject, as is apparent from beginning to end. What could Mr. Cromek possibly know in detail of the ongoings at trystes, kirns, and weddings, as are here described? Literally nothing. A hasty and brief visit to the locality could never have inspired him with such a minute knowledge of Scottish sentiments, customs, habits, and feelings as are here recorded. Therefore we think an injustice was done to Allan Cunningham in not putting him prominently in the foreground, instead of keeping him out of sight almost altogether. We do not think that a mere recognition of his aid in the preface was sufficient, when the whole work devolved upon himself.

> " Hos ego versiculos feci, tulit alter honores,
>   Sic vos non vobis nidificatis aves.
>   Sic vos non vobis vellera fertis oves.
>   Sic vos non vobis mellificatis apes.
>   Sic vos non vobis fertis aratra boves."

One of the finest ballads of the first class—the Sentimental—is, "Thou hast sworn by thy God, my Jeanie," to which the following note is prefixed :—

"These verses are copied from the recitation of a worthy old man, now 'raked i' the mools,' as the Scotch phrase is. With him have perished many beautiful songs, remnants of the tunes which were. He was a Dissenter from the Church of Scotland, and had all that stern severity of demeanour and rigidness of mind which belong to those trained in the old school of divinity, under the iron discipline of Scottish Presbyterianism. Yet when kept aloof from religious dispute, when his native goodness was not touched with the sour leaven of bigotry, he was a man, as we may truly say with Scripture, 'after God's own heart.' There is a characteristic trait of him which will lighten the darkness of superstition which gave it birth. In that violent persecution in the reigns of James the Seventh, and the Second Charles, one of the persecuted preachers took refuge among the wild hills behind Kirkmahoe, in the county of Dumfries. On a beautiful green-topped hill, called the *Wardlaw*, was raised a pulpit of sods, where he preached to his congregation. General Dalzell hastened on with his dragoons and dispersed the assembly—this consecrated the spot. Our worthy old patriarch, in the fine Sabbath evenings, would go with his wife and children to the Wardlaw, though some miles of rough road distant, seat himself in the preacher's place, and '*take the Beuk*,' with his family around him. He kneeled down, and with all the flow of religious eloquence, held converse with his God. This song was his favourite, and he usually sang it at halloweens, at kirk-suppers, and other trystes"—

"THOU HAST SWORN BY THY GOD, MY JEANIE.

"Thou hast sworn by thy God, my Jeanie,
  By that pretty white hand o' thine,
And by a' the lowing stars in heaven,
  That thou wad aye be mine!
And I hae sworn by my God, my Jeanie,
  And by that kind heart o' thine,
By a' the stars sown thick owre heaven
  That thou shalt aye be mine!

"Then foul fa' the hands that wad loose sic bands,
  An' the heart that wad part sic love;
But there's nae hand can loose the band,
  Save the finger o' God above.
Tho' the wee, wee cot maun be my bield,
  An' my claithing e'er sae mean,
I wad lap me up rich i' the faulds o' love,
  Heaven's armfu' o' my Jean!

"Her white arm wad be a pillow to me,
  Fu' safter than the down,
An' Love wad winnow owre us his kind, kind, wings,
  An' sweetly I'd sleep an' soun'.
Come here to me, thou lass o' my love,
  Come here and kneel wi' me;
The morning is fu' o' the presence o' God,
  An' I canna pray but thee.

"The morn-wind is sweet 'mang the beds o' new flowers,
  The wee birds sing kindly an' hie,
Our gude-man leans owre his kail-yard dyke,
  An' a blythe auld body is he.
The Book maun be taen when the carle comes hame,
  Wi' the holie psalmodie,
An' thou maun speak o' me to thy God,
  An' I will speak o' thee!"

In the second part of the volume much humour is displayed in the several pieces, though mixed with not a little of what would be called *coarseness* of expression in the present day, not to use a stronger term, but the difference of times and manners must be taken into account. From one of the ballads in this class an extract is taken, for the purpose of introducing a traditional feud which long existed between the two neighbouring parishes of Dunscore and Kirkmahoe, and to which Cunningham here refers. It seems that various versions of the well-known song, "Tibbie Fowler," were afloat in Nithsdale, one of which is here produced, along with what is known as the complete original, printed in Johnson's "Musical Museum." We quote the first three verses of this variation as a specimen :—

> " The brankit lairds o' Gallowa,
> The hodden breeks o' Annan Water,
> The bonnets blue of fair Nithsdale,
> Are 'yont the hallan wooing at her.

> " Tweedshaw's tarry neives are here,
> Braksha' gabs frae Moffat Water,
> An' half the thieves o' Annandale
> Are come to steal her gear and daute her.

> " I mind her weel, in plaiden gown,
> Afore she got her uncle's coffer;
> The gleds might pyked her at the dyke,
> Before the lads wad shoved them off her."

These variations used to be sung at the public trystes or merry-makings held in the surrounding parishes, and sometimes out of mischief or frolic sarcastic allusions were interpolated by the performer, which led to bruilzie and bloodshed in the end :—

> " The Dunscore *Salt Lairds* stilt the Nith,
> And muddle a' our supper water ;
> The gray-beard solemn-leaguing lowns
> Thraw by the beuk o' God to daute her.
> The birds hae a' forhoo'd their nests,
> The trouts hae ta'en the Cairn and Annan,
> For holdin breeks and stilting shanks,
> Between the sunset and the dawnin'."

These lines were instantly retorted by this blithesome effort of local parish pleasantry:—

> " Kirkmahoe louped on her sonks,
> Wi' new creeshed shoon and weel darned hosen ;
> And cry'd to maw an acre kail,
> And hing the pan wi' water brose on ;
> And wha will lend us brydal gear,
> Sheep amang the kale to simmer,
> Gullies for to sheer their cloots,
> Swats to foam aboon the timmer ?

> " Dunscore sent her spauls o' sheep,
> Sent her owre our big brose ladle ;
> Pewter plates and hansel gear,
> To mense her wi' at Tibbie's brydal.
> Ye've pyked the banes o' yere leap-year's cow,
> Yere aught day's kale's a' finished fairly ;
> Yere big brose pot has nae played brown
> Sin' the Reaver raid o' *gude Prince Charlie*."

The tradition referred to above is, that at a time when *salt*, as a household commodity, could with difficulty be procured, on account of its high price before the duty was removed, the Lairds of Dunscore, out of poverty, clubbed together and purchased a peck or a stone of salt, which they divided among themselves with a horn-spoon to ensure an equal distribution. Whether the story was true or not it was generally held to be so by those outside the parish, who took certain opportunities for using the taunt of poverty, such as at a losing bonspiel of curling on the ice, or when other disagreements arose. With regard to Kirkmahoe, the same taunt of poverty was employed by neighbouring enemies when they thought themselves in any way aggrieved. Pride and poverty would appear to have been in those days the besetting sin of both parishes. It was asserted that the parishioners of Kirkmahoe were so ill-bestead as to the necessaries of life that they could not afford to provide flesh-meat to enrich the broth-pot even once a week, and had recourse to the economical device of borrowing from one another when the great cooking day came round. A bone, denuded of its fleshly integuments, was procured at a small price by one of them from a butcher's shop in Dumfries, and served, *pro tempore*, the whole coterie of Duncow. "Lend me your bane the day, and I'll lend you mine the next time." The bone, be it observed, was not *boiled* in the broth, but merely dipped in the cold water previous to its being placed upon the fire, so that some of the meat particles adhering might give a *flavour* to the soup. This was called the *"Gustin' bane."* An enterprizing shoemaker, thinking to add a little to his means of livelihood, purchased several bones of this description, which he gave out to hire at a halfpenny each for a single use. The hirer was allowed to dip it three times and make one whisk round in the cold water. Some wag turned the circumstance into the following doggerel distich, which was spread far and wide, and which continued to be repeated for nearly a century, whenever passion or prejudice rose high:—

"Wha'll buy me, wha'll buy me,
Three plumps and a wallop for a bawbee?"

At fair or market, dance or wedding, the words "Gustin' bane," uttered in the hearing of those for whom they were intended, were sufficient to raise a riot. At the close of a marriage dinner in the neighbouring parish of Kirkmichael, where a number of the bridegroom's party from Kirkmahoe were present, and enjoying themselves most heartily, the bride's father, who had been carving and supplying his guests most hospitably, without a thought of the consequences, lifted a large shank-bone before him, which had done substantial service on the occasion, and said, "This wad still mak' a gude Gustin' bane." The words were most innocently uttered, and nothing was farther from the glad father's heart than the intention to wound the feelings of any of his friends. Indeed, he said it in the jubilance of enjoyment, meaning that there had been enough and to spare. Notwithstanding all his good intentions, however, in a moment the house was in an uproar, all were on their feet, and angry words were neither "few nor far between." The tables were overturned with all upon them. Dishes, glasses, tumblers, and bottles were

demolished, and formed a dismal scene of confusion
—"rudis indigestaque moles,"—while the bridecake
required no special cutting up, but lay scattered in
fragments among the *debris*—"apparent rari nantes
in gurgito vasto." The two parties were smashing
each other with whatever they could lay hold of, the
blood streamed, the women fainted, and the men swore
and fought. Old James Smith, ycleped the "Baillie o'
Carzield," firmly set his back against a wall, as he was
lame, and, in the spirit of Fitz-James in his encounter
with Roderick Dhu, said, in sentiment at least—

> " Come one, come all! this rock shall fly
> From its firm base as soon as I!"

His opponents immediately came forward with a rush,
and, in less time than we tell it, he had knocked five of
them down, who, on regaining their senses and their
legs, showed no desire to renew the combat. So runs
the tradition of the "Saut lairds" of Dunscore, and
the " Gustin' bane" of Kirkmahoe.

Having given a short outline of the contents and
nature of the volume now fairly launched on the wide
sea of public opinion, it will be interesting to notice
what the great critics think of the work. One may
easily imagine the state of excitement Cunningham
especially would be in as to the verdict about to be
pronounced upon the performance. Mr. Cromek, too,
would doubtless be anxious as to the reception of
what he considered his masterpiece, with regard to
Scottish ballad lore of the olden time. He had privately boasted of its great merits to his literary friends

while it was in the process of production, and now that it was before them, the verification of his own eulogium would cause some concern. The opinion of private literary friends, of course, came first, as the great lever of the public press generally takes time for its operations in forming a judgment. Two things were certain to be taken into consideration by both parties—the genuineness of the ballads as ancient, and their poetical merit. Poor Allan! trembling in the balance of suspense as to the verdict about to be given upon your poetical genius, stand forward and hear the judgment pronounced. Throw aside your long, dark locks, and let your intellectual brow be seen in all its massiveness. Your black, piercing eye and your manly form have no cause to be concealed. The world is with you, though as yet you know it not, and your name will go down with approbation to the latest ages!

The general impression on the appearance of the volume was that it was "too good to be old," and suspicions were hinted in confirmation of what Mr. Cromek had said in his own criticism of the first two pieces he had received from Cunningham, " Bonnie Lady Anne," and " She's gane to dwall in Heaven." The rhymes were too generally correct, some of the epithets were at variance with ancient phraseology, and even several of the sentiments had a tinge of modern times. Such things as these weighed greatly in the minds of the literary critics of the metropolis, and made them suspect the pseudo character of several of the songs, as well as the true personage who had produced them. Bishop Percy, Professor Wilson, Sir Walter Scott, Lord Woodhouselee, Mr. Roscoe, Mr. Graham, Mr. Montgomery, and the Ettrick Shepherd, were all of this opinion, though, at the same time, they declared that the songs "would hold up their heads to unnumbered generations."

Professor Wilson said of the volume:—" In Dumfriesshire he (Cromek) became acquainted with Mr. Allan Cunningham, at that time a common stonemason, and certainly one of the most original poets Scotland has produced, who communicated to him a vast quantity of most amusing and interesting information concerning the manners and customs of the people of Nithsdale and Galloway. Much of this is to be found in the appendix to this volume. That appendix is ostensibly written by Mr. Cromek, and perhaps a few sentences here and there are from his pen; but no person of ordinary penetration can for a moment doubt that, as a whole, it was fairly composed and written out by the hand of Allan Cunningham. Everything is treated of in the familiar and earnest style of a man speaking of what he has known from his youth upwards, and of what has influenced and even formed the happiness of his life. . . . But the best of the poetry too belongs to Allan Cunningham. Can the most credulous person believe that Mr. Cromek, an Englishman, an utter stranger in Scotland, should have been able in a few days' walk through Nithsdale and Galloway to collect, not a few broken fragments of poetry only, but a number of finished and perfect poems, of whose existence none of the inquisitive literary men or women of Scotland had ever before heard, and that too in the very country which Robert Burns had beaten to its every bush?　But, independently of all this, the poems speak for themselves, and for Allan Cunningham.　The following beautiful song, 'Thou hast sworn by thy God, my Jeanie,' though boldly said to have been written during the days of the Covenant, cannot, as we feel, be thought of in any other light but an exquisite imitation."

This was high commendation from the source whence it came, when it is borne in mind that the writer of it was himself a poet of the highest standing among the sons of Scotland, and one whose prose was poetry in depicting the sentiments, the loves, and. the various vicissitudes of Scottish life.

Another writer, the Ettrick Shepherd, equally, if not better, acquainted with the same subject, said:—" When Cromek's Nithsdale and Galloway Relics came to my hand, I at once discerned the strains of my friend, and I cannot describe with what sensations of delight I first heard Mr. Morrison read 'The Mermaid of Galloway,' while at every verse I kept naming the author.　Gray, of the High School, who had an attachment to Cromek, denied it positively on his friend's authority.　Grieve joined him.　Morrison, I saw, had strong lurking suspicions; but then he stickled for the ancient genius ' of Galloway.　When I went to Sir Walter Scott (then Mr. Scott), I found him decidedly of the same opinion as myself; and he said he wished to God that we had that valuable and original young man fairly out of Cromek's hands again.　I next wrote a review of the work, in which I laid the saddle on the right horse, and sent it to Mr. Jeffrey; but, after retaining it for some time, he returned it with a note, saying that he had read over the article, and was convinced of the fraud which had been attempted to be played off on the public, but he did not think it worthy of exposure."

As was to be expected, certain of the songs were adopted as favourites, according to the taste of the reader, and were specially noted for their excellence in antique sentiment and expression.   Besides those which we have already quoted, as forming part of the volume, and which were forwarded to Mr. Cromek when the first proposal of such a work was mooted, Sir Walter Scott was greatly delighted with the following ballad, which he said his daughter, Mrs. Lockhart, sang with "such uncommon effect."   It is said to be printed from a copy found in Burns' Commonplace Book, in the editor's possession, that it had long been popular in Galloway and Nithsdale, and that it had many variations, of which this one is the best.   We have failed to find it in any of the editions of Burns' works, and are at a loss to understand how he should have omitted to introduce it:—

"IT'S HAME AND IT'S HAME.

" It's hame and it's hame, hame fain would I be,
   O, hame, hame, hame to my ain countrie!
There's an eye that ever weeps, and a fair face will be fain,
As I pass through Annan Water with my bonnie bands again;
When the flower is in the bud, and the leaf upon the tree,
The lark shall sing me hame in my ain countrie.

" It's hame and it's hame, hame fain would I be,
   O, hame, hame, hame to my ain countrie!
The green leaf of loyalty's beginning for to fa',
The bonnie white rose it is withering and a',
But I'll water't with the blood of usurping tyrannie,
And green it will grow in my ain countrie.

> " It's hame and it's hame, hame fain would I be,
>   O, hame, hame, hame to my ain countrie !
> There's nought now from ruin my country can save,
> But the keys of kind heaven to open the grave,
> That all the noble martyrs who died for loyaltie
> May rise again and fight for their ain countrie.
>
> " It's hame and it's hame, hame fain would I be,
>   O, hame, hame, hame to my ain countrie !
> The great now are gane, a' who ventured to save ;
> The new grass is growing aboon their bloody grave ;
> But the sun through the mirk blinks blithe in my ee,
> I'll shine on ye yet in your ain countrie."

The *Scots Magazine* gave the volume a favourable review, with copious extracts as specimens of its composition, but at the same time gently hinting that certain expressions might have been improved by a little refinement. Speaking of the character of the pieces, it said :—

" None of them relate to the ancient scenes of ' feud and fight;' nor are any earlier than the middle of the sixteenth century, from which period they extend down to the present day. Some are the productions of living poets; for Dumfries has produced among her peasantry several truly inspired with the genius of song. The earliest poems are chiefly amorous, with some of a humorous cast; chiefly levelled against the wives of these days, many of whom appear to have kept their ' lords' under a very severe thraldom. . . The most modern songs return to the standard subject of love, and indulge also in a certain rude humour, which does not, in our opinion, form their brightest ornament.

" The love songs may be traced back to the time of the Covenanters, and are of a character very peculiar, different from what we have seen belonging to Scotland, or perhaps to any other country. This singularity consists in the intimate manner in which that spirit of devotion, which then prevailed to even an enthusiastic degree, is blended with this human passion. The two sentiments are sometimes so intermingled, as, combined with that familiarity with which the devotionists of those days were accustomed to address the Deity, makes the extreme of piety sometimes border on its opposite."

This last reflection has reference to the song, already quoted, "Thou hast sworn by thy God, my Jeanie," which we think is one of the finest in the volume, and was mentioned as such at the time it appeared. Nothing in our opinion can be finer than the two lovers agreeing to pray to God on behalf of each other:—

> " The *Beuk* maun be taen when the carle comes hame,
>   Wi' the holie psalmodie,
> And thou maun speak o' me to thy God,
>   And I will speak o' thee !"

The following song seems to us so exquisitely tender and heart-touching that we cannot refrain from quoting it, and many of our readers will thank us for doing so:—

" A WEARY BODIE'S BLYTHE WHAN THE SUN GANGS
DOWN.

> " A weary bodie's blythe whan the sun gangs down,
> A weary bodie's blythe whan the sun gangs down:
> To smile wi' his wife, and to daute wi' his weans,
> Wha wadna be blythe whan the sun gangs down !

" The simmer sun's lang, and we're a' toiled sair,
　　Frae sunrise to sunset's a dreigh tack o' care;
　　But at hame for to daute 'mang our wee bits o' weans,
　　We think on our toils an' our cares nae mair.

" The Saturday sun gangs aye sweetest down,
　　My bonnie boys leave their wark i' the town;
　　My heart loups light at my ain ingle side,
　　Whan my kin' blythe bairn-time is a' sitting roun'.

" The Sabbath morning comes, an' warm lowes the sun,
　　Ilk heart's fu' o' joy a' the parishen roun';
　　Round the hip o' the hill comes the sweet psalm tune,
　　An' the auld fowk a' to the preaching are bowne.

" The hearts o' the younkers loup lightsome, to see
　　The gladness that dwalls in their auld grannie's ee;
　　An' they gather i' the sun, 'side the green haw-tree,
　　Nae new-flown birds are sae mirthsome an' hie.

" Tho' my sonsie dame's cheeks nae to auld age are prief,
　　Tho' the roses that blumed there are smit i' the leaf;
　　Tho' the young blinks o' luve hae a' died in her ee,
　　She is bonnier an' dearer than ever to me!

" Anee poortith came in 'yont our hallan to keek,
　　But my Jeanie was nursing an' singing sae sweet,
　　That she laid down her powks at anither door check,
　　An' steppit blythely ben her auld shanks for to beek.

" My hame is the mailen weel stockit an' fu,
　　My bairns are the flocks an' the herds that I loo;—
　　My Jeanie is the gowd an' delight o' my ee,
　　She's worth a hale lairdship o' mailens to me!

" O wha wad fade awa like a flower i' the dew,
　　An' nae leave a sprout for kind heaven to pu'?
　　Wha wad rot 'mang the mools, like the trunk o' the tree,
　　Wi' nae shoots the pride o' the forest to be!"

We ask if there is any one who, after reading the above song, does not experience a peculiar sensation about the heart, and a well-known moisture in the eyes? We ourselves confess to both.

CHAPTER VII.

THE "MERMAID OF GALLOWAY"—PREFATORY NOTE AND
ACCOMPANYING LETTER.

WHAT was generally considered the gem of the volume
was the " Mermaid of Galloway," with its prefatory note,
and its accompanying letter:—

" Tradition is yet rich with the fame of this bewitching
Mermaid; and many of the good old folks have held most
edifying and instructing communion with her by her favourite
moonlight banks, and eddyed nooks of streams. She was wont
to treasure their minds with her celestial knowledge of household economy, and would give receipts to make heavenly salve
to heal the untimely touch of disease. A charming young
girl, whom consumption had brought to the brink of the
grave, was lamented by her lover. In a vein of renovating
sweetness the good Mermaid sung to him—

> ' Wad ye let the bonnie May die i' yere hand,
> An' the mugwort flowering i' the land?'

" He cropped and pressed the flower-tops, and adminis-
tered the juice to his fair mistress, who arose and blessed her
bestower for the return of health.

" The Mermaid's favourite haunts and couches were along
the shores of the Nith and Urr, and on the edge of the
Solway sea, which adjoins the mouths of these waters. Her

beauty was such that man could not behold her face but his heart was fired with unquenchable love. 'Her long hair of burning gold,' through the wiling links of which appeared her white bosom and shoulders, were her favourite care; and she is always represented by tradition with one hand shedding her locks, and with the other combing them.

"Tradition tells that this world is an outer husk or shell which encloses a kernel of most rare abode, where dwell the Mermaids of popular belief. According to Lowland mythology, they are a race of goddesses corrupted with earthly passions. Their visits to the world, 'though few and far between,' are spoken of and remembered with awe. Their affections were bestowed on men of exalted virtue and rare endowments of person and parts. They wooed in such a strain of syren eloquence that all hearts were fettered by the witcheries of love. When their celestial voice dropt on the ear every other faculty was enthralled. They caught the beloved object in their embrace, and laid him on a couch, where mortal eyes might search in vain into the rites of such romantic and mysterious wedlock.

"Though possessed of the most soft and gracious qualities, yet, when a serious premeditated indignity was offered them, they were immediately awakened to revenge. A devout farm dame, in the time of the last persecution, was troubled in spirit at the wonted return of this heathenish visitant. A deep and beautiful pool, formed in the mouth of Dalbeattie Burn by the eddy of Urr Water, was a beloved residence of the Mermaid of Galloway. 'I' the first come o' the moon' she would seat herself on a smooth block of granite on the brink of the pool, comb her golden links of hair, and deliver her healing oracles. The good woman, in a frenzy of religious zeal, with her Bible in her hand, had the temerity to tumble this ancient chair into the bottom of the pool. The next morning her only child was found dead in its cradle, and a voice from the pool was often heard at day-close by the distracted mother :—

> ' Ye may look i' yere toom cradle,
> And I'll look to my stane;
> And meikle we'll think, and meikle we'll look,
> But words we'll ne'er ha'e nane!'

"All the noxious weeds and filth that could be collected were thrown into the pool, until the stream was polluted; and the Mermaid departed, leaving a curse of barrenness on the house, which all the neighbours for several miles around are ready to certify has been faithfully fulfilled.

"William Maxwell, Esq. of Cowehill, is the bridegroom ' Willie' of this romance. According to popular history, he was nephew to the ' Lily of Nithsdale,' heroine of the sublime song, ' She's gane to dwall in Heaven.'"

"THE MERMAID OF GALLOWAY.

> " There's a maid has sat on the green merse side,
> These ten lang years and mair;
> An' every first night o' the new moon
> She kames her yellow hair.

> " An' aye while she sheds the yellow burning gowd,
> Fu' sweet she sings an' hie,
> Till the fairest bird that wooes the green-wood,
> Is charm'd wi' her melodie.

> " But wha e'er listens to that sweet sang,
> Or gangs the dame to see,
> No'er hears the sang o' the laverock again,
> Nor wakens an earthlie ee.

" It fell in about the sweet simmer month,
   I' the first come o' the moon,
 That she sat o' the tap of a sea-weed rock,
   A-kaming her silk locks down.

" Her kame was o' the whitely pearl,
   Her hand like new-won milk,
 Her breasts were a' o' the snawy curd,
   In a net o' sea-green silk.

" She kamed her locks owre her white shoulders,
   A fleece baith bonny and lang;
 An' ilka ringlet she shed frae her brows,
   She raised a lightsome sang.

" I' the very first lilt o' that sweet sang,
   The birds forsook their young,
 An' they flew i' the gate o' the grey howlet,
   To listen the maiden's song.

" I' the second lilt o' that sweet sang,
   Of sweetness it was sae fu',
 The tod leap'd out frae the bughted lambs,
   And dighted his red-wat mou'.

" I' the very third lilt o' that sweet sang,
   Red lowed the new-woke moon;
 The stars drapp'd blude on the yellow gowan tap,
   Sax miles that maiden roun'.

" I hae dwalt on the Nith, quo' the young Cowehill,
   These twenty years an' three,
 But the sweetest sang e'er brake frae a lip
   Comes thro' the green-wood to me.

" O is it a voice frae twa earthlie lips
   Whilk make sic melodie!
 It wad wyle the lark frae the morning lift,
   And weel may it wyle me!

" I dreamed a dreary thing, master,
    Whilk I am rad ye rede;
  I dreamed ye kissed a pair o' sweet lips,
    That drapp'd o' red heart's-blede.

" Come haud my steed, ye little foot-page,
    Shod wi' the red gold roun';
  Till I kiss the lips whilk sing sae sweet:
    An' lightlie lap he down.

" Kiss nae the singer's lips, master,
    Kiss nae the singer's chin;
  Touch nae her hand, quo' the little foot-page,
    If skaithless hame ye'd win.

" O wha will sit on yere toom saddle,
    O wha will bruik yere gluve?
  An' wha will fauld yere erled bride
    I' the kindlie clasps o' luve?

" He took aff his hat, a' gold i' the rim,
    Knot wi' a siller ban';
  He seemed a' in lowe wi' his gold raiment,
    As thro' the green-wood he ran.

" The summer-dew fa's saft, fair maid,
    Aneath the siller moon;
  But eerie is thy seat i' the rock,
    Washed wi' the white sea faem.

" Come wash me wi' thy lilie white hand,
    Below and aboon the knee;
  An' I'll kame these links o' yellow burning gold,
    Aboon thy bonnie blue ee.

" How rosie are thy parting lips,
    How lilie-white thy skin,
  An' weel I wat these kissing een
    Wad tempt a saint to sin.

" Take aff these bars an' bobs o' gold,
    Wi' thy gared doublet fine;
An' thraw me aff thy green mantle,
    Leafed wi' the siller twine.

" An' a' in courtesie, fair knight,
    A maiden's love to win;
The gold lacing o' thy green weeds
    Wad harm her lilie skin.

" Syne coost he aff his green mantle
    Hemm'd wi' the red gold roun';
His costly doublet coost he aff,
    Wi' red gold flow'red down.

" Now ye maun kame my yellow hair,
    Down wi' my pearlie kame;
Then rowe me in thy green mantle,
    An' take me maiden hame.

" But first come take me 'neath the chin,
    An' syne come kiss my cheek;
An' spread my hanks o' wat'ry hair
    I' the new-moon beam to dreep.

" Sae first he kissed her dimpled chin,
    Syne kissed her rosie cheek;
An' lang he wooed her willin' lips,
    Like heather-hinnie sweet!

" O, if ye'll come to the bonnie Cowehill,
    'Mang primrose banks to woo;
I'll wash ye ilk day i' the new milked milk,
    And bind wi' gold yere brow.

" An' a' for a drink o' the clear water,
    Ye'se hae the rosie wine;
An' a' for the water white lilie,
    Ye'se hae these arms o' mine.

·" But what'll she say, yere bonnie young bride,
    Busked wi' the siller fine;
Whan the rich kisses ye kept for her lips,
    Are left wi' vows on mine ?

" He took his lips frae her red-rose mou',
    His arm frae her waist sae sma';
Sweet maiden, I'm in bridal speed,
    It's time I were awa.

" O gie me a token o' luve, sweet May,
    A leal luve token true;
She crapped a lock o' yellow gowden hair,
    An' knotted it roun' his brow.

" O tie nae it sae strait, sweet May,
    But wi' love's rose-knot kind ;
My head is fu' o' burning pain,
    O saft ye maun it bind.

" His skin turned a' o' the red-rose hue,
    Wi' draps o' bludie sweat ;
An' he laid his head 'mang the water lilies—
    Sweet maiden, I maun sleep.

" She tied ae link o' her wet yellow hair,
    Aboon his burning bree ;
Amang his curling haffet locks
    She knotted knurles three.

" She weaved owre his brow the white lilie,
    Wi' witch-knots more than nine ;
Gif ye were seven times bridegroom owre,
    This night ye shall be mine.

" O twice he turned his sinking head
    An' twice he lifted his ee ;
An' twice he sought to loose the links
    Were knotted owre his bree.

" Arise, sweet knight, yere young bride waits,
    An' doubts her ale will sour;
An' wistly looks at the lily-white sheets,
    Down spread in ladie-bower.

" An' she has preened the broidered silk
    About her white hause-bane;
Her princely petticoat is on,
    Wi' gold can stan' its lane.

" He faintlie, slowlie, turn'd his cheek,
    An' faintlie lift his ee,
An' he strave to loose the witching bands
    Aboon his burning bree.

" Then took she up his green mantle,
    Of lowing gold the hem;
Then took she up his silken cap,
    Rich wi' a siller stem;
An' she threw them wi' her lilie hand
    Amang the white sea-faem.

" She took the bride ring frae his finger,
    An' threw it in the sea;
That hand shall mense nae ither ring
    But wi' the will o' me.

" She faulded him i' her lilie arms,
    An' left her pearlie kame;
His fleecy locks trailed owre the sand,
    As she took the white sea-faem.

" First rose the star out owre the hill,
    An' neist the lovelier morn;
While the beauteous bride o' Galloway
    Look'd for her blithe bridegroom.

" Lightly she sang while the new moon rose,
    Blithe as a young bride may,

　　　Whan the new moon lights her lamp o' luve,
　　　　An' blinks the bride away.

" Nithsdale, thou art a gay garden,
　　Wi' monie a winsome flower;
　But the princeliest rose o' that garden
　　Maun blossom in my bower.

" Oh, gentle be the wind on thy leaf,
　　An' gentle the gloaming dew;
　An' bonnie an' balmy be thy bud,
　　O' a pure an' steadfast hue;
　An' she who sings this sang in thy praise
　　Shall love thee leal an' true.

" An' aye she sewed her silken snood,
　　An' sung a bridal sang;
　But aft the tears drap't frae her ee
　　Afore the grey morn cam'.

" The sun leam'd ruddie 'mang the dew,
　　Sae thick on bank an' tree;
　The plow-boy whistled at his darke,
　　The milk-maid answered hie;
　But the lovely bride o' Galloway
　　Sat wi' a tear-wet ee.

" Ilk breath o' wind 'mang the forest leaves—
　　She heard the bridegroom's tongue,
　An' she heard the bridal-coming lilt
　　In every bird which sung.

" She sat high on the tap-tower stane,
　　Nae waiting May was there;
　She loosed the gold busk frae her breast,
　　The kame frae 'mang her hair;
　She wiped the tear-blobs frae her ee,
　　An' looked lang and sair.

" First sang to her the blythe wee bird,
    Frae aff the hawthorn green ;
Loose out the love curls frae yere hair,
    Ye plaited sae weel yestreen.

" An' the spreckled lark frae 'mang the clouds
    Of heaven came singing down—
Take out the bride-knots frae yere hair,
    An' let these lang locks down.

" Come, bide wi' me, ye pair o' sweet birds,
    Come down an' bide wi' me ;
Ye shall peckle o' the bread, an' drink o' the wine,
    An' gold yere cage shall be.

" She laid the bride-cake 'neath her head,
    An' syne below her feet ;
An' laid her down 'tween the lily-white sheets,
    An' soundly did she sleep.

" It seem'd i' the mid-hour o' the night,
    Her siller bell did ring ;
An' soun't as if nae earthlie hand
    Had pou'd the silken string.

" There was a cheek touch'd that ladye's,
    Cauld as the marble stane,
An' a hand cauld as the drifting snaw
    Was laid on her breast-bane.

" O cauld is thy hand, my dear Willie,
    O cauld, cauld is thy cheek ;
An' wring these locks o' yellow hair,
    Frae which the cauld draps dreep.

" O seek another bridegroom, Marie,
    On these bosom faulds to sleep ;
My bride is the yellow water lilie,
    Its leaves my bridal sheet !"

Among many others, Mr. Roscoe was captivated with this ballad, and made repeated inquiries about Jean Walker (Cunningham's future wife), to whom was attributed the letter at the end accompanying it, which he said was the finest thing ever written, and had more than the spirit of Burns. She was also accredited with the songs—"She's gane to dwall in Heaven," "Thou hast sworn by thy God, my Jeanie," "The Pawkie Loon the Miller," and "Young Derwentwater." The letter accompanying the "Mermaid of Galloway" was addressed to Mr. Cromek:—

" . . . A weed turns a flower when it is set in a garden. Will these songs be better or bonnier in print? I enclose you a flower new pou'd frae the banks of blythe Cowehill. It has long grown almost unkend of. Gentility disna pou' a flower that blooms i' the fields: it is trampled on as a weed when it is no' in a flower-pot. I see you smiling at the wretched lilts of the sweet-singing Mermaid. Well, come again to Galloway—sit down i' the gloaming dewfall on the green merse side amang the flowers; and if a pair of lilie arms, and twa kissing lips and witching een, forbye the sweet music of a honey-dropping tongue, winna gaur ye believe in the lilting glamour of the Mermaid ye may gang back to England singing—'Praise be blest!' How will your old-fashioned taste and the new-fangledness of the public's agree about these old songs? But tell me, can a song become old when the ideas and imagery it contains are drawn from nature! While gowans grow on our braes, and lilies on our burn-banks, so long will natural imagery and natural sentiment flourish green in song.

"I am, perhaps, too partial to these old songs: it is

because they recall the memory of parental endearments. The posies of our fathers and our mothers I hold it not seemly for a daughter to let wither."

Well done, Jean Walker! if you wrote this. You are entitled to be the mate` of Allan Cunningham. Your spirit seems to be entirely akin to his, and you write poetically even in prose. At the close of this letter the editor appends the following note:—

" That the peasantry of Scotland possess a greater portion of natural taste and information than the vulgar class of any other nation is considered paradoxical by their unbelieving brethren on this side of the Tweed. Were evidence required to establish this fact, a Scottish peasant would exclaim— ' Where are your ballads and songs, the beauteous fugitives of neglected or unknown rustic bards? Where are your sacred reliques of poetic devotion, with which every Scotchman's heart is filled?—the plaint of despair, the uplifting raptures of love, or the heart-warming lament of domestic misfortune? With us they live; with you they have never existed, or have perished!'"

We have not yet done with the volume, but only with the poetical part of it, and in another chapter we shall refer to what is given in prose, to which we attach special importance. While we now know that the ballads were in a great measure only imitations, we have confidence, from personal knowledge and otherwise, in the truth of what is described in the latter portion of the work. We must say, however, that, with regard to some of the songs, our opinion is that certain expressions, lines, and even verses, had better been omitted; but, as we have already said, our countrymen sixty years ago were not so fastidious as now. Besides, it should be remembered that the ballads profess to be of far older date than this; and as we know from the musings of some of the ancient ballad-mongers, they were anything but refined, it behoved that these imitations, as relics of bygone ages, should be in conformity with the style when these prevailed, otherwise their pretended genuineness would have been at once detected. Compared with some of the songs in Herd's Collection of 1769 they are almost purity, and Herd was not alone. So that there was almost an absolute necessity to have some unrefinement to preserve the mystification intended. When Cunningham avowedly wrote, in his own name, songs of his own day, no coarseness of expression was introduced, or anything but what might be chanted in the presence of parents by the maiden without a blush.

CHAPTER VIII.

CUNNINGHAM DISCLOSES THE SECRET OF THE "REMAINS" TO M'GUIE
—EXTRACTS FROM THE APPENDIX: FAMILY WORSHIP—THE
WITCHES—THE FAIRIES.

THOUGH Cunningham did not care to disclose the
secret that the ballads were imitations, such as the
literary critics surmised, yet he acknowledged the
fact to a certain extent in replying to his friend
George, who had hinted his own opinion in the same
direction:—

"You edify me by your opinion on the 'Remains of Nithsdale and Galloway Song.' The critics are much of the same
mind as yourself. Your conjecture is not very far wrong as
to my share of the book. Was it the duty of a son to show
the nakedness of his own land? No, my dear friend. I went
before and made the path straight. I planted here and
there a flower—dropped here and there a honeycomb—
plucked away the bitter gourd—cast some jewels in the
by-paths and in the fields, so that the traveller might find
them, and wonder at the richness of the land that produced
them! Nor did I drop them in vain. Pardon the confession,
and keep it a secret."

A third part of the volume contains an appendix in
prose, in which are given very graphic and interesting

descriptions of Scottish customs, amusements, superstitions, and beliefs, some of which have entirely died away, their departure not to be regretted; but one custom especially, which should ever remain, we are sorry to fear is not so religiously observed now throughout the country as in olden times, that of Family Worship. From this last we shall quote an extract, as being truly descriptive of what was a common practice in the peasant's dwelling, and as entirely in accord with Burns' immortal poem, "The Cottar's Saturday Night." It is named "Taking the Beuk":—

"On entering a neat thatched cottage, when past the partition or hallan, a wide, projecting chimney-piece, garnished with smoked meat, met your eye. The fire, a good space removed from the end wall, was placed against a large whinstone, called the cat-hud. Behind this was a bench stretching along the gable, which, on trysting nights, was occupied by the children—the best seat being courteously proffered to strangers. The Cottar sire was placed on the left of the fire, removed from the bustle of housewifery. A settee of oak, antiquely carved, and strewn with favourite texts of Scripture, was the good man's seat, where he rested after the day's fatigue, nursing and instructing his children. His library shelf above him displayed his folio Bible, covered with rough calf skin, wherein were registered his children's names and hour of birth; some histories of the old reforming worthies (divines who waded through the blood and peril of persecution), the sacred books of his fathers, lay, carefully adjusted, and pretty much used; and the acts and deeds of Scotland's saviour, Wallace, and the immortal Bruce, were deemed worthy of holding a place among the heroic divines who had won the heavenly crown of martyrdom. Above these were hung a broadsword and targe, the remains of ancient warfare, which, happily, the hand of peace had long forgot to wield.   From the same pin depended the kirn-cut of corn (the name sometimes given to the last handful of grain cut down on the harvest field) braided and adorned with ribbons.   Beside him was his fowling-piece, which, before the enaction of Game Laws, supplied his family with venison and fowls in their season.   At the end of the lang settle was the window, which displayed a few panes of glass, and two oaken boards that opened like shutters for the admission of air.   On the guidwife's side appeared her articles of economy and thrift.   A dresser replenished with pewter plates, with a large meal chest of carved oak, extended along the side-wall.   Bunches of yarn hung from a loft or flooring made of small wood or rye spread across the joisting, and covered with moor turf.   The walls, white with lime, were garnished with dairy utensils (every cottar almost having one or two kye).   At each side of the middle entry was a bed, sometimes of very curious and ingenious workmanship, being posted with oak, and lined with barley straw, finely cleaned, and inwoven with thread; these were remarkably warm, and much valued.

"Family worship was performed every evening, but on the Sabbath morning it was attended with peculiar solemnity.   At that season all the family, and frequently some of the neighbours, presented themselves before the aged village apostle.   He seated himself on a lang-settle, laying aside his bonnet and plaid.   His eldest child came submissively forward, and, unclasping the Bible, placed it across his father's knees.   After a few minutes of religious silence, he meekly lifts his eyes over his family to mark if they are all around him, and decorous.   Opening the Bible, he says—in a tone of simple and holy meekness—' Let us reverently worship our God by singing the (eighth) Psalm.' He reads it aloud, then gives or recites line after line, leading the tune himself. The ' Martyrs' is a chosen air, so called in honour of those men who displayed a zeal worthy of the name, and perished in the persecution. All the family join in this exquisitely mournful tune till the sacred song is finished. A selected portion of Scripture is then read, from the sublime soarings of Isaiah, or the solemn morality of Job. As the divine precepts of his Saviour are the sacred rules by which the good man shapes the conduct of his children, Isaiah's fifty-third chapter, where the coming of the Redeemer is foretold, is the soul-lifting favourite of rustic devotion. It is read with an exalted inspiration of voice accordant with the subject. The family rise as he clasps the book, fall down on their knees, bowing their heads to the ground. The good man, kneeling over his Bible, pours his prayer to Heaven in a strain of feeling and fervent eloquence. His severity of church discipline relaxes in the warmth of his heart.—' May our swords become plough-shares, and our spears reaping-hooks : may all find grace before Thee !' There is not, perhaps, a more impressive scene than a Scottish Sabbath morn presents, when the wind is low, the summer sun newly risen, and all the flocks at browse by the waters and by the woods. How glorious then to listen to the holy murmur of retired prayer, and the distant chaunt of the cottarman's psalm spreading from hamlet and village!"

The belief in witchcraft was as strong in Nithsdale as it was in Ayrshire, or, indeed, anywhere else; and although there are no scenes to record equal to that which Tam o' Shanter saw in Alloway Kirk, yet there are traditions of the ongoings of witches and warlocks ludicrous in the extreme. There were trystes or meetings held of these parties in several quarters of the district, when they performed their cantrips in the usual fashion:—

"The noted tryste of the Nithsdale and Galloway warlocks and witches was held on a rising knowe four miles distant from Dumfries, called *Locharbrigg Hill.* There are yet some fragments of the witches' "Gathering Hymn" too characteristically curious to be omitted:—

> ' When the gray howlet has three times hoo'd,
> When the grimy cat has three times mewed,
> When the tod has yowled three times i' the wode,
> At the red moon cowering ahin the clud;
> When the stars hae cruppen deep i' the drift,
> Lest cantrips had pyked them out o' the lift,
> Up horsies a', but mair adowe,
> Ryde, ryde, for Locharbrigg Knowe!'

"Roused by this infernal summons, the earth and the air groaned with the unusual load. It was a grand though a daring attempt for man, or aught of mortal frame, to view this diabolical hurry. The wisest part barred their doors, and left the world to its own misrule. Those aged matrons, deep read in incantation, says tradition, 'could sit i' the coat tails o' the moon,' or harness the wind to their ragweed chariot—could say to the west star, 'byde thou me!' or to the moon, 'hynte me in thy arm, for I am weary!' Those carlins of garrulous old age, who had suffered martyrdom on the brow for the cause, rode on chosen broom-sticks, shod with murdered men's bones. These moved spontaneously to tho will of the possessor. But the more gay and genteel kimmers loved a softer seat than the bark of a broomstick. A bridle shredded from the skin of an unbaptized infant, with bits forged in Satan's armoury, possessed irresistible power when shaken above any living thing.

"Two young lads of Nithsdale once served a widow dame, who possessed a bridle with these dangerous qualifications. One of them, a plump, merry young fellow, suddenly lost all his gaiety, and became lean, as if '*ridden post by a witch.*' On his neighbour lad's inquiry about the cause, he only said, 'Lie at the bed stock an' ye'll be as lean as me.' It was on a Hallowmas e'en, and though he felt unusual drowsiness he kept himself awake. At midnight his mistress, cautiously approaching his bedside, shook the charmed bridle over his face, saying, 'Up Horsie,' when, to his utter astonishment, he arose in the form of a gray horse! The cantrip bit was put in his teeth, and, mounted by the carlin, he went off like the wind. Feeling the prick of infernal spur, he took such leaps and bounds that he reached Locherbrigg Knowe in a few moments. He was fastened by the bridle to a tree, with many more of his acquaintance, whom he recognized through their brutal disguise. He looked petrified with affright when the father of cantrips drew a circle around the *knowe*, within which no baptized brow could enter.

"All being assembled, hands were joined, and a ring of warlocks and witches danced in the enchanted bound with many lewd and uncouth gestures. In the centre he beheld a thick smoke, and presently arose the piercing yells and screams of hellish baptism which the new converts were enduring. Startled and terrified to furious exertion, he plunged, pulled, and reared; and, praying ardently to Heaven, he shook off the bridle of power; and, starting up in his own shape, he seized the instrument of his transfor-

I

mation.　It was now gray daylight when the conclave dispersed, for their ogres could not endure the rebuke of the sun. He watched his mistress, who, all haste and confusion, was hurrying to her steed.　Shaking the bridle over her brow, she started up a 'gude gray mare,' and was hastened home with such push of spur that all competitors were left far behind !　The sun was nigh risen as he hurried into the stable.　Pulling off the bridle, his cantrip-casting mistress appeared with hands and feet lacerated with travel, and her sides pricked to the bone.　On her rider's promising never to divulge his night's adventure, she allowed him to keep the bridle as a pledge of safety. . . . .

"Caerlaverock and New Abbey are still celebrated as the native parishes of two midnight caterers in the festivals of glamour.　They were rivals in fame, in power, and dread. On the night of every full moon they met to devise employment for the coming month.　Their confederacy and their trysting haunts had been discovered, and were revealed by chosen and holy men who ministered to their Creator and fulfilled His dictates.

"Debarred from holding secret conference on the solid sward, they fixed their trystes on the unstable waters which separate their parishes.　This tale, so full of character, was taken down by the Editor from the word-of-mouth evidence of the man who saw all that passed ; and it must be told in his own simple, expressive language.

"'I gaed out ae fine simmer night to haud my halve at the Pow fit.　It was twal' o'clock, an' a' was lowne; the moon had just gotten up—ye mought a gathered preens !　I heard something firsle like silk, I glowered roun', an', 'lake ! what saw I but a bonnie boat wi' a nob o' gowd, an' sails like new-coined siller.　It was only but a wee bittie frae me—I mought amaist touch't it.　'Gude speed ye gif ye gang for gude,' quo' I, for I dreed our auld carlin was casting some o' her pranks.   Another cunning boat cam' aff frae Caerla'rick to meet it.   Thae twa bade a stricken hour thegither, sidie for sidie.   'Haith,' quo' I, 'the deil's grit wi' some!' sae I crap down amang some lang cowes till Luckie cam' back. The boat played bowte again the bank, an' out loups kimmer, wi' a pyked naig's head i' her han'.   'Lord be about us!' quo' I, 'for she cam' straught for me.   She howked up a green turf, covered her bane, an' gaed her wa's.   Whan I thought her hame, up I gat, and pou'd up the bane and haed it.   I was fley'd to gae back for twa or three nights lest the deil's minnie should wyte me for her uncannie boat, an' lair me 'mang the sludge, or may be do waur.   I gaed back, howsoever, an' on that night o' the moon wha comes to me but kimmer!   'Rabin,' quo' she, 'fand ye an auld bane amang the cowes?'   'Deed, no, it may be gowd for me!' quo' I.   'Weel, weel,' quo' she, 'I'll byde and help ye hame wi' your fish.'   God's be my help, nought grippit I but tades an' paddocks!   'Satan, thy neive's here,' quo' I. 'Ken ye,' quo' I, 'o' yon new cheese our wyfe took but frae the chessel yestreen? I'm gaun to send't t'ye i' the morning; ye're a gude neebor to me.   An', hear'st thou me! there's a bit auld bane whomeled aneath thae cowes; I kentnae it was thine.'   Kimmer drew't out.   'Aye, aye, it's my auld bane; weel speed ye.'   I' the very first pou I gat sic a louthe o' fish that I carried till my back cracked again.' . . .

"The way of restoring milk to the udder of a cow bewitched is curious, and may benefit posterity. A young virgin milked whatever milk the cow had left, which was of bloody mixture and poisonous quality. This was poured warm from the cow into a brass pan, and (every inlet to the house being closed) was placed over a gentle fire until it began to heat. Pins were dropped in, and closely stirred with a wand of rowan tree. When boiling, rusty nails were thrown in, and more fuel added. The witch instantly felt, by sympathetic power, the boiling medicine rankling through her bosom, and an awful knocking announced her arrival at the window. The sly ' Gudewife' instantly compounded with the mother of cantrips for ' *her hale loan of kye,*' the pan was cooled, and the cows' udders swelled with genuine milk."

We give an extract from a long and interesting account of Fairy superstition as it existed in Nithsdale; and, indeed, the description holds true with regard to every district in the South of Scotland. We can speak from personal knowledge as to the famous Ayrshire haunt of that weird people on the banks of the Doon, the Cassills Downans, immortalized by Burns; but though in our young enthusiasm we searched the place at all hours of the night, in the hope of seeing some of the elfin band, for long all was silence and desertion, till at last we did, in our perseverance, meet with the Fairy Queen who afterwards became our wife. No wonder, then, we have such an attachment to the fairy superstition:—

" There are few old people who have not a powerful belief in the influence and dominion of fairies; few who do not believe they have heard them on their midnight excursions, or talked with them amongst their woods and their knowes, in the familiarity of friendship. So general was this superstition that priestly caution deemed it necessary to interpose its religious authority to forbid man's intercourse with these ' *light infantry of Satan!*'

"They were small of stature, exquisitely shaped and proportioned, of a fair complexion, with long fleeces of yellow hair flowing over their shoulders, and tucked above their brows with combs of gold. A mantle of green cloth, inlaid with wild flowers, reached to their middle; green pantaloons, buttoned with bobs of silk, and sandals of silver, formed their under dress. On their shoulders hung quivers of adder slough, stored with pernicious arrows; and bows fashioned from the rib of a man buried where '*three Lairds' lands meet,*' tipped with gold, ready bent for warfare, were slung by their sides. Thus accoutred, they mounted on steeds, whose hoofs would not print the new ploughed land, nor dash the dew from the cup of a harebell. They visited the flocks, the folds, the fields of coming grain, and the habitations of man; and woe to the mortal whose frailty threw him in their power! A flight of arrows, tipped with deadly plagues, was poured into his folds, and nauseous weeds grew up in his pastures; his coming harvest was blighted with pernicious breath, and whatever he had no longer prospered. These fatal shafts were formed of the bog reed, pointed with white field flint, and dipped in the dew of hemlock. They were shot into cattle with such magical dexterity that the smallest aperture could not be discovered but by those deeply skilled in fairy warfare, and in the cure of elf-shooting. Cordials and potent charms are applied, the burning arrow is extracted, and instant recovery ensues.

"The fairies seem to have been much attached to particular places. A green hill, an opening in a wood, a burn just freeing itself from the uplands, were kept sacred for revelry and festival. The Wardlaw, an ever green hill in Dalswinton barony, was, in olden days, a noted fairy tryste. But the fairy ring being converted into a pulpit, in the times of persecution, proscribed the revelry of unchristened feet.

Lamentations of no earthly voices were heard for years around this beloved hill. In their festivals they had the choicest earthly cheer; nor do they seem to have repelled the intrusion of man, but invited him to partake of their enjoyments.

"A young man of Nithsdale, being on a love intrigue, was enchanted with wild and delightful music, and the sound of mingled voices, more charming than aught that mortal breath could utter. With a romantic daring peculiar to a Scottish lover, he followed the sound and discovered the fairy banquet. A green table, with feet of gold, was placed across a small rivulet, and richly furnished with pure bread and wines of sweetest flavour. Their minstrelsy was raised from small reeds and stalks of corn. He was invited to partake in the dance, and presented with a cup of wine. He was allowed to depart, and was ever after endowed with the second sight. He boasted of having seen and conversed with several of his earthly acquaintances whom the fairies had taken and admitted as brothers!

"Mankind, measuring the minds of others by their own enjoyments, have marked out set times of festivity to the fairies. At the first approach of summer is held the 'Fairy Raid;' and their merry minstrelsy, with the tinkling of their horses' housings, and the hubbub of voices, have kept the peasantry in the Scottish villages awake on the first night of summer. They placed branches of rowan tree over their doors, and gazed on the fairy procession safely from below the charm-proof twig. This march was described to the Editor with the artless simplicity of sure belief by an old woman of Nithsdale :—' I' the night afore Roodsmas, I had trysted wi' a neighbour lass, a Scots mile frae hame, to talk anent buying braws i' the fair. We hadna sutten lang aneath the haw-buss till we heard the loud laugh o' fowk riding, wi' the jingling o' bridles, and the clanking o' hoofs. We banged up, thinking they would ryde owre us ; we kent nae but it was drunken fowk riding to the fair i' the fore nicht. We glowred roun' and roun', an' sune saw it was the *Fairie Fowks' Raid.* We cowered down till they passed by. A leam o' light was dancing owre them, mair bonnie than moonshine : they were a' wee, wee fowk, wi' green scarfs on, but ane that rade foremost, an' that ane was a gude deal langer than the lave, wi' bonnie lang hair bun' about wi' a strap, whilk glented lyke stars. They rade on braw wee whyte naigs, wi' unco lang swooping tails, an' manes hung wi' whustles that the win' played on. This, an' their tongues whan they sang, was like the soun' of a far awa Psalm. Marion an' me was in a brade lea fiel' whare they cam' by us. A high hedge o' haw trees keepit them frae gaun through Johnnie Corrie's corn, but they lap a' owre't like sparrows, an' gallop't into a green knowe beyont it. We gade i' the morning to look at the tredded corn, but the fient a hoof mark was there nor a blade broken.'

"In the solitary instances of their intercourse with mankind there is a benevolence of character, or a cruelty of disposition, which brings them down to be measured by a mortal standard. In all these presiding spirits there is a vein of earthly grossness which marks them beings created by human invention.

"It is reckoned by the Scottish peasantry ' *Unco sonsie* ' to live in familiar and social terms with them. They will borrow or lend, and it is counted *uncanny* to refuse a fairy request. A woman of Auchencreath, in Nithsdale, was one day sifting meal warm from the mill : a little cleanly-arrayed beautiful woman came to her, holding out a basin of antique workmanship, requesting her courteously to fill it with her new meal. Her demand was cheerfully complied with. In a week the comely little dame returned with the borrowed meal. She breathed over it, setting it down basin and all, saying aloud, '*Be never toom.*' The gudewife lived to a goodly age, without ever seeing the bottom of her blessed basin. When an injury was unwittingly done them they forgave it, and asked for amends like other creatures.

"A woman who lived in the ancient burgh of Lochmaben was returning late one evening to her home from a gossipping. A little, lovely boy, dressed in green, came to her, saying—'*Coupe yere dish-water farther frae yere doorstep, it pits out our fire!*' This request was complied with, and plenty abode in the good woman's house all her days.

"There are chosen fields of fairy revelry, which it is reckoned unsonsie to plough or to reap. Old thorn trees in the middle of a field are deemed the rallying trystes of fairies, and are preserved with scrupulous care. Two lads were opening with the plough one of these fields, and one of them had described a circle around the fairy thorn, which was not to be ploughed. They were surprised when, on ending the furrow, a green table was placed there, heaped with the choicest cheese, bread, and wine. He who marked out the thorn sat down without hesitation, eating and drinking heartily, saying '*fair fa' the hands whilk gie.*' His fellow-servant lashed his steeds, refusing to partake. The courteous ploughman 'thrave,' said my informer, 'like a breckan, and was a proverb for wisdom, and an oracle of local rural knowledge ever after!'

"Their love of mortal commerce prompted them to have their children suckled at earthly breasts. The favoured nurse was chosen from healthful, ruddy complexioned beauty, one every way approved of by mortal eyes. A fine young woman of Nithsdale, when first made a mother, was sitting singing and rocking her child, when a pretty lady came into her cottage, covered with a fairy mantle. She carried a beautiful child in her arms, swaddled in green silk. '*Gie my bonnie thing a suck*,' said the fairy. The young woman, conscious to whom the child belonged, took it kindly in her arms, and laid it to her breast. The lady instantly disappeared, saying, '*Nurse kin' an' ne'er want!*' The young mother nurtured, the two babes, and was astonished whenever she awoke at finding the richest suits of apparel for both children, with meat of most delicious flavour. This food tasted, says tradition, like loaf mixed with wine and honey. It possessed more miraculous properties than the wilderness manna, preserving its relish even over the seventh day.

"On the approach of summer the fairy lady came to see her child. It bounded with joy when it beheld her. She was much delighted with its freshness and activity. Taking it in her arms, she bade the nurse follow. Passing through some scraggy woods, skirting the side of a beautiful green hill, they walked mid-way up. On its sunward slope a door opened, disclosing a beauteous porch, which they entered, and the turf closed behind them. The fairy dropped three drops of a precious dew on the nurse's left eyelid, and they entered a land of most pleasant and abundant promise. It was watered with fine looping rivulets, and yellow with corn; the fairest trees enclosed its fields, laden with fruit which dropped honey. The nurse was rewarded with finest webs of cloth, and food of ever-enduring substance. Boxes of salves for restoring mortal health, and curing mortal wounds and infirmities, were bestowed on her, with a promise of never needing. The fairy dropt a green dew over her right eye, and bade her look. She beheld many of her lost friends and acquaintances doing menial drudgery—reaping the corn and gathering the fruits. 'This,' said she, 'is the punishment of evil deeds!'   The fairy passed her hand over her eye, and restored its mortal faculties.   She was conducted to the porch, but had the address to secure the heavenly salve. She lived and enjoyed the gift of discerning the earth-visiting spirits till she was the mother of many children; but happening to meet the fairy lady who gave her the child, she attempted to shake hands with her.   'What ee d'ye see me wi'?' whispered she.   'Wi' them baith,' said the dame. She breathed on her eyes, and even the power of the box failed to restore their gifts again!   .   .   .

"For the stealing of handsome and lovely children they are far famed, and held in great awe.   But their pernicious breath has such power of transformation that it is equally dreaded.   The way to cure a breath-blasted child is worthy of notice.   When the mother's vigilance hinders the fairies from carrying her child away, or changing it, the touch of fairy hands, and their unearthly breath, make it wither away in every limb and lineament, like a blighted ear of corn, saving the countenance, which unchangeably retains the sacred stamp of divinity.   The child is undressed, and laid out in unbleached linen, new from the loom.   Water is brought from a *blessed well* in the utmost silence, before sunrise, in a pitcher never before wet, in which the child is washed, and its cloths dipped by the fingers of a virgin.   Its limbs, on the third morning's experiment, plump up, and all its former vigour returns.

"But matron knowledge has frequently triumphed over these subtle thieves, by daring experiments and desperate charms.   A beautiful child of Caerlaverock, in Nithsdale, on the second day of its birth, and before its baptism, was changed, none knew how, for an antiquated elf of hideous aspect.   It kept the family awake with its nightly yells; biting the mother's breasts, and would neither be cradled nor nursed. The mother, obliged to be from home, left it in charge of the servant girl. The poor lass was sitting bemoaning herself—'Wer't nae for thy girning face I would knock the big, winnow the corn, and grun' the meal!' 'Lowse the cradle-band,' quoth the elf, 'and tent the neighbours, an' I'll work yere wark.' Up started the elf, the wind arose, the corn was chaffed,·the outlyers were foddered, the hand-mill moved around as by instinct, and the *knocking mell* did its work with amazing rapidity. The lass and her elfin servant rested and diverted themselves till, on the mistress' approach, it was restored to the cradle, and began to yell anew. The girl took the first opportunity of slyly telling her mistress the adventure. *' What'll we do wi' the wee diel?'* said she. 'I'll work it a pirn,' replied the lass. At the middle of the night the chimney top was covered up, and every inlet barred and closed. The embers were blown up until glowing hot, and the maid, undressing the elf, tossed it on the fire. It uttered the wildest and most piercing yells, and, in a moment, the fairies were heard moaning at every wonted avenue, and rattling at the window boards, at the chimney head, and at the door. 'In the name o' God bring back the bairn,' cried the lass. The window flew up, the earthly child was laid unharmed on the mother's lap, while its grizzly substitute flew up the chimney with a loud laugh."

A long account of the Brownies and their peculiar characteristics is also given, especially of one attached to the Maxwell family of Dalswinton; but, though highly interesting, we must omit it, after what has been already extracted at such length. There is also inserted Lady Nithsdale's wonderful narrative of her husband's escape from the Tower of London, on the 23rd of February, 1715, disguised in female apparel, a story which now all the world knows. We do not wonder that the volume created a sensation when it appeared; but it needed little sagacity or penetration on the part of the Ettrick Shepherd to "lay the saddle on the right horse," after his knowledge of Cunningham's lyric powers and legendary lore, and the special references to incidents, real or imaginary, in Kirkmahoe. One thing is clear, Mr. Cromek could not have written the "Remains of Nithsdale and Galloway Song."

CHAPTER IX.

HIS MARRIAGE—LETTER TO M'GHIE—INTRODUCTION TO MR. JERDAN OF THE "LITERARY GAZETTE"—PUBLISHES A VOLUME OF SONGS —NOTICES OF THESE—EXTRACTS—LETTER TO HIS MOTHER.

ABOUT the middle of the following summer, Jean Walker, the "Lovely Lass of Preston Mill," left her native vale for good and all, to link her fate with Allan Cunningham in London. Her journey thither, like his own, had an incident on the way, of the most friendly character, which he himself thus describes:—"In the house of Gray, Master of the High School of Edinburgh, she met the attention due to a daughter, was introduced to Dr. Anderson, and had the pleasure of hearing a letter read from Bishop Percy, in which he spoke well of the talents of her future husband. In James Hogg, also, and his comrade, Grieve, she met with attentive friends, who showed her the beauties of Edinburgh, conveyed her to the pier of Leith, and saw her safely embarked on the waves. Of her and my sister Jean, who accompanied her, Hogg thus wrote to my eldest brother James:—'I had the pleasure of waiting on your two sisters for a few days, and I am sure there never was a brother took the charge of sisters more pleasantly than I did. But one of them, at least, needs nobody to take care of her—I mean the beauteous mermaid of

Galloway, who is certainly a most extraordinary young woman. I introduced her to some gentlemen and ladies of my acquaintance, who were not only delighted, but astonished at her.' Jean Walker was then twenty years of age; her complexion was fine, and her eyes bright; and her prudence equalled her looks." No .doubt the merit with which she had been credited in supplying some of the ancient ballads contributed in some measure to the admiration.

The marriage was celebrated on the 1st of July, 1811, in the Church of St. Saviour, Southwark; and, notwithstanding the joyous excitement of the occasion, Cunningham naïvely says, that he "did not fail to remark that James I., the poet-king of Scotland, had been married there also, and that we joined hands nigh the monument of Gower, and not far from the grave of Massinger." The marriage was a happy one in every sense of the term. Mrs. Allan Cunningham seems to have been a most sensible, intelligent, and prudent woman, highly esteemed in society, and well worthy of all her husband sang in her praise. Mr. S. C. Hall, who was an intimate friend, says, in a memento after her death in 1864:—"She was a charming woman in her prime, and must have been very lovely as a girl. I have never known a better example of what natural grace and purity can do to produce refinement. Though peasant-born, she was in society a lady— thoroughly so. There was not only no shadow of vulgarity in her manners, there was not even rusticity, while there was a total absence of assumption and pretence; and she was entirely at ease in the 'grand' society—men and women of rank, as well as those eminent in Art, in Science, and in Letters—I have met as guests at her home."

Cunningham has now fairly entered upon a new career, not only in a matrimonial sense, but also in a literary view, for upwards of thirty volumes of prose and poetry are to flow from his pen before that career shall close, in addition to physical labour, though a concealing Providence did not vouchsafe to him the secret. Desultory employment, in which he was engaged, occasionally roused fears for the future in regard to the permanent comfort of his family home, as he well knew that something more than literature was necessary for the support of domestic life.

Exactly a month after his marriage, while " basking in the beams of the honeymoon," he thus playfully and also instructively wrote to his friend M'Ghie:—

"London, 1st August, 1811.

" My Trusty Fier,—I look back, like the seed of Jacob in their wilderness wanderings, to the divinity of their fathers, after they had made them a molten god to worship from the golden ornaments they filched from the Egyptians. Ah! cried I, work of mine own hands, I have worshipped thee long enough. I will turn me back to the friend I have not written to these many moons. So I awoke, and thought on thee, vain recreant to looms, free grace, and substantial prayer 'à la Cameronian.' And how fares my friend? Basking in the beams of the honeymoon of wedlock, I have still so much time as awakes the pleasant remembrance of other years. I know you deserved an earlier letter than this from me, but I excused myself from day to day, like the wicked in repentance, and now I am obliged to write under the pleasant prospect of being every moment called from it. . . . .

" On the whole, George, with a pleasant and good-hearted woman, you would prefer it to the lonesome life which late I led. You wrote me a pithy but very short epistle last time, and, really, I expect one of alarming size this forthcoming month. You were, however, so vague in your mode of expression that one part of your letter I could not understand after the most adroit scrutiny. Whether you expected some uncommon tidings soon from me, or that you might have some extraordinary occurrence to relate concerning yourself, you left it for those gifted in the unraveling of prophecy to decide. I fondly believe my friend may have an elegant recantation of the heresies of Bachelorism to make unto his friend, and nothing, I do assure you, would more sensibly touch me with pleasure than to find you, in your next letter, sending me the respects of a sweet and beloved fine woman whom you have wedded. This is not counsel, it is only wishing; for, matrimony without affection, I pray heaven to keep you from the hell of it.

" Permit me now to give you counsel of another kind. Instruct yourself in grammar, and learn French until you have ability to translate it. Read, and faithfully treasure up in your mind, the history and most prominent events of your native country; acquaint yourself with its revolutions, civil commotions and their causes. These you will find in Hume and Robertson, and I counsel you to prefer these authors, for while they are instructing you in history, they familiarize you to the most beautiful and vigorous modes of expression, the most lucid and perspicuous arrangement of language. Gibbon's Decline and Fall of the Roman Empire is a work written with an eye to the taste of my friend. Plutarch's Lives of Eminent Grecians and Romans you should take into bed with you, as long as you are unmarried, and dream on it. A history of the world in abridgment will, after these, be almost sufficient to acquaint you with History. Elegant literature is the soul which agitates, in conjunction with that of genius, the whole range of your learning, and sets it in motion. Blair's Lectures on Rhetoric —the Elements of Criticism—some of the articles in the *Edinburgh Review*—many articles in the *Spectator*—and the whole of Samuel Johnson's prose works.

"These will assist you to judge. Then Milton, Shakspeare, Dryden, with his translation of Virgil—Pope, with his translation of Homer—Butler, Akenside, Thomson, Cowper, Campbell, Burns, and Scott, must be treasured in your heart, and practised in your life. All this range of knowledge might be acquired in your leisure hours, and on rainy Sundays. When you have such knowledge as this, you can be an overmatch for any ordinary reader, and then you are ready to accept of any place which may cast up to you in the lottery of life.

"Present my love to your father and your mother, your sister Rachel, and your brother James. I have no very remarkable occurrence to edify you with. You will find some Hudibrastic verses enclosed, which I struck off at a heat; accept them rough-hewn. . . . Write me soon. I hope you are highly improved by your attendance at Maxweltown's School. Write me any little short notices of local news which you can find. Yours, sleeping or waking,

"ALLAN CUNNINGHAM.

"Mr. Geo. D. M'Ghie,
    "Quarrelwood, Kirkmahoe."

With regard to the latter part of this letter, in which the course of instruction is laid down, we humbly think that such a formidable array of literature was enough to upset any mechanic, however numerous his "leisure hours," and frequent the "rainy Sundays" might be; but the advice was kindly intended, and possibly a desire was felt that M'Ghie should, like himself, come out in the literary line.

Soon after his arrival in London he introduced himself to several editors of the magazines, with the view of obtaining employment as a contributor, literary work being the great object of his ambition. Some received him favourably, while others treated him as an unknown stranger. Of the former class was Mr. Jerdan, editor of the *Literary Gazette*, who was himself a Scotchman, being a native of Kelso, and who afterwards became one of Cunningham's most intimate and valued friends, as we shall afterwards see from their correspondence. The first meeting, however, was productive of an anecdote worthy of rehearsal, as showing the poet's dogged adherence to his own ideas of composition. Cunningham appeared one day in the office of the *Literary Gazette*, and presented some verses to the editor for insertion in that periodical. Mr. Jerdan read them carefully over, expressed satisfaction with them, but pointed out a grammatical error, which he requested him to correct. "Na, na," was the abrupt reply, "I will make no alteration. Grammar, or no grammar, it must go in as I wrote it, or not at all. What do I care for the gender of pronouns? We care naething for such things in Nithsdale, and I won't in London." So the *which* was printed instead of the *who*, the editor, no doubt, sympathizing with his fellow-countryman's sturdy exhibition of the national motto, *Nemo me impune lacessit.*

The honeymoon is all very well while it lasts, but it is soon discovered that something more than love is necessary for the sustenance of life and the maintenance of domestic comfort. This feeling naturally becomes the keener when the olive plants begin to appear, soon to take their places around the table; therefore, we do not wonder to find him expressing anxiety and concern for the future, especially with the aim of literary distinction never relaxed. He possessed, however, one sterling quality which is often awanting in persons holding his position, and cherishing his aspirations; he wisely and prudently resolved to earn his bread by the sweat of his brow, and not to rely upon the produce of his pen, except as an auxiliary, in supplying the wants of the household. He hoped that both connected would carry him and his along, so he made the resolution, and carried it out to the last.

We should like to have had a peep unseen into the young folk's dwelling, in the winter evening, when the windows were closed and the curtains drawn. Beside a "cozy fire and clean hearthstane" is Jean Walker sitting on one side, and Allan Cunningham on the other, with a table between them on which a lamp is brightly burning. She is busy with the needle—darning stockings for her young husband's comfort, making up some frills for her own adornment, altering a dress from the fashion of Kirkbean to that of London, and, in anticipation of some forthcoming event, shaping and sewing certain pieces of very little apparel, which she would willingly conceal, or wish not to be noticed. On his part, the mallet and the chisel has been thrown aside for the day, and he, too, is busy with pencil and paper, cogitating a new song, which, verse by verse, as they start into creation, he sings or recites aloud for the criticism and gratification of his "bonnie Jean." Happy pair! with the world before them smiling in hope, blest in each other's love, and, conscious of manly talent, artistic and mental, if health is vouchsafed he fears not the future.

In the summer of 1812 the first of a distinguished family of sons was born, who was named Joseph Davy, after one of his old associates when engaged on the *Day* newspaper. His cares now increased with his joys, and he strove the more ardently to maintain a position of credit as well as comfort, with literary distinction still in view. Writing to Professor Wilson, many years afterwards, he said:—

" My life has been one continued struggle to maintain my independence, and support wife and children; and I have, when the labour of the day is closed, endeavoured to use the little talent which my country allows me to possess as easily and as profitably as I can. The pen thus adds a little to the profits of the chisel, and I keep my head above water, and on occasion take the middle of the causeway with an independent step."

Well said! all the more independent that you have the good sense to use the pen only as a subsidiary means of support. The pen, however, has not been idle, and we are now to see what it has produced.

In 1813 he collected his musings, and published them in a volume, with the title "Songs, chiefly in the Rural Language of Scotland." It consisted of forty-nine songs, and was dedicated to Henry Phillips, Esq., New Bond Street, London. Like many of his predecessors, a considerable number of the songs have "Bonnie Jean" as their subject. There are two, which, though different, have the same title, "The Lovely Lass of Preston Mill." The volume was well received by the public, and was soon out of print, which stimulated the author to further efforts in the same line. As it is not now to be had, and is even unknown to many, we shall the more readily give some account of it. In the Dedication, which is somewhat lengthy, the author says:—

"After seriously meditating, therefore, upon the characteristic excellences of those songs, which the approval of the public has made popular, I have consented to censure, as wholly unworthy of future imitation, half-a-dozen deviations from the natural tone of British lyrical composition."

Well, we are anxious to know who these offenders are, who have so deviated, and are in consequence to be ostracized. The first class are those "courtly poets of ancient date," who have been succeeded to the present day, by endeavouring to please their mistresses with "metaphysical subtleties and sprightly sallies of wit, which appertain not to the customary feelings of the human race." The second are those who introduce the names of the heathen goddesses in describing the objects of their adoration, such as Venus, Diana, Apollo, Cupid, and the Graces. The next class is very much akin to the preceding—they lament the degeneracy of the present race, and, in imagination, seek to restore a resemblance of the beautiful world which has been lost by peopling it with a race of beings perfectly pure, and who inhabit regions of beatific splendour and fertility. We are introduced to Pan, and Sylvander, and Chloris, and the Arcadian lute, an arbour of woodbine, nuptial engagements, ruddy-countenanced shepherds, and 'the flocks of Admetus. He next attacks the lyrical sentimentalists with " a professed veneration and high-toned affection for everything which excites no emotions in any breasts but their own." The next batch under denunciation are similar to a previous one, who introduce into Christian song the names of the heroines of heathen lyrics. The last brought under ban are those who sing of shepherds and shepherdesses in luxuriant pastures, and beside murmuring streams, swains and nymphs finding themselves unconsciously in close proximity to one another.

He acknowledges that he is perfectly aware of the sweeping character of his censure, as it comprehends some whose songs are the masterpieces of lyrical excellence, but he says in extenuation—" I have been wholly desirous of fixing an accurate idea of what I hold to be the natural elements of British song, by disencumbering it of those gorgeous trappings and unnatural decorations with which injudicious innovators have obscured its beauties." Then, with regard to the songs in the volume, he says:—"I have attempted to preserve inviolable what I conceived to be the primitive rules of lyrical composition, and associate with the emotions of love the rural imagery of my native land." The volume gives indication that the author was following in the footsteps of some who had gone before him, by adopting similar titles, phrases, and measures. For instance, one is addressed "To Jean in Heaven;" doubtless suggested by Burns' "Mary in Heaven." It runs thus:—

"TO JEAN IN HEAVEN.

" Dalswinton holms are soon in bloom,
   And early are her woods in green;
Her clover walks are honey-breathed,
   And pleasant riv'lets reek between:
For lonesome lovers they are meet,
Who saunter forth with tentless feet,
The gowan bending 'mang the weet,
   When evening draws her shady screen;
Retired from the noting eye,
Unloosing all the seals of joy.

" Far in a deep untrodden nook,
   A fragrant hawthorn there is seen;
Beside it trills a babbling brook,
   That loops the banks of primrose green.
When spring woos forth its blossom fair,
In solemn gait I hie me there,
And kneeling unto God in prayer,
   I call upon thy shade, my Jean;
And soon I feel as thou wert near,
And heavenly whispers meet mine ear.

" I treasure all thy tokens, love;
    Thy ring, thy raven fillet fair,
Which curled o'er thy blooming cheek,
    And swan-white neck beyond compare;
Bright as it glisters with my tears,
The beauteous cheek again appears,
O'er which I passed the silver shears,
    And cut the sacred pledge I wear:
Drenched from my troubled eyes with weet,
I dry it with my bosom's heat.

" Oft thou descendest in my dreams,
    And seem'st by my bedside to stand;
Around thy waist, and on thy cheek,
    Are marks of a celestial hand:
Divinely wakening I see,
The glances of thy dove-like ee,
Which, smiling, thou dost bend on me,
    To go with thee to angel's land:
My arms outstretching thee to take,
I sleep of heaven, on earth I wake."

Then there is another song, at once suggesting the
source:—

"MY HEART IS IN SCOTLAND.

" My heart is in Scotland, my heart is not here,
    I left it at home with a lass I love dear;
When the ev'ning star comes o'er the hill-tops of green,
I bless its fair light, and I think on my Jean,
What distance can fasten, what country can bind,
The flight of my soul, or the march of my mind?
Though hills tower atween us, and wide waters flow,
My heart is in Scotland wherever I go.

" When I bade her farewell on the flow'r-blossomed knowe,
The bright lamps of heaven more lovely did lowe;
The ocean return'd back the moon's silver beam,
The wood tops and fountains were all in a leam;
Our wet eyes to heaven in transports we threw,
Our souls talk'd of love, for our hearts were owre fou;
Her warm parting kiss on my lips aye will glow,
For my heart is in Scotland wherever I go.

" How silent we met, and how lonesome the grove,
The rising moon welcom'd and kend of our love;
The wind 'mongst the branches hung listening and lown,
The sweet flowers blushed love, with their bloomy heads down,
The hours seemed but miuutes, so lightsome they flew,
Her arms clasped kinder, more sweet her lips grew;
Till Aurora, gold-lock'd, set the land in a lowe,
O my heart is in Scotland wherever I go.

" Now where are love's gloaming walks 'mang the new dew,
The white clasping arms, and the red rosie mou'?
The eloquent tongue dropping honey of love,
And the talk of two eyes which a statue might move:
I left them by Criffel's green mountain at hame,
And far from the heaven that holds them I came;
Come wealth, or come want, or come weal, or come woe,
My heart will be with them wherever I go."

This is evidently an imitation of "My heart's in the Highlands," and other songs in the volume may also be traced to their original source. We cannot well account for this, except on the ground of his adoration of Burns, and his admiration of previous poets. Perhaps, too, there was a feeling of want of self-reliance, and of mistrust in his own originality; but however this may be, he is pluming his wing for further and higher flight, and the pinion is growing apace. He becomes more confident as he moves along, and at last he launches out on his own resources, and after his own manner, the most satisfactory of all.

An especial characteristic of the Cunningham family was their filial affection towards their mother, the only remaining parent, whose widowhood was cheered by their kind attention to her, even when far away, and by the endeavours they made to afford her the comforts which declining years required. No one of all the family was more affectionate and helpful than Allan. The letters he wrote to her are full of the warmest love and the deepest gratitude, and must have greatly gladdened her heart, and cheered her loneliness, while she ruminated on the days of other years. True, one at least of her daughters was always with her, and made the descent of life as smooth as possible; but what mother could avoid following her sons into distant lands, and throbbing with delight when the post brought her, from time to time, tokens of their remembrance and affection, as well as tidings of their well-doing in the world. Did far distant sons know only half the pleasure which their letters impart to a mother's breast, they would not be so remiss as they often are in putting pen to paper, and telling all the news. With her, above all others, out of sight is not out of mind, but rather the reverse, and the thought of her *boys*—for they are always *boys* in her mind—causes many a wakerife night, and constitutes many a dream. The following letter is creditable to the hearts and heads of the two sons who sent it:—

"8 Ranelagh Place, Pimlico, London,
"20th October, 1814.

"Dear and Honoured Mother,—Distance has not diminished our affection, nor long absence altered our regard for a parent whom we reverence for her tenderness and love, and venerate for her motherly care and affection for all her children. Though we have not punctually corresponded with you, and though by living in a remote land we have been prevented from conversing with you face to face, and from being cheered by your conversation, and guided by your counsel like others of your children, yet our hearts entertain your image as dearly, and our minds are filled with as much respect, as if we wrote to you daily, or lived beside you.

"Our situations and prospects in life are now much altered, and perhaps sobered, since we parted from you. Both husbands, and both parents, we have become settled and sedate. Our chief felicities consist in the pleasures which our own homes afford, the love of our wives, and the artless affection of our children; and if one moment more tender than another occurs, it is, when on Sabbath evening we turn our minds from business and the ordinary anxieties of life to think on our former home, on a mother whose whole heart is composed of kindness and tenderness and care, and on a father unequalled for excellence of heart and soundness of understanding. To console our minds for absence from our native land, and separation from those whom it is our duty to love and esteem, we frequently picture out the felicities of our earlier years; our old house at the Roads, with our beloved mother, and brothers, and sisters, always composing a prominent part in the Drawing—we fancy ourselves seated happily beside you, and thus we comfort ourselves through many an hour, which all the pleasures of London could not render supportable.

"We lament the distance at which we are placed from our beloved mother, now in the decline of life, because we might help to make her situation more comfortable by the tender assiduities of affectionate children, and by many little attentions which cheer old age and render life more pleasant; but it is in vain to bewail what is not to be remedied. Desirous, however, of rendering every assistance in our power, we authorized our brother James, with the goodness of whose heart no one who knows him is a stranger, to assist you in any manner which might be most conducive to your comfort and your health, and it will bring a bitter pang to our hearts to think that our mother accuses us of neglect, or want of affection.

"It would delight us much would our dear mother send us a letter, no matter how short or how long; the sight of words, written by that venerable hand which nursed and watched over us, would be a gratification which we cannot describe. Our wives desire to be remembered to their mother, and have the warmest wishes for her welfare. We are anxious to be remembered to our brothers and sisters. We sincerely hope that your health is better, and that your mind is cheered by the presence of your children who have the happiness to be nearer you than ourselves. With most earnest prayers for your welfare, we remain your affectionate and dutiful sons,

"ALLAN CUNNINGHAM.
"THOS. M. CUNNINGHAM.

"P.S.—Present my compliments to my brother James, and say that nothing but some of those rough occurrences which bewilder and perplex the human mind, making resolves vain, and giving fortitude itself the look of desperation, could have prevented me from writing him long ago. I will certainly write to him before you read this.

"A. CUNNINGHAM.

"Mrs. Cunningham, Dalswinton."

Such a letter as this must have come like balm to the mother's heart, and it was succeeded by many others of a similar import on the part of Allan, some of which we shall give anon. Of the part which the other sons took in correspondence with home we have not had opportunity to show, but though even none but Allan had existed, the mother's heart must have been delighted above measure. How kind and grateful and affectionate are all his letters to her, when with many others family claims would have diverted the attention from the parent tree! But we are now to enter upon a new era in the biography, which closed only with his death.

CHAPTER X.

AFTER Cunningham had been a short time in London, and had finished the " Remains of Nithsdale and Galloway Song," Mr. Cromek introduced him to a rising young sculptor, Francis Chantrey, as a young man of very considerable literary genius and artistic ability. The sculptor, however, did not require an assistant at that time; he was as yet unknown to fame, and had barely work sufficient for himself alone, but he promised to keep the young stranger in view should times improve. In the course of three or four years times did improve, and Cunningham was not forgotten. When from indifferent health, caused by late and long hours, he quitted the reporters' gallery, Bubb, his former master, was in ecstacy at the prospect of again receiving him into his studio, and ran to Chantrey intimating the likelihood of good fortune by his return; but Chantrey, having improved in business, engaged Cunningham as his assistant, greatly to the chagrin and disappointment of Bubb. Of course ill-feeling was

engendered on the part of the disappointed sculptor towards the other two parties, but they judiciously took no notice of it, and in course of time it died away. Cunningham was now permanently established, and his fears for the future were considerably done away. Though his wages at first were comparatively small for the duties he undertook, yet they were afterwards increased, and he had ample leisure for gratifying his literary taste, and adding to his resources by the fruits of his pen.

Some little account of Francis Chantrey may be interesting to the reader, as he and the subject of our memoir were so long and intimately associated together, death alone causing the separation. He rose from almost the humblest origin to the pinnacle of artistic fame. He was born at Norton in 1782, and was, therefore, only some sixteen months older than his future coadjutor, Allan Cunningham. Though his father rented a small piece of land, yet it could scarcely be called a farm, and the boy Francis carried sand from it on a donkey's back, and sold it in the town of Sheffield, riding home in one of the empty creels. His father having died while he was young, his education, though attended to by the widowed mother, was very desultory, and, as might be expected, not very satisfactory, seeing that he was oftener engaged in field operations than in school, and what he learned the one day was forgotten when he returned again. Like some others who rose to eminence in science or art, he gave early indication of his future greatness by showing a decided taste for modelling in common clay whatever objects came before him; and it is said that on great occasions he assisted his aunt, an aristocratic housekeeper, by forming figures out of the dough with which to ornament the pastry for the table.

When he had attained the age of seventeen, he took it into his head that he would enter the legal profession, and was desirous to become an apprentice under a certain Sheffield solicitor. On the day fixed for his introduction to this gentleman, in his eagerness he was in town an hour too soon, and while he awaited the arrival of his friends who were to accompany him to the office, he sauntered through the streets, gazing at all and sundry, as a country lad would do. He was arrested by some figures he saw in the window of a carver and gilder named Ramsay, a Scotchman by birth. His early taste at once sprang up anew, his former resolution was entirely given up, and when his friends arrived, to their great astonishment, he intimated that a "change had come o'er the spirit of his dream," and that he desired to be apprenticed with Ramsay instead. In order to gratify his wishes this was accordingly done, and he immediately entered upon the trade of an incipient carver and gilder. Ramsay's business was not flourishing, as work was not plentiful, and, consequently, the hours of labour were limited. This was all the better for the new apprentice, who employed his leisure time in gratifying his favourite taste for modelling and drawing. Unaccountable as it may seem, when his master discovered what his private labours were, instead of encouraging him in the exercise of his taste, seeing that it did not interfere with his legitimate duties, he ordered all his figures to be destroyed, and the making of them discontinued! The modelling, however, was still carried on, the place of operation being transferred from the workshop to his own lodgings, and there, night after night, beyond the latest hour, he wrought away with none to disturb him in his artistic amusement. He felt anything but comfortable in this situation, with such a prohibition hanging over his head, and after enduring it for three years, he bought up the remaining portion of his indenture, and the two separated with mutual satisfaction.

He now went up to London and began operations there as a sculptor; but not succeeding up to his expectations, he set out on a course of travel through Ireland and Scotland, but was stricken down with a dangerous fever in Dublin, from which he did not entirely recover for several months. When his health was completely restored he returned to London in the autumn of the following year, where he began his studies anew, and carried them on with an ardour, a perseverance, and success which commanded public acknowledgment, though not without envy and jealousy on the part of some in the same profession ; and after a considerable time, notwithstanding this party feeling, he was raised to the high honour of a Royal Academician, after first having been made a member of the Royal Society, and also a member of the Society of Antiquaries. The crowning honour of all, however, was receiving the honour of knighthood from his Sovereign.

The first bust which he contributed to the Exhibition of the Royal Academy was one of Raphael Smith, an engraver, and a man of no ordinary talent, who had proved a kind friend, and given him good advice before he came to London, greatly encouraging him in the pursuit of excellence in the art. It was considered so good that the great Nollekens, who was far beyond rival competition, and died leaving £200,000 derived from bust making, caused one of his own works to be removed that Chantrey's might take its place, saying, "It's all there; he'll do it; it's in him." Chantrey had also a talent for painting, and many of his performances in this line, which are said to be of very great merit, still remain. This acquisition, however, nearly proved fatal to his success on a very important occasion. When the City of London resolved to erect a statue of George III., designs were called for, and several candidates sent in drawings, of whom Chantrey was one. His design was considered preferable to the others, but one of the Common Council objected, on the ground that the successful artist was a painter, and consequently could not be considered qualified for the execution of a work in sculpture. Sir William Curtis, who presided, said, " You hear this, young man, what say you—are you a painter or a sculptor ?" " I live by sculpture," Chantrey replied, and, thereupon, the work was entrusted to his execution.

His forte was in bust sculpture, though in full length figures he was also highly successful. He cared not for the higher flights of the art, the allegorical and ideal, but contented himself with taking from nature or the life. This reminds us of an expression of a late artist in Dumfries, John Maxwell, whom Thomas Aird characterized as "the best likeness-taker on earth," on our asking him why he did not attempt a fancy picture, "My faith," he said, "I have enough ado to paint what I see." As illustrative of this distaste of the ideal, Cunningham once requested Chantrey to look at a painting done by a young artist, when he inquired, "What is the subject?" "Adam," was the reply. "Have you seen it?" "Yes." "And do you think it like him?" with which sarcastic hit the matter dropped without any opinion being given.

Cunningham engaged with Chantrey as superintendent of the works, but in his new position he was more than this. He acted also as secretary and amanuensis, while, from his connection with the Press, he had the most favourable opportunities, and he embraced them, of bringing his master's productions into public notice. He conducted all the correspondence, for Chantrey himself had neither the inclination nor the ability to do so, as may be inferred from the character of his education while a youth. An anecdote of this has been told us by Cunningham's sister, with regard to the Washington Statue, which went from Chantrey's studio. A number of American students in London one evening over their wine, while discussing the merits of the work, adverted to the beauty of the penmanship in the correspondence, and the elegant style of the composition. Some doubted that the sculptor had had anything to do with it, and others took the opposite side. A keen controversy ensued, and a heavy bet was laid on the subject. To settle the affair, a deputation of their number immediately started for the studio to ascertain the truth, and finding Cunningham present, they told him the object of their errand, who at once admitted that he himself was the author of the correspondence, verifying the fact by showing them a specimen of his handwriting in the letter books of the office.

He was also helpful to Chantrey in another way, by making suggestions which only a poet could, with regard to certain details of the figures. One of Chantrey's masterpieces of sculpture is that of the two Sleeping Children in Lichfield Cathedral. The two sisters are represented asleep in each others arms, the younger with a bunch of new plucked snow-drops in her hand, a sight which has brought the tears over many a cheek while contemplating this emblem of infant innocence. The design of the group was made by Stothard, the eminent London artist, but the bunch of snow-drops which imparts such a charm, was inserted at the suggestion of Cunningham. Chantrey made the model in clay, and a Frenchman named Legee, in his employment, carved it in marble. . This was Chantrey's mode of operation, only to take the model in clay, and leave the rest to his workmen, under the superintendence of Cunningham, of course subject to his own inspection as the finishing touches approached. After the clay model was finished, which was generally done at one performance, a cast was taken in plaster of Paris, from which the marble or bronze bust was copied, and with which it was always minutely compared. Cunningham's position, therefore, was one of very great responsibility, requiring both taste and discernment, in addition to the care necessary for a faithful and safe completion of the work. How efficiently he discharged the duty may be inferred from the fact that he held the situation for twenty-eight years, when death called him away. Chantrey had the greatest affection for him, and always regarded him as a bosom friend. When he was about to build his mausoleum, some time before his death, that it might be ready when the occasion required, he offered to enclose additional ground for the remains of his friend also, that they might lie together. "No, no," said Cunningham, "I wont be built over, but be buried where the daisies will grow upon my grave, and the lark sing above my head." But he was "built over" after all.

But Cunningham's responsibilities were even of a weightier character than we have described, although they were weighty enough. Under the eye of the master the burden of care and anxiety is considerably lightened, for attention can be immediately called should difficulty arise, and counsel be received ; but when he is far away, self-reliance must then be depended upon, whatever may be the result. Chantrey was in the habit of going away for several months every year, visiting Paris, Rome, Venice, and Florence, as his taste inclined him, during which absence Cunningham was left entirely in charge, to receive orders, answer inquiries, receive visitors, and see properly and faithfully executed the works in operation. In short, he was Chantrey's second self, and what he undertook, or performed in the absence, was cordially approved of on the return. Never were master and servant more united or confident in one another.

If Chantrey received advantage from his connection with Cunningham, as his secretary and superintendent, Cunningham also received advantage from Chantrey, so that the benefit was reciprocal. Apart from pecuniary remuneration, he was thereby introduced into a class of society which was otherwise beyond his reach, for here he met with the titled and the great who visited the studio, to whom he descanted in the most fascinating manner on the merits of several works of art which they examined and admired. In short, he became a favourite, and almost a familiar, with all, although his good sense and innate modesty preserved him from using too much freedom on that account. We know that by this means he was invited and welcomed into the families of many distinguished personages, whose kindness and hospitality he was ever ready to acknowledge, and which he reciprocated with those who either offered him a visit, or whom he could judiciously invite under his roof, and partake at his board. We are naturally desirous to know what was his appearance and bearing on his introduction to the literary and other magnates of the great city. Mrs. S. C. Hall, in one of her admirable and graphic sketches, thus describes him:—

"I can clearly recall the first interview I had with him. It was before I had been much in literary society, and when I was but little acquainted with those whose works had found places in my heart. I remember how my cheek flushed, and how pleased and proud I was of the few words of praise he gave to one of the first efforts of my pen. He was then a stout man, somewhat high-shouldered, broad-chested, and altogether strongly proportioned; his head was firm and erect, his mouth close, yet full, the lips large, his nose thick and broad, his eyes of intense darkness (I could never define their colour), beneath shaggy and flexible eye-brows, and were, I think, as powerful, yet as soft and winning, as any eyes I ever saw. His brow was expansive, indicating, by its breadth, not only imagination and observation, but, by its height, the veneration and benevolence so conspicuous in his character. His accent was strongly Scotch, and when he warmed into a subject, he expressed himself with eloquence and feeling; but generally his manner was quiet and reserved—quiet more from a habit of observing than from a dislike to conversation. . . . In after years, when it was my privilege to meet him frequently, it was a pleasure to note the respect he commanded from all who were distinguished in Art and in Letters. He had a sovereign contempt for anything that approached affectation —literary affectation especially; and certainly lashed it, even in society, by words and looks of contempt that could not be easily forgotten. 'Wherever,' I have heard him say, 'there is nature, wherever a person is not ashamed to show a heart, there is the germ of excellence. I love nature!' His dark eyes would often glisten over a child or a flower; and a ballad, one of the songs of his native land, would move him to tears (I have seen it do so more than once), that is to say, if it were sung 'acording to nature,' with no extra 'flourish,' no encumbering drapery of form to disturb the 'natural' melody."

This description is endorsed by Mr. S. C. Hall himself in the following tribute to his memory, after the remains of his friend had been laid in the dust:—

" Allan, as I have said, was a man of stalwart form; it was well knit, and, apparently, the health that had been garnered in childhood and in youth was his blessing when in manhood. Certainly, to all outward seeming, he had ample security for a long life. His brow was large and lofty; his face of the Scottish type—high cheek-bones and well rounded; his mouth flexible and expressive, yet indicative of strong resolution; his eyes were likened, by those who knew both persons, to those of Burns, and no doubt they were so; they were deeply seated, and almost black, surrounded by a dark rim, and shadowed by somewhat heavy dark eyebrows. His manners conveyed conviction of sincerity; they were not refined, neither were they rugged, and the very opposite of coarse. It was plain that for all his advantages he was indebted to nature, for although he mixed much in what is called 'polite society,' and was a gentleman whose companionship was courted by the highest—statesmen and peers—up to the last he had ' a smack of the heather.'

" Nothing seemed to irritate him so much as affectation, either with pen or pencil, or in word, or look, or manner. I have seen him exasperated by a lisp in a woman, and by a mincing gait in a man. Any pretence to be what was not, made him, so to say, furious. I would close this memoir so as, I think, may best convey an idea of his peculiar character and worth, by quoting a favourite phrase of his own—

' Love him, for he loved Nature.' "

From these descriptions of candid and intimate friends, in which prominence is given to his love of artless simplicity, and his great dislike to all kinds of affectation, one sees the strong link of connection which bound Chantrey and him so closely together. They were both lovers of what was true, natural, and unaffected, and despised what was artificial, constrained, or assumed.

Their minds in this, as in many other respects, were congenial, so that mutual esteem and affection could not fail to be the result.

Being now in a measure secured against anxiety for family comfort, should health and strength be continued, he set himself resolutely down in the evenings by his "ain fireside," and wielded the pen with a will which was not to be resisted. He contributed prose articles of various kinds to several magazines, and wrote a series of tales, chiefly illustrative of Scottish character, mostly connected with his own native Nithsdale, which had to appear month by month when begun, thus entailing an incessant drudgery upon the pen as well as the brain. The Muse, however, was not altogether willing to be set aside by this description of work, but he was enabled to gratify her longings in this respect by inserting in his prose compositions occasional flights she made, thus to prevent her wing from becoming stiffened, and her fancy dulled. So his prose tales are interspersed with ballads, and songs, and snatches of poems, which give a lightsomeness to the reader, and impart variety to the theme. But, besides this, he is preparing works of a higher style and aim, which are not permitted to see the light in monthly piecemeals, but are reserved in secret till they are ready to issue forth to the public as a compact whole, then to stand or fall by their own merits or demerits, to receive praise or censure, without having the benefit of monthly criticism and suggestion.

Though always thus engaged, either in the studio by day or the study by night, he never forgot his native district, and the many friends he had there left behind.

Every now and again, however, he learned directly or indirectly that they were becoming fewer, which made him cling the more closely to those who remained. One of his special friends, for whom he had the deepest regard, was Mr. James M'Ghie of Quarrelwood, the father of his " trusty fier" George, in whose household he had spent many a joyous evening. The following letter sent to this worthy is interesting and amusing:—

" Eccleston Street, Pimlico, 28th Jan., 1817.

" Dear James,—The warlike offspring of auld minstrel Hugh has undertaken to carry this to your fireside, and along with it my warmest hopes that it continues to be gladdened with the same kindness of heart, social mirth, and hospitality, for which it claims a kind place in my early remembrance. I recognized the kenspeckle aspect of a Paisley whenever Hugh presented his front at my door, and immediately the hours when our feet made the Kirkmahoe barn-roofs wag to the remotest rafter, to the compound melody of auld Hugh's fiddle, came upon my mind, and I could scarcely restrain my feet from making a movement similar to the first step in Shan Trews.

" Thoughts which gave me pleasure might well recall your family and fireside to my mind, which I must always associate with all that gave delight to my youthful days, and I hope the hour is not remote when I may open the door latch and step ben among you all with a patriarchal ' Peace be here,' and take my seat with the same consciousness of a soul-warm welcome as if I had not been absent an hour.   How are George, and James, and Rachel, and how is Katy? She would never, you know, tolerate me to call her Mrs. M'Ghie. I wish I were beside her to have one of her laughs and shakes by the hand; and, man, how are you yourself, my dear and worthy friend? May the cloven foot of Envy never touch one of your treddles, nor Trouble draw her black hand across the white warp and weft of your existence.

"I understand that many of the old faces that gladdened the social circles in my native place have passed into the consecrated earth; that Hugh Paisley is now listening to melody superior even to his own, and that James Macrabin has ceased to pickle in saltpetre the decaying bodies of his neighbours, or admonish the easy morality of honest Thomas M'Ghie with the terrors of his gird rung.

"Do Mirth and the Muses continue to haunt the groves and streams of Quarrelwood, and do you, now and then, hang the chastening rod of poetic sarcasm over the vices and follies of the proud and the titled around you? I wish I could tell you good tidings of myself, but I have nothing better to tell you than that I am toiling eidently for 'saps o' cream' to three boy bairns, and coats of callimanco to my wife. I preserve a decent silence in verse and prose, and I believe some of my best friends think I have '*steeked my gab for ever.*' Believe not one word of it. I will come out among them all some morning like a trumpet sounding in a lonely glen.

"I wished to introduce my wife to you and Katy in a long description, but Jean declares she is perfectly well acquainted with you all, and that the manner in which I have so often talked to her of you both has done as much as half a century's friendship of visits given and received. Give my kind respects to George and James and Rachel, and especially to Katy, and my wife desires the same from her to you all.

"I hope you will all be as much delighted with our towns-man Hugh as I have been; he possesses all the manners of a gentleman, with a mind keen and inquiring, and stocked with useful knowledge, and he relates his adventures in the perils of war with the spirit, the conciseness, and elegance of a historian.   Now, I entreat you not to wait till you find a messenger to convey the answer which I know your kindness will dictate to this; write by the post-office whenever your inclination stirs you.   With the kindest wishes for your welfare, I remain, dear James,

 "Your most faithful friend,

 "ALLAN CUNNINGHAM.

 "Mr. James M'Ghie,
 "Quarrelwood, Kirkmahoe."

A few months afterwards he sent the following letter to his brother James :—

 "London, 24th August, 1817.

"My dear James,—I have received both your kind and brotherly letters, and I assure you when my indolence interrupts our correspondence, I deprive myself of one of the chief comforts of existence.   It gives me unmingled satisfaction to find that you have plenty of work, and that your future affairs promise to be so prosperous.   It will increase that delight much if circumstances enable us to unite our hearts and hands in one pursuit, and at present I cannot contemplate any situation so gratifying to my feelings, so consoling to my best affections, as that of returning to my native land, with the prospect of work before me, to awaken the echoes of gray cairns of Nithsdale and Annandale once more with the clank of our whinstone hammers.   In the meantime I enjoy good health, plenty of work and its produce, and I might be happy, if a man may be happy who stoops himself in the command of others, whose genius he finds to be that of the Roman rebuked by his own (slave ?), and who feels more pleasure in being the chief of a village than the first courtier of a palace.

"I have commenced a search for the book you mentioned, and I despair not of finding it soon. Books of songs are what you must want much, and I think I will fall in with some esteemed works of that kind during the course of the year, which I will treasure past me, and profit by their knowledge, and bring them with me if fortune favours us. I think you act prudently in maintaining the good graces of the Factor, and, indeed, one ought to do all he can to have the good word of every one, for the meanest of mankind may sow abundance of mischief. During the next week I depart for Lichfield to put up two marble monuments. I will be a week away; at my return I will expect another letter from you.

"I am much amused with the manner you extracted payment from ——, and I certainly felt disappointed in the conduct of ——, whom I reckoned an upright, honourable man; but bad times and ruin in trades bring the villainous part of man's character into action, and show how much of the fiend remains unsubdued by religion and virtue. The death and removal of so many masons from Dumfries certainly opens a fair path for adventure, for I scarcely know a single person whose talents one would have to dread among all those who remain. A step so decisive of one's future fate must be taken prudently, and pursued with industry.

"We are on the point of going into our new house, and it really seems a place calculated to give many happy days, and comforts to human life, but I hope my destiny is yet of a brighter hue.

"This is a period of great poetical dulness with me; the distractions of my place overwhelm all poetical broodings, and the agitated current of business bears down my resolves like a flood. But winter is coming, and I have tasked myself to collect, collate, and correct my songs, which are neither numerous nor excellent, and dress up my little poems, among which the 'Bard's Winter Night,' must not be forgotten. Besides all this, I have covenanted with myself to rough-hew my tragedy, balance all its parts, portion out its actions, and make it ready for the finishing touches. These are tasks which will require as much resolution and leisure as I will be able to muster. Of Geraldine I have not heard one word for a twelvemonth, except by verbal report, and I was much surprised at your mentioning its being in the hands of a publisher, which I hope is incorrect, for I would look at a work where I was conscious of its incorrectness with horror. I should like much to have it returned, for I meditate great improvements. I am perfectly conscious of the progressive state of my judgment, and though I do not think my poetical powers have received any reinforcement of late, yet I can wield them with much more certainty of effect than formerly, and I don't think I alter a single line without improving it.

"I am concerned at Mr. Hogg's losses. His genius may easily repair such disasters as those you mention; besides, the farm he holds on so torch-like a tenure might keep him above the absolute pressure of want. Considering these circumstances, I was concerned to see an advertisement of his poem in the Dumfries newspaper, which seemed penned in rather a supplicating tone. I hope it was the well-meant work of the good-hearted editor.

"I have enclosed you a sheetful of extracts from a ballad called *Lord Percy's Mantle*, founded on the ballad of *Chevy Chase*. Lord Douglas hastens to encounter Lord Percy, his rival in fame, and his lady, disguising herself like a page, accompanied by the family bard, follows and awaits the closing of the armies from the summit of a hill on the opposite side of the stream of Teviot. I can only extract what will give you some idea of the manner in which it is written, without unravelling the plan, or explaining the catastrophe.

"My wife joins me in love to you and our sister, and a' the lave. We hope to see her next year.—I remain, dear James, yours faithfully and affectionately,

"ALLAN CUNNINGHAM.

"Mr. Cunningham,
"Hoddam Cross, Ecclefechan."

We are now about to enter upon another period of his literary career, which has been foreshadowed in the foregoing letter to his brother, in which work after work will be published with amazing rapidity, filling one with astonishment, how time could have sufficed, and energy sustained, the mental strain and manual labour necessary for their production. But if evidence were required to illustrate the truth of the adage, "Where there is a will there is a way," it is to be found in the doings of Allan Cunningham.

CHAPTER XI.

CONTRIBUTES TO "BLACKWOOD"—WINNING THE HARVEST KIRN—
NOTICE OF THE CAMERONIANS—CAMERONIAN BALLADS: "THE
DOOM OF NITHSDALE," "ON MARK WILSON, SLAIN IN IRON-
GRAY," "THE VOICE LIFTED UP AGAINST CHAPELS AND
CHURCHES," "THE CAMERONIAN BANNER."

BESIDES the *London Magazine*, and other periodicals
to which he was a regular contributor, we find him
engaged also on the literary pabulum of *Blackwood*,
after it had become fairly afloat. To this Magazine he
supplied monthly, in 1819-21, a series of tales under the
title of "Recollections of Mark Macrabin, the Cameronian," which for humour, and glowing description of
Scottish manners, sectarian feeling, and superstitions,
are inimitable. The scenes of the tales are laid in
Nithsdale, but the declared narrator of them was too
" Kenspeckle," which somewhat roused the ire of himself
and his friends of the Cameronian connection, for the
freedom taken with his name and his doings. He kept
a grocery store, with a sign above his door entrance, on
which was painted in flaming colours an open Bible,
and underneath, in prominent letters, " Mark Macrabin,
Cameronian, Dealer in Scottish Hose, and Cheap Tracts,
Religious and Political." This was a sufficiently catching
signboard for the "guid and the godly" of Kirkmahoe,
and Mark drew largely by the clap-trap he adopted.

Although Cunningham disavowed any desire on his part to hold the Cameronians up to ridicule, yet their religious propensities and doings were enlarged upon in a way which made them suspicious of being exposed as a laughing-stock to the community at large. Old James M'Ghie, George's father, belonged to the covenanting body, not by original descent, however, but by a " tender conscience." He had been precentor in the Parish Church of Kirkmahoe before the induction of the Rev. Dr. Wightman to the charge, but on the Rev. Doctor one day appearing in the pulpit arrayed in a black gown, which had been presented to him by a distinguished lady in the parish, James took fright at the " rag of Popery," and went over to the Cameronians, who were then a pretty strong body at Quarrelwood. Mark Macrabin, Cameronian, general dealer in groceries, hose, and cheap religious and political tracts, is made to narrate a series of tales, the principal incidents of which had come under his own experience. Among them are an account of the Buchanites, who, fleeing from Irvine, took up their residence at Cample, in the parish of Closeburn; Adventure with the Gipsies; the Witch of Ae; the Last of the Morisons; Janet Morison's Lyke-Wake; and the Harvest Kirn of Lillycross. These are all descriptive of Scottish life in its most natural and characteristic forms.

What, in our opinion, greatly enhances the value of Cunningham's tales is their descriptiveness, true to the life, of scenes and customs which have now gone by, but which are deserving of remembrance. In the series of tales contributed to *Blackwood*, there are many such;

but there is one especially to which we would refer, which was great in its time, but has now of necessity passed entirely away. This was the closing day of the cutting of the harvest, called the Har'st Kirn, when the grain was wholly cut by the hook, before the invasion of scythes and reaping machines. On the harvest-field, as on the battle-field, there were often scenes of deftness displayed, though not with the same sanguinary issue, save in a cut finger or so; but the blood occasionally got up from a jealousy of superior prowess, and then a " Kemp" was the result : this was who should cut their rig of corn soonest by dexterity and force of arm. When this took place, the greatest effort was made to " cut the gumpin'" on the rival; to advance so far ahead of him as to be able to cut across his rig, which was considered the greatest insult to the lagging fellow, intimating his inferior skill and want of ability in the contention. When the cutting of the harvest was about to be finished, the greatest struggle arose, so as not to be the last at the landing, which was called " couping the kirn" on the luckless reaper, which was regarded a disgrace, and dreadful were the efforts put forth by all parties, half-divested of their clothing, and the perspiration streaming, to be the first out, or at all events not the last. As a man and a woman were employed on each rig, it was often painful to witness the fair one in distress, with her neck and bosom bare, thrusting in the sickle with a will greater than her strength, and then to hear the cry of her brawny partner, " Mak' straps, mak' straps, and I'll do the cutting," and away he went like a whirlwind, a sheaf in every "louchter." Cunningham gives the following graphic description of such a scene in the vale of Ae, the correctness of which we guarantee from personal experience on like occasions forty years ago :—

"My fair Cameronian looked over the field while she whet her sickle, and whispered to me, in a tone approaching to intercession, 'Dinna forget that I have bribed thee to do thy best wi' the promise o' a gliff at gloaming under the Tryste bower birks. I would rather add a whole night to the hour than Ronald Rodan and yon govan widow should waur us. Sae nae a single word—that look was a full vow to do thy utmost—sae here's for the kirn.' And the harvest-horn winding as she spoke, the sickles were laid to the root of the ripe grain, and the contest commenced. Those on the haft and those on the point of the hook exerted themselves with so much success, that Hamish Machamish was compelled to cheer up his lagging mountaineers by the charms of his pipe. But the music which breathed life and mettle into the men of the mountains seemed not without its influence on those of the plains.

"The Highland sickles, though kept in incessant and rapid motion, could not prevent the haft and the point from advancing before them, forming a front like the horns of a crescent. The old bandsmen enjoyed the contest, and, from their conversation alone, I learned how the field was likely to go. 'I'se tell thee what, Lucas Laurie,' said Saunders Creeshmaloof, 'as sure as the seven stars are no aught—and the starry elwand will never measure the length o' the lang Bear—that sang-singin' haspin' o' a callant, Ronald Rodan, and that light-ended, light-headed—I mean, widow woman, Keturah, will win the kirn o' Crumacomfort—they are foremost by a lang cat loup at least.'　'Heard ever ony body the like o' that, Saunders Creeshmaloof,' said his fellow expounder of shooting stars : 'ye have an ee that couldnae tell that a pike-staff was langer than ane o' Tam Macgee's spoolpins ! I sall eat a' the corn, chaff and a', without butter, that the ballad-making lad has cut afore our ain sonsie lass o' Lilly-cross, and this mettled stripling that's her marrow.　I wish, however, that the lad bairn wad take counsel, and no lose time by keeking aye in the maiden's face ilka· louchter he lays down ; and may I be suppered wi' shooten stars on the summit o' Queensberry gin they dinna win the kirn.'　I adopted this self-denying counsel, and rejoiced to find the sacrifice was rewarded with success.

"'It's a bonnie sight, gudeman o' Crumacomfort,' said another bandsman, as he hooded a stook behind me ; 'I say it's a bonnie sight to see sae mony stark youths and strapping kimmers streaking themselves sae cidently to the harvest darke.　Hech ! but that sonsie widow, Keturah, be a prood ane—she's marrowed wi' the proodest piece o' man's flesh in the vale o' Ae.　He's a clever lad, though he be a prood ane ; he casts his sickle sae glegly round the corn, and rolls a louchter like a little sheaf, and yet looks sae heedless a' the while, as gin he were framing some fule ballad.　I wad counsel him to cast aside that black-and-blue bird bonnet wi' its hassock o' feathers.　See, see, how he makes them fan the hot brow o' the widow, and oh ! but she blinks blithely for't.　Conscience, gudeman ! wer't no for thy well-faured Mary and her marrow, they wad win the kirn—they're within a stane-cast o' the landing.'

" The Highland piper, whose music had augmented as we proceeded, now blew a perfect hurricane, and the sickles moved faster and faster ; but though they kept time with the music like the accuracy of a marching regiment, they failed to obtain the smallest visible advantage, and the unintelligible clattering and murmuring they raised resembled the outcry of a disturbed flock of geese. ‘Deel blaw ye south for a pose o’ gowd, and take ye to the Highlands wi’ the same wind again, gin I can make ye gain the half length o’ my chanter on thae brainwude bairns on the haft and point. God, gin I had them in Glentourachglen, where deel hate grows but brakens, wi’ a straught blade, instead o’ a bowed ane in my neeve, I wad turn the best o’ them !’ So saying, Hamish Machamish relinquished the contest in despair, and the wind, as it forsook his instrument, grunted a long and melancholy whine, like the wind in a cloven oak. As we approached the landing, the old bandsmen ran on either side, and looked on the concluding contest with accuracy of eye which counted every handful that remained unshorn. ‘Conscience ! but that sonsie woman, Keturah, merits to be married,’ said an old man, whose chin as he walked almost touched the stubble ; ‘and she sha’na want a man though I should take her mysel’—she maks the corn fa’ afore her like the devouring fire.’ ‘And she wad be a useful woman t’ye, Roger,’ said another old man, whose prolonged cough as he spoke seemed like a kirkyard echo ; ‘she wad make ye a drib buttered gruel, and have ‘aye something cozie and warm for ye whan ye daundered hame at gloaming.’ ‘And I can tell ye,’ said one of their companions, ‘gin that callant, Ronald Rodan, wad give up the gowk-craft o’ ballad making, and bide by the craft o’ cutting corn, and passing the sharp coulter through the green-sward, he wadnae hae his fellow atween Corsincon and Caerlaverock ; and I should nae grudge him my daughter Penny Holiday, wi’ a tocher o’ twal hundred as bonnie merks as e’er were minted.’

“While this conversation passed, the exertions of all seemed redoubled. It was a beautiful sight to see the rows of tall stooks ranked behind—the standing corn before, diminished to a mere remnant, with half a hundred bright sickles glimmering in perpetual motion at its root, and the busy movement of so many fair and anxious faces shining with the dews of toil—the motion of curling haffet locks and white hands, and so many grey-haired men awaiting to commend the victor. 'I may gae seek out the kirn-cut o' corn,' said old Hugh Halbertson, 'and dress and deck it out wi' lily white ribbons as gaily as I please, and a' for my ain bonny Mary o' Lillycross.' Even as the old man spoke, the four sickles on the haft and point reached the end at once, and so close were their companions, that ere John Macmukle concluded his flourish on the harvest horn, the corn was all lying on the bands. Ronald Rodan taking at the same time his horn from the hands of one of the bandsmen, winded it so loud, and even melodious, that Ae water returned the echo from every double of her stream, the shepherd shouted on the hill, and the numerous reapers of neighbour boons, staying their sickles, waved them around their heads at every repeated flourish of the horn. An old bandsman conversant with the traditional ceremonies of winning harvest kirns, took the last and reserved cut of corn, and, braiding it into two locks, crowned my fair Cameronian partner with one, and the buxom Keturah with the other, who stood shedding the moisture with her white hands from her long hair, and giving the cooling breeze free admission to a white and shapely neck, glancing her blue eyes all the while on Ronald Rodan."

Talk not of the excitement of the Turf—winning the Derby was nothing in comparison to winning the Harvest Kirn !

Though neither Cunningham nor any of his father's family belonged to the Cameronian body, yet many of them, besides the M'Ghies, were his intimate associates while he attended the Dame's school at Quarrelwood, and during his apprenticeship as a mason. And though he talks sometimes rather lightly of them in the way of raillery, yet he cherished for them a great regard, for the noble manner in which they had stood out for their religious principles, some of them even to the death. In his "Recollections of Mark Macrabin" he refers to them at considerable length, and also in an article in *Blackwood*, 1820, he gives a series of Cameronian ballads, prefaced with a brief account of the sect.

"THE DOOM OF NITHSDALE.

" I stood and gazed—from Dalswinton wood
  To Criffel's green mountain, and Solway flood
  Was quiet and joyous. The merry loud horn
  Called the mirthsome reapers in bands to the corn;
  The plaided swain, with his dogs, was seen
  Looking down on the vale from the mountain green;
  The lark with his note, now lowne, now loud,
  The blue heaven breathed through the white cloud,
  Round a smiling maid, white as winter snowing,
  The Nith clasped its arms, and went singing and flowing—
  Yet all the green valley, so lovely and broad,
  Lay in black nature, nor breathed of a God.

" And yet it was sweet, as the rising sun shone,
  To stand and look this fair land upon,
  The stream kissed my feet, and away to the sea
  Flow where the wild sea-fowl went swimming free.
  In the town the lordly trumpet was blowing,
  From the hill the meek pipe sent its sweet notes flowing,

And a fair damsel set her brown tresses a-wreathing,
And looking of heaven, and perfume breathing,
And, stretched at her feet, despairing and sighing,
Lay a youth on the grass, like a creature dying.
But mocked was the Preacher, and scorned was the Word,
Green Nithsdale, I yield thee to gunshot and sword.

" And yet, green valley, though thou art sunk dark,
And deep as the waters that flowed round the ark;
Though none of thy flocks, from the Nith to the Scarr,
Wear Calvin's choice keel or the Covenant's tar—
Come, shear thy bright love-locks, and bow thy head low,
And fold thy white arms o'er thy bosom of snow,
And kneel, till the summer pass with its sweet flowers,—
And kneel, till the autumn go with her gold bowers,
And kneel, till rough winter grows weary with flinging
Her snows upon thee, and the lily is springing,
And fill the green land with thy woe and complaining;
And let thine eyes drop like two summer clouds raining—
And ye may have hope, in the dread dooms-day morning,
To be snatched as a brand from the sacrifice burning.

" But if ye kneel not, nor in blood-tears make moan,
And harden your heart like the steel and the stone,
Oh! then, lovely Nithsdale—even as I now cast
My shrunk hand to heaven, thy doom shall be passed;
Through thy best blood the war-horse shall snort and career,
Thy breast shall be gored with the brand and the spear—
Thy bonnie love-locks shall be ragged and reft—
The babe at thy bosom be cloven and cleft;
From Queensberry's mountain to Criffel below,
Nought shall live but the blood-footed hawk and the crow!
Farewell, thou doomed Nithsdale—in sin and asleep—
Lie still—and awaken to wail and to weep.

" I tried much to bless thee, fair Nithsdale, there came
Nought but curses to lay on thy fate and thy fame !

Yet still do I mind—for the follies of youth
Mix their meteor gleams with the sunshine of truth—
A fair one, and some blessed moments, aboon,
Gleaming down the green mountain gazed on as the moon,
The kisses and vows were unnumbered and sweet,
And the flower at our side, and the stream at our feet,
Seemed to swell and to flow so divinely.—Oh ! never,
Thou lovely green land, and thou fair flowing river,
Can man gaze upon you and curse you.   In vain
Doth he make his heart hard.—So I bless you again."

Another is entitled:—

"ON MARK WILSON, SLAIN IN IRONGRAY.

" I wandered forth when all men lay sleeping,
　And I heard a sweet voice wailing and weeping,
　The voice of a babe, and the wail of women,
　And ever there came a faint low screaming;
　And after the screaming a low, low moaning,
　All adown by the burnbank in the green loaning.
　I went, and by the moonlight I found
　A beauteous dame weeping low on the ground.

" The beauteous dame was sobbing and weeping,
　And at her breast lay a sweet babe sleeping,
　And by her side was a fair-haired child,
　With dark eyes flushed with weeping, and wild
　And troubled, he held by his mother, and spake,
' Oh mither ! when will my faither awake?'
　And there lay a man smitten low to the ground,
　The blood gushing forth from a bosom wound.

" And by his side lay a broken sword,
　And by his side lay the opened ' Word,'
　His palms were spread, and his head was bare,
　His knees were bent, he had knelt in prayer ;

> But brief was his prayer, for the flowers where he knelt
> Had risen all wet with his life's-blood spilt,
> And the smoke of powder smelled fresh around,
> And a steed's hoof-prints were in the ground.
>
> " She saw me, but she heeded me not,
> As a flower she sat, that had grown on the spot;
> But ever she knelt o'er the murdered man,
> And sobbed afresh, and the loosed tears ran;
> Even low as she knelt, there came a rush
> Like a fiery wind, over river and bush,
> And amid the wind, and in lightning speed,
> A bright RIDER came, on a brighter steed.
>
> " 'Woe! woe! woe!' he called, and there came
> To his hand as he spake, a sword of flame;
> He smote the air, and he smote the ground,
> Warm blood, as a rivulet, leapt up from the wound,
> Shriek followed on shriek, loud, fearful, and fast,
> And filled all the track where this dread one passed;
> And tumult and terrible outcry there came,
> As a sacked city yields when it stoops to the flame;
> And a shrill low voice came running abroad,
> ' Come, mortal man, come, and be judged by God!'
> And the dead man turned unto heaven his face,
> Stretched his hands and smiled in the light of grace."

The following one is truly descriptive of what was the stern determination of the Cameronians not to enter a building for the purpose of religious worship; a striking example of which was given when a meeting-house was erected at Quarrelwood, in Kirkmahoe, by a goodly number of the congregation, assisted by friends; a portion of them stood firmly out against entering it when it was ready for sacred service, saying, " We were driven to the hills, and on the hills we shall remain !"   By-and-by, however, they came round and worshipped along with the other brethren.   We think it likely that Cunningham had that occasion in view when this ballad was written :—

"THE VOICE LIFTED UP AGAINST CHURCHES AND CHAPELS.

" And will ye forsake the balmy, free air,
The fresh face of heaven, so golden and fair,
The mountain glen, and the silver brook,
And Nature's free bountith and open book,
To sit and worship our God with a groan,
Hemmed in with dead timber and shapen stone?
Away—away—for it never can be,
The green earth and heaven's blue vault for me.

" Woe ! woe ! to the time when to the heath-bell
The seed of the Covenant sing their farewell, .
And leave the mount written with martyr story,
The sun beaming bright in his bridegroom glory;
And leave the green birks, and the lang flowering broom,
The breath of the woodland steeped rich in perfume;
And barter our life's sweetest flower for the bran,
The glory of God for the folly of man."

"THE CAMERONIAN BANNER.

" O Banner ! fair Banner ! a century of woe
Has flowed on thy people since thou wert laid low;
Hewn down by the godless, and sullied and shorn,
Defiled with base blood, and all trodden and torn !
Thou wert lost, and John Balfour's bright steel-blade in vain
Shed their best blood as fast as moist April sheds rain—

Young, fierce, gallant Hackstoun, the river in flood
Sent rejoicing to sea with a tribute of blood;
And Gideon Macrabin, with bible and brand,
Quoted Scripture, as Am'lek fell 'neath his right hand—
All in vain, thou fair Banner, for thou wert laid low,
And a sport and a prey to the Covenant's foe.

" Fair Banner ! 'gainst thee bloody Claver'se came hewing
His road through our helms, and our glory subduing;
And Nithsdale Dalzell—his fierce deeds to requite,
On his house darkest ruin descended like night—
Came spurring and full on the lap of our war,
Disastrous shot down like an ominous star.
And Allan Dalzell—may his name to all time
Stand accurs'd, and be named with nought nobler than rhyme—
Smote thee down, thou fair Banner, all rudely, and left
Thee defiled, and the skull of the bannerman cleft.
Fair Banner ! fair Banner ! a century of woe
Has flowed on thy people since thou wert laid low.

" And now, lovely Banner ! led captive and placed
'Mid the spoils of the scoffer, and scorned and disgraced,
And hung with the helm and the glaive on the wall,
'Mongst idolatrous figures to wave in the hall,
Where lips, wet with wine, jested with thee profane,
And the minstrel, more graceless, mixed thee with his strain,
Till the might and the pride of thy conqueror fell,
And the owl sat and whoop'd in the halls of Dalzell.
O thou holy Banner ! in weeping and wail,
Let me mourn thy soiled glory, and finish my tale.

" And yet, lovely Banner ! thus torn from the brave,
And disgraced by the graceless, and sold by the slave,
And hung o'er a hostel, where rich ruddy wine,
And the soul-cheering beverage of barley divine,
Floated glorious, and sent such á smoke—in his flight
The lark stayed in the air, and sang, drunk with delight.

> Does this lessen thy lustre? or tarnish thy glory?
> Diminish thy fame, and traduce thee in story?
> Oh, no, beauteous Banner! loosed free on the beam,
> By the hand of the chosen, long, long shalt thou stream!
> And the damsel dark-eyed, and the Covenant swain,
> Shall bless thee, and talk of dread Bothwell again."

This interesting relic is carefully preserved by a very worthy family in the parish of Kirkmahoe. It is in a very sad-looking condition, from the brunt of battle and the decay of time, but its bullet-holes render it almost sacred in the eyes of those who possess it, and the stranger, while gazing upon them, has a feeling of reverence for the memory of the brave men who fought and fell under this inspiring Banner.

When and where Cunningham picked up these ballads we cannot tell, but perhaps he got them from the same fair hand who gave him the "Mermaid of Galloway;" or, what is likelier still, from his own fertile imagination—the same source.

His tales of Mark Macrabin were certainly not of a nature to give entire satisfaction to the sect of religionists to which that worthy belonged. "Indeed," as the author said, "he had no idea when he invested his hero with the name of Macrabin, of doing honour to that singular and selfish old being. It was a good name, and as the London apprentice says in Launcelot Greaves, 'a good travelling name,' and he made use of it." But notwithstanding this, he speaks kindly of the sect, for he says—"A frequent visitor of their preachings, I have hearkened with delight and edification to the poetical and prophetic eloquence of their discourses. A guest at their hearths and their tables, I have proved the cheerful and open hospitality of their nature, and have held converse and fellowship with almost all the burning and the shining lights that have distinguished the present house of Cameron. I have made their character my study, and their pursuits my chief business, and collected many curious sayings, and songs, and adventures, which belong to this simple and unassuming race. . . . Certainly the most wondrous part of the Cameronian character is the poetical warmth and spirit which everywhere abounds in their sermons and their sayings ; and, though profane minstrelsy was wisely accounted as an abomination, yet poetry, conceived and composed in the overflowing and passionate style of their compositions, has been long privately cherished among the most enlightened of the flock. But I by no means claim rank for the Cameronian bards with those who lent their unstinted strength to the strings. Their glimpses of poetical inspiration cannot equal the fuller day of those who gloried in the immortal intercourse with the muse." Who, after reading the foregoing extract, could find fault with the author of the Cameronian Ballads, though in some places flippant expressions may be detected; but yet, after all, there was nothing but a kindly feeling towards them at bottom? No one can possibly doubt this, after reading the affectionate M'Ghie letters, a family who belonged to the denomination. And we all the more respect Cunningham on account of this affection, that while adhering to his own creed he was neither bigoted nor sectarian.

CHAPTER XII.

INTRODUCTION TO SIR WALTER SCOTT—SCOTT SITTING FOR HIS BUST TO CHANTREY—EQUIPMENT TO RECEIVE HIS BARONETCY AT THE KING'S LEVEE—ON HIS RETURN HOME RECEIVES THE MANUSCRIPT OF "SIR MARMADUKE MAXWELL," A TRAGEDY—LETTERS FROM SIR WALTER SCOTT—MEMORANDA.

IT will be recollected that on the appearance of "Marmion," by Sir Walter Scott, Cunningham travelled on foot from Dalswinton to Edinburgh, upwards of seventy miles, to get a glimpse of the author, which he fortuitously did, though he was not successful in obtaining an introduction, which, perhaps, he did not then desire. A time, however, has now come when he is to be gratified to his heart's fullest wish, and under circumstances which he could scarcely, even in his most sanguine moments, anticipate. When Scott went up to London to receive his baronetcy, in 1820, Chantrey was exceedingly desirous to execute a marble bust of the great novelist, and present it to him as a mark of admiration and esteem. For this purpose he commissioned Cunningham to call and make the request. This was the more gladly complied with, as Cunningham himself was anxious to call and express his acknowledgments for "some kind message he had received, through a common friend, on the subject of those 'Remains of Nithsdale and Galloway Song,' which first made his poetical talents known to the public."

Cunningham thus describes the introduction:—" It was about nine in the morning that I sent in my card to him at Miss Dumergue's, in Piccadilly. It had not been gone a minute when I heard a quick heavy step coming, and in he came, holding out both hands, as was his custom, and saying, as he pressed mine—'Allan Cunningham, I am glad to see you.' I said something about the pleasure I felt in touching the hand that had charmed me so much. He moved his hand, and with one of his comic smiles said, 'Ay, and a big brown hand it is.' I was a little abashed at first; Scott saw it, and soon put me at my ease; he had the power—I had almost called it the art, but art it was not—of winning one's heart, and restoring one's confidence, beyond any man I ever met." He then complimented him upon his lyric powers, and urged upon him to try some higher flight than the " Remains;" and as he was engaged to breakfast in a distant part of the city the interview abruptly ended. He agreed most cheerfully to Chantrey's request with regard to the bust, and promised to call early at the studio on the following morning, which he did. The sitting was so interesting that we quote the description of it given by Lockhart, in his " Life of Sir Walter Scott," from memoranda furnished by Cunningham :—

" Chantrey's purpose had been the same as Lawrence's—to seize a poetical phasis of Scott's countenance ; and he proceeded to model the head as looking upwards, gravely and solemnly. The talk that passed, meantime, had equally amused and gratified both, and, fortunately at parting,

Chantrey requested that Scott would come and breakfast with him next morning before he recommenced operations in the studio. Scott accepted the invitation, and, when he arrived again in Eccleston Street, found two or three acquaintances assembled to meet him—among others, his old friend, Richard Heber. The breakfast was, as any party in Sir Francis Chantrey's house is sure to be, a gay and joyous one; and not having seen Heber in particular for several years, Scott's spirits were unusually excited by the presence of an intimate associate of his youthful days."

Then follow Cunningham's Memoranda:—

" Heber made many inquiries about old friends in Edinburgh, and old books, and old houses, and reminded the other of their early socialities. 'Ay,' said Mr. Scott, 'I remember we once dined out together, and sat so late that when we came away the night and day were so neatly balanced that we resolved to walk about till sunrise. The moon was not down, however, and we took advantage of her ladyship's lantern, and climbed to the top of Arthur's Seat; when we came down we had a rare appetite for breakfast.' 'I remember it well,' said Heber, 'Edinburgh was a wild place in those days,—it abounded in clubs—convivial clubs.' 'Yes,' replied Mr. Scott, 'and abounds still; but the conversation is calmer, and there are no such sallies now as might be heard in other times. One club, I remember, was infested with two Kemps, father and son. When the old man had done speaking the young one began, and before he grew weary the father was refreshed, and took up the song. John Clerk, during a pause, was called on for a stave. He immediately struck up, in a psalm-singing tone, and electrified the club with a verse which sticks like a burr to my memory—

'Now, God Almighty judge James Kemp,
    And likewise his son John,
And hang them over Hell in hemp,
    And burn them in brimstone.'

" In the midst of the mirth which this specimen of psalmody raised, John (commonly called Jack) Fuller, the member for Surrey, and standing jester of the House of Commons, came in. Heber, who was well acquainted with the free and joyous character of that worthy, began to lead him out by relating some festive anecdotes. Fuller growled approbation, and indulged us with some of his odd sallies; things which he assured us 'were damned good, and true too, which was better.' Mr. Scott, who was standing when Fuller came in, eyed him at first with a look, grave and considerate; but as the stream of conversation flowed, his keen eye twinkled brighter and brighter, his stature increased, for he drew himself up, and seemed to take the measure of the hoary joker, body and soul. An hour or two of social chat had meanwhile induced Mr. Chantrey to alter his views as to the bust, and when Mr. Scott left us, he said to me privately, 'This will never do—I shall never be able to please myself with a perfectly serene expression. I must try his conversational look, take him when about to break out into some sly funny old story.' As Chantrey said this, he took a string, cut off the head of the bust, put it into its present position, touched the eyes and the mouth slightly, and wrought such a transformation upon it, that when Scott came to his third sitting, he smiled and said—'Ay, ye're mair like yoursel now! Why, Mr. Chantrey, no witch of old ever performed such cantrips with clay as this.'

"These sittings were seven in number; but when Scott revisited London a year afterwards, he gave Chantrey several more, the bust being by that time in marble. Allan Cunningham, when he called to bid him farewell, as he was about to leave town on the present occasion, found him in Court dress, preparing to kiss hands at the Levee, on being gazetted as Baronet. 'He seemed anything but at his ease,' says Cunningham, 'in that strange attire; he was like one in armour—the stiff cut of the coat—the large shining buttons and buckles—the lace ruffles—the queue—the sword—and the cocked hat, formed a picture at which I could not forbear smiling. He surveyed himself in the glass for a moment, and burst into a hearty laugh. 'O Allan,' he said, 'O Allan, what creatures we must make of ourselves in obedience to Madam Etiquette! See'st thou not, I say, what a deformed thief this fashion is?—how giddily she turns about all the hotbloods between fourteen and five-and-thirty?' ('Much Ado About Nothing,' Act iii., Scene 3.)"

Sir Walter returned home to Edinburgh highly elated with his newly received dignity, which was the more valuable as being the King's personal desire, and from the kind words with which he conferred the honour— "I shall always reflect with pleasure on Sir Walter Scott's having been the first creation of my reign." Shortly after his return, Cunningham transmitted to him the manuscript of a long historical drama or tragedy, requesting his opinion of it, and whether he thought it suitable for the stage. He did this the more confidently from the intimacy he had contracted with Sir Walter while sitting for his bust in Chantrey's studio. That opinion was frankly given in a long and friendly letter,

of which the following sentences are the kernel:—" I
have perused twice your curious and interesting manuscript. Many parts of the poetry are eminently beautiful,
though I fear the great length of the piece, and some
obscurity of the plot, would render it unfit for dramatic
representation. There is a fine tone of supernatural
impulse spread over the whole action, which I think a
common audience would not be likely to adopt or comprehend—though I own that to me it has a very
powerful effect." This was criticism kind, and at the
same time explicit, although it was not the opinion
which the author expected. But the letter is deserving
of being given at length, and therefore we insert it :—

" Edinburgh, 14th November, 1820.

" My dear Allan,—I have been meditating a long letter
to you for many weeks past; but company, and rural business,
and rural sports, are very unfavourable to writing letters. I
have now a double reason for writing, for I have to thank
you for sending me in safety a beautiful specimen of our
English Michael's talents in the cast of my venerable friend
Mr. Watt. It is a most striking resemblance, with all that
living character which we are apt to think life itself alone
can exhibit. I hope Mr. Chantrey does not permit his distinguished skill either to remain unexercised, or to be lavished
exclusively on subjects of little interest. I would like to see
him engaged on some subject of importance, completely
adapted to the purpose of his chisel, and demanding its highest
powers. Pray remember me to him most kindly.
" I have perused twice your curious and interesting manuscript. Many parts of the poetry are eminently beautiful,

though I fear the great length of the piece, and some obscurity of the plot, would render it unfit for dramatic representation. There is also a fine tone of supernatural impulse spread over the whole action, which I think a common audience would not be likely to adopt or comprehend—though I own that to me it has a very powerful effect. Speaking of dramatic composition in general, I think it is almost essential (though the rule may be most difficult in practice) that the plot, or business of the piece, should advance with every line that is spoken. The fact is, the drama is addressed chiefly to the eyes, and as much as can be, by any possibility, represented on the stage, should neither be told nor described. Of the miscellaneous part of a large audience, many do not understand, nay, many cannot hear, either narrative or description, but are solely intent upon the action exhibited. It is, I conceive, for this reason that very bad plays, written by performers themselves, often contrive to get through, and not without applause; while others, immeasurably superior in point of poetical merit, fail, merely because the author is not sufficiently possessed of the trick of the scene, or enough aware of the importance of a maxim pronounced by no less a performer than Punch himself (at least he was the last authority from whom I heard it)—*Push on, keep moving!* Now, in your ingenious dramatic effort, the interest not only stands still, but sometimes retrogrades. It contains, notwithstanding, many passages of eminent beauty — many specimens of most interesting dialogue; and, on the whole, if it is not fitted for the modern stage, I am not sure that its very imperfections do not render it more fit for the closet, for we certainly do not always read with the greatest pleasure those plays which act best.

" If, however, you should at any time wish to become a candidate for dramatic laurels, I would advise you, in the first place, to consult some professional person of judgment and taste.   I should regard friend Terry as an excellent mentor, and I believe he would concur with me in recommending that at least one-third of the drama be retrenched, that the plot should be rendered simpler, and the motives more obvious; and I think the powerful language and many of the situations might then have their full effect upon the audience.   I am uncertain if I have made myself sufficiently understood; but I would say, for example, that it is ill explained by what means Comyn and his gang, who land as shipwrecked men, become at once possessed of the old lord's domains merely by killing and taking possession.   I am aware of what you mean—namely, that being attached to the then rulers, he is supported in his ill-acquired power by their authority.   But this is imperfectly brought out, and escaped me at the first reading.   The superstitious motives, also, which induced the shepherds to delay their vengeance, are not likely to be intelligible to the generality of the hearers.   It would seem more probable that the young Baron should have led his faithful vassals to avenge the death of his parents; and it has escaped me what prevents him from taking this direct and natural course.   Besides, it is, I believe, a rule (and it seems a good one) that one single interest, to which every other is subordinate, should occupy the whole play,—each separate object having just the effect of a mill-dam, sluicing off a certain portion of the sympathy, which should move on with increasing force and rapidity to the catastrophe.   Now, in your work there are several divided points of interest.   There is the murder of the old Baron—the escape of his wife—that of his son—the loss of his bride—the villanous artifices of Comyn to possess himself of her person—and, finally, the fall of Comyn, and acceleration of the vengeance due to his crimes.   I am sure your own excellent sense, which I admire as much as I do your genius, will give me credit for my frankness in these matters. I only know, that I do not know many persons on whose performances I would venture to offer so much criticism.

"I will return the manuscript under Mr. Freeland's Post-office cover, and I hope it will reach you safe.—Adieu, my leal and esteemed friend—Yours truly,

"WALTER SCOTT.

"To Mr. Allan Cunningham
"(Care of F. Chantrey, Esq., R. A., London)."

When Cunningham wrote for his manuscript, which had been retained by Sir Walter for a considerable time, and which he was afraid had been mislaid or forgotten, he intimated that he was about to undertake a "Collection of the Songs of Scotland, with Notes,"—a proposal which Sir Walter approved of in the most complimentary terms, promising to give him all the assistance in his power :—

"My dear Allan,—It was as you supposed—I detained your manuscript to read it over with Terry. The plot appears to Terry, as to me, ill-combined, which is a great defect in a drama, though less perceptible in the closet than on the stage. Still, if the mind can be kept upon one unbroken course of interest, the effect even in perusal is more gratifying. I have always considered this as the great secret in dramatic poetry, and conceive it one of the most difficult exercises of the invention possible, to conduct a story through five acts, developing it gradually in every scene, so as to keep up the attention, yet never till the very conclusion permitting the nature of the catastrophe to become visible,—and all the while to accompany this by the necessary delineation of character and beauty of language. I am glad, however, that you mean to preserve in some permanent form your very curious drama, which, if not altogether fitted for the stage, cannot be read without very much and very deep interest.

"I am glad you are about Scottish Song. No man—not Robert Burns himself—has contributed more beautiful effusions to enrich it. Here and there I would pluck a flower from your Posey to give what remains an effect of greater simplicity; but luxuriance can only be the fault of genius, and many of your songs are, I think, unmatched. I would instance, 'It's Hame and it's Hame,' which my daughter, Mrs. Lockhart, sings with such uncommon effect. You cannot do anything either in the way of original composition, or collection, or criticism, that will not be highly acceptable to all who are worth pleasing in the Scottish public—and I pray you to proceed with it.

"Remember me kindly to Chantrey. I am happy my effigy is to go with that of Wordsworth, for (differing from him in very many points of taste) I do not know a man more to be venerated for uprightness of heart and loftiness of genius. Why he will sometimes choose to crawl upon all-fours, when God has given him so noble a countenance to lift to heaven, I am as little able to account for as for his quarrelling (as you tell me) with the wrinkles which time and meditation have stamped his brow withal.

"I am obliged to conclude hastily, having long letters to write, God wot, upon very different subjects. I pray my kind respects to Mrs. Chantrey.—Believe me, dear Allan, very truly yours, &c.,

"WALTER SCOTT.

"To Mr. Allan Cunningham."

The reference here made to Wordsworth arose from an intimation to Sir Walter by Cunningham that his bust was to be sent to the Royal Academy's Exhibition, along with that of Wordsworth.

Cunningham gives the following interesting memoranda of his meeting with Sir Walter in the following year, when he went up to London to attend the Coronation:—

"I saw Sir Walter again, when he attended the Coronation in 1821. In the meantime his bust had been wrought in marble, and the sculptor desired to take the advantage of his visit to communicate such touches of expression or lineament as the new material rendered necessary. This was done with a happiness of eye and hand almost magical; for five hours did the poet sit, or stand, or walk, while Chantrey's chisel was passed again and again over the marble, adding something at every touch.

"'Well, Allan,' he said, when he saw me at this last sitting, 'were you at the Coronation? it was a splendid sight.' 'No, Sir Walter,' I answered; 'places were dear and ill to get. I am told it was a magnificent scene; but having seen the procession of King Crispin at Dumfries, I was satisfied.' I said this with a smile. Scott took it as I meant it, and laughed heartily. 'That's not a bit better than Hogg,' he said. 'He stood balancing the matter whether to go to the Coronation or the Fair of Saint Boswell—and the Fair carried it.'

"During this conversation, Mr. Bolton, the engineer, came in. Something like a cold acknowledgment passed between the poet and him. On his passing into an inner room, Scott said, 'I am afraid Mr. Bolton has not forgot a little passage that once took place between us. We met in a public company, and in reply to the remark of some one he said, 'That's like the old saying,—in every quarter, of the world you will find a Scot, a rat, and a Newcastle grindstone.' This touched my Scotch spirit, and I said, 'Mr. Bolton, you should have added—*and a Brummagem button.*' There was a laugh at this, and Mr. Bolton replied, 'We make something better in Birmingham than buttons—we make steam-engines, Sir.'

"'I like Bolton,' thus continued Sir Walter; 'he is a brave man—and who can dislike the brave? He showed this on a remarkable occasion. He had engaged to coin for some foreign prince a large quantity of gold. This was found out by some desperadoes, who resolved to rob the premises, and as a preliminary step tried to bribe the porter. The porter was an honest fellow,—he told Bolton that he was offered a hundred pounds to be blind and deaf next night. 'Take the money,' was the answer, 'and I shall protect the place.' Midnight came—the gates opened as if by magic—the interior doors, secured with patent locks, opened as of their own accord—and three men with dark lanterns entered and went straight to the gold. Bolton had prepared some flax steeped in turpentine—he dropt fire upon it, a sudden light filled all the place, and with his assistance he rushed forward on the robbers. The leader saw in a moment he was betrayed, turned on the porter, and shooting him dead, burst through all obstruction, and with an ingot of gold in his hand, scaled the wall and escaped.'

"'That is quite a romance in robbing,' I said; and I had nearly said more, for the cavern scene and death of Meg Merrilees rose in my mind. Perhaps the mind of Sir Walter was taking the direction of the Solway too, for he said, 'How long have you been from Nithsdale?'—'A dozen years.' 'Then you will remember it well. I was a visitor there in my youth. My brother was at Closeburn school, and there I found Creehope Linn, a scene ever present to my fancy. It is at once fearful and beautiful. The stream jumps down from the moorlands, saws its way into the freestone rock of a hundred feet deep, and, in escaping to the plain, performs a thousand vagaries. In one part it has actually shaped out a little chapel,—the peasants call it the Sutor's Chair. There are sculptures on the sides of the Linn too, not such as Mr. Chantrey casts, but etchings scraped in with a knife perhaps, or a harrow-tooth.—Did you ever hear,' said Sir Walter, ' of Patrick Maxwell, who, taken prisoner by the King's troops, escaped from them on his way to Edinburgh, by flinging himself into that dreadful Linn on Moffat water, called the Douglases Beef-tub?'—'Frequently,' I answered; 'the country abounds with anecdotes of those days: the popular feeling sympathizes with the poor Jacobites, and has recorded its sentiments in many a tale and many a verse.'—'The Ettrick Shepherd has collected not a few of those things,' said Scott, and I suppose many snatches of song may yet be found.'— C.—'I have gathered many such things myself, Sir Walter, and as I still propose to make a collection of all Scottish songs of poetic merit, I shall work up many of my stray verses and curious anecdotes in the notes.' S.—I am glad that you are about such a thing. Any help which I can give you, you may command. Ask me any questions, no matter how many, I shall answer them if I can. Don't be timid in your selection. Our ancestors fought boldly, spoke boldly, and sang boldly too. I can help you to an old characteristic ditty not yet in print:—

> 'There dwalt a man into the waat,
>   And O gin he was cruel,
> For on his bridal night at e'en
>   He gat up and grat for gruel.

> They brought to him a gude sheep's head,
>   A bason, and a towel;
> Gar take thae whim-whams far frae me,
>   I winna want my gruel.'

"*C.*—'I never heard that verse before. The hero seems related to the bridegroom of Nithsdale:—

> 'The bridegroom grat as the sun gade down;
> The bridegroom grat as the sun gade down;
> To ouy man I'll gie a hunder marks sae free,
> This night that will bed wi' a bride for me.'

"*S.*—'A cowardly loon enough. I know of many crumbs and fragments of verse which will be useful to your work. The Border was once peopled with poets, for every one that could fight could make ballads, some of them of great power and pathos. Some such people as the minstrels were living less than a century ago.' *C.*—'I knew a man, the last of a race of district tale-tellers, who used to boast of the golden days of his youth, and say, that the world, with all its knowledge, was grown sixpence a-day worse for him.' *S.*—'How was that? How did he make his living? By telling tales, or singing ballads?' *C.*—'By both. He had a devout tale for the old, and a merry song for the young. He was a sort of beggar.' *S.*—'Out upon thee, Allan. Dost thou call that begging? Why, man, we make our bread by story-telling, and honest bread it is.'"

It would be impertinent to say that Sir Walter's friendship and esteem for Cunningham was sincere. The very fact of his writing him at such length on the merits and defects of his tragedy, giving him the best of counsel, and at the same time encouragement, is an evidence of this, as he himself expressly states; and when in 1826 he again went up to London, he breakfasted one morning with "Honest Allan," of which he makes the following jotting in his diary:—"We breakfasted at honest Allan Cunningham's—honest Allan—a leal and true Scotchman of the old cast. A man of genius, besides, who only requires the tact of knowing when and where to stop to attain the universal praise which ought to follow it. I look upon the alteration of ' It's Hame and it's Hame,' and 'A wet sheet and a flowing sea,' as among the best songs going. His prose has often admirable passages; but he is obscure, and overlays his meaning, which will not do now-a-days, when he who runs must read." Future instances of friendship from the same source will meet us as we proceed.

He had now ceased contributing to *Blackwood*, for reasons not necessary to be here stated in full. He acknowledged that he had received considerable kindness from the publisher, but at last he "became weary," especially as he was required to limit his pen to that work alone. As he received more liberal terms from the *London Magazine*, he resolved to devote himself entirely to its columns, the more especially as he was a favourite with the publishers, and had obtained much kindness at their hands. Writing to his brother James at this time, he says—"I am proceeding rapidly with my Collection of Songs, and shall spare no pains to render it creditable to me. I have had several liberal offers for the work, and as it will extend to four volumes with a preface—with characters of our best lyric poets, and notes, together with many hitherto unpublished songs, I have no doubt I will make something handsome by it. I have many good offers for other works—a Novel particularly, for which my friends seem to think me very fit, and for which I have this morning been offered Two Hundred Pounds; but my songs devour up all lesser things at present, except the communications with the *Magazine.*" In the same letter he says—" I still work as hard as I ever did—rise at six and work to six. I shall amend this presently, for it prevents me profiting by literary pursuits; and I think I could live handsomely by my pen alone, and perhaps obtain a little fame too. But I have no wish to leave Mr. Chantrey, who is a man of genius and a gentleman, and treats me with abundance of kindness and distinction." " Rise at six and work to six!" He wrought till far on in the morning, when the wearied body often refused to countenance and support the busy brain.

He here speaks of living by his pen alone; but though he had this ambition, he very prudently did not carry out the suggestion, and in this respect he shines admirably above many of his predecessors, by making literature a staff and not a crutch, by engaging in it rather as a relaxation and a pleasure than as a profession, and so avoiding the chasm into which many have fallen, poverty and misfortune. One of his great characteristics was the exemplification of one of his nation's proverbs, " Look before ye leap," and hence he attained a distinguished reputation and position in the world.

CHAPTER XIII.

PUBLISHES "SIR MARMADUKE MAXWELL"—HIS OWN OPINION OF THE
WORK—SIR WALTER SCOTT'S NOTICE OF IT ON ITS PUBLICATION
—EXTRACT SPECIMENS OF THE TRAGEDY—LETTER FROM SIR
WALTER SCOTT—SONG, "MY NANIE, O."

NOTWITHSTANDING the genial tone and friendly manner
in which Sir Walter criticized the manuscript of "Sir
Marmaduke Maxwell," and the kind advice he gave with
regard to that kind of composition, it cannot be doubted
that Cunningham was greatly disappointed in the opinion
expressed by such a distinguished author. He had expected a very different judgment, because to his own
mind it was a highly creditable production, and certain
to create a sensation among the literary public. He had
set his whole heart upon the matter, and he was exceedingly desirous to see it have a place on the stage. That
might be the making of his fortune, and other pieces of
a similar kind would be sure to follow. Then, to his
imagination, there was the applause of the audience,
the thunder of the gods, and the calls for the author
before the curtain, and the bowing of his acknowledgments. All this, however, was knocked on the head by
the magic wand of the great Wizard. The advice as to
remodelling the piece, effecting excisions and curtail-
ments, and making another dramatic attempt, was not
adopted, and he seems to have become soured at it

himself, from the long list of defects and superfluities and inconsistencies which had been pointed out for revision and correction.

Adverse as the private criticism was, he resolved to test public opinion on the subject, for he was unwilling that his first and great attempt at dramatic composition should be thrown aside, without giving it an opportunity of ventilation. So, in March, 1822, it was issued from the press, accompanied with " The Mermaid of Galloway," "Richard Faulder," and twenty Scottish Songs, most of which had previously seen the light. The scene of the tragedy is Caerlaverock Castle, and its adjoining precincts on the Solway shore. The time is under the second Cromwell, at the close of the Commonwealth. Of course the story is almost wholly imaginary, and "the manners, feelings, and superstitions are those common to the Scottish peasantry." He intimates that though the piece "is not, perhaps, unfitted for representation," yet it was not written altogether with that view, but rather "to excite interest in the reader by a natural and national presentation of action and character." One of the earliest copies was sent to Sir Walter Scott, who prominently referred to it in his introduction to "The Fortunes of Nigel" in the following terms:—

" *Author.*—You are quite right—habit's a strange thing, my son. I had forgot whom I was speaking to. Yes, plays for the closet, not for the stage—

" *Captain.*—Right, and so you are sure to be acted; for the managers, while thousands of volunteers are desirous of saving them, are wonderfully partial to pressed men.

"*Author.*—I am a living witness, having been, like a second Laberius, made a dramatist whether I would or not. I believe my muse would be *Terryfied* into treading the stage, even if I should write a sermon.

"*Captain.*—Truly, if you did, I am afraid folks might make a farce of it; and, therefore, should you change your style, I still advise a volume of dramas like Lord Byron's.

"*Author.*—No, his lordship is a cut above me—I won't run my horse against his, if I can help myself.   But there is my friend Allan has written just such a play as I might write myself, in a very sunny day, and with one of Bramah's extra patent pens.   I cannot make neat work without such appurtenances.

"*Captain.*—Do you mean Allan Ramsay?

"*Author.*—No, nor Barbara Allan either.   I mean Allan Cunningham, who has just published his tragedy of 'Sir Marmaduke Maxwell,' full of merry-making and murdering, kissing, and cutting of throats, and passages which lead to nothing, and which are very pretty passages for all that. Not a glimpse of probability is there about the plot, but so much animation in particular passages, and such a vein of poetry through the whole, as I dearly wish I could infuse into my Culinary Remains, should I ever be tempted to publish them.   With a popular impress, people would read and admire the beauties of Allan—as it is, they may perhaps only note his defects—or, what is worse, not note him at all. But never mind them, honest Allan, you are a credit to Caledonia for all that.   There are some lyrical effusions of his, too, which you would do well to read, Captain.   'It's Hame and it's Hame' is equal to Burns."

Though "Sir Marmaduke Maxwell" may be called a closet drama, fitter for private reading than representa-

tion on the stage, yet there are some scenes in it quite
of a sensational character, and which could not have
failed to receive popular applause.   We quote the
following :—

ACT IV.

Scene I.—*Cumlongan Castle.*

MARY DOUGLAS *and* MAY MORISON.

May Morison.   This grief's a most seducing thing.   All
      ladies
Who wish to be most gallantly woo'd must sit
And sigh to the starlight on the turret top,
Saunter by waterfalls, and court the moon
For a goodly gift of paleness.   Faith! I'll cast
My trick of laughing to the priest, and woo
Man, tender man, by sighing.
Mary Douglas.   The ash bough
Shall drop with honey, and the leaf of the linn
Shall cease its shaking, when that merry eye
Knows what a tear-drop means.   Be mute! be mute!
May Morison.   When gallant knights shall scale a dizzy
      wall
For the love of a laughing lady, I shall know
What sighs will bring i' the market.   (*Sings.*)

    If love for love it may na be,
      At least be pity to me shown;
    A thought ungentle canna be,
      The thought o' Mary Morison.

Mary Douglas.   No tidings of thee yet—my love, my love;
Didst thou but live as thou camest yesternight

In visioned beauty to my side, 'twere worth
The world from east to west.
   May Morison.   O lady! lady!
This grief becomes you rarely; 'tis a dress
That costs at most a tear o' the eye—the sweetest
Handmaid that beauty has.   How thou wouldst weep
To see some fair knight, on whose helmet bright
A score of dames stuck favours—see him leave
His barb'd steed standing in the wood to preach
Thee out of thy virgin purgatory, to taste
The joys of wedded heaven.
                                [A knock is heard at the gate.
   Mary Douglas.   See who this is
That knocks so loud and late.   *[Exit May Morison.*
                       Ye crowded stars,
Shine you on one so wretched as I am?
You have your times of darkness, but the cloud
Doth pass away; and you shine forth again
With an increase of loveliness—from me
This cloud can never pass. So now, farewell,
Ye twilight watchings on the castle top,
For him who made my glad heart leap and bound
From my bosom to my lip.

               Enter HALBERT COMYNE.

   Comyne.   Now, beauteous lady,
Joy to your meditations: your thoughts hallow
Whate'er they touch; and aught you think on's blest.
   Mary Douglas.   I think on thee, but thou'rt not therefore
      bless'd.
What must I thank for this unwished-for honour?
   Comyne.   Thyself thank, gentle one: thou art the cause

Why I have broken slumbers and sad dreams,
Why I forget high purposes, and talk
Of nought but cherry lips.
    Mary Douglas.   Now, were you, sir,
Some unsunn'd strippling, you might quote to me
These cast-off saws of shepherds.
  Comyne.   The war trump
Less charms my spirit than the sheep boy's whistle.
My barbed steed stamps in his stall, and neighs
For lack of his arm'd rider.   Once I dream'd
Of spurring battle steeds, of carving down
Spain's proudest crests to curious relics; and
I cleft in midnight vision the gold helm
Of the proud Prince of Parma.
    Mary Douglas.   Thanks, my lord;
You are blest in dreams, and a most pretty teller
Of tricks in sleep—and so your dream is told:
Then, my fair sir, good-night.
    Comyne.   You are too proud,
Too proud, fair lady; yet your pride becomes you;
Your eyes lend you divinity.   Unversed
Am I in love's soft silken words—unversed
In the cunning way to win a gentle heart.
When my heart heaves as if 'twould crack my corselet,
I'm tongue-tied with emotion, and I lose
Her that I love for lack of honey'd words.
    Mary Douglas.   Go school that rank simplicity of thine:
Learn to speak falsely in love's gilded terms;
Go, learn to sugar o'er a hollow heart;
And learn to shower tears, as the winter cloud,
Bright, but all frozen; make thy rotten vows
Smell like the rose of July.   Go, my lord;
Thou art too good for this world.

Comyne.   My fair lady,
Cease with this bitter but most pleasant scoffing;
For I am come upon a gentle suit,
Which I can ill find terms for.
    Mary Douglas.   •   Name it not.
Think it is granted; gô now.   Now, farewell:
I'm sad, am sick—a fearful faintness comes
With a rush upon my heart; so now, farewell.
    Comyne.   Lo! how thé lilies chase the ruddy rose—
What a small waist is this!
    Mary Douglas.   That hand! that hand!
There's red blood on that right hand, and that brow;.
There's motion in my father's statue; see,
Doth it not draw the sword?   Unhand me, sir.
    Comyne.   Thou dost act to the life; but scare not me
With vision'd blood-drops, and with marble swords;
I'm too firm stuff, thou'lt find, to start at shadows.
    Mary Douglas.   Now, were thy lips with eloquence to drop,
As July's wind with balm; wert thou to vow
Till all the saints grew pale; kneel i' the ground
Till the green grass grew about thee; had thy brow
The crowned honour of the world upon it;
I'd scorn thee—spurn thee.
    Comyne.   Lady, scorn not me.
O! what a proud thing is a woman, when
She has red in her cheek.   Lady, when I kneel down
And court the bridal gift of that white hand
Thou wavest so disdainfully, why then
I give thee leave to scorn me.   I have hope
To climb a nobler, and as fair a tree,
And pull far richer fruit.   So scorn not me:
I dream of no such honour as thou dread'st.
    Mary Douglas.   And what darest thou to dream of?

Comyne.   Of thee, lady.
Of winning thy love on some bloom'd violet bank,
When nought shines save the moon, and where no proud
Priest dares be present: lady, that's my dream.
    Mary Douglas.   Let it be still a dream, then; lest I beg
From heaven five minutes' manhood, to make thee
Dream it when thou art dust.
    Comyne.   Why, thou heroine,
Thou piece o' the rarest metal e'er nature stamp'd
Her chosen spirits from, now I do love thee,
Do love thee much for this; I love thee more
Than loves a soldier the grim looks of war,
As he wipes his bloody brow.

Enter Sir MARMADUKE MAXWELL, *unseen.*

Sir Marmaduke.   (*Aside.*)   What! what is this?
She whom I love best—he whom I hate worst?—
Is this an airy pageant of the fiends?
    Mary Douglas.   (*Aside.*)   Down! down! ye proud drops
            of my bosom, be
To my dull brain obedient.   (*To Comyne.*)   My good lord,
Much gladness may this merry mood of yours
With a poor maiden bring you.   I thank you much
For lending one dull hour of evening wings
To fly away so joyous.
    Sir Marmaduke.   (*Aside.*)   Mine ears have
Turn'd traitors to my love; else they receive
A sound more dread than doomsday.   Oh! thou false—
Thou didst seem purer than the undropt dew,
Chaste as the unsunn'd snow-drops' buds disclosed
Unto the frosty stars; and truer far
Than blossom to the summer, or than light

Unto the morning.　And dost thou smile too,
And smile on him so lovingly? bow too
That brow of alabaster? Woman—woman.
　　Comyne.　O! for a month of such sweet gentle chiding
From such ripe tempting lips! Now, fair young lady,
As those two bright eyes love the light, and love
To see proud man adore them, cast not off
For his rough manner, and his unpruned speech,
A man who loves you.　Gentle one, we'll live
As pair'd doves do among the balmy boughs.
　　Sir Marmaduke.　(*Aside.*)　Painted perdition, dost thou
　　　　smile at this?
　　Mary Douglas.　This is a theme I love so well, I wish
For God's good daylight to it; so, farewell.
　　Comyne.　An hour aneath the new risen moon to woo
Is worth a summer of sunshine : a fair maid
Once told me this ; and lest I should forget it,
Kiss'd me, and told it twice.
　　Sir Marmaduke.　(*Aside.*)　Dare but to touch
Her little finger, faithless as she is ;
Yea, or her garment's hem—My father's sword,
Thou hadst thy temper for a nobler purpose ;
So keep thy sheath : for did I smite him now,
Why men would say, that for a father's blood
Mine slept like water 'neath the winter ice ;
But when a weak sweet woman chafed my mood,
And made sport of her vows, then my blood rose,
And with my spirit burning on my brow
I sprang wi' my blade to his bosom.　So, then, sleep
Fast in thy sheath.　Before that lovely face,
Those lips I've kiss'd so fondly, and that neck
Round which mine arms have hung, I could not strike
As the son of my father should.

Mary Douglas.   Now, fair good-night
To thee, most courteous sir.   I seek the chase
From dark Cumlongan to green Burnswark top,
With hawk and hound, before to-morrow's sun
Has kiss'd the silver dew.   So be not found
By me alone beneath the greenwood bough,
Lest I should woo thee as the bold dame did
The sire of good King Robert.   [*Exit.*
    Comyne.   Gentle dreams
To thee, thou sweet one : gladly would I quote
The say of an old shepherd : mayst thou dream
Of linking me within thy lily arms;
And leave my wit, sweet lady, to unravel't.   [*Exit.*
    Sir Marmaduke.   And now there's nought for me in this
        wide world
That's worth the wishing for.   For thee, false one,
The burning hell of an inconstant mind
Is curse enough; and so we part in peace.
And now for THEE—I name thee not; thy name,
Save for thy doom, shall never pass my lips—
Depart untouch'd.   There's something in this place
Which the stern temper that doth spill men's blood
Is soften'd by.   We're doom'd once more to meet,
And never part in life.   . [*Exit.*

Sir Marmaduke is under a false impression as to
Mary Douglas's affection for Halbert Comyne.   She
loves himself alone, and only in consciousness of fixed
love there, she had in her playfulness dallied with the
tempter.   She is as firm to her vows as ever, and Sir
Marmaduke discovers this in a future scene, where all
again is well :—

SCENE V.—*Cumlongan Wood.*

Sir MARMADUKE MAXWELL *and* MARY DOUGLAS.

Sir Marmaduke.   Thou art free, stripling—use thy feet—
  fly fast,
The chasers' swords may yet o'ertake us both.
When thou dost fold thy flocks and pray, oh! pray
For one whom woe and ruin hold in chase;
Who wears the griefs of eighty at eighteen;
Upon whose bud the canker-dew has dropt;
Whose friends, love, kindred are cold, faithless, dead.
O! weeping youth, pray not for me; for God
Has left me, and to pray for me might bring
My fate upon thee too.   Away, I pray thee.
  Mary Douglas.   The wretched love the wretched.   I love
    thee
Too well to sunder thus.   I will go with thee;
Friends, kindred, all, are all estranged or dead;
An evil star has risen upon my name,
On which no morn will rise.
  Sir Marmaduke.   Thou art too soft
I' the eye—too meek of speech—and thou dost start
For the falling of the forest leaf, and quakest
As the thrush does for the hawk.   Who lives with me
Must have eyes firmer than remorseless steel,
And shake grim danger's gory hand, nor start
For the feather of his bonnet.
  Mary Douglas.   O! I shall learn.
I'll sit and watch thee in thy sleep, and bring
Thee clustering nuts; take thee where purest springs
Spout crystal forth; rob the brown honey bees

Of half their summer's gathering, and dig too
The roots of cornick.   I will snare for thee
The leaping hares—the nimble fawns shall stay
The coming of mine arrow.   We will live
Like two wild pigeons in the wood, where men
May see us, but not harm us.   Take me, take me.

   Sir Marmaduke.   Come, then, my soft petitioner, thou
          plead'st
Too tenderly for me.   And thy voice, too,
Has caught the echo of the sweetest tongue
That ever blest man's ear.   Where is thy home?
That little sunburnt hand has never prest
Aught harder than white curd.

   Mary Douglas.   I served a lady.
And all my time flew past in penning her
Soft letters to her love; in making verses
Riddling, and keen and quaint; in bleaching white
Her lily fingers 'mong the morning dew;
In touching for her ear some tender string;
And I was gifted with a voice that made
Her lover's ballads melting.   She would lay
Her tresses back from her dark eyes, and say,
Sing it again.

   Sir Marmaduke.   Thou wert a happy servant.
And did thy gentle mistress love this youth
As royally as thou paint'st?

   Mary Douglas.   O! yes, she loved him,
For I have heard her laughing in her sleep,
And saying, O! my love, come back, come back;
Indeed thou'rt worth one kiss.

   Sir Marmaduke.   And did her love
Know that she dearly loved him?   Did he keep
Acquaintance with the mighty stars, and watch

Beneath her window for one glance of her,
To glad him a whole winter?
   Mary Douglas.   Aye! he talk'd much
To her about the horn'd moon, and clear stars;
How colds were bad for coughs, and pangs at heart:
And she made him sack posset, and he sung
Songs he said he made himself, and I believe him,
For they were rife of braes, and birks, and burns,
And lips made of twin cherries, tresses loop'd
Like the curling hyacinth.   Now in my bosom
Have I the last song which this sighing youth
Framed for my mistress.   It doth tenderly
Touch present love: there future sadness is
Shadow'd with melting sweetness.—
   Sir Marmaduke.   This small hand—
This little trembling lily hand is soft,
And like my Mary's.   O! my love—my love,
Look up! 'tis thou thyself! now blessed be
The spot thou stand'st on, and let men this hour
For ever reverence—heaven is busy in it.
   Mary Douglas. O! let us fly! the hand of heaven, my love,
And thine, have wrought most wondrously for me.
   Sir Marmaduke.   And wilt thou trust thy gentle self
      with me?
   Mary Douglas. Who can withhold me from thee—I had
      sworn
To seek thee through the world—to ask each hind
That held the plough, if he had seen my love;
Then seek thee through the sea—to ask each ship
That pass'd me by, if it had met my love;—
My journey had a perilous outset, but
A passing pleasant end.   Thine enemy came:
I pass'd a fearful and a trembling hour.

Sir Marmaduke.   I know—I heard it all—O! I have
        wrong'd thee much;
So come with me, my beautiful, my best;
True friends are near: the hour of vengeance, too,
Is not far distant.   Come, my fair one, come.   (*Exeunt.*)

The following is a specimen of the author's power of
sustaining soliloquy:—

ACT II.

Scene I.—*Caerlaverock Castle.*

Halbert Comyne *alone.*

Comyne.   'Tis said there is an hour i' the darkness when
Man's brain is wondrous fertile, if nought holy
Mix with his musings.   Now, whilst seeking this,
I've worn some hours away, yet my brain's dull,
As if a thing called grace stuck to my heart,
And sickened resolution.   Is my soul tamed
And baby-rid wi' the thought that flood or field
Can render back, to scare men and the moon,
The airy shapes of the corses they enwomb?
And what if't 'tis so?   Shall I lose the crown
Of my most golden hope because its circle
Is haunted by a shadow?   Shall I go wear
Five summers of fair looks,—sigh shreds of psalms,—
Pray i' the desert till I fright the fox,—
Gaze on the cold moon and the clustered stars,
And quote some old man's saws 'bout crowns above,—
Watch with wet eyes at death-beds, dandle the child,
And cut the elder whistles of him who knocks

Red earth from clouted shoon.   Thus may I buy
Scant praise from tardy lips; and when I die,
Some ancient hind will scratch, to scare the owl,
A death's head on my grave-stone.   If I live so,
May the spectres dog my heels of those I slew
I' the gulph of battle; wise men cease their faith
In the sun's rising; soldiers no more trust
The truth of tempered steel.   I never loved him.—
He topt me as a tree that kept the dew
And balmy south wind from me : fair maids smiled;
Glad minstrels sung; and he went lauded forth,
Like a thing dropt from the stars.   At every step
Stooped hoary heads unbonneted; white caps
Hung i' the air; there was clapping of hard palms,
And shouting of the dames.   All this to him
Was as the dropping honey; but to me
'Twas as the bitter gourd.   Thus did I hang,
As his robe's tassel, kissing the dust, and flung
Behind him for boys' shouts,—for cotman's dogs
To bay and bark at.   Now from a far land,
From fields of blood and extreme peril I come,
Like an eagle to his rock, who finds his nest
Filled with an owlet's young.   For he had seen
One summer's eve a milkmaid with her pail,
And 'cause her foot was white, and her green gown
Was spun by her white hand, he fell in love.
Then did he sit and pen an amorous ballad;
Then did he carve her name in plum-tree bark;
And, with a heart as soft as new pressed curd,
Away he walked to woo.   He swore he loved her.
She said cream curds were sweeter than lord's love.
He vowed 'twas pretty wit, and he would wed her.
She laid her white arm round the fond lord's neck,

And said his pet sheep ate her cottage kale,
And they were naughty beasts.   And so they talked;
And then they made their bridal bed i' the grass,
No witness but the moon.   So this must pluck
Things from my heart I've hugged since I could count
What hours the moon had.   There has been with me
A time of tenderer heart, when soft love hung
Around this beadsman's neck such a fair string
Of what the world calls virtues that I stood
Even as the wildered man who dropped his staff,
And walked the way it fell to.   I am now
More fiery of resolve.   This night I've wiped
The milk of kindred mercy from my lips.
I shall be kin to nought but my good blade,
And that when the blood gilds it that flows between
Me and my cousin's land.—Who's there?

It is probable that while the author sent an early copy of his tragedy to Sir Walter Scott, out of gratitude and esteem, he did so also under the belief that a perusal of it in print would lead to a more favourable impression with regard to its representation on the stage than the manuscript had done.   The following letter was received in acknowledgment of the gift, with a few more counsels on dramatic composition:—

"Abbotsford, 27th April [1822].

"Dear Allan,—Accept my kind thanks for your little modest volume, received two days since.   I was acquainted with most of the pieces, and yet I perused them all with renewed pleasure, and especially my old friend, Sir Marma-duke, with his new face, and by the assistance of an April sun, which is at length, after many a rough blast, beginning to smile on us. The drama has, in my conception, more poetical conception and poetical expression in it than most of our modern compositions. Perhaps, indeed, it occasionally sins in the richness of poetical expression; for the language of passion, though bold and figurative, is brief and concise at the same time. But what would, in acting, be a more serious objection, is the complicated nature of the plot, which is very obscure. I hope you will make another dramatic attempt; and, in that case, I would strongly recommend that you should previously make a model or skeleton of your incidents, dividing them regularly into scenes and acts, so as to insure the dependence of one circumstance upon another, and the simplicity and union of your whole story. The common class of readers, and more especially of spectators, are thick-skulled enough, and can hardly comprehend what they see and hear, unless they are hemmed in, and guided to the sense at every turn.

"The unities of time and place have always appeared to me fopperies, so far as they require close observance of the French rules. Still, the nearer you can come to them it is always, no doubt, the better, because your action will be more probable. But the unity of action—I mean that continuity which unites every scene with the other, and makes the catastrophe the natural and probable result of all that has gone before—seems to me a critical rule, which cannot safely be dispensed with. Without such a regular deduction of incidents, men's attention becomes distracted, and the most beautiful language, if at all listened to, creates no interest, and is out of place. I would give, as an example, the suddenly entertained, and as suddenly abandoned, jealousy of Sir Marmaduke, p. 85, as a useless excrescence in the action of the drama.

"I am very much unaccustomed to offer criticism, and when I do so, it is because I believe in my soul that I am endeavouring to pluck away the weeds which hide flowers well worthy of cultivation. In your case, the richness of your language, and fertility of your imagination, are the snares against which I would warn you. If the one had been poor, and the other costive, I never would have made remarks which could never do good, while they only give pain. Did you ever read Savage's beautiful poem of the Wanderer? If not, do so, and you will see the fault which, I think, attaches to Lord Maxwell—a want of distinct precision and intelligibility about the story, which counteracts, especially with ordinary readers, the effect of beautiful and forcible diction, poetical imagery, and animated description.

"All this freedom you will excuse, I know, on the part of one who has the truest respect for the manly independence of character which rests for its support on honest industry, instead of indulging the foolish fastidiousness formerly supposed to be essential to the poetical temperament, and which has induced some men of real talents to become coxcombs— some to become sots—some to plunge themselves into want —others, into the equal miseries of dependence, merely because, forsooth, they were men of genius, and wise above the ordinary, and, I say, the manly duties of human life.

'I'd rather be a kitten and cry, Mew!'

than write the best poetry in the world, on condition of laying aside common-sense in the ordinary transactions and business of the world; and, therefore, dear Allan, I wish much the better to the muse whom you meet by the fireside in your hours of leisure, when you have played your part manfully through a day of labour. I should like to see her making those hours also a little profitable. Perhaps something of the dramatic romance, if you could hit on a good subject, and combine the scenes well, might answer. A beautiful thing, with appropriate music, scenes, &c., might be woven out of the Mermaid of Galloway.

"When there is any chance of Mr. Chantrey coming this way, I hope you will let me know; and if you come with him, so much the better. I like him as much for his manners as for his genius—

> 'He is a man without a clagg;
> His heart is frank without a flaw.'

"This is a horrible long letter for so vile a correspondent as I am. Once more, my best thanks for the little volume, and believe me yours truly,

"WALTER SCOTT.

"To Mr. Allan Cunningham,
    Eccleston Street, Pimlico."

With all due deference to so eminent and able a critic as Sir Walter Scott, we think the foregoing extracts show that Cunningham was in no small degree qualified to write for the stage, and the scenes laid before the reader would have certainly met with approbation there. However, the critic, no doubt with the best intention for the literary success of his *protégé*, perhaps went a little too far in his fault-finding, and thus unconsciously threw a wet blanket over the whole concern, as Cunningham never again attempted dramatic composition. Sensitiveness to criticism, as we saw in his brother Thomas, seems to have been a family feeling, and, while grateful for useful hints, when carried out to some extent, the hereditary independence at once took its own stand. He had still, notwithstanding this scattering of fondly cherished hopes, a hankering after the stage, and in a letter to his brother James he speaks of preparing a second edition of Sir Marmaduke, on which he had made some amendments, and expresses his gratification at finding that its reception had been so very favourable, and that his songs had obtained more notice than he had any reason to hope. The "Mermaid of Galloway," which appeared in the volume, we have already quoted, and no further allusion to it is necessary. "Richard Faulder" is a poem occupying sixteen pages; it is a tale of the Solway sea, written in three "Fyttes," and entitled "The Spectre Shallop." It is deeply interesting, and the various incidents it narrates show very considerable imagination and versifying power. Some of the songs had previously appeared, but others were new, and of no small merit. One of these is a fair rival to that of Burns bearing the same name, and has been equally popular among those whose condition it represents, and for whom it was specially intended:—

"MY NANIE O.

"Red rowes the Nith 'tween bank and brae,
  Mirk is the night and rainie O,
Though heaven and earth should mix in storm,
  I'll gang and see my Nanie O.
My Nanie O, my Nanie O;
  My kind and winsome Nanie O,
She holds my heart in love's dear bands,
  And nane can do't but Nanie O.

"In preaching time sae meek she stands,
   Sae saintlie and sae bonnie O,
I cannot get ae glimpse of grace,
   For thieving looks at Nanie O;
My Nanie O, my Nanie O;
   The world's in love with Nanie O;
That heart is hardly worth the wear
   That wadna love my Nanie O.

"My breast can scarce contain my heart,
   When dancing she moves finely O;
I guess what heaven is by her eyes,
   They sparkle sae divinely O;
My Nanie O, my Nanie O;
   The flower of Nithsdale's Nanie O;
Love looks frae 'neath her long brown hair,
   And says, I dwell with Nanie O.

"Tell not, thou star at gray daylight,
   O'er Tinwald-top sae bonnie O,
My footsteps 'mang the morning dew
   When coming frae my Nanie O;
My Nanie O, my Nanie O;
   Nane ken o' me and Nanie O;
The stars and moon may tell't aboon,
   They winna wrang my Nanie O!"

In a future note to the first half of the third stanza of this song the author says, "In the Nanie O of Allan Ramsay, these four beautiful lines will be found; and there they might have remained, had their beauty not been impaired by the presence of Lais and Leda, Jove and Danae." The reader will remember how Cunningham formerly vented his objurgations against the introduction of the names of heathen gods and goddesses into Scottish song. With regard to the last stanza he makes this note—"Tinwald-top belongs to a range of fine green hills, commencing with the uplands of Dalswinton, and ending with those of Mouswald, and lies between Dumfries and Lochmaben. Tradition says that on Tinwald-hill Robert Bruce met James Douglas as he hastened to assert his right to the crown of Scotland."

CHAPTER XIV.

PUBLISHES TWO VOLUMES OF TALES—SONG, "THE FAIRY OAK OF CORRIE-
WATER"—ANECDOTE OF CUNNINGHAM ON FAIRY MYTHOLOGY—
SONG, "LADY SELBY"—ESSAY ON BURNS AND BYRON, A CONTRAST.

DURING the same year which brought his tragedy to
the light he published, in two volumes, "Traditional
Tales of the English and Scottish Peasantry," which
had all, with one exception, previously appeared in the
London Magazine. He had been urgently persuaded
to collect them, make such alterations as he thought
might improve them, and send them forth to the public
in a permanent form. In making the announcement
of their forthcoming publication to his brother James,
he says:—"I cannot anticipate what their success may
be, but I shall be satisfied with little, as the fire-edge
has been taken off them already, and they cannot have
the charm of novelty. In the drama I have made some
amendments, and I am pleased to find that its reception
has been so very favourable—indeed, the songs have
obtained more notice than I had any reason to hope.
. . . I am exceedingly busy in the way of my
business, and can hardly call an hour of the day my
own. I have some hopes of lessening this regular
pressure of labour, for my health' has never been very
flourishing here, and the study which my little intercourse with the Press requires increases the trouble. I

know not how my present endeavours may end, but I am labouring to insure some relaxation of bodily exertion, and my future comfort." He was no doubt the more anxious about the success of his publications as his family was increasing, London living was expensive, and for school fees alone for his three boys he was paying thirty guineas a-year.

These tales are very interestingly narrated, brimful of description, and are freely interspersed with songs of varied measure and tone. They are sixteen in all, one of them extending over three parts. Of the Scottish tales, "Ezra Peden," a Presbyterian minister, and the "Placing of a Scottish Minister," perhaps verge a little too close on exaggeration, if not caricature, but a general idea may be obtained from them of what took place in olden times in connection with the kirk. Many customs now fallen into desuetude, and some altogether forgotten are there described with the vividness of one who had been an eye-witness of all that occurred. The minister's man in those days seems to have been an important personage, and performed a work in a small way something akin to that of the pioneers of Christianity into Scotland. "He contented himself with swelling the psalm into something like melody on Sunday, visiting the sick as a forerunner of his master's approach, and pouring forth prayers and graces at burials and banquetings as long and dreary as a hill sermon. He looked on the minister as something superior to man; a being possessed by a divine spirit, and he shook his head with all its silver hairs, and uttered a gentle groan or two, during some of the more rapt and glowing passages of Ezra's sermons." Such was the minister's man in the days of old.

"The Placing of a Scottish Minister" refers undoubtedly to an ordination in Newabbey, in the Presbytery of Dumfries, when the assistance of the military required to be called in to effect the settlement. The minister was hooted, hissed, and pelted with mud, by a refractory people, who were indignant and furious because by the law of Patronage they had no voice in the choosing of their pastor. We have reason to believe that the narrative is a true description of what occurred on the occasion, and is therefore historical. Of course fictitious names are given, but the whole story is too strongly marked to be mistaken. Perhaps the most amusing and popular tale of the whole is " Elphin Irving, the Fairies' Cup-bearer." The scene is laid in a romantic vale in Annandale, and Elphin was taken away by the Fairy Queen, to be retained in her service for a term of seven years, his remuneration to be a kiss of her own sweet lips at the end of that period. His sister Phemie Irving was desirous to win him back, and one night, at a great gathering of the Fairies on Corriewater, she attempted the rescue, but failed at a certain stage of the procedure. The story bears a strong resemblance to young Tamlane, only it had a different result. It contains the following song:—

"THE FAIRY OAK OF CORRIEWATER.

" The small bird's head is under its wing,
    The deer sleeps on the grass;
  The moon comes out, and the stars shine down,
    The dew gleams like the glass:

There is no sound in the world so wide,
  Save the sound of the smitten brass,
With the merry cittern and the pipe
  Of the fairies as they pass.
But, oh! the fire maun burn and burn,
And the hour is gone, and will never return.

"The green hill cleaves, and forth, with a bound,
  Come elf and elfin steed;
The moon dives down in a golden cloud,
  The stars grow dim with dread;
But a light is running along the earth,
  So of heaven's they have no need:
O'er moor and moss with a shout they pass,
  And the word is spur and speed:
But the fire maun burn, and I maun quake,
And the hour is gone that will never come back.

"And when they came to Craigyburn-wood,
  The Queen of the fairies spoke:
'Come bind your steeds to the rushes so green,
  And dance by the haunted oak:
I found the acorn on Heshbon Hill,
  In the nook of a palmer's poke,
A thousand years since; here it grows!'
  And they danced till the greenwood shook:
But, oh! the fire, the burning fire,
The longer it burns it but blazes the higher.

"'I have won me a youth,' the elf Queen said,
  'The fairest that earth may see;
This night I have won young Elph Irving
  My cup-bearer to be.
His service lasts but for seven sweet years,
  And his wage is a kiss of me.'
And merrily, merrily, laughed the wild elves
  Round Corrie's greenwood tree:
But, oh! the fire it glows in my brain,
And the hour is gone, and comes not again.

"The Queen she has whispered a secret word,
  'Come hither, my Elphin sweet,
And bring that cup of the charmed wine,
  Thy lips and mine to weet.'
But a brown elf shouted a loud, loud shout,
  'Come, leap on your coursers fleet,
For here comes the smell of some baptized flesh,
  And the sounding of baptized feet:'
But, oh! the fire that burns, and maun burn,
For the time that is gone will never return.

"On a steed as white as the new-milked milk,
  The elf Queen leaped with a bound,
And young Elphin a stud like December snow
  'Neath him at the word he found.
But a maiden came, and her christened arms
  She linked her brother around,
And called on God, and the steed with a snort
  Sank into the gaping ground:
But the fire maun burn, and I maun quake,
And the time that is gone will no more come back.

"And she held her brother, and lo! he grew
  A wild bull waked in ire;
And she held her brother, and lo! he changed
  To a river roaring higher;
And she held her brother, and he became
  A flood of raging fire;
She shrieked and sank, and the wild elves laughed
  Till mountain rang and mire:
But, oh! the fire yet burns in my brain,
And the hour is gone, and comes not again.

"'O maiden, why waxed thy faith so faint,
  Thy spirit so slack and slaw?
Thy courage kept good till the flame waxed wud,
  Then thy might began to thaw;
Had ye kissed him with thy christened lip,
  Ye had won him frae 'mang us a.'

> Now bless the fire, the elfin fire,
>   That made thee faint and fa';
> Now bless the fire, the elfin fire,
>   The longer it burns it blazes the higher.'"

Cunningham had a strong regard for the belief in the "Fairy Folk," as it enabled him to exercise his luxuriant fancy at will. The following anecdote is told of him on the subject. "Do you believe in fairies, Mac?" he said to a Celtic acquaintance one day in the course of conversation. "Deet, I'm no ferry shure," was the characteristically cautious reply of the mountaineer; "but do you pelieve in them your nainsel, Mister Kinnikum?" "I once did," said the burly poet, "and would to God I could do so still! for the woodland and the moor have lost for me a great portion of their romance, since my faith in their existence has departed." He then quoted the following lines from Campbell's address to the Rainbow:—

> " When Science from Creation's face
>   Enchantment's veil withdraws,
> What lovely visions yield their place
>   To cold material laws !"

Another poetic piece is worth extracting from these interesting volumes. The "Selbys of Cumberland" is the most imposing of the tales, and is written at greater length and in higher language than most of the others. As the song is complete in itself, it is unnecessary to give any summary or explanation of the story, which could scarcely be done in moderate space with anything like satisfaction:—

"LADY SELBY.

" On the holly tree sat a raven black,
    And at its foot a lady fair
Sat singing of sorrow, and shedding down
    The tresses of her nut-brown hair:
And aye as that fair dame's voice awoke,
The raven broke in with a chorusing croak.

" ' The steeds they are saddled on Derwent banks;
    The banners are streaming so broad and free;
The sharp sword sits at each Selby's side,
    And all to be dyed for the love of me:
And I maun give this lily-white hand
To him who wields the wightest brand.'

" She coost her mantle of satin so fine,
    She kilted her gown of the deep-sea green,
She wound her locks round her brow and flew
    Where the swords were glimmering sharp and sheen:
As she flew, the trumpet awoke with a clang,
And the sharp blades smote, and the bow-strings sang.

" The streamlet that ran down the lonely vale,
    Aneath its banks, half seen, half hid,
Seemed melted silver—at once it came down
    From the shocking of horsemen—recking and red;
And that lady flew—and she uttered a cry,
As the riderless steeds came rushing by.

" And many have fallen—and more have fled:—
    All in a nook of the bloody ground
That lady sat by a bleeding knight,
    And strove with her fingers to staunch the wound:
Her locks, like sunbeams when summer's in pride,
She plucked and placed on his wounded side.

" And aye the sorer that lady sighed,
    The more her golden locks she drew—

> The more she prayed—the ruddy life's-blood
>   The faster and faster came trickling through:—
> On a sadder sight ne'er looked the moon,
> That o'er the green mountain came gleaming down.
>
> " He lay with his sword in the pale moonlight;
>   All mute and pale she lay at his side—
> He, sheathed in mail from brow to heel—
>   She, in her maiden bloom and pride:
> And their beds were made, and the lovers were laid,
> All under the gentle holly's shade.
>
> " May that Selby's right hand wither and rot,
>   That fails with flowers their bed to strew!
> May a foreign grave be his who doth rend
>   Away the shade of the holly bough!—
> But let them sleep by the gentle river,
> And waken in love that shall last for ever."

From the varied and humorous character of the volumes, and their being so descriptive of ancient usages and stirring events in both countries, especially in Scotland, many of the former having entirely passed away, they speedily obtained an extensive circulation, and produced a suitable remuneration to the author in pocket and in fame. This stimulated him the more for new endeavours in " fresh fields and pastures new." While thus engaged in the preparation and publication of his works he still wrote steadily for the monthly periodicals, sometimes attempting higher flights than he had previously ventured on, assuming the position of a critic, as if feeling his way for another description of literary effort which was looming in the distance.

As the following clever essay on Burns and Byron

is almost unknown, we give it *in extenso* from the *London Magazine* of August, 1824:—

"ROBERT BURNS AND LORD BYRON.

"I have seen Robert Burns laid in his grave, and I have seen George Gordon Byron borne to his. Of both I wish to speak, and my words shall be spoken with honesty and freedom. They were great, though not equal, heirs of fame. The fortunes of their birth were widely dissimilar; yet in their passions and in their genius they approached to a closer resemblance. Their careers were short and glorious, and they both perished in the summer of life, and in all the splendour of a reputation more likely to increase than diminish. One was a peasant, and the other was a peer; but Nature is a great leveller, and makes amends for the injuries of fortune by the richness of her benefactions. The genius of Burns raised him to a level with the nobles of the land; by nature, if not by birth, he was the peer of Byron. I knew one, and I have seen both. I have hearkened to words from their lips, and admired the labours of their pens, and I am now, and likely to remain, under the influence of their magic songs. They rose by the force of their genius, and they fell by the strength of their passions. One wrote from a love, and the other from a scorn of mankind; and they both sang of the emotions of their own hearts with a vehemence and an originality which few have equalled, and none surely have surpassed. But it is less my wish to draw the characters of those extraordinary men than to write what I remember of them; and I will say nothing that I know not to be true, and little but what I saw myself.

"The first time I ever saw Burns was in Nithsdale. I was then a child, but his looks and his voice cannot well be forgotten; and while I write this I behold him as distinctly as I did when I stood at my father's knee, and heard the bard repeat his 'Tam o' Shanter.' He was tall and of a manly make, his brow broad and high, and his voice varied with the character of his inimitable tale; yet through all its variations it was melody itself. He was of great personal strength, and proud too of displaying it; and I have seen him lift a load with ease which few ordinary men would have willingly undertaken.

"The first time I ever saw Byron was in the House of Lords, soon after the publication of 'Childe Harold.' He stood up in his place on the Opposition side, and made a speech on the subject of Catholic freedom. His voice was low, and I heard him but by fits; and when I say he was witty and sarcastic, I judge as much from the involuntary mirth of the benches as from what I heard with my own ears. His voice had not the full and manly melody of the voice of Burns; nor had he equal vigour of frame, nor the same open expanse of forehead. But his face was finely formed, and was impressed with a more delicate vigour than that of the peasant poet. He had a singular conformation of ear; the lower lobe, instead of being pendulous, grew down and united itself to the check, and resembled no other ear I ever saw save that of the Duke of Wellington. His bust by Thorvaldsen is feeble and mean; the painting of Phillips is more noble and much more like. Of Burns I have never seen aught but a very uninspired resemblance; and I regret it the more because he had a look worthy of the happiest effort of art—a look beaming with poetry and eloquence.

"The last time I saw Burns in life was on his return from the Brow-well of Solway. He had been ailing all spring, and summer had come without bringing health with it; he had gone away very ill and he returned worse. He was brought back, I think, in a covered spring cart, and when he alighted at the foot of the street in which he lived, he could scarce stand upright. He reached his own door with difficulty. He stooped much, and there was a visible change in his looks. Some may think it not unimportant to know, that he was at that time dressed in a blue coat, with the undress nankeen pantaloons of the volunteers, and that his neck, which was inclining to be short, caused his hat to turn up behind, in the manner of the shovel hats of the Episcopal clergy. Truth obliges me to add, that he was not fastidious about his dress; and that an officer, curious in the personal appearance and equipments of his company, might have questioned the military nicety of the poet's clothes and arms. But his colonel was a maker of rhyme, and the poet had to display more charity for his commander's verse than the other had to exercise when he inspected the clothing and arms of the careless bard.

"From the day of his return home till the hour of his untimely death, Dumfries was like a besieged palace. It was known he was dying, and the anxiety, not of the rich and the learned only, but of the mechanics and peasants, exceeded all belief. Wherever two or three people stood together, their talk was of Burns and of him alone; they spoke of his history—of his person—of his works—of his family—of his fame, and of his untimely and approaching fate, with a warmth and an enthusiasm which will ever endear Dumfries to my remembrance. All that he said or was saying—the opinions of the physicians (and Maxwell was a kind and a skilful one), were eagerly caught up and reported from street to street, and from house to house.

"His good humour was unruffled, and his wit never forsook him. He looked to one of his fellow-volunteers with a smile, as he stood by the bedside with his eyes wet, and

said, 'John, don't let the awkward squad fire over me.' He
was aware that death was dealing with him. He asked a
lady who visited him, more in sincerity than in mirth, what
commands she had for the other world. He repressed with a
smile the hopes of his friends, and told them he had lived
long enough. As his life drew near a close, the eager yet
decorous solicitude of his fellow-townsmen increased. He
was an exciseman, it is true—a name odious, from many
associations, to his countrymen—but he did his duty meekly
and kindly, and repressed rather than encouraged the desire
of some of his companions to push the law with severity. He
was therefore much beloved, and the passion of the Scotch
for poetry made them regard him as little lower than a spirit
inspired. It is the practice of the young men of Dumfries
to meet in the street during the hours of remission from
labour, and by these means I had an opportunity of witnessing the general solicitude of all ranks and of all ages. His
differences with them in some important points of human
speculation and religious hope were forgotten and forgiven;
they thought only of his genius—of the delight his compositions had diffused—and they talked of him with the same
awe as of some departing spirit, whose voice was to gladden
them no more. His last moments have never been described. He had laid his head quietly on the pillow, awaiting
dissolution, when his attendant reminded him of his medicine,
and held the cup to his lip. He started suddenly up, drained
the cup at a gulp, threw his hands before him like a man
about to swim, and sprang from head to foot of the bed—
fell with his face down, and expired with a groan.

"Of the dying moments of Byron we have no minute nor
very distinct account. He perished in a foreign land among
barbarians or aliens, and he seems to have been without the
aid of a determined physician, whose firmness or persuasion

might have vanquished his obstinacy. His aversion to bleeding was an infirmity which he shared with many better regulated minds; for it is no uncommon belief that the first touch of the lancet will charm away the approach of death, and those who believe this are willing to reserve so decisive a spell for a more momentous occasion. He had parted with his native land in no ordinary bitterness of spirit; and his domestic infelicity had rendered his future peace of mind hopeless. This was aggravated from time to time by the tales or the intrusion of travellers, by reports injurious to his character, and by the eager and vulgar avidity with which idle stories were circulated, which exhibited him in weakness or in folly. But there is every reason to believe that long before his untimely death his native land was as bright as ever in his fancy, and that his anger conceived against the many for the sins of the few had subsided, or was subsiding.

"Of Scotland, and of his Scottish origin, he has boasted in more than one place of his poetry; he is proud to remember the land of his mother, and to sing that he is half a Scot by birth, and a whole one in his heart. Of his great rival in popularity, Sir Walter Scott, he speaks with kindness; and the compliment he has paid him has been earned by the unchangeable admiration of the other. Scott has ever spoken of Byron as he has lately written, and all those who know him will feel that this consistency is characteristic. I must, however, confess his forgiveness of Mr. Jeffrey was an unlooked-for and unexpected piece of humility and loving-kindness, and, as a Scotchman, I am rather willing to regard it as a presage of early death, and to conclude that the poet was 'fey,' and forgave his arch enemy in the spirit of the dying Highlander—'Weel, weel, I forgive him; but God confound you, my twa sons, Duncan and Gilbert, if you forgive him.' The criticism with which the *Edinburgh Review* welcomed the first flight which Byron's Muse took would have crushed and broken any spirit less dauntless than his own; and for a long while he entertained the horror of a reviewer which a bird of song feels for the presence of the raven. But they smoothed his spirit down, first by submission and then by idolatry, and his pride must have been equal to that which made the angels fall, if it had refused to be soothed by the obeisance of a reviewer.

"One never forgets, if he should happen to forgive, an insult or an injury offered in youth—it grows with the growth, and strengthens with the strength, and I may reasonably doubt the truth of the poet's song when he sings of his dear Jeffrey. The news of his death came upon London like an earthquake; and the common multitude are ignorant of literature, and destitute of feeling for the higher flights of poetry, yet they consented to feel by faith, and believed that one of the brightest lights in the firmament of poesy was extinguished for ever. With literary men a sense of the public misfortune was mingled, perhaps, with a sense that a giant was removed from their way; and that they had room now to break a lance with an equal, without the fear of being overthrown by fiery impetuosity and colossal strength. The world of literature is now resigned to lower, but, perhaps, not less presumptuous poetic spirits. But among those who feared him, or envied him, or loved him, there are none who sorrow not for the national loss, and grieve not that Byron fell so soon, and on a foreign shore.

"When Burns died I was then young, but I was not insensible that a mind of no common strength had passed from among us. He had caught my fancy and touched my heart with his songs and his poems. I went to see him laid out for the grave; several elderly people were with me. He lay in a plain unadorned coffin, with a linen sheet drawn over his face, and on the bed, and around the body, herbs and flowers were thickly strewn, according to the usage of the country. He was wasted somewhat by long illness; but death had not increased the swarthy hue of his face, which was uncommonly dark and deeply marked—the dying pang was visible in the lower part, but his broad and open brow was pale and serene, and around it his sable hair lay in masses, slightly touched with gray, and inclining more to a wave than a curl. The room where he lay was plain and neat, and the simplicity of the poet's humble dwelling pressed the presence of death more closely on the heart than if his bier had been embellished by vanity and covered with the blazonry of high ancestry and rank. We stood and gazed on him in silence for the space of several minutes—we went, and others succeeded us—there was no jostling and crushing, though the crowd was great—man followed man as patiently and orderly as if all had been a matter of mutual under-standing—not a question was asked—not a whisper was heard. This was several days after his death. It is the custom of Scotland to 'wake' the body—not with wild howlings and wilder songs, and much waste of strong drink, like our mercurial neighbours, but in silence or in prayer—superstition says it is unsonsie to leave a corpse alone; and it is never left. I know not who watched by the body of Burns—much it was my wish to share in the honour—but my extreme youth would have made such a request seem foolish, and its rejection would have been sure.

"I am to speak the feelings of another people, and of the customs of a higher rank, when I speak of laying out the body of Byron for the grave. It was announced from time to time that he was to be exhibited in state, and the progress of the embellishments of the poet's bier was recorded in the pages of a hundred publications. They were at length completed, and to separate the curiosity of the poor from the admiration of the rich, the latter were indulged with tickets of admission, and a day was set apart for them to go and wonder over the decked room and the emblazoned bier. Peers and peeresses, priests, poets, and politicians, came in gilded chariots and in hired hacks to gaze upon the splendour of the funeral preparations, and to see in how rich and how vain a shroud the body of the immortal had been hid. Those idle trappings in which rank seeks to mark its altitude above the vulgar belonged to the state of the peer rather than to the state of the poet; genius required no such attractions; and all this magnificence served only to divide our regard with the man whose inspired tongue was now silenced for ever. Who cared for Lord Byron the peer, and the Privy Councillor, with his coronet, and his long descent from princes on one side, and from heroes on both—and who did not care for George Gordon Byron the poet, who has charmed us, and will charm our descendants, with his deep and impassioned verse! The homage was rendered to genius, not surely to rank—for lord can be stamped on any clay, but inspiration can only be impressed on the finest metal.

"Of the day on which the multitude were admitted I know not in what terms to speak—I never surely saw so strange a mixture of silent sorrow and of fierce and intractable curiosity. If one looked on the poet's splendid coffin with deep awe, and thought of the gifted spirit which had lately animated the cold remains, others regarded the whole as a pageant or a show, got up for the amusement of the idle and the careless, and criticized the arrangements in the spirit of those who wish to be rewarded for their time, and who consider that all they condescend to visit should be according to their own taste. There was a crushing, a trampling, and an impatience, as rude and as fierce as ever I witnessed at a theatre; and words of incivility were bandied about, and questions asked with such determination to be answered, that the very mutes, whose business was silence and repose, were obliged to interfere with tongue and hand between the visitors and the dust of the poet. In contemplation of such a scene, some of the trappings which were there on the first day were removed on the second, and this suspicion of the good sense and decorum of the multitude called forth many expressions of displeasure, as remarkable for their warmth as their propriety of language. By five o'clock the people were all ejected—man and woman—and the rich coffin bore tokens of the touch of hundreds of eager fingers, many of which had not been overclean.

"The multitude who accompanied Burns to the grave went step by step with the chief mourners; they might amount to ten or twelve thousand. Not a word was heard; and, though all could not be near, and many could not see, when the earth closed on their darling poet for ever, there was no rude impatience shown, no fierce disappointment expressed. It was an impressive and mournful sight to see men of all ranks and persuasions and opinions mingling as brothers, and stepping side by side down the streets of Dumfries, with the remains of him who had sang of their loves, and joys, and domestic endearments, with a truth and a tenderness which none perhaps have seen equalled. I could, indeed, have wished the military part of the procession away—for he was buried with military honours—because I am one of those who love simplicity in all that regards genius. The scarlet and gold—the banners displayed—the measured step, and the military array, with the sound of martial instruments of music, had no share in increasing the solemnity of the burial scene; and I had no connexion with the poet. I looked on it then, and I consider it now, as an idle ostentation, a piece of superfluous state, which might have been spared, more especially, as his neglected, and traduced, and insulted spirit had experienced no kindness in the body from those lofty people who are now proud of being numbered as his coevals and countrymen.

His fate has been a reproach to Scotland. But the reproach comes with an ill grace from England. When we can forget Butler's fate—Otway's loaf—Dryden's old age, and Chatterton's poison-cup, we may think that we stand alone in the iniquity of neglecting pre-eminent genius. I found myself at the brink of the poet's grave, into which he was about to descend for ever—there was a pause among the mourners, as if loath to part with his remains; and when he was at last lowered, and the first shovelful of earth sounded on his coffin-lid, I looked up and saw tears on many cheeks where tears were not usual. The volunteers justified the fears of their comrade by three ragged and straggling volleys. The earth was heaped up, the green sod laid over him, and the multitude stood gazing on the grave for some minutes' space, and then melted silently away. The day was a fine one, the sky was almost without a cloud, and not a drop of rain fell from dawn to twilight. I notice this—not from my concurrence in the common superstition—that 'happy is the corpse which the rain rains on,' but to confute a pious fraud of a religious magazine, which made heaven express its wrath at the interment of a profane poet in thunder, in lightning, and in rain. I know not who wrote the story, and I wish not to know; but its utter falsehood thousands an attest. It is one proof out of many, how divine wrath is found by dishonest zeal in a common commotion of the elements, and that men, whose profession is godliness and truth, will look in the face of heaven and tell a deliberate lie.

"A few select friends and admirers followed Lord Byron to his grave—his coronet was borne before him, and there were many indications of his rank; but, save the assembled multitude, no indications of his genius. In conformity to a singular practice of the great, a long train of their empty carriages followed the mourning coaches—mocking the dead with idle state, and impeding the honester sympathy of the crowd with barren pageantry. Where were the owners of those machines of sloth and luxury—where were the men of rank among whose dark pedigrees Lord Byron threw the light of his genius, and lent the brows of nobility a halo to which they were strangers? Where were the great Whigs? Where were the illustrious Tories? Could a mere difference in matters of human belief keep those fastidious persons away? But, above all, where were the friends with whom wedlock had united him? On his desolate corpse no wife looked, and no child shed a tear. I have no wish to set myself up as a judge in domestic infelicities, and I am willing to believe they were separated in such a way as rendered reconciliation hopeless; but who could stand and look on his pale manly face, and his dark locks which early sorrows were making thin and grey, without feeling that, gifted as he was, with a soul above the mark of other men, his domestic misfortunes called for our pity as surely as his genius called for our admiration. When the career of Burns was closed, I saw another sight—a weeping widow and four helpless sons; they came into the streets in their mournings, and public sympathy was awakened afresh. I shall never forget the looks of his boys, and the compassion which they excited. The poet's life had not been without errors, and such errors, too, as a wife is slow in forgiving; but he was honoured then, and is honoured now, by the unalienable affection of his wife, and the world repays her prudence and her love by its regard and esteem.

"Burns, with all his errors in faith and in practice, was laid in hallowed earth, in the churchyard of the town where he resided. No one thought of closing the church gates against his body because of the freedom of his poetry and the carelessness of his life. And why was not Byron laid among the illustrious men of England in Westminster Abbey? Is there a poet in all the Poet's Corner who has better right to that distinction? Why was the door closed against him, and opened to the carcases of thousands without merit and without name? Look round the walls, and on the floor over which you tread, and behold them encumbered and inscribed with memorials of the mean, and the sordid, and the impure, as well as of the virtuous and the great. Why did the Dean of Westminster refuse admission to such an heir of fame as Byron? If he had no claim to lie within the consecrated precincts of the Abbey, he has no right to lie in consecrated ground at all. There is no doubt that the pious fee for sepulture would have been paid—and it is not a small one. Hail! to the Church of England, if her piety is stronger than her avarice."

Well written, Allan Cunningham! though probably a little too democratic in your estimate of the two poets; but your admiration of the peasant bard was certainly natural, as belonging to your own dear land, and it might, perhaps, be said in this case, as said in others, that "the light which led astray was light from heaven."

CHAPTER XV.

PREPARATION OF HIS COLLECTION OF SONGS—ITS PUBLICATION—"A WET SHEET AND A FLOWING SEA"—ACCOUNT OF THE WORK—TRIBUTE TO THE MEMORY OF HIS FATHER—"LAMENT FOR LORD MAXWELL"—ANECDOTE REGARDING AN ENGLISH DRAGOON AND A NITHSDALE WIDOW—CRITICISMS—"THE POET'S BRIDAL-DAY SONG"—LETTER TO THE ETTRICK SHEPHERD.

THE intensity with which Cunningham prosecuted his efforts in gathering materials for his newly projected work, "The Songs of Scotland," ancient and modern, was greater than he had ever devoted to any of his previous publications. Sir Walter Scott had greatly encouraged him in the undertaking, promising to give him what assistance he could, and other distinguished persons had done the same. He applied everywhere for old songs, or scraps of such, as he thought he might make up defects himself where the original was awanting. In addition to his own knowledge of Scottish songstry, he knew several sources to which he could successfully apply with regard both to the songs and their elucidations. One of these sources was the M'Ghies of Quarrelwood, Kirkmahoe, at whose fireside he had heard so many ballads lilted, and stories told. Writing in the fullest exuberance of spirits to his friend George on the subject, he says:—"I have been writing and printing books since I saw you, and am become a great man in rhyme and prose. Even lords and knights—mighty men whom the King delighteth to honour—have praised me and my offspring. I mean the offspring of my pen, for I have other progeny, of which more anon. I am at present busied in a Collection of Scottish Songs, which I expect will be a very curious work, and my friend Sir Walter Scott has already given me some valuable assistance, and has promised me more. I have no doubt but your father and you could give me some aid in this; half verses, or whole songs—anything will be welcome, and the older the better." We have reason to know that he was largely assisted from this source, as the whole family were musical, and had store of songs almost without end.

It is interesting to note in the same letter of application for ballad lore, his humorous reference to the times of old, indicating the friendly and familiar terms on which he stood with the M'Ghies:—"I often think of the auld clachan, and the glorious evenings I had among the M'Ghies—even now, I behold all the family faces laughing around the fire, and honest Thomas M'Ghie is entering at the partition door, with the same face with which he sought to associate the eighth psalm with its kindred tune of 'Martyrs.' My wife is now sitting beside me, and seems pleased that I am writing to her old acquaintance. She looks little the worse—sometimes I think, and oftentimes say, *better*, than when you saw her in Dumfries, and four boys and a little girl, with my sister Mina, and a 'servan' hizzie,' a southron quean, make up the amount of my household. Three of the boys are great in the mystery of Latin and English grammar, and are promising chiels; but when can either your sons or mine hope to rival the genius of their fathers?" Such snatches as these, which were never intended to be seen by any other than the person to whom they were addressed, afford glimpses of the real nature of the writer, which a more formal document could not have done, intended to see the light.

While making this preparation he had also formed an intention of *regenerating*, as he called it, "Mark Macrabin the Cameronian," which had appeared by instalments in *Blackwood*, and of sending it into the world in two volumes, as, at first, it had been exceedingly popular. He cherished a great respect for the name and the followers of Cameron, and he was desirous to honour them a little, so far as he could, as he thought they deserved it. But in the meantime, while intentions like this are cropping up, the main thing in hand is his Collection of Songs, for which he is to receive from the publisher £200, and as to his other works, author and publisher are to share the profits between them. This had hitherto been his greatest undertaking, and he braced himself manfully for its performance. The pecuniary remuneration was encouraging, where thirty guineas a-year had to be paid for the school fees of three boys alone, besides their food and clothing, and the parents kept in hodden-grey and calimanco for week-days, and broadcloth and silk for the Sunday.

After much research, and correspondence, and study, and many late hours, no other time being afforded, the work was completed, and appeared in four volumes, under the title of "The Songs of Scotland, Ancient and

Modern; with an Introduction and Notes, Historical and Critical, and Characters of the Lyric Poets." The songs were numerous, the best known having been taken from reliable authorities, and the rest from where they could be found. A number of them came from the author's own pen. One of the best, a nautical one, is the following, which has obtained a wide-spread popularity to the present day:—

"A WET SHEET AND A FLOWING SEA.

> " A wet sheet and a flowing sea,
>   A wind that follows fast,
> And fills the white and rustling sail,
>   And bends the gallant mast;
> And bends the gallant mast, my boys,
>   While, like the eagle free,
> Away the good ship flies, and leaves
>   Old England on the lee.
>
> " O for a soft and gentle wind!
>   I heard a fair one cry;
> But give to me the snoring breeze,
>   And white waves heaving high;
> And white waves heaving high, my boys,
>   The good ship tight and free—
> The world of waters is our home,
>   And merry men are we.
>
> " There's tempest in yon horned moon,
>   And lightning in yon cloud:
> And hark the music, mariners!
>   The wind is piping loud;
> The wind is piping loud, my boys,
>   The lightning flashing free—
> While the hollow oak our palace is,
>   Our heritage the sea."

The greater part of the first volume contains a long, elaborate, and eloquent disquisition on Scottish Song, which is gratefully dedicated to Sir Walter Scott, for the friendship he had shown and the assistance given in the preparation of the work. It bears evidence of extensive research and intimate acquaintance with the subject, as well as a keen discrimination of what constitutes the merits and beauties of our national lyrics. Unlike Burns, Cunningham was musical, and could not resist chanting what he read in poetry. From his boyhood he was accustomed to put an air to every song he met with, and, curiously enough, he afterwards found that the air which the words suggested to himself generally corresponded with the proper tune. Burns lamented his deficiency in this respect, and was indebted to others to test the musical cadence of his songs, but with Hogg and Cunningham there was the greatest advantage, as they could throw their whole soul into the melody, and so make words and music harmonize.

With regard to the coarseness of the songs which were popular before the Reformation, they were, he acknowledges, such as would now " cover us with blushes," and greatly required amendment, but still, he says:—" It would be unjust to pretend that this age has more virtue, and unwise to suppose that it has a better taste, than the age which produced some of our brightest spirits. The songs which our great-grandmothers sang, we may suppose, gave them delight; and we are not to imagine that their delight came from a source less pure than our own. They were a simple people, who had not learned the art of attiring sensuality in a dainty dress, nor had they found it necessary to live like us in 'decencies for ever. Yet I am no admirer of that primitive mode of expression which speaks bluntly out the hopes and wishes of the heart, nor am I sure that this direct and undisguised style is half so mischievous to innocence and youth as those strains which, like the angler's hook, hide their sting among painted plumes." The Reformation produced a change upon the character of our lyrics by the ecclesiastical discipline exercised, but that change could scarcely be said for the better, as the lewdness or profanity became mixed up with seeming holiness, under a very thin disguise.

It seems strange what a reverse has taken place in public opinion with regard to poetizing and song-making. Those gifted with the "faculty divine" are now held in the highest estimation, laurels are placed upon their brow while they live, and monuments are erected to their memory when they die. In olden times it was far otherwise, as those who practised the art of versifying were considered godless and profane. So late as the commencement of the present century this was generally the opinion of the lower and uneducated classes, and we believe that there are still some at the present day who hold that ballad-making has some connection with the " Black Art." The reader will, perhaps, remember how in the extract we gave, " Winning the Harvest Kirn," Ronald Rodan was stigmatized by some of the elder harvesters as a "sang-singin' haspin' o' a callant," and was advised to "give up the gowk-craft o' ballad-making' as being a godless trade. To be sure, this advice was given by those who belonged to a religious denomination who were generally considered very strict in their morals, who would not listen to any music save that of psalms, hymns, and spiritual songs, and who would not tolerate dancing on any account, as John the Baptist had lost his head through the bewitching performance of a dancing damsel; but, besides these, a great body of worthies entertained a similar conviction. Cunningham was right when he said that "Poesy languished beneath the austere or morose enthusiasm of some of our fondest reformers; and as many of our voluntary minstrels were silenced from a sense of the unholiness of rhyme, or from the admonitions of the Kirk, minstrelsy became less popular than formerly."

The disquisition, which, as we have said, is very elaborate, and often highly eloquent, is followed up with short biographical notices of thirty-three song-makers, from King James the Fifth downwards, which are full of interest, and oftentimes throw light upon events and ballads which had heretofore been obscure. In one of these, that of the Rev. James Muirhead, D.D., minister of Urr, and author of "Bess the Gawkie," the only song he wrote, Cunningham pays the following tribute to the memory of his father, who was intimate with the reverend divine:—"That he was the author, I had the assurance of my father—a man fond of collecting all that was characteristic of his country, and possessing a warm heart, lively fancy, benevolent humour, and pleasant happy wit. To him I owe much of the information concerning song which I have scattered over these pages; and in all things connected with our national poetry, so much did our tastes correspond, that in recording my own opinions I am only expressing his. A poet himself, and a correct judge of poetry, his curiosity was unbounded and his reading extensive. He had by heart many a historical and romantic tradition, many a moving story, and many an ancient verse; and so well did he feel, and so happily could he utter what others wrote, that I have heard many say they would rather hear him read songs than others sing them." This is very creditable to filial affection for a parent who had now been five-and-twenty years in the grave.

The work contained upwards of five hundred songs, many of them accompanied with variations obtained from several sources named, and criticisms as to their genuine or spurious character. The following pathetic one is by Cunningham himself:—

"LAMENT FOR LORD MAXWELL.

"Green Nithsdale, make moan, for the leaf's in the fa',
The lealest of thy warriors are drapping awa';
The rose in thy bonnet, that flourished sae and shone,
Has lost its white hue, and is faded and gone!
Our matrons may sigh, our hoary men may wail,—
He's gone, and gone for ever, the Lord of Nithsdale!
But those that smile sweetest may have sadness ere lang,
And some may mix sorrow with their merry, merry sang.

"Full loud was the merriment among us ladies a',
They sang in the parlour and danced in the ha'—
O Jamie's coming hame again to chase the Whigs awa':
But they cannot wipe the tears now so fast as they fa'.
Our lady does do nought now but wipe aye her een—
Her heart's like to burst the gold lace of her gown;
Men silent gaze upon her, and minstrels make a wail—
O dool for our brave warrior, the Lord of Nithsdale!

   " Wae to thee, proud Preston!—to hissing and to hate
   I give thee: may wailings be frequent at thy gate!
   Now eighty summer shoots of the forest I have seen,
   To the saddle laps in blude i' the battle I hae been,
   But I never kenn'd o' dool till I kenn'd it yestreen.
   O that I were laid where the sods are growing green!—
   I tint half mysel' when my gude lord I did tine—
   He's a drop of dearest blood in this auld heart of mine.

   " By the bud of the leaf, by the rising of the flower,—
   By the song of the birds, where some stream tottles o'er,
   I'll wander awa' there, and big a wee bit bower,
   To hap my gray head frae the drap and the shower;
   And there I'll sit and moan till I sink into the grave,
   For Nithsdale's bonnie Lord—aye the bravest of the brave!—
   O that I lay but with him, in sorrow and in pine,
   And the steel that harms his gentle neck wad do as much for mine!"

To this song is added the following note:—" The hero of this song, the Earl of Nithsdale, was taken prisoner, along with Viscount Kenmure and many other noblemen, at Preston in Lancashire, and sentenced to be beheaded. His Countess, a lady of great presence of mind, contrived and accomplished his escape from the Tower. Her fortitude, her patience, and her intrepidity are yet unrivalled in the history of female heroism. A letter from the Countess, containing a lively and circumstantial account of the Earl's escape, is in Terregles House in Nithsdale, dated from Rome in the year 1718. From the woman's cloak and hood, in which the Earl was disguised, the Jacobites of the north formed a new token of cognizance—all the ladies who favoured the Stuarts wore ' Nithsdales,' till fashion got the better of political love."

An original interesting anecdote inserted in the notes is the following:—"At the close of the last rebellion a party of the Duke of Cumberland's dragoons passed through Nithsdale; they called at a lone house, where a widow lived, and demanded refreshments. She brought them milk; and her son, a youth of sixteen, prepared kale and butter—this, she said, was all her store. One of the party inquired how she lived on such slender means. 'I live,' she said, 'on my cow, my kale-yard, and on the blessing of God.' He went and killed the cow, destroyed her kale, and continued his march. The poor woman died of a broken heart, and her son wandered away from the inquiry of friends and the reach of compassion. It happened, afterwards, in the continental war, when the British army had gained a great victory, that the soldiers were seated on the ground, making merry with wine, and relating their exploits. 'All this is nothing,' cried a dragoon, 'to what I once did in Scotland. I starved a witch in Nithsdale; I drank her milk, I killed her cow, destroyed her kale-yard, and left her to live upon God—and I daresay He had enough ado with her.' 'And don't you rue it?' exclaimed a soldier, starting up—'don't you rue it?' 'Rue what?' said the ruffian; 'what would you have me rue? she's dead and damned, and there's an end of her.' 'Then, by my God!' said the other, 'that woman was my mother—draw your sword—draw.' They fought on the spot, and while the Scottish soldier passed his sword through his body, and turned him over in the pangs of death, he said, 'Had you but said you rued it, God should have punished you, not I.'"

The work on its appearance received quite an ovation by the general public, and the leading magazines and reviews spoke highly in its praise. Professor Wilson noticed it favourably in his "*Noctes Ambrosianæ*" in *Blackwood*, in the following terms:—"A very good collection indeed. Allan is occasionally very happy in his ardent eulogy of his country's lyrical genius, and one loves to hear a man speaking about a species of poetry in which he has himself excelled." He then sings, to the delight of the Ettrick Shepherd, Allan's song, "*My ain Countrie.*" In a subsequent *Noctes* he reverts to the subject, and says,—"Some of Allan's songs too, James, will not die." To which the Shepherd is represented as replying, "Mony a bonny thing dies— some o' them, as it would seem, o' theirsels, without onything hurtin' them, and as if even gracious Nature, though loth, consented to allow them to fade awa' into forgetfulness; and that will happen, I fear, to no a few o' baith his breathin's and mine. But that ithers will surveeve, even though Time should try to ding them down wi' his heel into the yird, as sure am I as that the night sky shall never lose a single star till the morning o' the Day o' Doom." The *Edinburgh Review* characterized it as "an exceedingly agreeable, and to Scotchmen, in many respects, a very delightful publication," while it gave the author credit for the "warm and unaffected interest he took in the subject— his deep feeling of the beauties of his favourite pieces, and the natural eloquence of the commendations by which he sought to raise kindred emotions in the minds of his readers."

The only hostile critic we have met with is Motherwell, who, instead of cherishing a fellow-feeling for a brother poet, seems to have borne Cunningham a grudge, as he speaks of his works in very disparaging terms. With regard to the " Remains of Nithsdale and Galloway Song" he says—"There never was, and never can be, a more barefaced attempt made to gull ignorance than this work exhibits." And again, "More pretension, downright impudence, and literary falsehood, seldom or ever came into conjunction." Why, he forgets that he himself palmed off as an ancient ballad one of his own invention! Then of "The Songs of Scotland" he thus writes:—"Nor did it ever occur that the celebrity these compositions had obtained would be sapped, and the spot they occupied in the affections and memories of the people be supplanted by their editor substituting his own compositions in their place, decorated with their names, and built upon their sentiments and incident. To his pious care had been willingly consigned the sacred duty of gathering, as it were, the sacred and unurned ashes of departed and of anonymous genius, and of placing these in a shrine at which posterity might bend the knee, without any of those misgivings regarding the genuineness of the reliques it contained which paralyze the devotion of the heart. Never, however, was it contemplated that these reliques should be made part and parcel of what the collector should find himself in the vein of fabricating in a similar style; nor was it asked of him to repair the devastations time and accident had wrought on these, with any interpolation, amendment, or addition, however appropriate, well-imagined, or cleverly executed. It is an unholy and abhorrent lust which thus ransacks the tomb, and rifles the calm beauty of the mute and unresisting dead." No doubt Cunningham saw this criticism, as it appeared the year following his publication, but he outlived the depreciation of his brother poet, lauded, and supported, and encouraged, as he was, by those whose opinion was accepted in the world of letters.

A clever critic in *Blackwood*, reviewing "The Literary Souvenir" for 1824, edited by Alaric A. Watts, and to which Cunningham had contributed, says:—"Perhaps the best poem in the volume is by Allan Cunningham. It is full of real warm human feeling of the best kind, finely tinged, too, with the spirit of poetry, and written in language almost Wordsworthian. Cunningham is far superior to Clare, and we say so without meaning any disrespect to that most amiable and interesting person. He has all, or nearly all, that is good in Hogg— not a twentieth part of the Shepherd's atrocities—and much merit peculiarly his own, which, according to our notion of poetry, is beyond the reach of the Ettrick bard." The piece here referred to is the following, which Mrs. Hemans, in a letter to the author, characterized as "beautiful," as introducing her to his wife, and making her feel greatly interested in the subject of the song:—

"THE POET'S BRIDAL-DAY SONG.

"O! my love's like the steadfast sun,
   Or streams that deepen as they run;
   Nor hoary hairs, nor forty years,
   Nor moments between sighs and tears,

Nor nights of thought, nor days of pain,
Nor dreams of glory dream'd in vain;
Nor mirth, nor sweetest song that flows
To sober joys and soften woes,
Can make my heart or fancy flee,
One moment, my sweet wife, from thee.

"Even when I muse I see thee sit
In maiden bloom and matron wit;
Fair, gentle as when first I sued,
Ye seem, but of sedater mood;
Yet my heart leaps as fond for thee,
As, when beneath Arbigland tree,
We stay'd and woo'd, and thought the moon
Set on the sea an hour too soon,
Or linger'd 'mid the falling dew,
When looks were fond and words were few.

"Though I see smiling at thy feet,
Five sons and ae fair daughter sweet,
And time and care and birthtime woes
Have dimm'd thine eye and touch'd thy rose,
To thee, and thoughts of thee, belong
Whate'er charms me in tale or song.
When words descend like dews unsought,
With gleams of deep enthusiast thought,
And fancy in her heaven flies free,
They come, my love, they come from thee.

"O, when more thought we gave, of old,
To silver, than some give to gold,
'Twas sweet to sit and ponder o'er,
How we should deck our humble bower:
'Twas sweet to pull, in hope, with thee,
The golden fruit of Fortune's tree;
And sweeter still to choose and twine
A garland for that brow of thine:
A song-wreath which may grace my Jean,
While rivers flow, and woods grow green.

> "At times there come, as come there ought,
> Grave moments of sedater thought,
> When Fortune frowns, nor lends our night
> One gleam of her inconstant light;
> And Hope, that decks the peasant's bower,
> Shines like a rainbow through the shower;
> O then I see, while seated nigh,
> A mother's heart shine in thine eye,
> And proud resolve and purpose meek,
> Speak of thee more than words can speak.
> I think this wedded wife of mine,
> The best of all things not divine."

After a long silence, his friendship with the Ettrick Shepherd was renewed, on the occasion of a nephew of the latter going up to London to engage in business, and who was confided to his good offices and attention. To this application he returned the following interesting letter, in which he recalls the scene long ago enacted on Queensberry hill, when but a lad not out of his teens:—

"27 Lower Belgrave Place, 16th Feb., 1826.

"My dear James,—It required neither present of book, nor friend, nor the recalling of old scenes, to render your letter a most welcome one. You are often present to my heart and fancy, for your genius and your friendliness have secured you a place in both. Your nephew is a fine, modest, and intelligent young man, and is welcome to my house for his own sake, as well as yours. Your 'Queen Hynde,' for which I thank you, carries all the vivid marks of your own peculiar cast of genius about her. One of your happiest little things is in the 'Souvenir' of this season—it is pure and graceful, warm, yet delicate; and we have nought in the language to compare to it, save everybody's 'Kilmeny.' In other portions of verse you have been equalled, and sometimes surpassed; but in scenes which are neither on earth, nor wholly removed from it—where fairies speak, and spiritual creatures act, you are unrivalled.

"Often do I tread back to the foot of old Queensberry, and meet you coming down amid the sunny rain, as I did some twenty years ago. The little sodded shealing where we sought shelter rises now on my sight—your two dogs (old Hector was one) lie at my feet—the 'Lay of the Last Minstrel' is in my hand, for the first time, to be twice read over after sermon, as it really was—poetry, nothing but poetry, is our talk, and we are supremely happy. Or, I shift the scene to Thornhill, and there whilst the glass goes round, and lads sing and lasses laugh, we turn our discourse on verse, and still our speech is song. Poetry had then a charm for us which has since been sobered down. I can now meditate without the fever of enthusiasm upon me; yet age to youth owes all or most of its happiest aspirations, and contents itself with purifying and completing the conceptions of early years.

"We are both a little older and a little graver than we were some twenty years ago, when we walked in glory and joy on the side of old Queensberry. My wife is much the same in look as when you saw her in Edinburgh—at least so she seems to me, though five boys and a girl might admonish me of change—of loss of bloom, and abatement of activity. My eldest boy resolves to be a soldier; he is a clever scholar, and his head has been turned by Cæsar. My second and third boys are in Christ's School, and are distinguished in their classes; they climb to the head, and keep their places. The other three are at their mother's knee at home, and have a strong capacity for mirth and mischief.

" I have not destroyed my Scottish poem. I mean to remodel it, and infuse into it something more of the spark of living life. But my pen has of late strayed into the regions of prose. Poetry is too much its own reward; and one cannot always write for a barren smile, and a thriftless clap on the back. We must live, and the white bread and the brown can only be obtained by gross payment. There is no poet and a wife and six children fed now like the prophet Elijah—they are more likely to be devoured by critics than fed by ravens. I cannot hope that Heaven will feed me and mine while I sing. So farewell to song for a season.

" My brother's (Thomas) want of success has surprised me too. He had a fair share of talent; and had he cultivated his powers with care, and given himself fair play, his fate would have been different. But he sees nature rather through a curious medium than with the tasteful eye of poetry, and must please himself with the praise of those who love singular and curious things. I have said nothing all this while of Mrs. Hogg, though I might have said much, for we hear her household prudence and her good taste often commended. She comes, too, from our own dear country—a good assurance of a capital wife and an affectionate mother. My wife and I send her and you most friendly greetings. We hope to see you both in London during the summer.

" You have written much, but you must write more yet. What say you to a series of poems in your own original way, steeped from end to end in Scottish superstition, but purified from its grossness by your own genius and taste? Do write me soon. I have a good mind to come and commence Shepherd beside you, and aid you in making a yearly pastoral *Gazette* in prose and verse for our *ain* native Lowlands. The thing would take.

" The evil news of Sir Walter's losses came on me like an

invasion.   I wish the world would do for him now what it will do in fifty years, when it puts up his statue in every town—let it lay out its money in purchasing an estate, as the nation did to the Duke of Wellington, and money could never be laid out more worthily.—I remain, dear James, your very faithful friend,

" ALLAN CUNNINGHAM."

CHAPTER XVI.

THE "FARMER'S INGLE" IN THE OLDEN TIME—PUBLICATION OF
"PAUL JONES"—CRITICISMS—REFLECTIONS ON DIBDIN—ROMANCE
OF "SIR MICHAEL SCOTT"—CORRESPONDENCE WITH MR. RITCHIE
OF THE "SCOTSMAN"—CADETSHIPS FOR HIS TWO SONS OBTAINED—
LETTER TO HIS MOTHER.

THE following graphic description of a "Farmer's
Ingle," from his Essay on Scottish Songs, is deserving
of quotation, not only for its faithfulness of detail, but
also because it is among the things connected with the
rural population which have passed away, succeeded,
shall we say, by a more heartsome and genial fireside?
We fear not.

"But I have no need to seek in trysts, or meetings of
love, or labour, or merriment, for the sources of song: a
farmer or a cottager's winter fireside has often been the
theme and always the theatre of lyric verse; and the
grey hairs of the old, and the glad looks of the young, may
aptly prefigure out the two great divisions of Scottish song—
the songs of true love, and those of domestic and humble joy.
The character of the people is written in their habitations.
Their kitchens, or rather halls, warm, roomy, and well
replenished with furniture, fashioned less for show than
service, are filled on all sides with the visible materials and
tokens of pastoral and agricultural wealth and abundance.
The fire is on the floor; and around it, during the winter
evenings, the family and dependents are disposed, each in

their own department, one side of the house being occupied by the men, the other resigned to the mistress and her maidens; while beyond the fire, in the space between the hearth-stone and the wall, are placed those travelling mendicants who wander from house to house, and find subsistence as they can, and lodgings where they may. The carved oaken settle, or couch, on which the farmer rests, has descended to him through a number of generations; it is embossed with rude thistles, and rough with family names; and the year in which it was made has been considered an era worthy of the accompaniment of a motto from Scripture. On a shelf above him, and within the reach of his hand, are some of the works of the literary worthies of his country: the history, the romance, the sermon, the poem, and the song, all well used, and bearing token of many hands."

Well, this is very faithful in its descriptiveness, but it is not complete. There is another party in the household that must not be overlooked:—

" Around the farmer's dame the evening has gathered all her maidens whom daylight has scattered about in various employments, and the needle and the wheel are busied alike in the labours required for the barn and the hall. Above and beside them, all that the hand and the wheel have twined from fleece and flax is hung in good order: the wardrobe is filled with barn-bleached linen, the dairy shelves with cheese for daily use, and with some made of a richer curd to grace the table at the harvest-feast. Over all, and among them, the prudent and experienced mistress, while she manages some small personal matter of her own, casts from time to time her eye, and explains or advises, or hearkens to the song, which is not silent amid the lapses of conversation. In households such as these, which present an image of our more primitive days, all the delights, and joys, and pursuits of our forefathers find refuge ; to them Hallow-eve is welcome with its mysteries, the new-year with its mirth, the summer with its sheep-shearing feast, and the close of harvest with its dancing and its revelry. The increasing refinement and opulence of the community has made this rather a picture of times past than times present; and the labour of a score of wheels, each with its presiding maiden, is far outdone by a single turn or two of a machine. The once slow and simple process of bleaching, by laving water on the linen as it lay extended on the rivulet bank, is accomplished now by a chemical process ; and the curious art of dyeing wool, and the admixture of various colours to form those parti-coloured garments so much in fashion among us of old, have been entrusted to more scientific hands. Out of these, and many other employments, now disused and formed into separate callings, song extracted its images and illustrations, and caught the hue and the pressure of passing manners, and customs, and pursuits."

Cabinet pictures, like these of the olden times, are like those paintings of the "old masters" which every one admires, and this the more as they recede into the past. Cunningham had an observant eye and a graphic pen; and one special value of his writings is, that he has preserved from oblivion Scottish habits and manners in which he was a participator, but which have now in great measure passed away.

Encouraged by the success which attended the " Songs of Scotland " he applied the pen with unremitting ardour, and in the following year he brought out three volumes of a romance, under the title of "Paul Jones," the subject being a sea-tale of the Solway. It had been eagerly waited for after its announcement by the publishers, and when it appeared it was rapidly read. The story is told very much in the Scottish vernacular, the various actors being mostly of the Doric type, and, consequently, using that language. The work, considered from a certain point of view, is exceedingly interesting, and many of its parts are brilliantly captivating; but regarded in another light, it is disappointing as a tale of the sea. The hero is captain of a ship and a pirate, and yet there is an absence of nautical phraseology, even when he is brought prominently forward in his professional capacity. Now, every one knows that of all men sailors in their conversation are the most addicted to the use of terms and phrases connected with their every-day life. Cunningham knew nothing of the sea and the phraseology common among those who live upon it, and yet he produces a story with the natural characteristics awanting, which could not pass without observation.

On the above ground the critics were not satisfied, and some of them did not hesitate to express an adverse opinion, though still attributing the fire of genius to the author. Professor Wilson, one of Cunningham's best friends and warmest admirers, declared it "a failure." In one of his *Noctes* he thus freely gives his criticism in an imaginary conversation with the Ettrick Shepherd:—
"'Paul Jones', James, is an amusing, an interesting tale, and will, on the whole, raise Allan's reputation. It is full of talent. . . There are many bold and striking incidents and situations; many picturesque and

poetical descriptions; many reflections that prove Allan to be a man of an original, vigorous, and sagacious mind. . . The character of Paul Jones is, I think, well conceived. . . Much may be forgiven in imperfect execution to good conception. In bringing out his *idea* of Paul Jones, Allan has not always been successful. The delineation wants light and shade; there is frequent daubing — great — or rather gross exaggeration, and continual effort after effort, that sometimes totally defeats its purpose. On the whole, the interest we take in the pirate is but languid. But the worst part of the book is that it smells not of the ocean. There are waves—waves—waves—but never a sea,—battle on battle, but as of ships in a painted panorama, where we feel all is the mockery of imitation—and almost grudge our half-crown at each new ineffectual broadside and crash of music from a band borrowed from a caravan of wild beasts. . . It is evident that Allan never made a cruise in a frigate or line-of-battle ship. He dares not venture on nautical terms—and the land-lubber is in every line. Paul Jones's face is perpetually painted with blood and gunpowder, and his person spattered with brains. . . A most decided failure. Still a bright genius like Allan's will show itself through darkest ignorance—and there are occasional flashes of war poetry in 'Paul Jones.' But he manœuvres a ship as if she were on wheels, and on dry land. All the glory of the power of sail and helm is gone. . . But I shall probably review Allan's book. You will see my opinion of its beauties and its deformities at great length in an early number. The article shall be a good one, depend on't—perhaps a leading one; for it is delightful to have to do with a man of genius." This is a wonderful criticism, being a pull with the one hand and a push with the other, but yet it was entirely friendly and candid, and as the Ettrick Shepherd interjected, its chief merits and its chief defects were "geyan equally balanced."

However strongly severe some of the above criticism might be, Cunningham took no umbrage at the writer of it, as we shall afterwards see, but addressed him in the most respectful and grateful terms for kind counsel and assistance. He knew the fault-finding was sincere, and was as much addressed to the author for his benefit, as to the general readers of a distinguished magazine, who looked to him for a candid review of the literature of the day. We might have now passed on sufficiently satisfied with the foregoing from such a master of criticism, but we wish to be *honest* in our remarks with regard to "Honest Allan." All the critics were not of the Professor Wilson type, though with less ability for making a judicious use of the pen. Cunningham, when writing his discursive and eloquent essay on Scottish Song, had, in a moment of forgetfulness, come into collision with Dibdin and his Sea-Songs. Dibdin was not a sailor, any more than was Cunningham, and knew little, if anything, of the sea—yet he produced sea-songs which were universally hailed with applause, and which continue to be appreciated at the present day.

A reviewer in *Blackwood*, a year before Wilson's criticism appeared, falls terribly foul of "Paul Jones," and the famous song by the same author which every one admired, "A wet sheet and a flowing sea," and gave vent to a little venom in his remarks, but followed it up by saying:—"Allan Cunningham knows our admiration of his genius, and our affection for himself; but the above diatribe dribbled from our pen, as we thought of the most absurd contempt with which in his 'Scottish Songs,' he chooses to treat Dibdin. Dibdin knew nothing, forsooth, of ships, or sailors' souls, or sailors' slang! Thank you for that, Allan—we owe you one. Why the devil, then, are his thousand and one songs the delight of the whole British navy, and constantly heard below decks in every man-of-war afloat. The shepherds of the sea must be allowed to understand their own pastoral doric, and Charles Dibdin is their Allan Ramsay." It was unfortunate that Cunningham laid himself open to such reprehension. But whatever the critics might say in their high ideal of what was right and proper to have been written on the subject, the general public, of course those who were not sea-faring, hailed the work with gratulation from the variety of topics introduced, the graphic, descriptions of its interesting scenes, the pathetic passages with which it abounded, the humour with which it sparkled, the legendary lore which assumed form and substance, and the weird narrations introduced from time to time. Author and publisher had good reason to be satisfied with the general reception which "Paul Jones" received, notwithstanding the severity of some of the criticisms, as it enhanced the fame of the one, and the pecuniary profits of both. As a specimen of the style of the work, we may extract the following, a duel scene:—

" While Cargill spoke, Lord Thomas retired a little way, and Paul, freeing himself from the impediment which the Cameronian had placed between them, confronted him at some six paces distance. They looked at each other—they raised their right hands at once, and the double flash and knell made the horses rear and the riders start. Down sprang Cargill, with all the alacrity of youth, and threw himself in between them. They both stood—their pistols reeking at touch-hole and muzzle. When the smoke flew up, Dalveen dashed his pistol on the ground, and exclaimed, ' Eternal God! have I missed him?' He pulled another pistol from his pocket, another was ready cocked in the hand of Paul; but Cargill exclaimed, ' Ye shall find each other's hearts through me; and seizing the right hand of the young nobleman, held him with as sure a grip as an iron manacle.

" All the castle windows flew open, and down the stair came Lady Phemie; while, with her antique silks rustling like frozen sails in a stiff gale, Lady Emeline tottered after her, crying, ' Oh! run between them!—hold them!—bind them!—are they hurt? ' Oh that I have lived to see this!' And, with eyes glistening with tears, she threw herself on the neck of her grandson, and said, ' This pride, this unhappy pride of thine will be the ruin of thy house.' She grew deadly pale as she spoke, and added faintly, ' He's wounded, mortally wounded!—there's blood flowing down his neck. All gathered round, while Lord Thomas smiled, and said, ' A drop, a mere drop—a touch, only a touch;' and putting his hand to the place, he drew it back covered with blood. His colour changed when he looked on it. ' Stand back, madam,' he said, ' and keep back your devout asses; this

blood must be atoned for;—back, I say, else by the fiends
I'll fire my pistol upon you.'   He cocked a pistol as he spoke,
and, stepping up to Paul, said, 'Back to back—step two
paces away—wheel round and fire—that's the Dalveen
distance.'   And each of them had taken a step, when Lady
Phemie caught her cousin in her arms, and sought to master
his right hand;—he snatched ·the pistol with his left, and
held it out. ·His better nature overcame him—he flung the
weapon from his hand with such velocity that it sung through
the air, and went off as it struck the bough of a large
chestnut tree."

So industrious was he with the pen during the hours
of evening, or rather we should say of night, after the
labours of the studio were over, that, in addition to
several magazine articles, towards the end of the follow-
year he produced, in three volumes, the mythical romance
of "Sir Michael Scott."   This work was not so successful
as the preceding ones, the public mind not being disposed to follow him into the region of the supernatural.
Still it had a satisfactory run.   A writer in the *Edinburgh Review* noticing it, along with some of the other
works by the author, says:—" In 'Paul Jones' alone there
is ten times as much glittering description, ingenious
metaphor, and emphatic dialogue, as would enliven and
embellish a work of twice the size; while, from the
extravagance of the fictions, and the utter want of
coherence in the events, or human interest in the
characters, it becomes tedious by the very redundance
of its stimulating qualities.   'Sir Michael Scott,' again—
being all magic, witchcraft, and mystery—is absolutely
illegible; and much excellent invention and powerful

fancy is thrown away on delineations which revolt by their monstrous exaggerations, and tire out by their long-continued soaring above the region of human sympathy. Mr. Cunningham is, beyond all question, a man of genius, taste, and feeling." Now, we do not object to the character of this criticism, for, though somewhat adverse, it appears to be candid, and we insert it with the same candid intent.

The publication of the romance of "Sir Michael Scott" brought the author into contact and friendship with a very excellent and distinguished man, Mr. Ritchie of the *Scotsman* newspaper, Edinburgh. Mr. Ritchie had very kindly noticed "Paul Jones" in one of his reviews, and Cunningham addressed to him the following letter, with a copy of his new work:—

27 Lower Belgrave Place, November, 1827.

"Dear Sir,—In laying on your table my romance of 'Sir Michael Scott,' I beg you will feel that I do so with no levity of nature like an author of full-grown reputation, who can cry to a critic, 'There, do your worst!' On the contrary, I feel that my works must be read with much indulgence, and even sympathy. In the present instance, I may fairly claim the protection of all true Scotsmen, because my romance is the offspring of the poetic beliefs and popular superstitions of *our* native land; and though I may not have made out my conception of the work to my full satisfaction, I may, nevertheless, expect some approbation, from the attempt to gather into one narrative, some of the marvellous legends and romantic beliefs of our Border.

"My chief object was to write a kind of Gothic Romance— a sort of British Arabian Nights, in which I could let loose my imagination among the mythological beings of fireside tales and old superstitions. As a work of imagination, therefore, it ought to be examined; and as the narrative, marvellous though it be, is guided by the visible landmarks of legendary belief, I hope it will be found to be in its nature as true to national lore as shadow is to substance.

"Your kind and liberal notice of my 'Paul Jones' I ascribed in some measure to your sympathy for my lot in life, and to your feeling that one who contested the matter so long and so hardly with fortune, deserved some little indulgence. My whole life has hitherto been spent in working for my daily bread, and my pen ekes out what the day fails to provide. My education, too, is such as I have gathered from books and from mankind, and I am consequently without the advantages of learning which embellishes genius by refining the taste and informing the judgment. I mention these things from no desire to soften the justice of criticism, but I own with some hope of awakening its mercy. I am sensible that, in general, my works, hasty and imperfect as they are, have met with some attention and much indulgence, and through them I have obtained some of the best friendships of my life. The editor of the *Scotsman* I consider as one of the number, and have much pleasure in saying I am his faithful friend and admirer,

"ALLAN CUNNINGHAM.

"To the Editor of the *Scotsman*."

His two eldest sons were now growing up towards manhood's estate, and he was naturally anxious to place them in positions where they might creditably discharge their portion of duty in the administration of affairs in the great and busy world. They were already good scholars, being, as we were told, great in the mysteries of Latin, Grammar, and Geography, and even Mathematics, if we remember aright; and, like every aspiring father, he wished them to aspire also, and gain for themselves a name among their fellow-men. For this purpose they had received a superior education— for this purpose he had toiled early and late, by chisel and pen, but, like Job of old, his way sometimes seemed "hedged in." However, he trusted to Providence, and worked and wrote with all his might, in the confidence that something suitable would arise, and that a rift in the sky would show the blue beyond. He believed firmly in the maxim, and strenuously acted upon it, that "Heaven helps those who help themselves," and he was not disappointed, as the following extract from Lockhart's " Life of Sir Walter Scott" will show :—

"Breakfasting one morning with Allan Cunningham, and commending one of his publications, Scott looked round the table, and said, 'What are you going to make of all these boys, Allan?' 'I ask that question often at my own heart,' said Allan, 'and I cannot answer it.' 'What does the eldest point to?' 'The callant would fain be a soldier, Sir Walter, and I have a half promise of a commission in the king's army for him, but I wish rather he could go to India, for there the pay is a maintenance, and one does not need interest at every step to get on.' Scott dropped the subject, but went an hour afterwards to Lord Melville (who was then President of the Board of Control), and begged a cadetship for young Cunningham. Lord Melville promised to inquire if he had one at his disposal, in which case he would gladly serve the son of honest Allan; but the point being thus left doubtful, Scott, meeting Mr. John Loch, one of the East India Directors, at dinner the same evening at Lord Stafford's, applied to him, and received an immediate assent. On reaching home at night, he found a note from Lord Melville intimating that he had inquired, and was happy in complying with his request. Next morning Sir Walter appeared at Sir Francis Chantrey's breakfast table, and greeted the sculptor (who is a brother of the angle) with, ' I suppose it has sometimes happened to you to catch one trout (which was all you thought of) with the fly and another with the bobber. I have done so, and I think I shall land them both. Don't you think Cunningham would like very well to have cadetships for two of those fine lads?' 'To be sure he would,' said Chantrey, 'and if you'll secure the commissions, I'll make the outfit easy.' Great was the joy in Allan's household on this double good news; but I should add that, before the thing was done, he had to thank another bene-factor. Lord Melville, after all, went out of the Board of Control before he had been able to fulfil his promise. But his successor, Lord Ellenborough, on hearing the circum-stances of the case, desired Cunningham to set his mind at rest; and both his young men are now prospering in the Indian service."

One may well conceive the flood of sunshine which irradiated 27 Belgrave Place, sending a thrill of joy through the heart of father and mother, when the glad-some appointment of the cadetships was intimated, and the outfits promised to be "made easy" by the great sculptor. Of course, such an affectionate son as Cun-ningham was not long in informing his mother of the happy tidings, desiring her blessing on his boys:—

"27 Belgrave Place, 16th August, 1828.

"My beloved Mother,—We were all much affected by your very kind and touching letter. We are now all well in health, and sad at heart at times, but the duties of the world must be done, and I have my share. You know that we have got cadetships for your two grandsons, and that they are preparing themselves for their situations. They will both go and receive your blessing before they sail. I hope you are well in health, and comfortable in all respects. Mina, I know and feel, will love and reverence you, and Jean, I am sure, will leave nothing deficient.

"I am very busy with my pen just now, making a little book, the most beautiful thing outwardly you ever saw. I hope it will also be good inwardly, for I have ministers of the gospel, and ministers of state, and poets, and lords, and ladies of high degree, among my contributors. I am a person of some importance, you observe, my dear mother. My wife joins me in love. I remain your ever affectionate son,

"Allan Cunningham.

"Mrs. Cunningham."

CHAPTER XVII.

PUBLICATION OF THE "ANNIVERSARY"—EXTRACTS FROM THE VOLUME—CORRESPONDENCE ON THE SUBJECT WITH PROFESSOR WILSON AND MR. RITCHIE OF THE "SCOTSMAN."

THE work alluded to in the foregoing letter to his mother was the "Anniversary" for 1829, an Annual he had undertaken to edit, at the desire of the publishers, and also to procure the necessary matter from among his literary acquaintances and friends. He wrought hard to make it a success, as it was a new field for operation, and he admirably succeeded. Some of the ablest pens willingly supported him. There was then considerable rivalry in that class of "entertainment for the million," and he exerted himself the more that he might not fail in the undertaking. He was aspiring to fame, and here was an opportunity for "making a spoon or spoiling a horn." He had literary friends on whom he thought he could count for assistance, and his applications were responded to in the most kindly manner.

The volume appeared in due time, with green cloth boards and gilt edges. It consisted of 336 pages, contained 60 pieces of poetry and prose, and was illustrated with 20 steel engravings by some of the most eminent artists. Among the most notable of the contributors were, Southey the Poet-Laureate, Professor Wilson, Lockhart, Montgomery, Hogg, Pringle, Croker, " Barry

Cornwall," Edward Irving, and Miss Strickland. Cunningham himself furnished seven pieces. For want of space various articles of merit were omitted, and the names of the authors of several valuable contributions were withheld for reasons satisfactory to the editor.

Of the poetry in the volume the best was that contributed by Southey and Wilson. The former sent a long poetic epistle in eulogy of Cunningham, and three inscriptions for the Caledonian Canal. From the "Epistle" we quote the following passage as illustrative of its nature. The Laureate has been in London, and, sick of city life, leaves it and returns home, glad once more to breathe the pure air of heaven, and revel amidst the beauties of rural scenery. Like a bird escaped from its cage after long confinement, he seems as if he could not spread his wings widely enough, soar highly enough, and carol joyously enough:—

"EPISTLE TO ALLAN CUNNINGHAM.

.   .   .   .

"Oh! not for all that London might bestow,
Would I renounce the genial influences
And thoughts, and feelings to be found where'er
We breathe beneath the open sky, and see
Earth's liberal bosom. Judge, then, from thyself,
Allan, true child of Scotland; thou who art
So oft in spirit on thy native hills,
And yonder Solway shores; a poet thou,
Judge from thyself how strong the ties which bind
A poet to his home, when, making thus
Large recompense for all that, haply, else
Might seem perversely or unkindly done,
Fortune hath set his happy habitacle
Among the ancient hills, near mountain streams

And lakes pellucid; in a land sublime
And lovely as those regions of romance,
Where his young fancy in its day-dreams roamed,
Expatiating in forests wild and wide,
Loegrian, or of dearest Fairy-land."

But the contribution above all, which Cunningham regarded as the gem of his book, was "Edderline's Dream," by Professor Wilson. The poem is too long to be extracted *in extenso*, though it was intended as only the first canto of a larger work ; but no more of it was ever produced by the author. The following opening lines will convey some idea of the writer's style:—

"EDDERLINE'S DREAM.

"First Canto.

"Castle-Oban is lost in the darkness of night,
    For the moon is swept from the starless heaven,
    And the latest line of lowering light
    That lingered on the stormy even,
    A dim-seen line, half cloud, half wave,
    Hath sunk into the weltering grave.
    Castle-Oban is dark without and within,
    And downwards to the fearful din,
    Where Ocean, with his thunder-shocks,
    Stuns the green foundation rocks,
    Through the grim abyss that mocks his eye
    Oft hath the eerie watchman sent
    A shuddering look, a shivering sigh,
    From the edge of the howling battlement!

"Therein is a lonesome room,
    Undisturbed as some old tomb
    That, built within a forest glen,
    Far from feet of living men,
    And sheltered by its black pine-trees,

From sound of rivers, lochs, and seas,
Flings back its archèd gateway tall,
At times to some great funeral.
Noiseless as a central cell
In the bosom of a mountain,
Where the fairy people dwell,
By the cold and sunless fountain!

" Breathless as the holy shrine
When the voice of psalms is shed!
And there upon her stately bed,
While her raven locks recline
O'er an arm more pure than snow,
Motionless beneath her head,—
And through her large, fair eyelids shine
Shadowy dreams that come and go,
By too deep bliss disquieted,—
There sleeps in love and beauty's glow,
The high-born Lady Edderline.

" Lo! the lamp's wan fitful light,
Glide, gliding round the golden rim!
Restored to life, now glancing bright,
Now just expiring, faint and dim,
Like a spirit loth to die,
Contending with its destiny.
All dark! a momentary veil
Is o'er the sleeper! now a pale
Uncertain beauty glimmers faint,
And now the calm face of the saint
With every feature reappears,
Celestial in unconscious tears!
Another gleam! how sweet the while,
Those pictured faces on the wall
Through the midnight silence smile;
Shades of fair ones in the aisle,
Vaulted the castle cliffs below,
To nothing mouldered, one and all,
Ages long ago!

. " From her pillow, as if driven
  By an unseen demon's hand
  Disturbing the repose of heaven,
  Hath fallen her head! The long black hair,
  From the fillet's silken band,
  In dishevelled masses riven,
  Is streaming downwards to the floor.

. . . .

" Eager to speak—but in terror mute,
  With chainèd breath and snow-soft foot,
  The gentle maid whom that lady loves,
  Like a gleam of light through the darkness moves,
  And leaning o'er her rosy breath,
  Listens in tears—for sleep—or death!
  Then touches with a kiss her breast—
  'O, Lady, this is ghastly rest!
  Awake, awake! for Jesus' sake!'
  Far in her soul a thousand sighs
  Are madly struggling to get free.

. . . .

" So gently as a shepherd lifts,
  From a wreath of drifted snow,
  A lamb, that vainly on a rock,
  Up among the mountain clefts,
  Bleats unto the heedless flocks
  Sunwards feeding far below,
  Even so gently Edith takes
  The sighing dreamer to her breast,
  Loving kisses soft and meek
  Breathing o'er bosom, brow, and cheek,
  For their own fair, delightful sakes,
  And lays her lovely limbs at rest;
  When, stirring like the wondrous flower
  That blossoms at the midnight hour,
  And only then—the Lady wakes!"

The "Anniversary" succeeded beyond the expectations of its most sanguine friends, and surpassed in literary and artistic ability its formidable rival the "Keepsake," of which it had been so much in dread.   Indeed, it had the reputation of excelling all its competitors in poetry, a compliment of which the editor was very proud.   Six thousand copies were sold before the day of publication! Any man, even of the largest experience in this line of literature, might well be proud of such a public appreciation of his labours, and especially after such difficulties as he had to contend with.   Accordingly, this success acted as a strong stimulus for the future, and we find him flirting with a new love ere he is off with the old.   Next year's "Anniversary" is already before him, and he is determined to excel himself if possible. He has enlisted several writers of distinction, such as Lockhart, and Southey, and Edward Irving.   He is not quite sure of Wordsworth, but he means to try him; and thus taking time by the forelock, he resolves to gain a march upon his rival the " Keepsake."   There is one above all others he lays siege to, who has done him such eminent service in the present, with his delightful " Edderline's Dream," and so the following letter is despatched to Edinburgh to Professor Wilson:—

" 27 Lower Belgrave Place, 11th September, 1828.

"My dear Friend,—I have cut and cleared away right and left, and opened a space for your very beautiful poem, and now it will appear at full length, as it rightly deserves. Will you have the goodness to say your will to the proof as quickly as possible, and let me have it again, for the printer pushes me sorely.

" You have indeed done me a great and lasting kindness. You have aided me, I trust effectually, in establishing my *Annual* book, and enabled me to create a little income for my family. My life has been one continued struggle to maintain my independence and support wife and children, and I have, when the labour of the day closed, endeavoured to use the little talent which my country allows me to possess as easily and as profitably as I can. The pen thus adds a little to the profit of the chisel, and I keep head above water, and on occasion take the middle of the causeway with an independent step.

" There is another matter about which I know not how to speak; and now I think on't, I had better speak out bluntly at once. My means are but moderate; and having engaged to produce the literature of the volume for a certain sum, the variety of the articles has caused no small expenditure. I cannot, therefore, say that I can pay you for 'Edderline's Dream;' but I beg you will allow me to lay twenty pounds aside by way of token or remembrance, to be paid in any way you may desire, into some friend's hand here, or re-mitted by post to Edinburgh. I am ashamed to offer so small a sum for a work which I admire so much; but what Burns said to the Muse, I may with equal propriety say to you—

' Ye ken—ye ken
That strong necessity supreme is
'Mang sons of men.'

" Now, may I venture to look to you for eight or ten pages for my next volume on the same kind of terms? I shall, with half-a-dozen assurances of the aid of the leading men of genius, be able to negotiate more effectually with the proprietor; for, when he sees that Sir Walter Scott, Professor Wilson, Mr. Southey, Mr. Lockhart, and one or two more, are resolved to support me, he will comprehend that the speculation will be profitable, and close with me accordingly. Do, I beg and entreat of you, agree to this, and say so when you write.

" Forgive all this forwardness and earnestness, and believe me to be your faithful servant and admirer,

" ALLAN CUNNINGHAM."

The following letter was also sent to Mr. Ritchie of the *Scotsman :—*

" 27 Belgrave Place, 20th Oct., 1828.

" My dear Friend,—I send for your acceptance my little embellished book, the 'Anniversary.' It is externally gaudy enough; internally there are graver and better things, with some of which I hope you will be much pleased. On the whole, I believe the book will be a successful one, and opposed as I have been by superior talents and superior wealth, I may be thankful that I can hold my head up as high as I do. The 'Keepsake' purchased authors and bribed lords at a prodigious expense, and when I commenced my work I found many of the mighty of the realms of genius arrayed against me, and a large proportion of the peerage. I have lived forty-three years in the world, and wish to live longer, without the clap-of-hand of the great, and I shall be glad if my book proves that there are men who write well without the advantage of coronets. I must make one exception. Lord F. Leveson Gower was exceedingly kind. Should this thing succeed, I shall add by it £250 a-year to my little income. Help me with your approbation, my dear friend.

"Our friend Miss Mitford has been here, and much have we talked of you, and many kind compliments did she charge me to send you. My wife and she became as intimate as two breast bones, and both being frank and jolly, weel-faured roundabout dames, they were well matched. Much they spoke and whispered about you and me. I wish we had had you with us, we should have

'Gien ae nicht's discharge to care.'

"I am also charged with an apology to you from James Montgomery for some abrupt interview he had with you. He seems very anxious to stand well with you, and I hope if aught happened unpleasant then it is forgotten now.

"I am busy with plans of new books, for my mind is never idle, and I have information upon many things which I wish to tell to the world. Can you inform me where I can find any satisfactory account of Jameson the painter, called the Scottish Vandyke, and any information respecting his works which can be depended on? What do you think of his portraits compared with his times? He is one of our earliest painters, island-born, and I wish to do him as much honour as he deserves, and no more. I remember a little about him in Stark's 'Picture of Edinburgh.' I have some notion of writing the Lives of the British Painters, on the plan of Johnson's 'Lives of the Poets.' I am full of information on the subject, have notions of my own in keeping with the nature of the art, and I think a couple of volumes would not be unwelcome from one who has no theory to support, and who will write with full freedom and spirit. I speak thus openly to you, my dear friend, because I know you wish me well, and rejoice in my success. Indeed, you have helped me not a little.

T

"I could say much more, but I have said enough to interest you, and more than enough, if my little book is not worthy of your friendly notice. Indeed, I have had hard measures dealt me by critics generally, the *Scotsman* and one or two others forming exceptions. They make no allowances for my want of time and skill, and seem to expect as clear and polished narratives from my pen as they receive from men of talent and education too. If they would try me as they have tried other rustic writers by their peers, I should not object. My wife joins me in esteem.—I am, my dear friend, yours most truly,

"ALLAN CUNNINGHAM.

"William Ritchie, Esq.,
"59 George Square, Edinburgh."

Here is another letter to the Professor:—

"27 Lower Belgrave Place, 7th November, 1828.

"My dear Friend,—My little Annual—thanks to your exquisite 'Edderline,' and your kind and seasonable words—has been very successful. It is not yet published, and cannot appear these eight days, yet we have sold 6000 copies. The booksellers all look kindly upon it; the proprietor is very much pleased with its success, and it is generally looked upon here as a work fairly rooted in public favour. The *first* large paper proof-copy ready shall be on its way to Gloucester Place before it is an hour finished. It is indeed outwardly a most splendid book.

"I must now speak of the future. The 'Keepsake' people last season bought up some of my friends, and imagined, because they had succeeded with one or two eminent ones, that my book was crushed, and would not be anything like a rival. They were too wily for me; and though I shall never be able to meet them in their own way, still I must endeavour to gather all the friends round me that I can. I have been with our mutual friend Lockhart this morning, and we have made the following arrangement, which he permits me to mention to you, in the hope you will aid me on the same conditions. He has promised me a poem, and a piece of prose to the extent of from twenty to thirty pages, for £50, and engaged to write for no other Annual. Now, if you would help me on the same terms, and to the same extent, I shall consider myself fortunate. It is true you kindly promised to aid me with whatever I liked for next year, and desired me not to talk of money. My dear friend, we make money of you, and why not make some return? I beg you will, therefore, letting bygones be bygones in money matters, join with Mr. Lockhart in this. I could give you many reasons for doing it, all of which would influence you. It is enough to say, that my rivals will come next year into the field in all the strength of talent, and rank, and fashion, and strive to bear me down. The author of ' Edderline,' and many other things equally delightful, can prevent this, and to him I look for help.

" I shall try Wordsworth in the same way. I am sure of Southey, and of Edward Irving. I shall limit my list of contributors, and make a better book generally than I have done. I am to have a painting from Wilkie, and one from Newton, and they will be more carefully engraved too.

" I am glad that your poem has met with such applause here. I have now seen all the other Annuals, and I assure you that in the best of them there is nothing that approaches in beauty to ' Edderline.' This seems to be the general opinion, and proud I am of it. —I remain, my dear friend, yours ever faithfully,

" ALLAN CUNNINGHAM."

Again, there is another letter to Professor Wilson:—

"27 Lower Belgrave Place, Nov. 19th, 1828.

"My dear Friend,—I send for your acceptance a large paper copy of my Annual, with proofs of the plates, and I send it by the mail that you may have it on your table a few days before publication. You will be glad to hear that the book has been favourably received, and the general impression seems to be, that while the 'Keepsake' is a little below expectation, the 'Anniversary' is a little above it. I am told by one in whose judgment I can wholly confide, that *our* poetry is superior, and 'Edderline's Dream' the noblest poem in *any* of the Annuals. This makes me happy; it puts us at the head of these publications.

"I took the liberty of writing a letter to you lately, and ventured to make you an offer, which I wish, in justice to my admiration of your talents, had been worthier of your merits. I hope and entreat you will think favourably of my request, and give me your aid, as powerfully as you can. If you but knew the opposition which I have to encounter, and could hear the high words of those who, with their exclusive poets, and their bands of bards, seek to bear me down, your own proud spirit and chivalrous feelings would send you quickly to my aid, and secure me from being put to shame by the highest of the island. One great poet, not a Scotch one, kindly advised me last season to think no more of literary competition with the 'Keepsake,' inasmuch as *he* dipt *his* pen exclusively for that publication. I know his poetic contributions, and fear them not when I think on 'Edderline.'

"I hope you will not think me vain, or a dreamer of un- attainable things, when I express my hope of being able, through the aid of my friends, to maintain the reputation of my book against the fame of others, though they be aided by some who might have aided me. Should you decline—which I hope in God you will not—the offer which I lately made, I shall still depend upon your assistance, which you had the goodness to promise. Another such poem as 'Elderline' would make my fortune, and if I could obtain it by May or June it would be in excellent time.

"If you would wish a copy or two of the book to give away, I shall be happy to place them at your disposal.—I remain, my dear friend, your faithful servant,

"ALLAN CUNNINGHAM."

The following is despatched to Mr. Ritchie on the same subject:—

"27 Lower Belgrave Place, 22nd Nov., 1828.

"My dear Friend,—I thank you most sincerely for your friendly criticism and your friendly letter. I am sensible of the value of both, and I hope I shall ever retain your good opinion both as a man and an author. You will find our dear friend Miss Mitford at 'Three-Mile-Cross, Reading.' I have in some sort prepared her to expect a commencement of your chivalrous correspondence. She is indeed a most delightful lady, and I hope some time to have the pleasure of seeing you both under my roof.

"I am, you may be assured, much pleased with your niece's good opinion. I always set down such things to the discernment of the fair party, and in this feeling I request the favour of her name, that I may think of it when I have my poetic pen in my hand, and a pleasant old Scotch air in my head. That we shall all meet in your *gude* town there can be no manner of doubt, for if I *be to the fore* Scotland shall see me before the harvest shoots over. This I have sworn as well as said.

"You will be glad to hear that my little Annual promises to be very successful, and that it has *now* the reputation of excelling all its competitors in poetry. This seems to be the universal opinion here, and I am very proud of it. In truth, the 'Keepsake' is below expectation, and mine is above it. Great names do not always produce great works, and so it has happened in this case. If the 'Keepsake' sells 25,000 copies, then it will have expended £11,000; if it sells 16,000 copies only, and that is the number printed, the expense cannot be near that sum. But round numbers sound well, and the public ear is gratified by swaggering accounts of lords hired, and large sums expended. For myself I go quietly on, minding no one's boast, making the best book I am able to do.

"I am much pleased that you approve of my new undertaking, and equally pleased with your sound and sensible advice. There will be ten engravings, eight on wood, and two on steel, in each volume, examples of the genius of the various artists, and in the letterpress will be interwoven all the authentic anecdotes, and all the snatches of clever criticism which are the property of these gentlemen. I shall not neglect to mention of the authorities. I have made some progress in the first volume, and I hope to make a popular book. It is much wanted. Artists themselves are far too busied to write it. Besides, they would overwhelm the narrative with the jargon of the studio, and with the jaundiced notions of their own school of art. I shall do the best I can.

"Of our friend of Oxford I have not heard for some time. There is so much indolence coupled with so much talent in him that I sometimes fear for his success in life. To sit and indulge in delightful speculations is very well if you start up and carry them into instant practice; but our friend is a splendid theorist; his practice is yet to come. He is certainly a right good fellow as ever trod the earth.

"My wife unites in good wishes for you and for Mrs. Ritchie, and all in whom you have an interest. I shall be most happy to hear from you when your inclination and leisure serve. I am, my dear friend, yours most truly,

"ALLAN CUNNINGHAM.

"William Ritchie, Esq.,
"59 George Square, Edinburgh."

The same subject draws forth another letter to the Professor:—

"27 Lower Belgrave Place, 12th Dec., 1828.

"My dear Friend,—I enclose you some lines for your friend's paper, and am truly glad of any opportunity of obliging you. I like Mr. Bell's *Journal* much. He understands, I see, what poetry is; a thing not common among critics. If there is anything else you wish me to do, say so. I have not the heart to refuse you anything.

"I was much pleased with your kind assurances respecting my next year's volume. Mr. Lockhart said he would write to you, and I hope you will unite with him and Mr. Irving in contributing for me alone. As I have been disappointed in Wordsworth, I hope you will allow me to add £25 of his £50 to the £50 I already promised. The other I intend for Mr. Lockhart. This, after all, looks like picking your pocket, for such is the rage for Annuals at present that a poet so eminent as you are may command terms. I ought, perhaps, to be satisfied with the kind assurances you have given and not be over greedy.

"One word about Wordsworth.   In his last letter to me he said that Alaric Watts had a prior claim.   'Only,' quoth he, 'Watts says I go about depreciating other Annuals out of regard for the "Keepsake." This is untrue. I only said, 'as the "Keepsake" paid poets best, it would be the best work.' This is not depreciating! He advised me, before he knew who were to be my contributors, not to think of rivalry in literature with the 'Keepsake.' Enough of a little man and a great poet.   His poetic sympathies are warm, but his heart, for any manly purpose, as cold as a December snail.   I had to-day a very pleasant, witty contribution from Theodore Hook.—I remain, my dear friend, yours faithfully,

" ALLAN CUNNINGHAM.

" *P.S.*—I have got Mr. Bell's letter and *Journals*, and shall thank him for his good opinion by sending *him* a trifle some time soon for the paper. If you think my name will do the least good to the good cause, pray insert it at either end of the poem you like.

"A. C."

CHAPTER XVIII.

PUBLISHES TWO ROMANCES, "LORD ROLDAN," AND "THE MAID OF ELVAR"—"LIVES OF THE PAINTERS, SCULPTORS, AND ARCHITECTS"—LETTERS TO MR. RITCHIE—CRITICISMS—REVISITS NITHSDALE, AND ENTERTAINED AT A BANQUET IN DUMFRIES—FAREWELL TO DALSWINTON.

NOTWITHSTANDING the great mental excitement and manual labour which attended the preparation of the "Anniversary Annual," he had other matters in hand, which speedily came forth in a three-volume romance, entitled "Lord Roldan," which does not appear, however, to have made much impression upon the public mind; and also another romance, "The Maid of Elvar," which seems to have shared the same fate. We fear that he now wrote too hurriedly, and too extensively, with the little time he had at disposal; but doubtless he had his own reasons for doing what he did. Still, like the eagle soaring to the sun, he undertook a work which required great reading, great research, and great judgment, namely, writing "The Lives of the most Eminent British Painters, Sculptors, and Architects," and which appeared in Murray's "Family Library." The work was published in six volumes, and of course embraced a great number of artists, with criticisms of their works. These were treated with very considerable taste and judgment, although some of them fell short of public expectation. The work was originally intended and advertised to be completed in three volumes, but the matter so increased that it extended to double that number.

Well, what said the critics about it? What said Professor Wilson, for whose opinion we have always had a high regard? When only two volumes had been published, he said in one of his *Noctes*:—" Allan Cunningham's Lives of the Painters—I know not which of the two volumes is best—are full of a fine and an instructed enthusiasm. He speaks boldly, but reverentially, of genius, and of men of genius; strews his narrative with many flowers of poetry; disposes and arranges his materials skilfully; and is, in few words, an admirable critic on art—an admirable biographer of artists." Nothing, surely, could be more complimentary —and coming from such a quarter. A writer in *Blackwood* said on the appearance of the first volume:—" The biographies included in this first volume are very interesting reading—the result apparently of much diligence —abounding certainly in masculine views and opinions, shrewd, terse common sense, and last, not least to our taste, in quiet graphic humour. The poet peeps out, as is fair and proper, here and there; but, on the whole, the style presents, in its subdued and compact simplicity, a striking and laudable contrast to the so often prolix and over-adorned prose of Mr. Cunningham's romances. He may depend upon it he has hit the right key here." What more encouraging and eulogistic could be said? The first volume, which contained the Lives of Hogarth, Wilson, Reynolds, and Gainsborough, was immediately transmitted to Edinburgh, with the following letter to Mr. Ritchie of the *Scotsman*:—

"27 Belgrave Place, 2nd July, 1829.

"My dear Friend,—I am your debtor for many kind words, kind deeds, and kind letters, and it is one of the chief miseries of my life that my hand has to keep up such a continual contest with the world for bread that it allows a debt of friendship to grow so enormously that it can only lessen and must never hope to pay it off. There is no man breathing, my dear Ritchie, with whom I would more gladly make a periodical interchange of social civilities than with yourself; and I hope and trust that fortune is not so much my enemy as may prevent me from yet having such an indulgence. Bairns, Bronze, Marble, Biography, and a periodical have united against me; and I can only say that if there be any passages in a little volume which, with my name on it, will along with this be put into your hands [*the letter is here mutilated*] . . . .

"To you I may plainly and openly state what I feel. This volume, then, containing the Lives of Hogarth, Wilson, Reynolds, and Gainsborough, ought to be the most popular of anything I have yet written, because I think it has more of human nature, more of shrewdness and sagacity, and more life and variety of narrative and anecdote than any of my works. I have read much, inquired much, and thought much, and formed my narratives from the best materials, and endeavoured to impress them with a popular stamp. I hope, my dear friend, that they will meet with your approbation. If I am successful now I shall have no further fear.

"My two eldest sons are preparing themselves for India, and are now in the Seminary of Addiscombe, where the eldest has distinguished himself much. My wife and the weans are also well. Why do I tell you of these matters?

Because, my dear friend, it is not my verse or my prose alone which interests you in me. Your feelings are tender [*the rest wanting*].

"William Ritchie, Esq., W.S.,
"59 George Square, Edinburgh."

When the second volume came out we have no doubt that it was also sent to the same quarter, but we cannot find any letter to that effect. However, the third volume was accompanied with the following interesting, genial, and affectionate account of how matters were going on :—

"27 Belgrave Place, 29th May, 1830.

"My dear Friend,—I send you another of my little books, and if you only think as favourably of it as of its elder brethren I shall be happy. I believe 12,000 copies are printed, for the sale of the others has risen to about 14,000, and the second edition of the second volume is already out of print. That I owe some of my popularity to the kind notices of my friends I am well aware, and who amongst them all has been so kind as yourself? This volume has been written in pain and suffering, for an evil spirit called Lumbago got on my back and punished me severely.

"When shall we see you again? When you arrive give us a day or two of your company; and to render it even more bewitching than it was, bring Mrs. Ritchie with you, and put her into the hands of my wife.

"Gray is now a married man. His wife is wealthy and weel-faured, and smiles like one of the syrens. She is a fine young creature. My wife is as plump and well-to-live as ever, and when she meets two or three North country friends sums up her estimate of happiness by saying, 'Oh, if we had but Mr. Ritchie here!' Our two eldest boys are at Addiscombe, and are distinguished mathematicians, standing at the head of their individual classes, and ranking first in *Merit* also. There can be little doubt of their success in the Engineers if they continue to study.

" I hope Mrs. Ritchie is well. As for yourself, I suppose you are never otherwise. I must include your niece also in my inquiries. I have forgot her name, but that is of no moment, as I imagine it is changed by this time. Do drop me a note now and then. In this wide world you have no one who likes you better, with the exception of the 'parties aforesaid.' I am a poor hard-working creature, toiling in marble and bronze all day, and at night dipping my pen in biographical ink to earn an honest penny for the bairns' bread. 'A blink of rest's a sweet enjoyment!' Do, therefore, thou worthiest, and pleasantest of all Scotchmen, write me a note and gladden me once more by the sight of thy well-known hand.—I am, my dear friend, yours most truly,

" ALLAN CUNNINGHAM.

" William Ritchie, Esq.
    " With Vol. 3rd of the Painters."

This is a most interesting letter in various ways—the grateful recognition of his friends in the great sale of his work—the strong desire to see Mr. and Mrs. Ritchie in London—the account of his boys studying at Addiscombe, and maintaining such distinguished places—and the statement of his own hard-wrought condition to keep the " bairns in bread." His boys in Addiscombe were a source of the greatest satisfaction, and his hope of their success in the Engineers every father must feel. As we shall afterwards see, they did not disappoint their parents' expectations when they had entered upon the field of their operations in India, but did the greatest credit to themselves, their country, and all connected with them.

"There is no place like home." Such is the opinion of all men, whatever their clime, condition, or generation. However bleak, barren, and poverty-stricken, there is no land like the land of our birth; and however humble, decayed, and dilapidated, there is no dwelling like home. The heart swells with emotion, and the eyes fill with tears, when, after long years of absence, we revisit the scenes of our childhood, and find ourselves again at home. Amid trackless prairies, and perpetual snows, the wild Indian thinks there is no wigwam like his own; and the hardy Highlander, inured to the fury of the mountain tempest, or secluded from the world in the lonely glen, sees no shieling like his own, and no flowers like the heather blooms. Home has a charm for the inferior creation as well as for man. The hare, however wide her circuit, returns to her old form at last; the swallow, having swept through distant climes, returns to her old nest in the window corner; the fish, having explored the depths of ocean, returns to its old fresh-water stream. And in like manner the emigrant, after traversing foreign lands in quest of fortune, returns, or desires to return, at last to lay his bones in the churchyard where his fathers sleep. The love of country and home is manifested in various ways. We show it in the fondness with which we speak of it when far away, in the eagerness with which we defend it in danger, and hazard life itself to maintain its honour and independence.

Allan Cunningham was very far from being an exception to this feeling. The great preponderance of his writings, prose and poetry, had reference to Nithsdale, and reflected his love for his native vale. Above the hum and the buzz and the roar of London he still heard the "craw" of the rooks in the Dalswinton woods—the soft murmur of the Nith, of which he had so melodiously sung. He saw the fertile holms of Kirkmahoe—the green hills of Tinwald—above all, the straggling village of Quarrelwood, where he had spent so many glorious evenings with the M'Ghies, and he had a longing desire to revisit the scenes of his youth. True, many of his former acquaintances had been removed by the hand of death, but a few still remained, especially George Douglas M'Ghie, with whom he had played so many pranks in youth, and brought on the terror of French invasion in the parish. So, in the summer of 1831, he carried out his desire, and visited Nithsdale with delight, though not unmixed with sadness. He saw Sandbed Farmhouse, to which he had been brought when little more than two years old, and where he had spent his early days; but where was the then family now? All gone! His worthy father, of whom he wrote so affectionately, had long since passed away, and the members of the family were also all absent. He saw Dalswinton village, where he had passed his apprenticeship under the tuition of his brother James; but there, also, all was changed. Strange faces looked out of the windows and the doors, but they had no sympathy with what was passing at the time in his own breast. Some rough voice would say, as he passed down the one street which the village contains—"Ay, is that Allan Cunningham? Wasn't he broucht up hereabouts? Didn't he mak' poems and sangs? He's a gey stout chield. Ken ye oucht aboot him particular?" It is this *unkendness* in our own locality which comes home to the heart. Our old friends and associates are not there to welcome us, and we acutely feel that there have arisen others who know not Joseph.

Taking advantage of his visit after a long absence, it was at once proposed, and speedily arranged, to offer him some ostensible testimony of the esteem in which he was held by his friends of Nithsdale, on account of his private character and literary merits. Accordingly, he was entertained at a public banquet in the Commercial Hotel, Dumfries, at which were present the leading gentlemen and others of the town and district, under the genial presidency of John M'Diarmid, Esq., of the *Dumfries Courier*, himself a distinguished poet, who shed a halo of enjoyment over the festive scene. One may easily conceive that Cunningham, greatly appreciating the honour which was being conferred upon him, was not quite at ease in his present position. The former days when he wrought in that town as a common stone-mason, and assisted in erecting the dwellings of several of those present, doubtless rose before his view, and he inwardly asked—"What am I or my father's house that Thou has brought me hitherto?" But still he had a consciousness that he had done something for his country, and his spirit of independence would not allow him to hang his head. So he sat in the "seat of honour" like a man who has honours thrust upon him, while all the time he wished, we believe, he had been somewhere else. In proposing the toast of the evening, Mr. M'Diarmid concluded a long and eloquent eulogium in the following terms :—

" We have met here this day to pay a merited tribute of respect to a man who, as Sir Walter Scott said long ago, is truly a 'credit to Caledonia,' and more particularly to his native district—a district which, in conjunction with Robert Burns, he has done much to illustrate and immortalize, and to which, if I may be allowed to judge from his writings, he still clings, both in fact and fancy, with all the fondness of a first love. More than twelve years have elapsed since he last feasted his eyes on the favourite scenery of Dalswinton, and nearly a quarter of a century since he first went forth to the wide world, with few advantages of birth or education, and fortified chiefly by a warm heart, a glowing fancy, and a good name, to exemplify, as he has done, nobly and well, the might that may slumber in a peasant's mind. There are two aspects in which we may view the character of Mr. Cunningham—as a man and as an author—and in both he has won the world's regard in a manner which, I must say, under all the circumstances, has been seldom equalled and rarely surpassed. In his presence it would be bad taste to say all, or even the half, that many of us may think of him; but this I may say without offence, that, considering the obstacles he has encountered and overcome, I am inclined to set him down not merely as a remarkable, but an extra-ordinary character. As a poet he leans to the ballad style of composition, and many of his lyrics are eminently sweet, graceful, and touching. As a novelist he is chiefly distin-guished for fancy and a power of sketching natural scenery; while his legends, illustrative of Scottish manners and

U

character, are nearly as perfect as any compositions of the kind with which I am acquainted. As a biographer, Mr. Cunningham excels greatly, from the graceful ease and spirit of his style, the extent of his information, and the peculiar opportunities he has enjoyed of conversing with a whole host of public men—authors, painters, sculptors, engravers, dramatists, actors, orators, and statesmen. Already the work I speak of has become prodigiously popular, and, if I am not mistaken, will go down to posterity a striking memorial of what genius and diligence can accomplish. In this happy country there are thousands of men who, not contented with the advantages of rank, fortune, and education, aspire to literary honours and distinctions; yet, if we except the master-spirits of the age, how few of the whole can be put in competition with our respected guest! To take only one example, what is even Lord Leveson Gower?—a nobleman of high rank and fortune, polished manners, and finished education—what, I say, are his translations from the German, and occasional contributions to periodical works, compared with the writings of plain Allan Cunningham?

"Here, therefore, I take my stand, and proceed to say that if all our poets and authors had been cast in the same happy mould, the world would have heard much less of their poverty and misfortunes. Industrious, temperate, and self-denying, it has been his pride to practise that genuine independence which too many only rave about. While his evenings were cheerfully devoted to the Muses, his days were more profitably employed, and he has never hitherto fallen into the egregious error of making that the staple of his mental industry for which there is rarely a regular demand. Voltaire tells, that while the Portuguese sailors, on entering battle, are prostrate on the deck imploring their saints to perform miracles in their favour, the British tars stand to their guns, and literally work miracles for themselves. This sagacious hint, which contains much wisdom under the guise of satire, has not been lost on our valued friend, who, in place of joining the crowd of adventurers, who frequently work to a thankless master, and persist in piping when there is none to dance, has studied human nature to better purpose, and shown his admirable good sense by making literature a staff rather than a crutch—a pleasure or pastime rather than a profession. It is somewhere finely said by Paley, that it is not the Lord Mayor seated in his coach of state that benefits society, but the feelings of the apprentice, whose emulation is roused by such a pageant. And, on the same principle, I would remark that, so far from assembling here this day for the vulgar purpose of eating and drinking, we have met for the noble one of marking the high sense we entertain of genius, industry, and good conduct, and of exciting others to persevere in the same paths of private worth and public usefulness, that in due time they may also meet a similar reward. And, finally, gentlemen, when all I now see around me shall have been removed from the stage of active life, other Allan Cunninghams may haply arise; and all I can add is an ardent wish that, when they chance to revisit the scenes of their youth, they may be welcomed with the same enthusiasm and cordiality, and that from Dumfriesshire, at least, may disappear now and hereafter, the old reproach, that a prophet has no honour in his own country."

It is unnecessary to add that the toast was received with the utmost enthusiasm.

Cunningham made a very modest reply. He said he was quite unaccustomed to public speaking, and could make but a poor return indeed for the great kindness and attention which had been shown him, and the manner in which his health had been proposed and received. In his case the saying had certainly been reversed, that a "Prophet had no honour in his own country." He was proud that he belonged to this district, for it was the first to own him—he was proud that his father and grandfather were freemen of this town—he was proud that all his earliest and most lasting feelings and associations were connected with a place such as this—and he was proud that any little knowledge he possessed had been gained amongst them. He could never forget the reception he had met with, and the kindness he had experienced since his arrival in Dumfries; and for the honour done to him on the present occasion, all he could do was to return his warmest and most fervent thanks.

Thomas Carlyle, now so celebrated as an author, and of world-wide fame, was also present, and made his first public speech, which it is interesting to note was in proposing the memory of Burns. In some preliminary observations he thus gracefully alluded to their guest, Mr. Cunningham:—" One circumstance had been stated, and he felt gratified that the Chairman had done so. He had certainly come down from his retreat in the hills to meet Allan Cunningham at a time when scarcely any other circumstance could have induced him to move half-a-mile from home. He conceived that a tribute could not be paid to a more deserving individual, nor did he ever know of a dinner being given which proceeded from a purer principle. When Allan left his

native place he was poor, unknown, and unfriended—
nobody knew what was in him, and he himself had only
a slight consciousness of his own powers. He now
comes back—his worth is known and appreciated, and
all Britain is proud to number him among her poets;
we can only say, be ye honoured, we thank you; you
have gratified us much by this meeting. It had been
said that a poet must do all for himself; but then he
must have a something in his heart, and this Mr. Cunningham possessed. He possessed genius, and the feeling to direct it aright. He covets not our silver and
gold—is sufficiently provided for within, and needs little
from without. It then remains for us (continued Mr.
Carlyle) to cheer him on in his honourable course, and
when he is told that his thoughts have dwelt in our
hearts, and elevated us, and made us happy, it must
inspire him with renewed feelings of ardour." This
was greeted with immense applause, and the speaker
went on to what he had risen to propose, the memory
of Burns.

Cunningham's old minister, the Rev. Mr. Wightman,
of Kirkmahoe, was present in the highest spirits, and
enlivened the evening by reciting a short poem he had
composed for the occasion, and which began thus:—

> " The Nith in lambent beauty glides,
>   To blend with Solway's briny tides;
>   The landscape all is fresh and fair,
>   And bland and balmy is the air;
>   Glad nature seems to swell the strain,
>   That welcomes Allan back again!"

During the evening Mr. Cunningham was, without

previous intimation, presented with the freedom of the incorporations of the town by Convener Thomson, who said he did so by the authority of the trades, "in testimony of the regard they bore him as a man of genius, an honest man, and one who was a credit to his country."

Mr. Cunningham, who was greatly affected at the unexpected honour conferred upon him, said, that while he had spoken of his father and grandfather being freemen of Dumfries, he did not anticipate that he was soon to be made one himself. He was pleased to think that he had been an apprentice in the town, and had worked as a mason in her streets and public places. He could still recognize the marks of his chisel on many an edifice, and even now observed the gentleman by whom he was treated as a friend, though still a servant. He had the other day made a pilgrimage to the mausoleum of Burns, and set down, among the signatures of many who performed the same errand, his name as a mason, for he was perfectly sure that he was a mason, although not so sure that he was anything else. Of course the room resounded with plaudits when he resumed his seat.

A compliment similar to Mr. Carlyle's was paid him eleven years afterwards, when he had passed from the scene of earthly eulogium, by another distinguished writer, who is also gone. Professor Aytoun, at the Burns' Festival in 1844, on the banks of the Doon, in proposing "The Memory of the Ettrick Shepherd, and Allan Cunningham," spoke of the latter in the following eulogistic terms:—"Of the other sweet singer, too—of

Allan Cunningham, the leal-hearted and kindly Allan—
I might say much; but why should I detain you further?
Does not his name alone recall to your recollections
many a sweet song that has thrilled the bosom of the
village maiden with an emotion that a princess need not
blush to own? Honour, then, to the poets! whether
they speak out loud and trumpet-tongued, to find
audience in the hearts of the great, and the mighty, and
the brave—or whether, in lowlier and more simple
accents, but not less sacred in their mission, they bring
comfort and consolation to the poor. As the sweep of
the rainbow, which has its arch in heaven and its shafts
resting upon the surface of the earth—as the sunshine
which falls with equal bounty upon the palace and the
hut—is the all-pervading and universal spirit of poetry;
and what less can we do to those men who have collected
and scattered it around us, than to hail them as the
benefactors of their race?"

On the day following this banquet, Cunningham and
a party of gentlemen, by invitation of Mr. Leny, dined
at Dalswinton House. They went out to Kirkmahoe a
considerable time before the dinner hour, in order to
have a ramble through the scenes and places where the
poet had spent the days of his youth. After strolling
about for some hours over the holms and the hills of
Dalswinton, so well known in days of yore, and even
still well known, with the tears oftentimes running
down his cheeks, in remembrance of youthful days, he
expressed to Mrs. Leny his desire to spend the evening
of his days on the banks of the Nith, with a cot, a kail-
yard, and a cow. Mrs. Leny, with her well-known

generosity and kindness of heart instantly replied to the poet's wish:—"Only come once more amongst us, and these, at least, I assure you, you shall have." The generous offer, highly appreciated, was never enjoyed. At the comparatively early age of forty-seven he thought he had not yet done with the great City, and, therefore, though the offer was not declined, but gratefully acknowledged, the fulfilment of its acceptance was delayed. The place was pointed out where the "cot" was to be built, and the "kail-yard" to be planted, a romantic spot on the edge of a deep glen, and commanding an extensive view of the vale of the Nith, from the hills of Blackwood to the Solway, and even, in a clear day, to the hills of Cumberland. But the intent was not carried into execution. On returning to London from his home-tour, he made a sketch of the intended cottage, but underneath he wrote the following stanzas, which he sent to Mrs. Leny:—

"A FAREWELL TO DALSWINTON.

" ' A cot, a kale-yard, and a cow,'
    Said fair Dalswinton's lady,
 ' Are thine,' and so the Muse began
    To make her dwelling ready.
She reared her walls, she laid her floors,
    And finished roof and rafter;
But looking on her handiwork
    She scarce refrained from laughter.
A cot sketched from some fairy's dream,
    In fancy's strangest tintin',
Would mock the beauteous banks and streams
    Of thee, my loved Dalswinton!

" When I look, lady, on thy land,
    It fills my soul with gladness,
Till I think on my youthful days,
    And then I sink in sadness.
With mind unfurnished with an aim
    Among your groves I wandered,
And dreaming much, and doing nought,
    My golden honrs I squandered;
Or followed Folly's meteor light,
    Oft till the sun came glintin',
And seemed to say, 'tis for thy sake
    I shine, my sweet Dalswinton!

" There stands the hill where first I roamed,
    Before the Muse had owned me—
There is the glen where first she wove
    Her web of witchcraft round me:
The wizard tree, the haunted stream,
    Where in my waking slumbers,
Fair fruitful fancy on my soul
    Poured fast her flowing numbers.
Dalswinton hill, Dalswinton holm,
    And Nith, thou gentle river,
Rise in my heart, flow in my soul,
    And dwell with me for ever.

" My father's feet seem on thy braes,
    And on each haugh and hollow;
I grow a child again, and seem
    His manly steps to follow,
Now on the spot where glad he sat,
    As bright our hearth was blazing,
The gowans grow, and harebells blow,
    And fleecy flocks are grazing.
Farewell Dalswinton's hill and grove,
    Farewell, too, its fair lady—
I'll think on all, when far I rove,
    By vale and woodland shady.

> " Farewell thy flowers, in whose rich bloom
>   The honey-bees are swarming—
> Farewell thy woods, with every smell
>   And every sound that's charming—
> Farewell thy banks of golden broom,
>   The hills with fox-gloves glowing,
> The ring-dove haunts, where fairy streams
>   Are in their music flowing.
> Farewell thy hill, farewell thy halls—
>   Dark fate to me is hintin',
> I've seen the last I e'er shall see
>   Of thee, my sweet Dalswinton!"

The prediction given in the last stanza was unfortunately only too true. The poet never saw Dalswinton again, but the tone and spirit which the effusion breathes show how closely and dearly it was enshrined in his heart. He never returned to the vale of Nithsdale any more. Cunningham, after all, did not see the M'Ghies on his visit, for which he was greatly sorry, and, writing afterwards to his friend George, he said:— " I was sorry I saw so little of you when I was in Dumfries, and the day I had laid out to see you in Kirkmahoe was one of much misery. I had nearly died in Crichope Linn, which would have been picturesque enough, but somehow one covets a bed in such times. When I make a descent on Scotland again, I will set up my standard in lodgings of my own, and rally the M'Ghies and others of the clans around me." He had done a great favour to George with respect to a friend, and this is a part of the letter stating what he succeeded in doing.

CHAPTER XIX.

PROPOSES A NEW EDITION OF THE WORKS OF BURNS, WITH A LIFE—
LETTERS FROM HIS SONS IN INDIA—LETTER TO THE LATE DR.
ROBERT CHAMBERS OF EDINBURGH—"THE POET'S INVITATION"—
LETTERS TO HIS MOTHER—PUBLISHES THE WORKS OF BURNS—
BIDS FAREWELL TO THE BARD.

HIS visit to Nithsdale was delightful in the extreme, as he anticipated it would be,' and produced a salutary effect upon both his bodily and mental constitution, which had been greatly exhausted by the labours he had undergone. He felt himself invigorated and almost an entirely new man. He had been highly gratified in looking upon the scenes of his youthful days—the famous loch from which he had removed Thomas M'Ghie's keen curling stone, and painted it all over the evening previous to a single-handed spiel, so that the owner did not know it again, and lost the game—Sand-bed, to which he was taken when a child, and where he first saw Burns—the Roads, where his father died—Foregarth, where was held many a tryst—the village of Dalswinton, where he lived when an apprentice—and Townhead, marked No. 14, in the great hoax of French invasion. He had been fêted by the *elite* of the district—his literary abilities had been eulogized—he had received the freedom of the Burgh of Dumfries, in which he had wrought as a common stone-mason, and he would have been unworthy of the honour conferred upon him had he not rejoiced. He highly appreciated the favours bestowed upon him, and resolved to make himself more worthy of them.

Accordingly, he now set himself to the performance of a task which he intended to be his great literary master-piece, to bring out an edition of the Works of Burns, with his Life. This was a great undertaking, but it was successfully accomplished. In a letter to his dear friend, Mr. Jerdan of the *Literary Gazette*, he gives, as his reasons for doing so, the following:—"His works have been heretofore ill-arranged; the natural order of composition has been neglected; poems have been printed as his which he never wrote, and his letters have had the accompaniment of epistles which were not necessary, and were the work of other hands. Poems, letters, and anecdotes, hitherto unpublished, are in my possession, and will appear in the course of the work. My desire is to arrange the poems, letters, songs, remarks, and memoranda of the bard in natural and intelligible order; to illustrate and explain them with introductions and notes, and to write a full and ample memoir, such as shall show his character as a man and his merits as a poet, and give freely and faithfully the history of his short and bright career." The work was to come out in six monthly volumes, and to be embellished with landscape vignettes of memorable scenes in the shires of Ayr and Dumfries.

In the meantime his sons Joseph and Alexander have sailed for India, under Government appointments, a circumstance which, however gratifying in the main, must have sent a pang through the hearts of the parents, at the thought that they might never see them again. However, they were noble fellows, and went on swimmingly, as the following interesting letters to their grandmother show. The first is from Joseph at Dinapore, on the Ganges :—

"I sailed, as you know, in the beginning of February, and though many people consider a ship as a mere prison, and a very dull one besides, yet I did not find it so, for to the novelty of the scene were added many entertaining passengers, and Captain Blair is a gentleman of parts and attainments, and very interesting in conversation. He had, besides, a good library, so that our time was spent cheerfully and usefully, while the capture of a shark, or of some enormous bird, would relieve the routine; and the sight of a green island would make us wish, in spite of everything, that we were on shore.

"The Bay of Biscay is a severe and proverbial trial for young sailors, and it proved so to me, though the time of our greatest pain and amusement was when we crossed the Line for the first time, when we were well dirtied with dung and tar, well shaved with an iron hoop, and well bruised with knocks, thumps, and tumbles. We landed upon a small island called Johanna, on the East Coast of Africa, and were much surprised at the sight of savages nearly naked, and delighted with the taste of fresh fruits and well water. Want of wind detained us in the neighbourhood of the Line —the weather was exceedingly hot and close, and exposure to the sun during a shooting excursion brought on a slight attack of fever, which will make me very cautious for the future.

"We sailed round Ceylon, and stopped at Madras for two days, which presents a most splendid appearance on approach-

ing it from the sea.   On the 12th of June I landed in
Calcutta, the capital of our empire in India, and a city of
palaces, as it is generally, though not deservedly, called.
The heat was excessive, for the thermometer was nearly 100°
for many days, and sometimes above it; but comfort and the
wealth of individuals have invented many artificial means of
cooling both their rooms and the water they drink.   I was
in Calcutta for six weeks, during which I was living with
Captain Blair, and visiting Government House and the best
society.   I am now proceeding up the great and holy river
Ganges in a large boat to join my corps at Delhi, the ancient
capital of India, and the seat of the Great Mogul.   We
proceed very slowly, and I shall be as long sailing 1000
miles of a river as I was in sailing from England to India.
We are passing through a rich and populous country, with
plenty of birds and game, but no tigers or wild boars near
the banks."

The next extract is from a letter written by Alexander,
at Moorshedabad, and is of a later date, but we introduce it here as there may not be an opportunity
again :—

"I daresay you have often wondered what has become of
that boy Sandie, and then my aunt Mina has said—'Ay,
he's a terrible boy that,—he'll no write to his auld grand-
mither, or his auld aunt, that kenn'd him for siccan a long
time.   He has a great aversion to women, and he so seldom
speaks to them that he canna be expected to write.'   But,
my dear grandmother, the reason that I did not write before
was, that I had not been settled, and could write nothing
but guesses about what would be my future destination.
Now I am appointed to Delhi, where Mr. Harley has been,

I believe, and where Joseph was for a short time.   It is the residence of the Great Mogul of the present age.

"I could not have arrived in India at a better time, for James Pagan was then in Calcutta, as an evidence on a court-martial, and my brother Joseph had just come in from his Survey, and came to Calcutta a week after, so that we were all three in Calcutta together.

> 'When shall we three meet again,
> In thunder, lightning, or in rain?'

"I was ordered up to Moorshedabad, within six miles of Berhampore, where James Pagan was stationed, and we lived together for about a month, when he was sent to a rather out-of-the-way, but healthy place, called Rungpore, in Bengal. Joseph stopped nearly a week here before recommencing his Survey, and I expect to see him again in about a fortnight.

"I like India very well; at least as a person fresh from London can be expected to do.   Like every one who has come, I must say that I am disappointed.   India is, according to what those who do not know it say, a place abounding with gold, silver, and precious stones; and every native that you may meet will have at least three Cashmere shawls about him.   The fact is, nothing but the sun is golden; and as for shawls, I have not seen any.   Lolling on beautiful couches, and being fanned by ladies, is very romantic and pleasing to read about, and would, no doubt, be much relished in England; but here you may be fanned by dozens of fans without any relief when the thermometer is 100°.

"The weather is beautiful just now—it is cold enough for a fire in the mornings and evenings, and not cold enough to make your fingers useless all day.   I shall have a very pleasant and solitary voyage up the river to Cawnpore for upwards of two months, when I shall commence marching along with the hot winds. The march will be about a month, through Agra to Delhi.

"I have been very happy all the time I have been here. Besides, it put me very much in mind of Scotland, where everybody is better acquainted with other people's families and affairs than with their own. In the last letter I had from James Pagan, he says:—'I used to think Berhampore a dull place, but I believe you will find few pleasanter stations in India; so don't look out for changes to a gayer station. You ought to be sent here for a week.' He was quite well, and 'sitting by the side of a good large fire.'

"Joseph will remain on his Survey till the middle of the year. He likes the stirring manner of life that he is leading very much, and I think it is more healthy than any other. I have just received a letter from him. He is quite well, and wants some more shooting materials. I was intending to say that my aunt Mina, being of a military disposition, would perhaps like a tiger or leopard better than a cat; but I am afraid that the leopard which Joseph has got would be rather too strong and rough an animal for a lady, as he has just sent to me for a strong iron chain to fasten him up.

"I daresay my aunt Mina, who still calls my brother Francis her boy, often says,—'Bless me ! I wonder what that puir wee fallow Sandie does amang a' thae great folk.' But Sandie is now a 'puir wee fallow' of six feet high, with breadth in proportion—has a constitution which bids defiance to all diseases, and spirits which would overcome anything."

How many grandmothers would rejoice to have such noble and affectionate grandsons ! The following opening of a correspondence with the late Dr. Robert Chambers, of *Chambers's Journal*, will be read with interest on various accounts:—

"27 Lower Belgrave Place, 27th October, 1832.

"My dear Sir,—Your letter was a welcome one. It is written with that frank openness of heart which I like, and contains a wish, which was no stranger to my own bosom, that we should be known to each other. You must not suppose that I have been influenced in my wish by the approbation with which I know your works have been received by your country. It is long since I took to judging in all matters for myself, and the 'Picture of Scotland' and the 'Traditions of Edinburgh,' both of which I bought, induced me to wish Robert Chambers among my friends. There was, perhaps, a touch or so of vanity in this—your *poetic, ballad-scrap, auld-world, new-world, Scottish* tastes and feelings seemed to go side for side with my own. Be so good, therefore, as send me your promised 'Book of Ballads,' and accept in return, or rather in token of future regard, active and not passive, my rustic 'Maid of Elvar,' who has made her way through reform pamphlets and other rubbish, like a lily rising through the clods of the spring. There's a complimentary simile in favour of myself and my book! You must not, however, think ill of it because I praise it; but try and read it, and tell me what you feel about it.

"I have been much pleased with your account of Sir Walter Scott; it wears such an air of truth, that no one can refuse credence to it, and is full of interesting facts and just observations. I have no intention of expanding, or even of correcting, my own hasty and inaccurate sketch. Mr. Lockhart will soon give a full and correct life of that wonderful man to the world. The weed which I have thrown on his grave—for I cannot call it a flower—may wither as better things must do. Some nine thousand copies were sold. This we consider high, though nothing comparable,

x

I know, to the immense sale of *Chambers's Journal.*　I am truly glad of your great circulation.　Your work is by a thousand degrees the best of all the latter progeny of the Press.　It is an original work, and while it continues so, must keep the lead of the paste and scissors productions. My wife, who has just returned from Scotland, says that your *Journal* is very popular among her native hills of Galloway.　The shepherds, who are scattered there at the rate of one to every four miles square, read it constantly, and they circulate it in this way: the first shepherd who gets it reads it, and at an understood hour places it under a stone on a certain hill-top; then shepherd the second in his own time finds it, reads it, and carries it to another hill, where it is found, like Ossian's chief, under its own gray stone by shepherd the third, and so it passes on its way, scattering information over the land.

"My songs, my dear sir, have all the faults you find with them, and some more.　The truth is, I am unacquainted with any other nature save that of the Nith and the Solway, and I must make it do my turn.　I am like a bird that gathers materials for its nest round its customary bush, and who sings in his own grove, and never thinks of moving elsewhere.　The affectations of London are as nothing to me. In my ' Lives of the Painters,' I have, however, escaped from my valley, and in other contemplated works I hope to show that, though I sing in the charmed circle of Nithsdale, I can make excursions in prose out of it, and write and think like a man of the world and its ways.—I remain, my dear Sir, with much regard, yours always,

"ALLAN CUNNINGHAM.

"To Robert Chambers, Esq."

If there is one social feature of Cunningham's character which we admire more than another, it is his affection for his family, and especially for his mother. How often does it happen that when sons grow up, leave their native place, and have families of their own, those near to them, if not forgotten, are neglected, and news of them are obtained at second-hand, or by chance! But it was not so with Allan Cunningham. He was a most dutiful and affectionate son, and amidst the greatest bustle of business he contrived time to write to his mother, and to add to her comfort in every way he could. Then, in his own home how genial he was! although in one of his letters he refers to his hasty temper, as contrasted with that of one of his sons, in his wife's estimation. This, however, we consider as a joke on his part. He had one daughter to whom he was devotedly attached, but who was early removed by death. We cannot avoid quoting the following poem addressed to her, on expressing a desire to leave Nithsdale and return to her home in London:—

"THE POET'S INVITATION.

" So thou wilt quit thy comrades, sweet,
    Nith's fountains, sweeping grove, and holme,
  For distant London's dusty street?
    Then come my youngest, fairest, come;
  For not the sunshine following showers,
  Nor fruit-buds to the wintry bowers,
  Nor ladye-bracken to the hind,
  Nor warm bark to the tender rind,
  Nor song-bird to the sprouting tree,
  Nor heath-bell to the gathering bee,
  Nor golden daylight to sad eyes,

Nor moon-star showing larks to rise,
Nor son long lost in some far part,
Who leaps back to his mother's heart.
Nor lily to Dalswinton lea,
Nor moonlight to the fairy,
Can be so dear as thou to me,
My youngest one, my Mary.

" Look well on Nithsdale's lonely hills,
Where they who loved thee lived of yore;
And dip thy small feet in the rills
Which sing beside thy mother's door.
There's not a bush on Blackwood lea,
On broad Dalswinton not a tree;
By Carse there's not a lily blows,
On Cowhill bank there's not a rose;
By green Portrack no fruit-tree fair,
Hangs its ripe clusters in mid-air,
But what in hours not long agone,
In idling mood were to me known;
And now, though distant far, they seem
Of heaven, and mix in many a dream.
Of Nith's fair land limn all the charms
Upon thy heart, and carry
The picture to thy father's arms,
My youngest one, my Mary.

" Nor on the lovely land alone,
Be all thy thoughts and fancy squander'd ;
Look at thy right hand, there is one
Who long with thee hath mused and wander'd,—
Now with the wild bee 'mongst the flowers,
Now with the song-bird in the bowers;
Or plucking balmy blooms and throwing
Them on the winds or waters flowing;
Or marking with a mirthsome scream,
Your shadows changing in the stream;
Or gay o'er summer's painted ground,

Danced till the trees seemed reeling round;
Or listening to some far-heard tune,
Or gazing on the calm clear moon.
        O! think on her whose nature sweet
            Would neither shift nor vary
        From gentle deeds and words discreet—
            Such Margaret was to Mary.

" The pasture hills fade from thy sight,
        Nith sinks with all her silver waters,
    With all that's gentle, mild, and sweet,
        Of Nithsdale's dames and daughters.
    Proud London, with her golden spires,
    Her painted halls and festal fires,
    Calls on thee with a mother's voice,
    And bids thee in her arms rejoice.
    But still when Spring, with primrose mouth,
    Breathes o'er the violets of the south,
    Thou'lt hear the far wind-wafted sounds
    Of waves in Siddick's cavern'd bounds,
    The music of unnumbered rills,
    Which sport on Nithsdale's haunted hills;
        And see old Molach's hoary back,
            That seems the cloud to carry,
        And dream thyself in green Portrack,
            My darling child, my Mary."

We shall now give some of his letters to his mother
before noticing his work, at which he is busy, the " Works
and Life of Burns":—

                    " Belgrave Place, 19th August, 1833.

"My dear Mother,—I am glad to learn that your health
and spirits are much the same as when I had the great satisfaction, I may say with a son's feeling, the honour of seeing
you in Scotland.   We are also very well.   Mary is taller and
stronger, and all are growing except myself.   My growth

must, I fear, be downwards; but such is the lot of life. My wife, with Poll and Frank, are living for the present at Blackheath, and the fresh, free air is, I can observe, beneficial. Peter is in London, and has written and published a book, a Life of Drummond the Poet, with selections from his poems. It has been well received, and, considering that it was written when he was but sixteen years old, is really wonderful for good taste and accuracy of thinking. Of Alexander, poor fellow, we have not yet heard, nor do we expect to hear before the end of next month. I hope he will meet his brother in Calcutta, and get on as well as he has done.

"We have had a letter from Joseph, dated from Rajmahal, the 1st of March. He was then well, in good spirits, and busy making his Survey. He says his name is now known in Bengal, and he is not afraid but that he will in future have staff appointments. His cousin, James Pagan, was with him, and living in his tent, on a visit for a month. James was very well, got Joseph's elephant every day to shoot upon, and generally succeeded in shooting as much game as served for dinner. He had nearly, I mean his elephant, stumbled on a sleeping tiger, but James prudently turned his elephant's head, and obeyed the old proverb of letting sleeping dogs lie. I am glad they are together. Will you tell this story to my dear sister Mary, and say that I wish to have a long letter from her own hand? I forgot to say that Joseph's appointment will, while it lasts, bring him £600 or £700 a-year above his pay. I summed up lately what my two engineers had cost me, and found it to exceed a thousand pounds.

"For my own part, I am busy beyond all example. I have twice as much to write as what I ought to do, but I have taxed my strength not beyond what it can bear, and I intend to give my body a month's pleasure, and my heart a month's joy, in coming and seeing you next year in the summer at your own fireside. I shall come when no one shall know. The first notice to yourself will be my alighting at your gate, and we shall have long conversations with no one to interrupt us. I am just now busy writing the Life of Burns. I am receiving new information from many sources, also letters, and even poems of his, and I expect to make a good work, such a one as the world will take. It will extend to six volumes. A painter is, I believe, even now in Nithsdale taking sketches of scenery to engrave for it. Among other things, he is making *me* a drawing of the Blackwood yews where our cottage stood in which I was born. This is a matter of vanity, so say nothing about it.

"Your grandson Allan is a quiet, steady lad, and a good workman, and will do very well there can be no doubt. Tell my sister at the village that he gives me full satisfaction, and will be able to save money. Tell my sister that we, that is, all of us, often talk of her, and that her boy Frank is grown tall, much like Joseph, and is an admirable scholar. Tell my sister Jean that she must find some anecdotes of Burns for me. I have got several more of his autographs, and expect a dozen or two of his letters which have never yet been published.

"My wife, for I have this moment returned from Blackheath, sends her kind love to you. She unites with me in love to my sisters.—I remain, my beloved Mother, your affectionate son,

"ALLAN CUNNINGHAM.

" Mrs. Cunningham."

" Belgrave Place, 15th March, 1835.

"My dear Mother,—I ought to have written this letter some time ago, but, to tell the truth, I had neither heart nor health for details of sorrow. We have suffered sad bereavements—you have lost a much-loved son—I have lost a dear brother, and my wife has been deprived of two brothers—all in the course of a few months. These events have kept us in a state of agitation and sorrow, but we are now becoming more composed, and are endeavouring to look forward, and, above all, upward, for true relief can only come from that quarter. It helps to soothe us, too, to hear that you are better. The spring suns are beginning to shine, and the spring flowers to appear, and you will be able to step over the door a little; and were your walks no wider than your own garden, it cannot fail to refresh you to see the daisies and lilies, and many other flowers which you taught me to be fond of, growing on every side. In the little spot of ground before my own window, I see, as I write now, the crocuses and snow-drops in full blow, and the lilies appearing, and I feel gratified, and think of the little nook at the Roads where I delved and dibbled, and thought my toils overpaid when I got you to come and look at my auriculas and roses.

" We had long letters on Saturday last from India. Alexander had been a second time promoted, but when he wrote his letter he had been for some time laid up with cold and fever. The fever, he said, was gone, but the cold and sore throat remained. Joseph's letter was three weeks later, and he had heard from Alexander two days before. He was then all but well, and on the point of riding out to begin his inspection of the public buildings of Central Bengal. He obtained this appointment through the kindness of Major Irvine, an eminent engineer, a native of Langholm. Joseph was quite well, and expected to be a twelvemonth more employed on the Canal. As soon as we hear from Alexander we will let you know. James Pagan was very well on the 12th of October, the date of his cousin's letter. Frank is at school at Twickenham, and is making great progress. Mary has a governess at home, and has learned to play Scotch tunes, and work flowers, and make puddings, though I hardly think she is equal to the construction of the pigeon pie, which I once heard you describe, with a dove-cote and doves on the top of it.

"Peter is, you know, a clerk in the Audit office. The situation begins at £90 a-year, and rises in course of time to £500 or £600. He has much leisure, and resolves to employ it like his father in making books. He is busy editing two volumes at present, and has good offers for original compositions. My only fear is that he will throw himself before the public sooner than his mind is informed and his taste matured. His place was given to me by my friend Sir Robert Peel, accompanied by a letter so complimentary and so kind as will ever endear him to my heart. My brother Peter is with us, and helps to make our fireside more cheerful. He is so equal of temper and mind, and so full too of all kinds of entertaining knowledge, that I hardly know whom to compare him to. Were I to say he is almost as good as I am, my wife would reply, 'He is far better natured than Allan,' and really I believe she would be right; yet I am not ill-tempered you know, as tempers go.

"We see our brother Thomas' widow and son and daughters often. It was fortunate for them that John was established in Mr. Rennie's before his father's death. They would have nearly been desolate (destitute?) also, for my brother had neglected to insure his life for the benefit of his family. Were I removed to-morrow, my wife would have £500 from the Life Insurance Office, besides what she may calculate on for my works, and what her children owe her. I pay £20 a-year to insure this sum. I shall not die a minute the sooner for it, and it helps to keep my mind easy.

"Now you must not imagine, that because I am not so well as I have been, I am at all in a dangerous state. In truth, I wrought too much and too anxiously. The education of my sons, and the outfit of the two eldest to India, have left me far from rich, and that made me toil more than was good for my health. I have not written twenty pages these three months, and am allowing my mind as well as body to lie fallow, as the farmers say, with the hope of a better crop at the next ploughing. If I can only get a couple of years or so over my head, I will, I think, leave my place with Mr. Chahtrey, and, taking a house and garden some three or four miles from London, try what three hours' writing in the day and a little gardening and amusement will do for me. I am not a person of expensive habits, and can, when Frank is provided for, live on a small income.

"My wife sends her best love to you, and to Mina, and Jean, and I add mine. Will you be so good as name us to Mr. David Rodan and Mrs. Rodan, also to Mrs. Burgess? When I am next on the Nith I shall take more leisure than I could obtain when I was down last. I particularly wish to spend some days with the Rodan family, the Robson family, the Taylor family, and, though last, not least in my esteem, with the M'Ghies, father and son. All these were friends of my father's family, and friends of mine, and are often present to my thoughts. There are others, but I have neither room nor leisure to be more particular.

"The stockings fitted me finely, and were made very welcome, particularly the pair which *you* knitted. Mina or Jean will be so good as write to say that the letter and enclosure have arrived; and if you could but write, were it only three lines yourself, they would be made most welcome by your loving and affectionate son,

" ALLAN CUNNINGHAM.

"Mrs. Cunningham."

"27 Belgrave Place, 4th April, 1835.

"My dear Mother,—I write to assure you that I am now quite as well as ever I was, reading, writing, and talking, as usual, during the evenings, and busy with marble and bronze during the day. Indeed, we are all as well as you can wish us. We had letters from India speaking of Alexander's illness, but a letter, dated 12th November, from Joseph says that he is quite as well as ever. We are looking for letters from the East every day, but winds and waves cannot be commanded.

"I almost envy you the little garden at your door. I have a small patch at mine where I persuade a lily or a daisy to bloom upon, with now and then a tulip and a rose. I miss a large garden much, and I feel persuaded that if I had one my health would be better, and I hope to have one soon in the neighbourhood of London. I was almost tempted to come down and dwell beside you lately, but luckily for myself I yielded not; for though I love the people, and the vale, and long to be among those whom I love, I cannot conceal from myself that London is the proper place for me. We are all in confusion here from the disputes between the Tories and the Whigs. The former propose measures which all who love their country cannot but approve, while the latter oppose them with all their might, and care nothing for either honour or consistency, so long as they can succeed in thwarting and upsetting them. Should the Whigs succeed, and I think they will, the Church of England will receive a blow from which it can never recover. If the revenues of the Established Church are bestowed on the Catholics in Ireland, the Dissenters of England, and I am, one you know, will demand the same concession, and so will the Dissenters of Scotland.

" My brother Peter is very well; so is my son Peter, and so likewise are Frank and Mary. I know not if we shall be in Scotland this year; the pain of parting with the North is not small, and the outlay is great. My wife joins me in love to Mina and Jean, and, above all, my beloved Mother, to yourself.—I remain, your affectionate son,

"ALLAN CUNNINGHAM.

" I shall write soon again.

" Mrs. Cunningham."

The Works and Life of Robert Burns came out in eight volumes, instead of six, as had been originally advertised, the matter having increased upon his hands, and he put forth all his energies to make the enterprize a success. After all his praying, pleading, and payment-promising, to certain distinguished writers, with regard to the "Anniversary Annual" for 1830, to which we have already referred, it came to nothing; for he descended from his editorial throne and ceased all connection with it, as the proprietor and publisher having twice changed its character, determined to change it again, by making it a monthly instead of an annual volume. Perhaps this stimulated his efforts the more, to show that in an independent capacity he was quite willing to risk public opinion on his side as he had hitherto done, and without regret. Poets, authors, and artists, are often-times, if not always, particularly sensitive in matters which belong to their several professions. The work appeared in a very elegant form, and was hailed with general approbation. Cunningham carried out his design most faithfully, and from the research he made, and the industry he bestowed in finding out fresh materials for the Life, as well as Notes, he deserves the acknowledgments of succeeding biographers of the great bard, seeing that they have made ample use of what he originally supplied. Of course, many things have come to light with reference to Burns since that work was issued, which Cunningham could not be expected to know at the time he wrote, but yet his edition is still considered a standard work on the subject. In a prefatory notice to the last volume he thus takes leave of his brother bard:—

> "My task is ended—fareweel, Robin!
> My 'prentice muse stands sad and sobbin',
> To think thy country kept thee scrubbin'
>   Her barmy barrels,
> Of strains immortal mankind robbin',
>   And thee of laurels.
>
> "Let learning's Greekish grubs cry humph!
> Hot zealots groan, cold critics grumph,
> And ilka starr'd and garter'd sumph
>   Yawn, hum, and ha;
> In glory's pack thou art a trumph
>   That sweeps them a'.
>
> "Round thee flock'd scholars mony a cluster,
> And dominies came in a cluster,
> In words three span lang 'gan they bluster
>   Of classic models,
> Of Tully's light and Virgil's lustre,
>   And shook their noddles.
>
> "Ye laugh'd, and muttering, 'Learning! d—n her!'
> Stood bauldly up, but start or stammer

Wi' Nature's fire for lore and grammar,
        And classic rules,
Crushed them as Thor's triumphant hammer
        Smash'd paddock stools.

"And thou wert right, and they were wrang—
The sculptor's toil, the poet's sang,
In Greece and Rome frae nature sprang,
        And, bauld and free,
In sentiment and language strang
        They spake like thee.

"Thy muse came like a giggling taupie
Dancing her lane; her sangs sae sappy
Cheer'd men like drink's inspiring drappie—
        Then, grave and stern,
High moral truths sublime and happy
        She made them learn.

"Auld grey-beard Lear, wi' college lantern,
O'er rules of Horace stoitering, venturin',
At song, glides to oblivion saunterin'
        And starless night;
Whilst thou, up cleft Parnassus canterin',
        Lives on in light.

"In light thou liv'st. While birds lo'e simmer,
Wild bees the blossom, buds the timmer,
And man lo'es woman—rosy limmer!
        I'll prophesie
Thy glorious halo nought the dimmer
        Will ever be.

"For me—though both sprung from ae mother,
I'm but a weakly young half-brother,
Sae O! forgive my musing swither,
        'Mid toils benighted,
'Twas lang a wish that nought could smother,
        To see thee righted.

"'Frae Kyle, wi' music in her bowers;
Frae fairy glens, where wild Doon pours;
Frae hills, bedropped wi' sunny showers,
              On Solway strand,
I've gathered, Burns, thy scatter'd flowers
              Wi' filial hand.

"And O! bright and immortal Spirit,
If ought that lessens thy rare merit
I've uttered—like a god thou'll bear it,
              Thou canst but know
Thy stature few or none can peer it
              Now born below."

A second edition of the work, in one volume, appeared the following year, so rapid had been the sale of the first.

CHAPTER XX.

BURNS—"WINSOME WILLIE"—TOM WALKER—"CUTTY SARK."

IN many of the earlier editions of Burns' poems, published after his death, and in some of the cheap editions still, there is found a humorous and scourging " Epistle to a Tailor," in reply to one which the said tailor had transmitted to the poet, admonishing him very severely with regard to his conduct and conversation.   This poem is now known to have been a forgery, but which Burns was made aware of at the time by its author, his friend and correspondent, "Winsome Willie."   So admirable an imitation was it of the language, style, and sentiment of the great bard himself, that it long passed without detection; and was even regarded as one of his choicest and raciest effusions, from the salient humour and keen satire which it contained.   Yet so great and penetrative was the sagacity of some of the early critics, that it was only after considerable hesitation they agreed to pass it as a genuine production.   But although not from the pen or the brain of Burns, yet, as we have said, he was cognizant of its existence; and the opinion he gave of it—not generally known—is one of the reasons why we refer to it at present.   Cunningham says he had heard it surmised that Burns wrote the epistle himself for the sake of the answer; and he seems to believe it, as he considers it a compliment to his genius, but not a just one, in being able to write down to the level

of the verses it contains. But it was not so. The
original letter in the tailor's autograph is now before us,
and could not by any possibility belong to Burns.

At the time that Burns was farmer at Mossgiel,
William Simpson was schoolmaster in Ochiltree, and
the two were on friendly—indeed, intimate—terms.
Simpson had been at first intended for the church, and
had proceeded some length in his college curriculum
towards the pulpit, when he suddenly stopped short,
bade farewell to the clergy, and adopted the humble
but no less important profession of a teacher of the
young. His abilities as a poet were considerably above
mediocrity, although he has been characterized by
Chambers as only a "rhymer," and he has left behind
him a large volume of poems in manuscript, which have
never been published. During his lifetime he was often
urged to give them to the world, but he always declined,
his constant reply being that he wrote for amusement
and not for profit. Burns, however, seems to have
thought him more than a "rhymer," when he addressed
him in the following strains:—

> " Auld Coila now may fidge fu' fain,
>   She's gotten poets o' her ain,
>   Chiels wha their chanters winna hain,
>   But tune their lays,
>   Till echoes a' resound again
>   Her weel-sung praise.

>   .   .   .   .

> " Ramsay and famous Fergusson
>   Gied Forth and Tay a lift aboon;

Y

Yarrow and Tweed to monie a tune
    Owre Scotland rings;
While Irwin, Lugar, Ayr, an' Doon,
    Naebody sings.

"Th' Illissus, Tiber, Thames, an' Seine
Glide sweet in monie a tunefu' line;
But, Willie, set your fit to mine
    An' cock your crest,
We'll gar our streams an' burnies shine
    Up wi' the best.

.   .   .   .

"Fareweel, my 'rhyme-composing brither!'
We've been owre lang unkenned to ither,
Now let us lay our heads thegither
    In love fraternal;
May envy wallop in a tether,
    Black fiend, infernal!"

It was with difficulty that we persuaded Simpson's brother to repeat to us any of William's poems, though he often spoke of him as a great crony with Burns, and to grant a copy was altogether out of the question. However, we secretly jotted down in shorthand one or two of them, as old Patrick, himself a poet, one evening at his fireside in the school-house of Ochiltree cast his broad shoulders back into his arm-chair, and his soul into the light of other days, when he brought the first copy of the "Twa Herds" to his father's house, and his brother began correspondence with the author. We shall give one or two of Simpson's poetic effusions. In the village of Ochiltree there lived an old pensioner, William Weir, who had seen much military service, and who thought himself entitled to greater remuneration than he received. His pay was one shilling a-day, which he thought too little for his wants, and therefore he caused a petition to be forwarded to the Duke of York for an increase; but he received no reply to his application. William boldly addressed a memorial in his own hand to the Duke, which procured him an additional sixpence. When he died, Simpson wrote the following epitaph for his tombstone :—

" EPITAPH ON WILLIAM WEIR.

" Faithfully is lodged here
　The mortal part of William Weir.
　William, full of martial mettle,
　Stood the brunt of many a battle;
　Hardships many underwent,
　Lived a hero—died a saint.
　Moments military past,
　Off his armour he has cast,
　Knapsack, sword, and gun flung by,
　Where his regimentals lie,
　Full of hope that when the last
　Trumpet sounds its potent blast,
　Starting all of every host,
　Dead and living to their post,
　William will (in armour clear,
　Never more to rust) appear,
　Ranked among the faithful few,
　Glorious at the Grand Review."

When the life of his Majesty George III. was attempted by James Hadfield, in 1800, fortunately without success, various congratulatory addresses were presented to the King on his providential escape. The following one was drawn up by Simpson for the Scottish schoolmasters to sign ; but whether or not it was forwarded for presentation in the proper quarter, we cannot say:—

"MOST GRACIOUS SOVEREIGN—

" While reverend priests, who through the nation
  Hold regicide in detestation,
  Crowd round, in keen congratulation,
        Britannia's throne,
  Adoring for your preservation
        Kind Heaven alone;

" We Dominies benorth the Tweed,
  Wha inly shudder at the deed
  Of firing at a monarch's head,
        In heartfelt strains
  The Power praised that wis'd the lead
        Out o'er your brains.

" For, like yoursel', we're monarchs a',
  Tho' mair despotic as to law;
  And shall, while treason we misca',
        Rejoice till death,
  That Hadfield neither made you fa',
        Nor did you scaith.

" Now Lon'on town rings like a bell,
  Wi' 'Jamie Hadfield's no himsel';'
  It may be sae, I canna tell;
        But this attempt,
  Unless ye hang him, argues well
        Ye're scant o' hemp.

" He's no himsel' ! what plague then is he ?
  Meg Nicholson, that hav'rel hizzy—

Wha blew the pipe till grown sae dizzy—
    Her rusty gully
Drew, and drave (the Deil's aye busy),
    Wi' murderous sally.

" To ettle death wi' sic a shaft,
    Convinced us a' that Meg was daft;
And therefore she's humanely left,
    Untwin'd o' life;
Of liberty alone bereft,
    And yon auld knife.

" But Meg's by far owre weel ta'en care o',
    And selfish Hadfield hearing thereo'—
Her lot to share, he coft a pair o'
    Pistols indeed;
And ane discharged within a hair o'
    Your royal head !

" If legislation prove sae callous,
    As wink at sic audacious fallows;
If rascals may get up to kill us,
    And no be snibbet,
What signify your laws, your gallows,
    Your jail, your jibbet ?

.   .   .   .

" May a' concerned in ony plot
    'Gainst you or yours be hanged and shot,
Amen.   When Satan thus has got
    His ain, we'll sing
The fervent prayer of every Scot,
    GOD SAVE THE KING !

The above specimens of Simpson's muse show that he was something more than a "rhymer." But we turn to another character. In a small cottage called

Pool, not far from the village of Ochiltree, lived, now upwards of a century ago, a man of the name of Thomas Walker, by trade a tailor, by propensity a poet. Of Walker's life little is now remembered, his position in society not being one which exposed him much to public notice beyond the bounds of his immediate neighbourhood. As a tradesman he was well skilled in his craft, and was greatly resorted to when the needle and shears were in requisition. He was a member of that portion of the dissenting Church called the Burghers, and during the whole course of his life he engaged in the ordinances of religion with a zeal and piety indicative of the pleasure he took in their observance. He was none of those, however, who consider an unbending gravity an indispensable requisite for the character of a Christian. He was gay and joyous, could break a joke upon his friend, and take one in return. Apart from his religious duties, his whole soul was wrapt in the worship of the Muses; and if he was favoured with but few visits from the celebrated Nine themselves, he had frequent intercourse with their nearest kin. As a poet he does not rank in the first class certainly, nor did he make any pretension to this. His ideas of poetry do not appear to have been the most correct. With him the whole charm of poetizing seemed to consist in a good jingle and a host of verses. From a long habit of throwing his thoughts into rhyme he had acquired great facility in making a stanza on the most trivial occurrence, and the shortest notice. Once on a time, while plying his vocation in a farm-house in the neighbourhood, one of the servants entered the kitchen,.

and in the absence of the mistress purloined a small slice of beef from a ham hanging overhead, at the same time addressing the tailor with—" Noo, Tam, ye're no to tell the guidwife, or mak' a sang on me, for takin' this bit thin skliffer," to which Tom immediately gave the following impromptu:—

> " Ye greedy-like thief,
>   Let be the hung beef,
> And meddle nae mair wi' the ham,
>   Or else the guidwife
>   Will raise up a strife,
> And lay a' the wyte o't on Tam."

At the time Simpson was enjoying the friendship and correspondence of Burns, his neighbour, the tailor, was ambitious of a similar honour, and did his utmost to secure it, but without success. Though labouring under the difficulties of a limited education, yet he possessed the feelings and affections of a poet. Many a late and early hour he devoted to the Muses, but the wants of a family were to be attended to, and the flow of some melodious stanza was cruelly interrupted by his having to mount the board. Yet there sat he, whistling, singing, joking, and rhyming from morning till night, with Rab Burns o' Mossgiel floating uppermost in his mind. Mustering courage, he sent the following letter to Burns, properly addressed, but weeks passed and no answer was returned:—

"EPISTLE TO ROBERT BURNS.

> " What fine amusement's this I hear,
>   That doth my dowie spirits cheer?

It's Robin, fam'd baith far and near
        For makin' rhyme,
Whilk sounded sweetly in my ear,
        Noo mony a time.

" Some cantie callan thou maun be;
  Altho' I never did thee see,
  Fain wad I shake a paw wi' thee,
        And crack a blink;
  But thou'rt owre far awa for me,
        I really think.

" Fine cantie chiel, I do declare,
  O, wert thou near a mile or mair,
  Tho' scant o' time, I wadna care
        To gang and crack,
  And sit wi' thee baith lang and sair
        Ere I cam' back.

" Or could we meet some Mauchline fair—
  I sometimes tak' a bottle there—
  Thou'd be as welcome to a share
        As thou could'st be;
  Wae worth the purse that wadna spair
        A drink to thee.

    .   .   .   .

" I'm yet but young, and new set out,
  My rhymes begin to rin about,
  And aye I ken I get a clout
        Frae you and Willie;
  Ye ken him weel, without a doubt,
        Your rhyming billie.

" He teaches weans the muckle A's,
  And keeps a pair o' leather taws,
  But ne'er lays on without a cause,
        Yet fleys them a';
  Lang may he wag about the wa's,
        And never fa'.

" Were you and Willie owre an ingle,
　　Where mutchkin stoups and glasses jingle,
　　You twa wad mak' a bonny pingle,
　　　　　I'm sure o' that;
　　A pair o' you is seen but single,
　　　　　In ony spat.

" Fair fa' ye, lads, ye're no that slack,
　　Fu' weel I like to hear your knack;
　　Can Will and Allan be come back,
　　　　　That lang are dead?
　　Hoot, no; ye're twa raised up to crack,
　　　　　Just in their stead.

" But, Robin, when cam' ye asteer?
　　It hasna been this mony a year;
　　Ye like auld warl' folk appear,
　　　　　That liv'd langsyne—
　　So your auld fashiont taunt and jeer
　　　　　Put me in min'

" O' some auld folk that I hae seen,
　　Sit roun' the ingle late at e'en,
　　Wi' lang e'ebrows out owre their een,
　　　　　And glower at me,
　　As if a ferlie I had been
　　　　　For them to see.

" They sat about the ingle lowes,
　　And fley'd me talking about cowes,
　　Witches and warlocks, dead men's pows,
　　　　　Till I was weary;
　　The sweat amaist ran aff my brows,
　　　　　I was sae eery.

.　　.　　.　　.　　.　　.　　.　　.

" But, Robin, between me and you,
　　Think ye, maun a' thae things be true?

> I ken ye're brawlie fit to show
>   Me what ye think;
> I heard some rhymes o' yours a' through,
>   And weel they clink.

> " O, but my heart wad be fu' light,
>   In Ochiltree to get a sight
>   O' your braw rhyme, sae trim and tight,
>   As ye can 'dite it;
>   So sit ye doon a while some night,
>   And rhyme and write it.

> " Direct to Tam that mak's the claes—
>   Some tell me that I jag the flaes;
>   But gin they ding me owre the braes,
>   They'll ne'er do mair,
>   For I might break baith shins and taes,
>   And that fu' sair.

"Thomas Walker."

Receiving no reply to this, he sent Burns another, in which he fully and freely gave his opinion of the poet's morality, but at the same time not exculpating himself. The following stanzas are a specimen of his second epistle:—

> " Fu' weel ye ken ye'll gang to hell,
>   Gin ye persist in doin' ill;
>   Wae's me, ye're hurlin' doon the hill
>   Withouten dread,
>   An' ye'll get leave to swear your fill
>   After ye're dead.

> " O Rab! lay by thae foolish tricks,
>   An' steer nae mair the female sex,

> Or some day ye'll come through the pricks,
> 　　An' that ye'll see;
> Ye'll fin't hard leevin' at auld Nick's—
> 　　I'm wae for thee.

> " We're owre like those wha think it fit,
> To stuff their noddles fu' o' wit,
> And yet content in darkness sit,
> 　　Wha shun the light,
> To let them see doon to the pit
> 　　That lang dark night.

> " But fareweel, Rab, I maun awa,
> May He that made us keep us a',
> For that would be a dreadfu' fa',
> 　　An' hurt us sair;
> Lad, ye would never mend ava,
> 　　Sae Rab, tak' care."

No answer was ever received to this letter either, and the poor tailor was sadly grieved, and almost demented, at the seeming slight. Day after day did he make his complaint to Simpson of Burns' unkindness in not writing him. To gratify Tom's ardent longings, Simpson wrote in Burns' name the poem to which we have referred, entitled "Epistle to a Tailor," and sent it up to Pool. Almost half-naked, and ecstatic with joy, Walker rushed into Simpson's school, crying, "O Willie, Willie, I hae got ane noo; a clencher; read it man, read it." With ill-restrained laughter he read it, and returned it to the tailor, who religiously preserved it till the day of his death without ever discovering the hoax which had been played upon him. A few days afterwards Simpson met Burns, and reproached him for not writing to the tailor.   Burns said, "Man, Willie, I aye intended to write the bodie, but never got it dune."   Simpson then told the whole story, and read to him the answer he had sent in his name.   Burns gave him a thump on the shoulder and said, "Od, Willie, ye hae thrashed the tailor far better than I could hae dune."   Many, many summers have come and gone, shedding a mellow lustre over fair Ochiltree, since "Winsome Willie" followed his famed correspondent and friend to "the land o' the leal."   A longer period has passed away since Tom Walker was gathered to his fathers; but the memory of all three is yet fresh among the old inhabitants of the village, and their names are never mentioned but with respect.

Among the minor celebrities of Burns' acquaintance who have given an interest to his musings, and who in return have been honoured with niches in the edifice of his fame, there is one who occupies a most prominent place, and who, we believe, will be among the very last to be forgotten.   Yet, conspicuous as her position is, and distinguished the part she is represented as having performed so well, we do not remember having seen recorded of her any notice, biographical, anecdotical, or obituary, beyond what has been transmitted in the poet's tale.   Others have had their historians and their commentators, tracing their genealogies, delineating their characters, describing their persons, and register- ing whatever else has been known or reported of them; but notwithstanding the havoc she wrought, the dread she inspired, and the prominence she held, the memorials of her history seem even more meagre and scanty than the famous garment which contributed to gain her an immortal name.

"Tam o' Shanter" we know as Douglas Graham, a gash, honest, Carrick farmer on the Culzean shore, somewhat addicted to sociality, late hours, and bibulous habits on market days in Ayr. His wife, Kate, we know as Helen M'Taggart, superstitious, credulous in witches and bogles, and peculiarly eloquent in a certain kind of discourse when her liege lord was himself both the subject and the principal auditor. "Souter Johnny" we also know as John Davidson, an itinerant house-to-house cobbler, common in olden times, and who repudiated the maxim that "the cobbler should ever stick to his last." But who was "Cutty Sark"? None can tell. Assuredly she was no myth. Yet what is known or remembered of her more than that she was the belle of the famous midnight carousal in Alloway Kirk, and occasionally practised disastrous pranks among the fishermen and farmers on the Carrick shore? We have lately obtained a few particulars respecting this notable weird woman from a respectable and trustworthy source, the friend of one who knew her intimately, and whom she presented, a few hours before her death, with a portion of her household chattels as a token of her gratitude for the kindness she had received from him during a long period of years—John Murdoch of Laighpark Kiln.

It may seem wonderful, but it is yet true, that however disreputable may be the character of a witch, there have been many claimants to the title of "Cutty Sark;" not, of course, by the parties themselves, but by their descendants, to whom "distance lends enchantment to the view," and who, now seeing the immortality the character has attained through the poet's genius, are anxious to claim kindred with the ill-starred quean. The real " Cutty Sark " was Katherine Steven, or, as curtailed in the dialect of the district, Kate Steen, by which she was commonly called, for no one dared to address her by her *sobriquet* through fear of the sad consequences which might ensue. She was born in a cottage near the Maidens, and was brought up by her grandmother at Laighpark, in the parish of Kirkoswald, on the Carrick shore, where she paid the debt of nature many years ago, in a state of extreme indigence, when she had attained a good old age, yet generally dreaded to the last.

When Burns was attending Kirkoswald school, he was intimately acquainted with the dwellers along the Turnberry coast. Shanter, the residence of Tam, Glenfit, the abode of " Souter Johnny," and Laighpark were placed in the immediate neighbourhood of each other, with other cottages around, such as those of the miller and the smith. Kate Steen, and her " reverend granny " were both well known to the poet, and many an hour he spent in their shieling, listening to the stories of the withered beldame about pirates and smugglers; and also spell-bound by the unconscious cantrips of the young witch Kate.

We usually associate the idea of witchcraft with extreme ugliness, deformity, and old age; but history informs us that the young and the fair have oftentimes been branded with the opprobrious epithet, and made to suffer the punishment which was accounted due.

Saturday, in the Devil's Calendar, was the witches' Sabbath; and it is interesting to mark the synchronical accuracy of the poet in fixing the time of the jubilant carousal—it was early on Saturday morning. The market-day in Ayr being then, as it still is, on Friday, the Carrick farmer had sat ". boozing at the nappy," till " the hour, of night's black arch the keystane," when he mounted his mare and took the road homeward. By the time he reached Alloway Kirk, the morning was in and the orgies were begun.

The title of " Cutty Sark " was not an original appellation of the poet's invention, though it was new in the use he made of it to the young wench of Kirkoswald shore. In a letter to Captain Grose, when collecting his " Antiquities of Scotland," he mentions three witch stories connected with Alloway Kirk, in one of which there is an account of a merry-making similar to that of his own tale, or which was rather the foundation of his tale, and when a belated farmer "was so tickled, that he involuntarily burst out with a loud laugh, ' Weel luppen, Maggie, wi' the short sark!' and, recollecting himself, instantly spurred his horse to the top of his speed." In this, then, we have the first idea of " Cutty Sark," and what was predicated of Maggie is happily converted into an appellation for Nanny. But why Nanny? There was doubtless the same reason for calling Kate Steen *Nanny*, as for calling Douglas Graham *Tam*, and his wife, Helen M'Taggart, *Kate* —a desire to avoid the delicacy, and the not over-agreeable consequences of direct personality. But to return.

Kate Steen was universally acknowledged to be a woman of very industrious habits, and was of necessity frugal and economical of whatever she obtained. She was accustomed when travelling from house to house to take her tow rock and spindle or twirling-pin with her, and spin as she went along. Her kind and obliging disposition secured her a warm reception among the farm-houses in the neighbourhood, and she always returned to her shieling at Laighpark Kiln laden with an abundant supply of the common necessaries of life. Her case was remarkable, but, we believe, by no means peculiar, in having the weird character forcibly thrust upon her. She not only made no pretensions, but repudiated the idea, of being considered a witch; yet a witch she was held to be in public estimation, and in those days that was enough. Her supposed insight into futurity, and acquaintance with the destinies of men, led also to the belief that she possessed a sway over fate from an intimate connection with Satanic power. In after life the peculiarity of her dress assisted in no small degree in investing her with supernatural agency; and, consequently, so much was she dreaded by young and old, that whenever she was espied on the highway afar off, with her rock and tow, a different road was taken to avoid coming in contact with her, as her presence produced great anxiety and fear, except when she was known to be favourably disposed. Doubtless she had the foibles and infirmities of her sex and calling; and it was, perhaps, not altogether exaggeration when it was said that she was not reluctant on certain occasions to tell, with an ominous shake of the head, that her meal barrel was nearly empty, and that kail and water made but thin broth. Yet it was seldom this necessity was pressed upon her; for, whether from love or fear, she received a seemingly cordial welcome, and her departure home gave her no cause to suspect its truth. Still, on some occasions, the complaint of Mause might have been hers:—

> " Hard luck, alake! when poverty and eild,
> Weeds out o' fashion, and a lonely bield,
> Wi' a sma' cast o' wiles, should, in a twitch,
> Gie ane the hatefu' name 'A wrinkled witch.'
> The fool imagines, as do mony sic,
> That I'm a witch, in compact wi' 'Auld Nick.'"

Kate Steen was of *low* stature, even for a woman, though we should infer differently from the description . given of her as—

> "Ae handsome wench and walie."

and also for the dexterous part she performed in *detail*ing "noble Maggie" at the "keystane o' the brig." But Burns must be here considered as using a poet's license, either for the sake of the rhyme, or to lend an additional grace to his heroine, even though a witch. A poet's *witches*, as well as his wenches, are oftentimes very exaggerated descriptions of humanity. Burns' lyric heroines, though adorned with the epithets "loveliest," "fairest," "bonniest," "sweetest," and "beyond compare," were many of them, after all, very mediocre specimens of the masterwork of nature. Nay, some of them, it is said, were scarcely up to what is generally regarded as the minimum standard of female beauty. So, in the description of "Cutty Sark," there is certainly much that is exaggerated, much intended to adorn the tale, though she was universally reported as in league with a certain dark conspirator. If not beautiful, she was doubtless powerful :—

> " For mony a beast to dead she shot,
> And perished mony a bonny boat,
> And shook baith muckle corn and beer,
> And kept the countryside in fear."

Among the cantrips imputed to Kate Steen in the above list is one which is but imperfectly understood, if known at all, in the present day—"Mony a beast · to dead she shot." What was the "shoot of dead?" It was a curse or denunciation of evil upon a living object, that bodily disease and death might speedily overtake it. And it was the popular belief in former days that if such an imprecation were made by any one, and especially by one reputed "no canny," it could not fail in producing the desired effect.

In the kirk-session records of the parish of Tinwald, Dumfriesshire, of date August, 1699, we find that the "shoot of dead" was a crime demanding more than ordinary church censure and discipline. A report having been laid before the session that "John Carruthers and Jean Wilson were scolding together, and that the said Jean *did imprecate him and his beasts,*" they were cited to appear at next meeting, which they did accordngly, but "John declared it was not Jean Wilson (who was brought up by another party on a like charge), but Bessie Kennedy, who, upon a certain Sabbath, did wish that his horse might *shoot to dead*—whereupon it fell sick, and he, bringing it home, and sitting at his house reading, the said Bessie Kennedy came by, and he telling her that his horse had not thriven since she cursed it, she wished that the *shoot of dead* might light on him and it both." Bessie was summoned and denied the charge; but acknowledged that when he told her his horse had eaten none since she cursed it, she replied that if the *shoot of dead* should come on him too, he might give her the blame. Bessie was found to have behaved unchristianly, was rebuked for the same and dismissed, after promising greater watchfulness for the future.

But witches, notwithstanding their cantrips, and charms, and incantations, are not invulnerable to the shafts of death; and however often they may have whidded over the green knowes, in the form of some sturdy grey maukin', with shot after shot rattling in their rear, when death draws the trigger the aim is sure. So the time came when "Cutty's" mortal career drew to a close; and the presentiment she had of the day and hour of her decease contributed not a little to confirm the popular reputation of her weird character. One morning she sent for one of her neighbours and addressed him in the following terms:—"Noo, John, this is my hinmost day in this warl, and the mid-day hour and me will hae an unco struggle. Ye hae lang befriended me and mine, when few cared little how ill we fared. There's my meal barrel in the corner by; mony a time ye hae filled it, but I shall need it nae mair. Tak' it as a present, along with the bake-brod

and the bread-roller on the tap o't, and when I'm gane
ye'll fin' a whisky bottle in the cupboard, wi' some
bread and cheese in the same place. Mak' yersel's
comfortable, and mourn na for me."

The meal barrel was a twenty-pint cask, which had
seen considerable service of a different kind—the bak-
ing-board was a few staves of a similar vessel nailed
together—and the bread-roller was a long-necked
brandy bottle. Such were the humble gifts conveyed
in the dying bequest of "Cutty Sark," and they were
till lately in the possession of her friend John, who has
followed his grateful neighbour over the unrepassable
bourne, and who presented these relics of a wondrous
character as a legacy to our informant.

One by one the morning hours crept wearily away,
and exactly at the predicted time the lingering spirit
of "Cutty Sark" departed to another scene. After the
necessary obsequies had been performed by some
female neighbours to the lifeless body, and the curtains
had been drawn closely around, they sat down before
the fire to refresh themselves, as directed, with the
comforts of the cupboard, when, lo! ere the first morsel
had been tasted or the cork drawn, down went the
hearth and all upon it, while the whole party fled in
terror to the door. After the consternation had been
somewhat abated, one bolder than the rest ventured to
look through the key-hole, in the fear lest another Alloway Kirk scene should be going on, but all was silent.
With trembling hand she lifted the latch and looked in.
The body was lying still in death upon the bed as when
they left it, and the hearthstone had disappeared save

a single corner.   They all returned and found that the
cause of their terror was a large vault underneath the
hearth, which had been used for the concealment of
illicit spirits and other smuggled goods, and also for
hiding renegades from the hand of justice.   The stone
had slidden off one of its end supports, and with its
superincumbent load was precipitated below.   With
considerable difficulty the stone was raised, and set
with earth from an adjoining field; the door was securely
fastened, and a few days after the mortal remains
of "Cutty Sark" were committed to the dust.   Some
time after the funeral it was found on entering the
cottage that the floor surrounding the hearth was
growing green, and bidding fair for a beautiful crop of
grain.   The earth with which the hearth was laid had
been taken from a lately sown field.   Though there
was nothing very remarkable in this, yet it spread like
wildfire with manifold exaggerations, and many a sigh
of relief was drawn that Laighpark shieling was now
without a tenant, and that Kate Steen would trouble
the district no more.   Poor woman! she never troubled
it, but the superstitious fears of its inhabitants did.
The troubler and the troubled, however, have long ere
now passed equally away.   The Maiden rocks still stand
as before, a landmark to the passing sailor; but Shanter,
Glenfoot, and Laighpark have long since been removed,
and the inquisitive traveller, with difficulty and doubt,
has pointed out to him the spots where they stood.

CHAPTER XXI.

REFLECTIONS ON OBTAINING PLACE-SITUATIONS—LETTERS TO MRS. AND MR. S. C. HALL—FAMILY LETTERS—MRS. COPLAND—LAST ILLNESS—DEATH AND BURIAL—CONCLUDING REMARKS.

ALTHOUGH Cunningham had attained eminence in literature, and could number several of the nobility among his friends, yet he did not receive the attention which he thought his due, with regard to place-situations for his sons in the Government offices. Writing to a near relative in Dumfries on the subject, he complains of this in the following terms:—"Frank is grown into a man almost. I have been trying to get him a clerkship in one of our public offices, but though Lord Melbourne spoke, nay wrote, very kindly, still the situation is not come, and I believe I *must* accept a cadetship to India for him, which a noble-minded friend holds for the purpose. Now, you see it is not quite my choice to send my son abroad, but then what can I do? There are many places at home in the gift of ministers, and they bestow them freely, but then they bestow them on men who have wealth or influence—not on those who write songs, and romances, and biographies. It was one of the dreams of my youth that patronage followed eminence in literature, but when I see hundreds obtain situations for their sons who have no eminence to plead in anything, I see that I only dreamed. But this is far from hurting my temper or disturbing my peace. For though these sad times have reduced the profits of literature to the wages of a harvest-reaper, and I have been, by the bankruptcy of one and the knavery of others, deprived of the fruits of my head and hand to the amount of £450, still it is my duty to endure the infliction with patience. With respect to my own health, I still keep out of the doctor's hands. I write much less than I used to do, and must write less yet, for the hard toils of my boyish days are making themselves felt; but as my hand-work has been long over, I must fatigue myself as little with the head as I can help." These last words were not mere matter of course, and were not written without a reason, as coming events were casting their shadows before them, though still at some considerable distance.

But we now turn to his home correspondence, which is always interesting, especially when he writes to his mother:—

"Belgrave Place, 2nd January, 1836.

"My beloved Mother,—When I last heard of you, and that was very lately, you were in excellent health. I need not say with what pain I hear that it is otherwise now, and that you are a sufferer. I have, however, much confidence in the excellence of your constitution, and expect to hear that you have got the better of this attack, as you did that very severe one when your son and grandson hastened from London to see you. The early loss of my father I have often felt was made up by your long life and good health; and as my grandfather lived till he was beyond ninety, I hope the Giver of all things will be equally indulgent to his daughter. We had a letter from Alexander on Thursday, and one from Joseph yesterday. They were both well, and so was your other grandson, James Pagan. The last account comes down to August 13.

"I am happy to learn that you have such skill at hand as that of the Rev. Mr. Kirkwood, who is the friend of his people both in and out of the pulpit, and also that your nephew Mr. Harley Maxwell is in Dumfries. But what must be your greatest consolation is the presence of your daughters, and the feeling that you have been a good and a kind mother. These are not my words alone, they are the last I remember having heard my father utter, and all your children must join in the sentiments.

"My brother Peter is writing. I shall therefore say no more, but add that your recovery has been the only wish, the sole prayer of my whole household this morning. I am quite well. My wife, who sends her love, has been suffering of late from a cold. Our love to Jean and Mina. I hope the next letter from Newington will tell us that you are better. —I remain, my beloved Mother, your ever affectionate son,

" ALLAN CUNNINGHAM.

"Mrs. Cunningham."

With Mr. and Mrs. S. C. Hall he was on the most intimate terms of friendship, and contributed several articles to the *Art Journal* on "Our Public Statues." The following reply was sent to a request for a piece of poetry from his pen:—

" Belgrave Place, 3rd August, 1836.

"My dear Mrs. Hall,—I will do anything for you, but my Muse, poor lassie, has lost much of her early readiness and spirit, and finds more difficulty in making words clink and lines keep time; but she will work for you, and as she loves you, who knows but some of her earlier inspiration may come to her again? for you must know, I think, her strains have lost much of their free, wild nature since WE came from the land of the yellow broom and the blossomed heather.—Yours ever and ever,

"ALLAN CUNNINGHAM."

The following acknowledgment was sent to Mr. S. C. Hall on receiving a copy of the first volume of his "Book of Gems;" and while giving due praise to the work, it also indicates what he himself had in view, and was preparing:—"Your 'Book of Gems' was welcome for your sake, painting's sake, poetry's sake, and my own sake. I have done nothing but look at it since it came, and admire the good taste of the selections, and the happy language—clear too, and discriminating—of the biographies. It will do good both to the living and the dead—directing and animating the former, and giving a fresh lustre to the latter. If it obtains but half the success which it deserves, both your publisher and yourself ought to be satisfied. I have made the characters of our poets my study—studied them both as men and as bards, looking at them through the eyes of nature, and I am fully warranted in saying that our notions very seldom differ, and that you come nearer my feelings on the whole than any other person, save one, whom I have ever met. You will see this when my 'Lives of the Poets' are published, and that will be soon, for the first volume is all but ready." This projected work of the 'Lives of the Poets,' after the manner of Johnson, was not carried into effect, so far as we are aware; but it is doubtless to be found among his literary manuscripts, and may yet be given to the public.

The following letters are interesting:—

"27 Belgrave Place, 17th May, 1838.

"My dear Mother,—We have thought of little else these two months but of your grandson Francis, and his visit to you in Scotland, his fitting-out here, and his departure for India. He is now on the sea. He sailed in the *Asia*, Captain Gillies, from Portsmouth, on Saturday, the 5th of this month; and as the wind was fair, we have no doubt that he is just now at Madeira, where the vessel was to touch and take in wine. He was fitted out in every way more suited to our hopes than to our pocket. He has a whole cabin to himself; he has a hundred guineas in his pocket; he has a full and more than full equipment of clothes, and an excellent little library of books, and three letters of introduction from first-rate men here to Lord Elphinstone, the Governor, and as he has good health, a clear head, an honest heart, and determination to do something worthy, I have no fears for him. He was much made of in Dumfries, he was the same here. All who met him liked him, and tried to do him service. By the direction of my friend the late Archdeacon of Madras he has undertaken to study the Persian language on his way out, for which I bought him Persian grammars and dictionaries; and by the advice of Sir Francis Chantrey he has undertaken for the sake of his health to shoot a little, not at men, but at birds and beasts, for which he gave him a beautiful double-barrelled gun, which cost forty guineas.

"Our eyes, my dear mother, have been a little wet since —from love, not from fear of your grandson, for 'an' he live to be a man,' he will be a distinguished one. It was remark-worthy that on the very morning before he left us he received a letter overland from his brother Alexander. It was from near Delhi, where he was encamped with the Governor-General. He was well, and so was Joseph, from whom he had heard on the 12th of February. His own letter was dated the 14th. Alexander said he had been on a visit with the Misses Eden, sisters of Lord Auckland, and the Prince of Orange, their visitor to Lucknow, where the Prince of the place gave them a public breakfast, and treated them to the show of a battle between elephants, rhinoceroses, antelopes, and rams. The combat of the elephants was fierce and fearful; tusks were broken and trunks gored, and they were separated by rockets; but neither fire nor water, Sandie says, could separate the rhinoceroses. The antelopes made a poor fight, and two tups in England fought better than the rams.

"He is making drawings of all the old temples, and taking notes of all the conversations with all the native princes, which he says he will send to me. He expects to see Joseph during their visit to Runjeit Sing, the King of the Punjab; but before that he thinks of making a journey into Cashmere. So much for your grandsons. Now for your poor son himself and his household here.

"Instead of writing books, I am busied arranging them. I have turned my wife and daughter, who are now well enough, into the drawing-rooms, and made my back and front parlours, by removing part of the partition, into one room, with book-cases all round, and called it my Library. Nor is it unworthy of the name, for with Pate, your grandson's volumes, there are in all little short of two thousand, mostly all good select books. I can now sit at my fireside, and in my arm-chair, and cast my eye, and put my hand, on any book I want. This arrangement was planned by your grandson Francis, who saw it begun before he set sail. I assure you the Library looks handsome. It has pictures too and busts, one of the former of Sir Francis Chantrey, one of the latter of Sir Walter Scott—both benefactors of my house.

Nelly, Thomas' widow, was here with my niece Betsy last night. They are all well. John has got a place at £75 a year; but I hope for his old situation under the Rennies. I shall see Sir John Rennie at the Duke of Sussex's on Saturday night, when I intend to speak in my nephew's favour, and offer myself as his security, if security should be required. Tell Mrs. Pagan that a friend of ours and Peter's, Lieut. Blackett of the Navy, a brother of Sir John Blackett, called the other day, and as he was bound for New Holland, on an excursion of pleasure, though he hopes profit, for he purposes to buy land, he requested introductions to my nieces and nephews on the Hunter River. I wrote to John, and Peter wrote to Jane, and sent her his volumes of Songs. I warned my young friend to beware of his heart and his £800 a-year, for all the ladies of the house of Cunningham were accounted handsome.

"When you see Miss Harley, the kind, the good Miss Harley, give my respects to her. I am concerned to hear that my old and esteemed friend David Rodan is unwell, and that he was compelled to relinquish his farm—also that Jane Taylor, a lady modest and fair, and one whom many loved, is dead and gone. She was my school-fellow at Duncow, and young as I was, I loved to be near her in the class. I heard of my brother Peter the other day; he was well at Athens on the 14th of March. My wife sends her love with mine to my *dear sisters three*, and Pate and Mary who is well and thriving, join us—Also to you, my beloved mother.—Your ever affectionate son,

" ALLAN CUNNINGHAM.

" Mrs. Cunningham."

" Belgrave Place, 29th March, 1839.

" My dear Sister,—I write in hope that my dear mother is so much recovered as to enable her to obtain some rest, and even converse with those who so anxiously and kindly attend her; nay, I trust that this setting in of sunny weather will be much in her favour. I wish I could send her some of the many coloured crocuses blooming in bunches, with snow-drops, at my door, for she is a lover of flowers, and has bestowed her taste on me. I wrote to Peter, and stated how ill our dear mother was at first, but that she was slightly better. He will likely be here soon. I am glad that my sister of Dalswinton has been with you; her's is well-timed attention, and my brother and I will remember her for it.

" We are all in our usual way, and anxious about our beloved mother. Frank says he wrote to his grandmother in December last. He was well on the 12th of January, and in great spirits, for the Bishop of Madras, who, with Sir Robert Comyne, has been very kind to him, has applied to Government to give him the command of the escort which is to accompany him on his Visitation journey through his diocese of Madras. This is high confidence in so young a man, and Francis hopes that his extreme youth will not hinder him from getting such an honourable appointment. Joseph and Alexander both wrote to us on the first day of the year. They were both well and in the Punjab, but Joseph, after having escorted Lord Auckland to the Sutlege, was to return to Lahore, and from thence go to Peshawur with the King of Cabool and the army.   He had hopes, he said, of being called on to besiege the Fortress of Peshawur. He is the only Engineer sent with the forces, and has to act as Political assistant likewise.   For all this he is well paid. His salary has been increased £250 a year, so that he has now about a thousand per annum, and expects further honours and higher pay.

"Alexander returns to Scinde with the Governor-General, but Joseph intimates that his brother will soon obtain a political appointment, one he hopes in Afghanistan, the land where his own place is.   They have no word of James Pagan, from whom they are now removed more than a thousand miles.   I wish that James had volunteered with the invading regiments; such boldness is expected, and always well looked on, and generally remembered when places are to be given away.

"We have our young friend John Harley Maxwell with us for a few days.   He is both anxious and clever, and have no doubt will be made an Engineer.   I like him very much. He has capital business habits, as well as a good business hand, and will be a credit to the Maxwells, and Hyslops, and Harleys.   We must have him appointed to Bengal.

"Will you give my love to my venerable and warm-hearted mother, also to my dear sister Mary, and do not forget my sister Jean, nor my sister Isabel?   I hope Allan will be established in due time in the Sandbed, and that he and his will prosper.   I trust also that good news have reached the Curriestanes from New Holland, and also from India.   My wife joins me in all these remembrances.   I wish you to write me soon, if you have not written already. —I remain, my dear Mina, your affectionate brother,

"ALLAN CUNNINGHAM.

"Miss Mina Cunningham."

"27 Lower Belgrave Place, 11th July, 1840.

"My dear Mother,—I have given myself too little time to write this letter, for I am anxious to send you the enclosed seven pounds, namely, a five pound note and two sovereigns, which I hope will arrive safe, and which I beg my sister Mina to acknowledge, for the post is by no means a safe mode of conveyance. I hope this will find you easy, if not quite well. It leaves all here in their usual health. Even I have picked up, as we Londoners say, of late; though I feel I must watch over myself, as you did over me, when I first ventured to walk under the Blackwood trees. I find that care, and above all vegetable diet, are the best things for me, and when I go out to dine, I resist all fine dishes and rich wines—indeed, I should like to retire on milk, porridge, and champed potatoes, such as I used to have at the Roads and the Sandbed, in the sunny days of my youth, when all was bright and full of hope before me. I saw it mentioned in the papers the other day that the *Asia* will be in England in August, which I trust will be the case, though Peter does not mention it in his last letters.

"We had letters from your three grandsons of my branch on Monday last—they were all well. Alexander was married at Simla on the 20th of March, and in the middle of April was in his own house at Lucknow with his young wife. Joseph was busy looking to the affairs of the Punjab, but when cold weather came he proposed to visit his brother at Lucknow; and Francis was about to get a year's leave of absence, to visit Calcutta and Lucknow and Lordiana. The three brothers have a strong regard for one another, and take no important steps without each other's concurrence. Give my regards to Mina and Mary, and all friends. My wife and Mary send their love to you.—I remain, my dear Mother, your affectionate son,

"ALLAN CUNNINGHAM.

"Mrs. Cunningham."

"27 Belgrave Place, 18th May, 1841.

"My dear Sister,—I heard through Helen Pagan that our dear mother had been ill, and was recovering, and I now hear from you that she continues to improve. That at her very great age she can have the health of other days may be prayed for, but can scarcely be hoped; yet I was not without that hope which is of the imagination, that as she had endured much when young, her old age would be calm and free from pain. When Helen's letters came I consulted our brother Peter, who did not feel any alarm, and regarded the attack, which frightened you so much, as an illness which would soon subside. Give my love to my dear mother, and say how I sympathize deeply, and would willingly, were such an exchange possible, take a share of her suffering. God knows I have little extra health to spare; for though Peter gave a flattering account of my appearance, my constitution is much shaken, and I feel what doctors close their eyes on. My business, in my declining health, grows no less; my patience in disposing of it lessens as I grow old, and I expect, one of these days, to be buried in the furrow like an old crow whose wing is broken, and cannot carry it out of harm's way.

"Yet I am cheerful, for why should a living man complain? The work which I am unable to do I leave undone, and the letters which I want leisure or power to reply to, I leave unanswered. I have for more than two years desisted from writing anything but letters, and even these are too numerous for a hand so weak and encumbered as mine. So you see, my dear sister, other people may be suffering as well as yourself, and yet must perform the duties of their station; but you are a complainer, one who often desires to die—you see the cloud and shut your eyes on the sunshine, and the joy of grief, of which Ossian sings, is the delight of your heart. Had my taste been like yours, I should have been in the dark and narrow house long ago. Continue to comfort our mother—do your duties as you have always done them in regard to her, for our business is not to die in despondency, and I have no doubt that you will find ten long years of enjoyment before you, and hope that I may live to see you enjoy them. We are all well—we heard from our three boys in India last mail. They are all well, and very busy. They all sent their love to you and to their grandmother. My wife sends her love to my mother, and Mary unites with her.—I remain, my dear Sister, your very affectionate brother,

" ALLAN CUNNINGHAM.

" Miss Cunningham."

We cannot omit to notice, in this concluding chapter, one to whom Cunningham was much indebted for his start in the world as a songster and a poet, Mrs. Copland. In the volume of " Remains of Nithsdale and Galloway Song," published by Cromek, but furnished by Cunningham, frequent reference is made to her, as having supplied songs, and snatches of songs, of the olden time for the work, which were used most gratefully, the interstices being supplemented where required. This lady was no myth as some have supposed, but was indeed what Cunningham has represented her to be, one of his main sources of ballad lore. She was brought up with her parents, who were highly respectable, at Gate-

2 A

side, in the parish of Newabbey, and when she had attained womanhood she was considered exceedingly good-looking, and was always spoken of as " Bonnie Mary Allan."　Her intellectual qualities were much superior to the ordinary standard of young ladies, as well as her physical lineaments, and therefore it was not to be wondered at that she became a special object of attraction to the young men around.　Cunningham was a weekly visitor at Gateside, when working in the neighbourhood, while Mary Allan was unmarried, and when he and other young men called there, the whisky bottle was of course produced.　Miss Allan was generally seated at the "Wee wheel" on such occasions, but it struck some of the lads that the "rock" continued from week to week about the same size, though it might have been frequently refurnished.　Besides, it was not a secret to them that some book or another received far more attention than did the wheel.　On one occasion, taking advantage of her temporary absence, a dram glass was removed from the table and secreted in the heart of the "rock and wee pickle tow."　Some weeks afterwards, when by any amount of diligence at all, several *rocks* should have been exhausted, the number of young men present being in excess of the dram glasses, one of them opened out the "tow" on the "rock" and brought out the secreted glass.　Among the many aspirants for her hand and heart she elected William Copland, Esq., merchant, Dalbeattie, and had a family of four daughters and two sons, one of the latter being John Copland, Esq., surgeon, residing in Dumfries.　After Mrs. Copland's marriage Cunningham was a frequent visitor at their residence of Greenhead, near Dalbeattie, previous to his removal to London, and his letters to her, after taking up his abode in the great metropolis, were neither "few nor far between;" but of these, it is sad to think, that there is not now one in existence, every scrap having been committed to the flames in the same way as those written to G. D. M'Ghie were, alluded to in a former chapter. Mrs. Copland died in Newabbey, in the spring of 1833, and must have been greatly gratified at the success which attended the writings of her friend Allan Cunningham.

Chantrey, as we formerly said, had the greatest affection for Cunningham, and left him an annuity of £100, with reversion to his widow, but he lived to receive only a single payment, for in the year succeeding that of Chantrey's death he followed his master and friend to "the land o' the leal." On Chantrey's death Cunningham was requested to execute the orders which had been received, but he declined to do so, saying it would take the longest lifetime to do that, but he would finish all that his master had modelled. We fear he did not survive to do even that.

On the morning of the 29th October, 1842, he was suddenly seized with paralysis, which was all the more ominous from his having had a similar attack some two years before, from which, however, he had completely recovered, though his health of late had caused some anxiety to his family and friends. Only two days before the attack he had revised the last proof-sheet of the "Life of Sir David Wilkie," which was published after his death. Medical assistance was found of no avail, and on the night of the following day the life and labours of Allan Cunningham were at an end. Apparently without any suffering, and "in a kind of solemn stillness," he passed away from the world at the comparatively early age of fifty-seven. On the following Friday, at one o'clock afternoon, a hearse and two mourning coaches left a house in Lower Belgrave Place, slowly wending their solemn way to the cemetery in Kensal Green, and there, in a plain grave, with only eight mourners standing round it, was laid the body of Allan Cunningham, far from his native Nithsdale that he loved so well.

He had acquired many friends in the course of his literary career, but none so intimate and valued as William Jerdan of the *Literary Gazette*, who at first so greatly roused his ire about the heretical pronoun. No one had better opportunities for knowing his real character and worth, and no one was better qualified to form a correct opinion. - In publicly noticing his death, he said, "few persons ever tasted the felicity of passing through the world with more of friendship and less enmity than this worthy and well deserving individual. He was straight-forward, right-minded, and conscientious; true to himself and to others." We believe this was the universal opinion. Few men ever had such delight in family and home as he, and few fathers ever had greater cause to be proud of his sons, who all distinguished themselves greatly in the literary world, as well as in their professional positions. His love for his wife was ardent, and many a tribute of affection he paid her in after days, as well as when he wooed her in the woods of Arbigland. After a separation of twenty-two years she now sleeps by his side.

As a writer his fancy was perhaps a little too luxuriant —he loved nature in her wildest tangles, and to have trimmed the wild-rose bush, or the hawthorn tree, would have been in his sight vandalism which he could not endure. While to the trained critic of modern literature there may appear in his works too great an exuberance of imagination, and too strong a fragrance of flowers, we are much mistaken if these are not the very things that will embalm his memory in the minds of those whom he sought most to please, the peasantry of his native land. We now reverentially let fall the curtain, and would inscribe upon the monolith which covers his grave—" Honest Allan—a credit to Caledonia!"

" Thou, like me, hast seen another grave would suit our Poet well,
Greenly banded by the breckan in a lonely Highland dell,
Looking on the solemn waters of a mighty inland sea,
In the shadow of a mountain, where the lonely eagles be ;
Thou hast seen the kindly heather blown around his simple bed ;
Heard the loch and torrent mingle dirges for the poet dead ;
Brother, thou hast seen him lying, as it is thy hope to lie,
Looking from the soil of Scotland up into a Scottish sky :
It may be such grave were better, better rain and dew should fall,
Tears of hopeful love to freshen Nature's ever-verdant pall

.   .   .   .

Better after-times should find him—to his rest in homage bound—
Lying in the land that bore him, with its glories piled around."

www.ingramcontent.com/pod-product-compliance
Lightning Source LLC
Chambersburg PA
CBHW032014120726
47902CB00013B/833